Son of Bhrigu

Christopher C. Doyle is the author of the hugely popular The Mahabharata Quest Series. Along the way to publishing his debut novel, Christopher pursued a career in the corporate world after graduating from St Stephen's College, Delhi and IIM, Calcutta. Christopher is also a musician and lives his passion for music through his band called Mid Life Crisis. He lives in New Delhi with his family.

Christopher can be contacted at:
Website: www.christophercdoyle.com
Email: contact@christophercdoyle.com
www.facebook.com/authorchristophercdoyle
The Quest Club: www.christophercdoyle.com/the-quest-club

D1195995

Also by Christopher C. Doyle

The Mahabharata Secret

The Mahabharata Quest Series
Book 1: The Alexander Secret
Book 2: The Secret of the Druids

A Secret Revealed

The Pataala Prophecy: Book I

Son of Bhrigu

Christopher C. Doyle

First published by Westland Publications Private Limited in 2018
61, 2nd Floor, Silverline Building, Alapakkam Main Road, Maduravoyal,
Chennai 600095

Westland and the Westland logo are the trademarks of Westland Publications
Private Limited, or its affiliates.

ISBN: 9789386850478

10 9 8 7 6 5 4 3 2 1

Typeset by R. Ajith Kumar
Printed at Thomson Press (India) Ltd.

*This book is dedicated to all the teachers in my life
who built me up as a person and made me what I am,
who enabled me to find my own special powers in the
gurukul of life
and
to the memory of Asha Michigan.*

Prologue

September, 1799

Giza, Egypt

Louis Alexandre Berthier looked around and shivered.

But not because it was cold.

It was their location.

The night had not yet begun its retreat before the advance of the sun, and its last vestiges still clung to the edges of the vast canopy of stars that stretched above the desert. It was cool but comfortably so; not frigid enough to cause a chill in the air.

It was something else that was getting to him. A veteran of many battles, there was little that could rattle him. Yet, tonight, he felt a sense of disquiet that he had never experienced before.

Berthier glanced at the faces of the two soldiers with him. In the light of the torches, their faces reflected his own anxiety, nervousness and — though he was loath to admit it — fear.

They had spent the better part of the night in a small, makeshift camp at the base of the largest pyramid of the three that towered over the Giza plateau. It soared hundreds of feet into the sky, its tip lost in the darkness and its base barely scratched by the flicker of the flames from their torches.

Not far away loomed another silhouette — the head of the enormous sculpture of the man-beast, with its inscrutable expression, commonly known as the 'Sphinx'. The inexorable advance of the sand dunes over centuries, had covered the bulk of the stone body of the Sphinx, leaving just the head exposed.

There was something unnerving about this place. He wouldn't have been here of his own accord. Yet, what choice had they been given?

Berthier reflected on the events that had brought them here. The last twelve months had been spent in military campaigns in Egypt, not all of them successful. But the highlight of the expedition led by Napoleon Bonaparte had been the wondrous architectural ruins — stone temples that soared towards the sky, defying gravity; giant statues sculpted thousands of years ago out of stone, depicting the rulers of yore — and the broken stone stele that had been discovered just a month ago by Captain Pierre Bouchard. Dubbed the 'Rosetta stone' it had caused unparalleled excitement among historians since it presented a means to finally decipher the hitherto incomprehensible Egyptian script that was so commonly inscribed in the temples and tombs of the country.

And then, Napoleon had suddenly decided that he would spend a night inside the largest pyramid of the trio that stood on the Giza plateau. Someone had told him that Alexander and Julius Caesar, too, had done this, and Napoleon was fired with the ambition of matching those great generals.

Berthier, who was Napoleon's chief of staff, had argued with his general, trying to dissuade him using logic, but to no avail.

'It is nothing more than a story, a myth,' Berthier had asserted. 'We know that the Great Pyramid was sealed and unviolated until Mohammed al-Mamoun tunnelled into it, thousands of years after it was built. How could Alexander and Caesar have entered it then? They lived centuries before the birth of our Lord.'

Napoleon, however, had made up his mind. So it was that, on the previous evening, Berthier and the two soldiers had accompanied the French general through the narrow and low ceilinged passageways that led from the hole, made by Al Mamoun centuries before, in the north face of the pyramid. They had clambered with great difficulty, by the light of torches, up the steeply sloping tunnels and into the highest chamber that contained the stone sarcophagus that was supposed to have been built to hold the body of the pharaoh, Khufu, who had constructed the pyramid as a grand tomb for himself. Of course, Khufu's body had never been found, the pyramid having been discovered to be empty, with no sign of either the Pharaoh's mummy or treasure and bereft of the ubiquitous inscriptions found in Egyptian tombs.

With grave misgivings, Berthier and the soldiers had left their general in the chamber and, in accordance with his instructions, gone from the building to camp outside and wait for his return at dawn.

Napoleon, himself, had shown no signs of anxiety or fear. He had appeared curious, excited even; poking into the corners of the room and the sarcophagus, examining the bare walls of the chamber in the light of the single lamp that was to be left with him.

Berthier shivered again. It was a mistake; he could feel it in his bones. The chamber that Napoleon had decided to conquer had an eeriness about it. He had felt it last night when he had accompanied Napoleon to settle him in. It was almost as if there was an invisible presence in the stone room. The sarcophagus may have been empty, but Berthier could not help feeling that there was something in that chamber. The pyramid had been empty and sealed shut for thousands of years, its original entrance concealed by the builders. Was it possible that some spirit or demon had taken up residence there in the intervening centuries?

He shook his head, trying to convince himself that he was imagining things. Others had been inside the pyramid since Al-Mamoun's intrusion. Yet, no one had ever spoken of hauntings or spirits.

A shout from one of the soldiers broke his reverie.

He glanced towards the base of the pyramid. A dark human figure could be seen, staggering and stumbling as it made its way towards them.

Napoleon!

Berthier rose swiftly and ran towards his general, the two soldiers hurrying behind him.

He reached Napoleon before the others and recoiled in shock as he saw his general's face.

The normally robust features had been replaced by an expression that combined horror and desperation. The excitement and confidence of the previous night were gone. His stricken look, on a face that seemed to have been drained of all blood, gave him the appearance of a cadaver and his arms were outstretched as if searching for succour; for a means of support, help and rescue.

Berthier grasped Napoleon by his arms and supported him as the mighty general leaned his weight upon him, as if collapsing with relief.

The two soldiers were still a short distance away.

'What happened?' Berthier demanded. 'What did you encounter inside that monstrosity? Tell me!'

Napoleon shook his head and looked Berthier in the eye for a fleeting moment of lucidity that seemed to cut through his confusion and fear.

Berthier's blood ran cold at Napoleon's response. The general's voice was hoarse with terror.

'You will never believe me if I told you.'

Chapter One

The History Teacher

Day One

Present Day
New Delhi, India

Dhananjay Trivedi hurried along, casting nervous glances around him as he walked.

A deep, dark fear seemed to engulf his very soul.

And he didn't understand it.

Dhananjay was a history teacher in a reputed school in New Delhi. A gold medallist from Allahabhad University, the world of academia had been waiting to welcome him with open arms. He had surprised many when he became a teacher. He loved his job and more importantly, his students at school loved him. There was hardly a student who wouldn't gush about Dhananjay's classes, which were known to be fun. He was a wonderful guide, walking his students through the trails of history with stories that kept them mesmerized in class. Dhananjay's strategy was simple. He believed that if his students enjoyed studying history, they would be more attentive, more curious and learn more.

Some of the other teachers would grumble about how devoted the students were to Dhananjay. It was almost as if he cast a spell upon them from the moment he walked into the classroom.

What no one knew, was that the much-adored history teacher had a secret of his own.

It was this very secret that had led to the encounter today, which had left him in his present state of disquiet.

It had started innocuously enough, with a young man approaching Trivedi as he stepped outside the school gate. The youth seemed to be in his late teens; definitely not more than nineteen or twenty.

'Good afternoon, sir,' he had greeted Trivedi with a disarming smile. 'I am Vishwaraj.' His voice had then lowered conspiratorially. 'Can I please have a word with you?'

Trivedi had recognized the name. He had heard of it before. The young man was a member of the *Gana*. Trivedi's curiosity had mounted. What could the young man want from him?

Without further ado, Vishwaraj had drawn him aside. His words were brief and to the point. Trivedi listened, astounded at what Vishwaraj had to say.

'So, you see, sir,' Vishwaraj concluded in the soft tones that he had adopted at the start of the conversation, 'I know that the boy is alive. And I want to know where he is. You will tell me or pay the price.'

Trivedi appraised the young man in front of him. This was an unforeseen development. A member of the *Gana* gone rogue. He couldn't fathom what Vishwaraj's intentions or motives were but he knew that the *Sangha* didn't know about Vishwaraj's apostasy. But there was nothing he could do for now. The *Sangha* would have to decide how to deal with this situation.

'I don't have to tell you anything,' he scoffed. 'Your words are an empty threat. If you try anything, you will find yourself in deep trouble. And you know it.' He paused, then added, 'In any case, I have no idea what you are talking about.'

Vishwaraj said nothing. His youthful face was hard as his eyes bored into the schoolmaster.

Suddenly, Trivedi felt a nameless fear in the depths of his heart. Despite his casual dismissal of the youth, he felt there was something that he was missing. Something that was gnawing at his subconscious mind, but wouldn't come out into the open.

He turned away. This meeting was over. But one thought ran through his mind repeatedly as he made his way home.

How did Vishwaraj know about the boy?

As he stood outside his apartment and fumbled with the keys to the front door, his mind raced with possibilities. This incident could not go unreported. Especially since it concerned the boy.

He opened the iron grill door, then unlocked the inner, wooden door and stepped in, locking both doors from the inside.

For a few moments, he leaned against a wall, breathing hard. He still couldn't understand his own anxiety. Vishwaraj was just a powerless youth, incapable of delivering on his threat. So why had the brief conversation with the boy unnerved him?

He whipped out his mobile phone and dialled a number. As the call connected, he began speaking rapidly, describing what had just happened. His breathing slowed as the person on the other end of the line seemed to offer him words of assurance, calming him down.

By the time the conversation was over, Trivedi had almost recovered his composure. He ended the call and placed his phone on the dining table.

That was when it struck him. The reason why he had been feeling uneasy since the encounter with Vishwaraj.

Why hadn't he seen it earlier?

As the realization dawned, the apartment erupted in flames. The fire was everywhere. It was as if every atom of the flat had spontaneously ignited at exactly the same moment.

Trivedi now knew that he had been wrong about Vishwaraj. He had made a big mistake. And he was going to pay with his life. But that didn't bother him as much as the fact that it was now too late to tell anyone else. He could only hope that his death would warn the others.

The future of the world was at stake.

Chapter Two

The Mystery Deepens

Day Two
New Delhi

Superintendent of Police, Raman Kapoor, stared at the preliminary autopsy report on his desk. An ambitious young police officer from the IPS, he had been put in charge of the Trivedi murder case by the Commissioner of Police himself.

And what a humdinger of a case this was. A history teacher murdered in his own flat, under mysterious circumstances. He reflected on the perplexing facts of the case even as he tried to digest the contents of the report. Nothing seemed to make any sense.

It was this sense of hopelessness — the lack of obvious clues or a direction to work towards — that made this case exciting for Kapoor. The challenge thrilled him. If the Police Commissioner hadn't assigned this case to him, there was a high degree of probability that he would have asked for it, just for the thrill of solving a case with no obvious clues. His outstanding investigative track record was the envy of many of his fellow batchmates from the IPS. Though his unorthodox methods of investigation were not always looked upon favourably by his superiors, even his detractors agreed that Kapoor's tenacity was unmatched. He would dig deep into a case, examine every lead, however insignificant, and sniff out clues that defied the possibilities, until the case was solved.

He had built up a fearsome reputation for solving the most complicated cases against all odds.

And this one was possibly the most difficult case he had come across so far. He was looking forward to the investigation. This case had the potential to be the highlight of his career.

Kapoor reviewed the report for the umpteenth time. By now, he knew its contents by heart.

Trivedi's neighbours had heard bloodcurdling screams and had rushed to the schoolmaster's flat only to find it locked and barred from inside. There was no way they could get in; the outer door was made of solid iron. Even as they had tried to break into the flat, while waiting for the police to arrive, Trivedi's screams had faded away, replaced by a deathly silence.

The police had arrived after an hour. It had taken another hour to get the tools to cut open the iron grill door and access the apartment.

Trivedi's lifeless body was lying on the floor next to the dining table, on which lay his mobile phone. A quick look around the flat revealed that nothing seemed to have been disturbed or removed. And how could anything have been stolen anyway? Both doors at the entrance had been locked from the inside — the police had had to break down the iron, as well as the wooden door to enter.

That was when the first mystery had reared its head. Despite the yells and agonizing screams that had tipped the neighbours off, there were no signs of trauma on the teacher's body. No possible indications of the cause of death. An autopsy was called for.

And now that the initial results of the autopsy were in, they had thrown up another set of questions.

The dead man's internal organs displayed all the symptoms of having been subjected to intense heat. It was as if Trivedi had been trapped in a blazing fire, unable to escape, and had finally been burnt alive. The report detailed the colour and texture of his organs to substantiate the conclusion, which was clear: fifth degree burns. The man had had no chance of survival.

Therein lay the mystery. Far from the charring normally associated with fifth degree burns, Trivedi's skin was unblemished. In fact even his clothing was intact. It was as if his skin and clothes had been untouched by the fire that had consumed his internal organs.

That was not all. Trivedi's lungs showed no indication of his having inhaled smoke or died of asphyxiation, a common killer of people trapped in infernos. His lungs and air passageways were clean, or as clean as they could be living in a polluted city like New Delhi.

Kapoor couldn't understand it. Had the autopsy missed something? How could a man die of internal burns when his clothing and skin were untouched by fire?

He picked up the phone and dialled a number.

Kapoor came straight to the point as soon as the call was answered. 'The last call on Trivedi's phone. I want to meet the man he spoke to. Tomorrow.'

He put the receiver down and leaned back in his chair, his brow furrowing as he tried to think his way through this one.

Whichever way he tried to analyze it, there was only one conclusion he could come to.

Things were not as they seemed. Something big was happening here. Something that he did not understand.

He could only hope that it wouldn't be too late before he discovered what they were.

Chapter Three

The Miseries of History

Day Three

Present Day
New Delhi

Damn History!

Arjun scowled at his text book, but he knew he was being unfair. It wasn't the subject that was to blame. In fact he had loved history until just two days ago.

That was when they had found out about the death of Dhananjay Trivedi, or DJ sir, as he was affectionately called by the students. The news had crushed him.

Arjun had been in this school for the past ten years, since nursery, and loved most of his teachers. He had never been one of the class toppers but was diligent in his studies, if a little talkative and fidgety.

He had always displayed a greater proclivity for sports, where he excelled. Not only had he won accolades in athletics, swimming and tennis but he also played football, basketball and cricket. He had represented the school in all these activities and had been a part of the winning team on several occasions at inter-school tournaments.

His teachers, through the years, had understood his talents and patiently nurtured him. Of course, they reprimanded him when he daydreamed in class or engaged in surreptitious conversations with the student sitting next to him; but they would also encourage him and try to bring out the best in him. Arjun appreciated their patience and was grateful for their guidance. It was one of the reasons he loved school so much — the teachers made all the difference.

And then there was DJ sir. The very best amongst all the teachers at school. He had been ... well, different. While the other teachers encouraged students, Dj sir had the ability to inspire them. His own love for History compelled his students to focus on the subject and do well in it. Arjun too had been drawn to the subject only because of him. And now his teacher was gone ...

'Arjun!' the voice of Sumitra, DJ sir's replacement cut through his thoughts. 'I don't know why your parents send you to school. Waste of their money and waste of my damn time!'

Arjun grimaced. In just two days, he had begun hating history with a vengeance. And he knew it was because of Sumitra.

With Dhananjay Trivedi's sudden demise, the school authorities had been left floundering. An immediate replacement was needed, and the history department had reallocated classes to Sumitra. She had taught history to the eleventh and twelfth grades for the last four years.

Her reputation among the senior classes had already filtered down to the ninth grade.

With a PhD in History from St. Stephen's College, Delhi, when Sumitra had joined the school, four years ago, there was much excitement amongst the children. The students had expected to welcome a teacher who was steeped in learning and loved the subject.

Instead, they soon learned that, far from being an enthusiastic teacher, she actually hated children. She had admitted as much privately to a couple of her favourite students. Of course, no one spoke about it publicly; doing so would have invited her wrath — and an F grade for sure. As it was, she was known to generously dole out E grades to any student she took a dislike to for reasons that she did not care to share.

And Arjun and his classmates had found her reputation to be well founded. If anything, she was more of a terror than they had expected.

Whether it was because she felt she had been demoted to teach the middle school, or that she resented the extra workload, she seemed to have become more vindictive and harsher than the stories about her had indicated. Of course, as per her routine practice, she had chosen four or five students to be her favourites in class. These students hung on to her every word and adored her. The rest of the grade loathed her.

Clearly, Arjun was not amongst the chosen few.

'You are going to fail in your terminals.' Sumitra hadn't finished with Arjun yet. 'I'm going to see to it.'

Arjun bit back the retort that threatened to burst out of him.

There was no point in responding to her, especially by way of argument.

It was better to keep mum, he decided.

He was saved by the bell going off, announcing the end of school. Relieved, he quickly stuffed his books in his bag and joined the throng of students in the corridor as they moved towards the school gates, all thoughts of Sumitra Ma'am forgotten.

There was a spring in his step. Not because school was over — he actually loved being in school — but because his uncle, Virendra Singh, had promised to teach him a new sword-fighting technique that day. Virendra had been teaching Arjun the art of sword fighting since the third grade. It was an unusual sport with little practical use since it really wasn't an organized, or even recognized, sport that he could compete in, but Arjun loved it anyway. His uncle had explained to him that this sport combined intelligence, alertness, strategy and speed of response with strength and agility, as few other sports did. They had started with wooden sticks for swords, but Arjun was a natural sportsman and had picked up the art well enough to graduate to training with real swords by the time he was in the seventh grade. He enjoyed the training and looked forward to it — it was intensive and exhausting, but somehow mentally rejuvenating.

When he was training he could banish all unpleasant thoughts from his mind. The thought of Sumitra, for example, especially today.

The technique Virendra had promised to teach Arjun today was one that could only be imparted to a swordsman who had reached a certain level of mastery; one that usually took anywhere between seven to ten years to accomplish. Arjun had been thrilled that his uncle had considered him worthy after just six years of training.

A girl waved to him and smiled broadly as he approached the gate. 'Hey AJ!' she called out.

Arjun grinned back. Maya and he weren't just close friends, they had grown up together. His uncle and her father were old mates from Allahabad and both had apparently come to Delhi at almost the same time. They also lived a short drive from each other's house and met almost every day. Maya and he went home together daily after school, except on days when he had to stay back for sports practice.

They ended up spending a lot of time together and their bond had only grown stronger over time. Maya was always cheerful and highly optimistic about everything. She was a great listener and a loyal friend. She was the only girl he felt he could trust with his secrets.

The two teenagers looked around for Arjun's uncle. Virendra would drop them in the morning and pick them up after school. On days when Arjun had sports practice, Virendra would first pick up Maya and then return later to pick up Arjun when he finished. This was a practice that had been established since the two children had joined school.

Last year, when Arjun had entered the eighth grade he had tried to break free of this daily routine.

'I'm old enough to go to school by myself,' he had argued with his mother, Pramila. 'Loads of kids do it. They come to school by auto, Metro or the bus. It's totally safe. Why do I need to be dropped and picked up?'

But Pramila had refused outright. 'When the time comes, you will be free to do as you wish,' she had said. Arjun had sulked and fumed but his mother had been unaffected. The daily chaperoning, to and from school, had continued.

Arjun had tried speaking to his uncle too, but his words had only echoed Pramila's.

'When you are ready,' Virendra had said, placing a hand on Arjun's shoulder, 'I will push you forward to be independent, to take charge even. You will shake off your reliance on your mother and me and take your place in the world. But that time has not yet come. This is a dangerous city. You don't realize it because ... well, we've sheltered you. You'll have to face it all someday, but only when you are prepared. Until then all I can say is, trust me. Please.'

Grownups could be so melodramatic. All he had wanted was some freedom ... sheesh! Arjun had seethed inwardly but had seen no point in raising the issue again. It would be futile. He didn't want to deal with their paranoia. Arjun wondered if Maya felt the same way as him, constrained and dependent. After all she, too, led a pretty sheltered life.

'Oh, look, it's your mom.' Maya tugged at Arjun's arm, having spotted Pramila among the parents standing outside the gate, each peering intently towards the school entrance, trying to catch sight of their wards.

They hurried towards Pramila. 'Where's uncle?' Arjun asked. 'We have sword practice today. He said he would ...'

'He had to go somewhere with Maya's dad,' Pramila cut in. 'They'll be back soon. Maya will stay with us till they return,' she said as the children piled into the car.

Chapter Four

Meeting the Police

SP Kapoor's office
New Delhi

SP Raman Kapoor regarded the two men sitting across the desk. Both seemed to be of the same age, in their early to mid-forties. The one who had introduced himself as Dr. Naresh Upadhyay was tall and gaunt with a prominent forehead. He was the head of the history department at a local school. The other, Virendra Singh, was tall and well-built and extremely fit for his age, which suited his occupation as the owner of a prominent gym that had branches all over the city. Both men claimed to be friends of the deceased, Dhananjay Trivedi.

'So, *you* were the last person to speak to the victim,' Kapoor addressed Upadhyay. It sounded like an accusation and Kapoor immediately regretted his tone. He was accustomed to dealing with hardened criminals, not genteel folk like the two men before him. He felt that he should have modified his usual way of interrogation.

Upadhyay nodded. He seemed not to have noticed Kapoor's insinuation. His eyes had a sad and weary look.

'And you, sir?' Kapoor shifted his gaze to Virendra Singh.

The big man shrugged. 'I wish I had spoken to him before he died. He was a close friend. The three of us were together for many years in Allahabad.'

'And by sheer coincidence, you all turned up in New Delhi.' It was a statement but Kapoor managed to insert a hint of scepticism, almost turning it into a question.

'I'm glad it happened that way,' Upadhyay responded. 'As Virendra said, we were good friends.'

Kapoor prided himself on being discerning. He was an astute officer and his judgment of people was rarely wrong. And he was getting the feeling that, although both men seemed honest, there was more to their story than they were letting on. He decided to get to the point.

'The reason I asked you to meet me,' Kapoor addressed Upadhyay, 'is because you spoke to Dhananjay Trivedi just before his murder.'

Upadhyay's eyes widened. 'Murder?' He exchanged a quick glance with Virendra, an action that did not go unnoticed by the SP.

'Yes, murder,' Kapoor affirmed, 'and a most mysterious one at that. I do not mind admitting that we are at our wit's end trying to figure this one out. I was hoping you could shed some light on this case. We need all the help we can get.'

'We will do whatever we can to help you,' Upadhyay assured Kapoor, gravely. 'We want nothing more than to bring Dhananjay's killer to justice.'

Kapoor nodded. 'Good. You can start by telling me what Trivedi and you spoke about during that last call.'

'Sure,' Upadhyay replied. 'He told me that he had met someone, a young man, outside school that day and he wanted to know if I knew this person.'

Kapoor's eyes narrowed. *Could this be the lead he was looking for?*

'And who was this young man?' he asked.

'A young student from Allahabad. He gave his name as Vishwaraj.'

'And did you know him?' Kapoor pressed.

'I have heard of him,' Upadhyay admitted, 'but I can't say I know him, and that's what I told Dhananjay. If he is the same Vishwaraj, then he studied in a school where I had taught for a while, so I am familiar with the name.'

'Vishwaraj,' Kapoor repeated, looking thoughtful, as if he was trying to etch the name in his memory. 'Any description?'

Upadhyay shook his head. 'Like I said, I don't know the boy.'

'I meant, did Trivedi give you a description?'

'No, he didn't,' Upadhyay paused. 'What makes you think it was murder?'

Kapoor contemplated the question for a few moments. These men seemed to be his only means to solve this case, at least for now. He decided to be candid. He told them about the preliminary autopsy report and its baffling conclusions.

It did not escape his notice that the two men exchanged another quick glance when he mentioned that while the victim had died of severe internal burns there were no external burn injuries on his body.

'So,' Kapoor concluded, 'what do you make of all this? And is there anything you would like to tell us about the victim which could help us find the person behind this?'

Virendra had sat, stoic and silent, until now. 'SP sahib,' he said, in a deep baritone, 'what you have described — the autopsy report's conclusion — is physically impossible.' He glanced yet again at his friend sitting next to him and then back to Kapoor. 'I am not a superstitious man, but if what you say is true, then this is not a matter for the police. It sounds like a case involving the supernatural.'

Kapoor stared at him, unsure if he was being facetious. But Virendra stared back at him, unblinking. The SP realized that the man was serious. He shook his head a little incredulously.

'I don't believe in the supernatural,' he said firmly. 'There has to be a rational explanation for the murder. And no matter who is behind this, we shall get to the bottom of it.' He looked at both men in turn. 'Thank you for your time and for coming in to meet me. I appreciate your cooperation.'

The two men rose to leave.

'One more thing,' Kapoor said as the men turned. 'Please don't leave town without informing me. I may want to ask you both a few more questions. This is a request.'

As the two men left his room, Kapoor picked up the phone and dialled a number. 'I want them watched,' he instructed. 'Yes, the two who came in to see me just now. They are hiding something and I want to find out what that is.'

Chapter Five

A Bolt from the Blue

Arjun's house
New Delhi

'But why are we leaving?' Arjun's mind was in turmoil. He couldn't understand what was suddenly happening.

His uncle and Maya's father had returned home a short while ago. The two men and Arjun's mother had shut themselves in a room since, apparently discussing something important.

Maya and he had sat talking about the history test that was scheduled for the next day. It was supposed to have been held three days ago, but two of Sumitra's favourite students hadn't come to school that day so she had rescheduled it.

'Better make it for the test tomorrow, AJ,' Maya chuckled. 'She won't reschedule it for you!'

'Oh, I'll be there alright,' Arjun had grinned back.

Just then, the adults had emerged from their 'secret meeting'. Maya and her father had left soon after.

That was when Virendra had dropped the bombshell.

'We're leaving town,' he announced. 'All three of us. Immediately.'

Shocked, Arjun had turned to his mother for an explanation. Pramila, seemingly unfazed, was already packing essentials. Only then had it dawned on him. She already knew! This was what they had been discussing with Naresh uncle.

But what could the reason be? And why the hurry? And where were they going? Would they ever return? When? What would he do about the history test? Sumitra would have his skin!

But there were no answers forthcoming. Both Virendra and Pramila were tightlipped.

'What about the gyms?' he asked desperate for a response.

'Sharma has been informed. He runs them anyway. I won't be missed,' Virendra had a ready answer. Sharma was the chief operating officer of Virendra's company, which owned the gyms.

Defeated, Arjun began throwing his clothes into a suitcase, in sullen despair. No one ever shared anything with him. It was the adults who made all the decisions. Neither of them bothered to consider what his feelings were, or if he would even like to move.

He felt a pang as he saw his books and his sporting gear, none of which he could take along. Virendra had been very clear: they were going to travel light. The only exception his uncle had made was for their set of practice swords, which Arjun now lovingly packed in a wooden case, crafted especially for the purpose of carrying the swords around.

Within no time, their suitcases were packed and loaded into Virendra's Land Cruiser.

Arjun took one last look at the house before they drove off. Would he ever see the house again? Or his school friends?

'What about Maya?' He suddenly realized he had not spoken to her. 'I need to call her.' He took out his phone.

'You can speak to her when we reach,' Virendra said firmly from behind the wheel. 'Anyway, I am sure her father will tell her.'

Pramila looked at her son, understanding his anguish at leaving his best friend behind. 'There's a reason for this, Arjun,' she said. 'I promise we will explain everything. Just be patient for a while. Please.'

Tears welled up in Arjun's eyes as he folded his arms tight and hugged himself. He looked out of the window, trying to hide his true feelings.

Only a few hours ago, he had been fretting about school work and Sumitra. And now, suddenly it seemed like his life had changed.

What he didn't know was that it would never be the same again.

Chapter Six

A Visitor

Maya's House
New Delhi

'What's the matter, Dad?' Maya asked. Her father's usually cheerful face was grave and dark today, like a storm on the horizon. He had been unusually silent and preoccupied during the drive home from Arjun's house. Maya had busied herself with her digital Walkman, listening to her favourite tunes. Now, as they reached the house, Maya thought she would try to find out what was bothering him.

Upadhyay seemed to awaken from a trance. He took a moment to respond. 'Oh, nothing, really,' he replied finally, attempting the shadow of a smile. 'Just some bad news that came in today.'

'Bad news, huh?' Maya put her headphones back on and returned to her music. Clearly, her father was disinclined to share any information with her. So, she figured, either it wasn't too important or she was not supposed to know. Either way, it seemed pointless to keep asking him about it. He would tell her when he wanted to.

'I'm going to be in my room if you need me, Dad. Have a test coming up tomorrow,' Maya told Upadhyay, as they entered the house.

Upadhyay nodded absently and made his way to the study. It was where he spent a lot of his time reading and researching. The walls of his study were lined with bookshelves on three sides. He headed for one in particular and began studying the titles on the shelf. Finally, he found what he was looking for. An old leather diary, well-thumbed and worn.

He opened the diary and flipped through the pages, which bore inscriptions in Sanskrit, written by hand.

When he reached the page he was looking for, he frowned and sat down at his desk, reading the inscription intently. Finally, he closed the book and sat for some time, looking into the distance, lost in thought.

After a while, he rose and made his way to one of the bookshelves and removed a few books to reveal the door of a safe built into the wall. He opened the safe and took out a sheet of paper. He studied it carefully before walking over to the desk and placing it in the notebook he had been reading a few moments ago.

Then, he returned to the safe and took out something. It was a golden amulet on a chain. He gazed at the amulet nestled in the palm of his hand, then closed his fingers around it and locked the safe.

After making sure everything was back to where it had been, he made his way to Maya's room and knocked on the door. 'Maya?'

'Ya, Dad, come in!'

He opened the door and stepped into the room.

'Sorry to disturb you, sweetheart, but I wanted to give you this.' He opened his palm, revealing the amulet. 'You must wear this at all times from now on.'

'Come on, Dad, what's this for?' Maya made a face. 'Not another of your rituals, is it? You know I don't …' she let her words trail. Her father already knew how she felt about these things.

Her disregard for such trinkets, as she thought of them, had deep roots. Her mother had died when she was still a baby. While her father had showered her with more love than most children get from both parents, she still missed having a mother around. Somehow, a father was different. There were some things that she could not say to him; things she could not share with him. Things she needed a mother for. She loved her father deeply, and didn't really have any recollection of her mother, but she did miss her.

And the question always stayed in her mind: if rituals, prayers, amulets and other such things had such immense power, why had her father not used them to save her mother?

It wasn't that she blamed him for not doing enough to save her mother; maybe he had tried—she didn't know and had never asked him; it would be intruding on not just his private thoughts but also on the grief she knew he had felt on losing his wife at such an early age. And whether he had tried or not, it only showed the limitations of rituals, prayers and baubles like the amulet. They really were of no use.

Upadhyay tried to smile, a weak, watery smile. 'This is for your protection, my dear. I hope to God that you won't need it, but just in case ... Promise me that you will wear this at all times and never let it leave you for even a moment.'

Maya started to protest but stopped when she saw her father's face. For just a moment, she thought she saw a flicker of fear and then it was gone.

She was taken aback. Ever since she could remember, she had known her father to be fearless. On one occasion, she remembered clearly, he had even taken on a mob which was hell bent on beating a driver, involved in a road accident, to death. He had waded into the rioting crowd and calmed them down with no fear for his own life or well-being. That was her dad; always ready to stand up for what he believed in, always fearless.

Yet, she was sure she had seen fear on his face for the first time today. A grim foreboding crept into her heart. What was her father afraid of?

Realizing that he was serious about his request, she wordlessly took the amulet from him and slipped it around her neck.

Just then, the doorbell rang.

'I'll see who it is. You carry on with your studies.' Upadhyay shut the door behind him as he left to answer the bell.

'Hi Diya,' he greeted the young girl at the door, with a smile. 'Come on in.'

Diya was a twelfth grade student in his school. But only Upadhyay and a few others knew that she was no ordinary student. She was also a member of the *Gana*.

'Why didn't you call?' he asked, indicating for her to sit down on the sofa. 'You know face to face meetings are to be avoided as far as possible.'

'This was too important, *Mahamati* Dhruv,' Diya explained, addressing Upadhyay by his real name and the respectful title given to the elder members of the *Sangha*.

'Diya, hush!' Upadhyay leaned forward. 'That name is not to be taken even in my house. Now tell me, is this to do with Vishwaraj?'

Diya nodded. 'We've discovered where he is hiding.' She looked around. 'Can I please have a pen and paper? I will draw you a map.'

Upadhyay rose and went to the study. He felt hopeful. The mists were clearing. He didn't know what role the boy had played in what had befallen Trivedi, and he certainly couldn't believe that Vishwaraj was powerful enough to have killed his friend. But Vishwaraj had threatened Trivedi. His friend had told him as much during their last conversation. And the boy had known something that only Upadhyay, Trivedi, Virendra, and a handful of others, were supposed to know. It was imperative that he meet Vishwaraj and find out more. He needed to know who was involved.

All the facts pointed in one direction. To one person. He involuntarily shuddered at the thought. It was not a pleasant one.

But only Vishwaraj could give them conclusive answers. Now that they had discovered his hideaway, it was just a matter of time.

He took a sheet of paper and a pen and turned around.

Upadhyay froze in his tracks.

The sofa, on which Diya was supposed to be sitting, was visible from his desk in the study through the open door.

But she wasn't sitting there anymore.

In her place, was a large man with an impressive physique, well over six and a half feet tall, with a black, bushy beard. His black hair grew long at the back, touching his shoulders, and he wore an eyepatch over one eye.

With his other eye, he was looking into the study, straight at Upadhyay.

A cold chill ran down the history teacher's spine. So he had been right about Trivedi's murder. It was this formidable man, whose involvement he had feared. But, even though he had expected to encounter him at some point, he had not thought it would be so soon. And definitely not in his own house.

He was totally unprepared for the confrontation he knew would follow.

Chapter Seven

New Suspects?

SP Kapoor's office
New Delhi

SP Raman Kapoor put the phone down and pondered the news he had just been given. Virendra Singh, one of the two friends of the victim, had gone straight home after their meeting and had just left his house with his sister and nephew. The man who had been assigned to shadow them had reported that they were carrying suitcases. Obviously the trio was leaving town.

A frown creased his forehead. What was going on here? Could this be a coincidence? Perhaps Virendra and family had already planned a vacation? Something told Kapoor that this was not the case. He had quite clearly requested both men to inform him if they intended to leave town. Singh had not mentioned anything about an upcoming trip. Surely he would have informed Kapoor had there been a plan.

If Singh had wanted to, that is.

That was the key. Whether this trip was planned or not, Singh had had no intention of informing Kapoor. While there was no obvious evidence that this sudden flight had any connection with the murder of Trivedi, Kapoor's intuition urged him to pursue that line of thought.

Another thought had started forming in his mind. He had convinced himself, after just one meeting with the men, that they were honest, upright folk who could have had nothing to do with the murder. But had he made a mistake?

Was it possible that he had let suspects in the case get away?

Kapoor could not believe his instincts would betray him. There had been nothing in the demeanour of the men, during his meeting with them, to indicate their direct involvement in the crime.

Upadhyay's house was still under surveillance. Kapoor had been informed that the teacher had received a visitor a short while ago. So Upadhyay, at least, was still in town. Was he in the clear, then? Kapoor remembered the glances that the men had exchanged every time he had brought up anything of significance. If Singh was involved, it was extremely likely that Upadhyay was too.

Too many possibilities and not enough evidence.

It didn't matter, Kapoor thought grimly. Singh's vehicle was still being tailed. His man had very clear instructions to follow Singh wherever he went.

He would get to the bottom of the matter.

Come what may.

Chapter Eight

Son of Bhrigu

Maya's House
New Delhi

The two men stood staring at each other, their eyes locked.

The silence was deafening.

Then the intruder spoke. His voice was deep, yet mellifluous, and in some ways at odds with his intimidating appearance.

'You don't seem surprised, Dhruv.'

Upadhyay forced himself to relax. 'I was expecting you,' he said simply, as he entered the sitting room and sat down facing the large man.

Diya was nowhere to be seen. He gestured around the room.

'Another of your illusions, Son of Bhrigu?' he asked.

The large man chuckled, apparently amused by Upadhyay's question. 'Yes. Even after being away for 5,000 years, meditating, I haven't lost my touch. You have to agree.'

Upadhyay felt a deep, dark fear take root in his soul. He had faced the intruder before and knew that he had never been a match for this man. Upadhyay was also painfully aware, that the son of Bhrigu had spent the last 5,000 years in meditation, gaining powers that he had never had before.

Still, he pulled himself together. The man was in his house now. There weren't too many options. He knew what was going to happen.

And he knew how it would end.

Another realization had struck him. If Diya had been an illusion, then this man knew about the *Gana*. He had known enough to track Upadhyay down.

'What did you do to Diya?' he demanded, concern for the girl overriding his fears.

The big man smiled; a smile that failed to reach his eyes. 'What do you think?' he shot back, then waved a hand. 'Let's not waste time in trifles.'

He looked Upadhyay in the eye. 'I want the boy. After disposing of Trivedi, I knew that whoever was responsible for the boy's escape would show their hand. And you did.' He shrugged. 'I mean, I always did suspect you but I had no evidence to back it up. But finally, I know. And, here we are. Just like old times, huh?' He spoke casually but Upadhyay knew the danger that lurked behind his humourless words.

'You killed Dhananjay?' Upadhyay was beside himself with rage. 'And you knew he was not involved with what happened in Allahabad?'

The stranger clicked his tongue impatiently. 'Trivedi was no more than bait. You see, he led me straight to you. So here I am. And I want the boy. This time, I will not let you come in my way, Dhruv.'

Upadhyay steeled himself for what was going to follow. He leaned forward and held the intruder's gaze. 'You will never reach the boy, Shukra.' His voice was hard. 'You forget the warning of the Saptarishis. Do not presume to continue what you started 5,000 years ago. You will be stopped.'

Shukra sprang to his feet, his face dark with fury. 'You dare threaten me with the Saptarishis?' he thundered. 'That powerless bunch? This is Kaliyuga, Dhruv. Even the Devas cannot stop me now! The whole lot of them can watch from their palaces and mansions, helpless and useless!'

He advanced menacingly towards Upadhyay. 'I will allow nothing to stop me now. Give me the boy. Tell me where he is and I will spare you.' His voice boomed in the small sitting room.

Upadhyay's eyes glinted with defiance. 'I don't know where he is,' he said, truthfully. 'But even if I did, I would not deliver him to you.'

'Very well. I gave you a chance and you refused. We'll do it the hard way then.'

Upadhyay's eyes widened as he realized what Shukra had in mind.

Chapter Nine

Maya's Amulet

Maya's House
New Delhi

Maya could hear the faint sound of a man shouting. She looked up from her book, concerned. It was not her father's voice. It must be the visitor who had rung the doorbell. She had, at first, heard the low murmur of voices as her father and his visitor seemed to be engaged in conversation. Then suddenly she heard raised voices. Disconcerted, Maya walked to her door, unsure of whether she should go out into the living room.

Her hand was still on the door handle, when the shouting abruptly stopped. There was silence now.

No voices.

An eerie calm prevailed. It unnerved her.

What was happening out there?

Her father's guests were always soft spoken, polite, usually scholarly people — like her father. While there were frequent discussions on various academic and political issues, she could never once remember hearing raised voices in her house.

Maya fingered the amulet that hung around her neck, making up her mind about what to do next.

The deafening silence persisted. Maya knew what she had to do. She opened the door of her room, and stepped into the corridor that led to the sitting area.

The sight that greeted her eyes filled her with horror.

Greater Noida
Taj Expressway

'Yes, sir,' the plainclothes constable in the unmarked Gypsy spoke into his earpiece. 'They made just one stop in Noida, to pick up something from a house. I don't know what it was but they sat for a few minutes in the car before starting off again.'

'Where are they now?' SP Kapoor's voice came over his earpiece.

'They're heading towards Agra. They don't know that I am following them.'

'And keep it that way, Harish. I want you to follow them right until their final destination. Call me anytime you find anything unusual. Even if it is at midnight!'

'Yes, sir,' Harish, Virendra Singh's shadow, signed off.

Chapter Ten

The Notebook

Maya's House
New Delhi

Maya stood transfixed by the scene before her.

She wanted to scream but couldn't.

Tears of horror and despair welled up in her eyes as she stared, terror stricken, at the sight of her father suspended in the air in an upright position, two feet above the floor. His body was stiff and his face contorted, though whether in pain or anger, she couldn't tell.

One thing was clear, though. The enormous man standing in front of her father, with his back towards her and his arms folded before him, had him in his control. The man seemed to be chanting something under his breath.

Maya caught the words.

Sanskrit.

Her father had taught her the language. She recognized it instantly.

It hit her like a ton of bricks.

The man was chanting mantras!

Maya couldn't believe what she was hearing. This was impossible!

She had come across some mantras in the ancient Vedic texts that her father had made her read. But she had never believed that they actually worked. They were part of the rituals that she didn't believe in.

Yet this man was definitely chanting mantras and, as she listened, she understood, with horror, what he was trying to do.

What was happening? Maya felt like her head would explode. All of a sudden, through her terror and despondency, she heard the whisper of a voice, caressing the surface of her mind.

'*Maya!*'

It was faint, as if emanating from far away. She almost dismissed it but then, she heard it again.

And again.

Like someone calling to her. The voice seemed familiar and yet sounded like nothing she had ever heard before.

The large man had not noticed her yet. Or, if he had, he was ignoring her, focusing all his attention on her father, concentrating on getting what he wanted.

Maya's helpless eyes fell on her father's face and she realized why it was contorted.

The voice was his! He was trying to speak to her using his thoughts!

Too many bizarre things were happening for Maya to pause and ponder on her father's telepathic powers. All she knew was that he was trying to communicate with her. She had to respond, somehow, anyhow.

She looked at him intently, noticing now how his eyes were fixed on his opponent, as if fighting back with his mind, trying to stave him off.

Slowly, she backed away from the sitting room, deeper into the corridor, trying to focus on the voice in her head. The harder she concentrated, the clearer the voice became.

'*Listen to me carefully,*' her father's voice urged. '*I cannot hold him off much longer without letting him know I am in contact with you. Take the handwritten diary on my desk and run! Get away from this house! Call Virendra. Tell him. Go now! Don't stop to think. Just do as I say. Don't look back. And don't come back.*' There was a pause. The voice seemed to be getting fainter now. '*Always remember this: I love you.*'

The voice died and an agonized cry sprang from Upadhyay's lips. His opponent had finally got the better of him.

'You ... will ... never ... succeed ... Shukra,' Maya heard her father struggle to get the words out. 'I have fulfilled my destiny. You will achieve nothing even if you kill me now.'

'It will be enough for me just to see you die, Dhruv,' the man growled angrily. 'You went to great lengths to cross me. Did you really think you would escape with your life?'

Maya had heard enough. She knew she had to act on her father's warning now or it would be too late. Holding back an urge to scream, she tore herself away from the painful scene that was unfolding in the sitting room. Unable to think straight through the clouds of fear and panic in her mind, she could only mechanically carry out the instructions her father had given her.

She slipped off her shoes and padded down the corridor in her bare feet, shoes in hand, careful to not make a sound. She did not think Shukra — as her father had called the big man — knew of her existence yet. She planned to keep it that way.

The corridor led through another door into the study, which was carpeted.

She slipped on her shoes and walked as quietly as possible to the desk.

There were three books on it.

Her hands shook with fear. She had to act fast.

Her father had mentioned a handwritten diary. She opened the first book. It was printed.

The second book was an old leather notebook.

Could this be it?

Maya opened it to a page at random. A sheet of paper slipped out of the notebook, and disappeared under the desk. Maya saw that the writing was in the Devanagari script.

A handwritten diary. This was it.

She kneeled on the carpet to see where the sheet of paper was. She spotted it under the desk. Maya rose and picked up the diary, preparing to tiptoe around the desk to retrieve it.

She found herself looking directly at Shukra. His gaze was fixed on her.

Maya stopped in her tracks. Her mind, numbed by fear and pain from witnessing her father's ordeal, desperately searched for a way out. Shukra was still in the sitting room, torturing her father but he seemed to have weakened him enough that he could now focus on Maya. He stared down at her.

Something was happening to her. She couldn't think straight.

Shukra's eyes bored into her, paralysing her. She felt as if they were invading the depths of her soul, reading her deepest emotions, rifling through her darkest thoughts. Something inside Maya made her resist it with all her might.

Suddenly, she found the mists clearing. She was able to think.

Something had broken Shukra's stranglehold on her mind.

It was her father. He was shouting.

'Run, Maya!'

She didn't stop to think. The urgency in her father's voice, the desperation in his plea, were enough.

Tearing her gaze away from Shukra's eyes, she sprinted away. The corridor outside the study led to the kitchen from where a back door opened out into a narrow lane behind the house.

Escape was so close.

Suddenly a blinding flash ripped through her head as she ran.

She went blank and stumbled.

There came a roar of anger from the sitting room.

It was accompanied by a cry of anguish. Of pain.

And death.

Maya found herself sprawled on the floor of the study, clutching the leather diary.

There was no time to wonder about what was happening. She had to keep going.

Picking herself up, she dashed for the study door.

This time, nothing stopped her. Down the corridor she ran, into the kitchen, where she struggled briefly with the bolts on the door leading outside.

Then she was in the lane behind the house. The kitchen door shut behind her.

Maya looked around, wild-eyed.

She didn't feel safe here.

Where could she go?

Chapter Eleven

Some Unexpected News

SP Kapoor's Office
New Delhi

Raman Kapoor snatched up his phone as soon as it rang. It was a call from Ajit, the constable who was assigned to shadow Upadhyay. His last report had been about the schoolmaster receiving a visitor. The man hadn't reported in since then.

'Yes?' Kapoor barked, eager to know the development.

Ajit's voice was low and serious. 'Sir,' he began, then hesitated. 'Upadhyay is dead.'

'Dead?' Kapoor echoed, shocked. This was the last thing he had expected to hear. The man had been hale and hearty just a few hours ago.

'Yes, sir,' the constable began to explain, 'I was waiting outside, keeping an eye on things as you had ordered. A few minutes ago, I heard screams coming from the house. Then, the man who had visited Mr. Upadhyay came striding out and walked away leaving the front door open.' He hesitated again. 'Sir, I know you had instructed me to keep a distance from Mr. Upadhayay and not contact him in any way. But the screams and the open door made me suspicious and I was concerned. So I decided to investigate.'

'And you found Upadhyay dead. Are you sure though? Have you called a doctor?'

'Um, sir, there can be no doubt of that. His body has been torn from limb to limb. There is blood all over the sitting room.'

Kapoor couldn't believe what he was hearing. He collected his thoughts. 'Call for a backup immediately. I am on my way.'

'I have already radioed for backup, sir. I did that before I called you.'

'Good man,' Kapoor nodded approvingly. 'Was there anyone else in the house?'

'No, sir.'

'I thought Upadhyay had a daughter?'

'Yes, sir. And they came home together. But I did a quick sweep of the house after finding the body. There is no one else in the house.'

'What do you mean? Where could she disappear to?' Kapoor was getting anxious. This case was getting more and more complicated.

'I can't say for sure, sir. I didn't see her leave the house. But I did find another exit. The kitchen door at the back of the house opens into a lane that runs behind it.'

'I suppose you checked out the lane as well?'

'Yes, sir. There was no sign of the girl.'

He rose. 'We must find the girl. She is the only one who can tell us exactly what happened in that house,' he said before disconnecting the phone.

Kapoor's mind raced as he considered the possibilities. The girl could have been a witness to what happened to her father. Or maybe she saw what was happening and ran for help. That seemed much more likely to Kapoor; a child seeing her father butchered may not find the strength to flee the spot. He only hoped the girl had not been harmed in any way.

As Kapoor signalled to a constable to get his car ready, he wondered if this murder was linked to the murder of Trivedi.

Two friends, two murders. There had to be a link.

But what was it?

The only way for him to find out was to locate Virendra Singh, and Upadhyay's daughter.

Now he had two people to hunt.

Near Upadhyay's House
New Delhi

Blinded by tears that streamed down her face, Maya sprinted down the lane, passing houses on both sides without stopping to think of asking for help. Her father had been emphatic about her leaving the house and not returning, even to help him. The sound of his screams and cries of pain still rang in her ears. She had to get as far from her house as possible.

Maya knew her father must be dead by now. The urgency in his tone, his absolute insistence that she flee, had told her that even he had known his fate. Staying there any longer would have meant certain death for her. Even though she didn't know who the stranger was or why he had burst into their house to kill her father, she knew that he would not hesitate to harm her.

Her hand tightly clutched the diary she had picked up from the study. She didn't know why her father had considered it to be important. But if he had asked her to retrieve it, even at the risk of being discovered by the man he had addressed as Shukra, there must be something special about it.

But what was she supposed to do with it? She didn't even know where she was headed at this moment.

Maya's world was a storm of confusion and terror.

So, she ran. It was the only thing she could do.

The lane opened out onto a larger side road. Maya didn't stop to choose. She turned left and kept running.

After several minutes, she slowed down and took stock of her surroundings, her breath coming in gasps. The streetlights had just begun to wink on. Before her, just a few hundred yards away loomed a metro station.

She stopped and thought for a moment. Her sides were aching and she needed to catch her breath. How far had she run? She didn't know but she felt that she had put enough distance between the house and herself. For now.

Her father's words came back to her as she tried to collect her wits. She remembered now that he had told her to call his friend, Virendra.

But she didn't have his number.

Arjun.

Of course.

She checked the pockets of her jeans and thanked her stars. She had her phone.

She pulled it out and dialled Arjun's number.

Chapter Twelve

An Urgent Call for Help

The Taj Express Highway
Uttar Pradesh

Arjun glanced at his phone as it rang.

'It's Maya,' he announced. 'I know you said that I could only speak to her when we reach wherever we are going,' he said, stressing on the ambiguity of their destination, 'but if she's calling now, it means her father has told her already. She wants to speak to me.'

'Fine,' Virendra said. 'Go ahead and take the call. I guess it is only fair.'

Just then the phone stopped ringing.

'It's okay, Arjun. No need to call back,' Virendra remarked, a bit too casually according to his nephew. 'If it is urgent, she'll call you.'

Arjun stared at the phone glumly, irritated. He badly wanted to speak to Maya. He couldn't understand why there were so many constraints. Why was their departure so sudden and hush hush that he hadn't even been allowed to call his best friend? He grimaced and fought back the resentment that was bubbling up within him.

He fixed the phone with a stony glare, trying to will it to ring again. But the phone didn't ring.

Come on, Maya, call back! I want to talk to you!

The phone remained silent.

Near the Metro Station
New Delhi

Maya fought back her tears. Arjun hadn't answered her call. The despair and helplessness of her situation were catching up with her.

The dark shadow of the night was creeping up stealthily, pushing away the twilight and suffusing through the fabric of the sky.

Maya tried to calm herself, she needed to be able to think. There was only one option left. Arjun lived a short distance away. It was a fifteen minute walk from where she stood.

With a new found determination, she wiped her tears and strode down the road. She would walk to Arjun's house and meet Virendra there. Maya didn't know where her strength was coming from. All she knew was that something within her was goading her on, not allowing her to give in or give up. She reached the main road of the colony — it was the same road that ran past her house. She still couldn't understand anything that had happened in her house a short while ago. But she didn't want to think about it. She feared if she did, it would debilitate her. The only way to keep her terror and panic in check was to avoid thinking and keep doing. The more she dwelt on the ordeal she had just been through, the worse she would feel.

Maya continued her walk down the lane to Arjun's house. She distracted herself by looking around, watching the cars, motorcycles, scooters and bicycles on the road, the birds in the trees twittering and chirping as they prepared to tuck themselves away for the night; and the occasional passerby. Anything to stop her thinking about her father.

As she approached Arjun's house, she noticed that the big Land Cruiser belonging to his uncle, was not parked in its usual place outside.

Her heart sank. If Virendra was not at home, what would she do? She could ask Pramila or Arjun to call him, but it would take time for him to return and accompany her back to her house.

The front door of the house was ajar.

That was strange. Virendra Singh was as fanatical about security as her father had been. The front doors of both houses had multiple bolts fitted on them. And, in both cases, there were clear instructions that the door would not be opened by the children under any circumstances. It would have to be one of the adults who answered the door.

Even when Updhyaya had to go out somewhere, as he often did, he would leave Maya with Virendra and Pramila. And in Virendra's house, the door had to be locked and bolted at all times, as a rule.

Something made her wary. She stepped up to the entrance and gingerly pushed the front door. It swung open.

The house was dark inside.

And deathly silent.

Even the curtains seemed to have been drawn shut.

Where were Arjun and Pramila? Her first instinct had been to call out for them, but a tight ball of fear, deep inside, made her check herself.

Where was everyone?

And why was the door open?

Maya gathered her strength, stepped inside the house, and stood still, looking around in the fading light of dusk that entered the room through the partly open door.

Abruptly, the air grew frigid and a cold blast hit her.

Something was not right.

Almost simultaneously, a foul odour assailed her nostrils. It seemed to be all pervasive, diffusing through the very air in the room and choking off the fresh air coming in from outside through the front door.

With a shock she realized that she was not alone. There was someone in the room.

Not someone.

Something.

She screamed.

Chapter Thirteen

Yet Another Mystery

Arjun's House
New Delhi

A strange and terrifying creature floated a few feet away from Maya. Its skin looked dull and desiccated and appeared to be rough, lined with seemingly dried up folds and ridges. There appeared to be very little muscle under the skin of the limbs, which were thin and atrophied. The whole being of the creature seemed to shimmer like black smoke on a still day with no breeze. It appeared to be solid yet shapeless at the same time, with a well-defined head atop a long neck, dark eyes sunk into its face, and a thin trunk from which a distended belly extruded.

Out of the corner of her eye, Maya saw a second creature of similar appearance approach her from the other side.

Both creatures stopped and hovered in mid-air, staring at her with lifeless, black, sunken eyes.

She screamed again.

Someone, or something, clattered down the stairs that led to the upper floor. The creatures were momentarily distracted.

Maya didn't have a minute to lose. Flinging open the front door, she dashed out of the house and sprinted down the street, in the direction from which she had come.

She didn't know what she had just seen in Arjun's house; or even if it had been a hallucination.

One thing was for sure. Arjun and his family were not in the house.

But something else was.

The Upadhyay House
New Delhi

SP Kapoor inspected the sitting room, treading carefully. The forensics team was busy at work and he didn't want to get in their way.

The man whom he had assigned to spy on Upadhyay had not been exaggerating.

This was, indeed, a bloodbath.

What could have happened?

Ajit had reported that the visitor had seemed to be unarmed when he entered and when he left his hands were empty, and there wasn't a spot of blood on him. If the mysterious visitor was the murderer, which was the most logical assumption, then where was the murder weapon?

And why was Upadhyay murdered in such a gruesome manner? This could not have been a simple burglary gone wrong. This seemed to be a murder born out of hate. There had to be a story behind it.

Just a few hours ago, the schoolmaster had been in his office, talking to him. And now.... Kapoor looked around and shuddered. This was not a sight for a weak stomach.

He stepped outside the house. There was nothing he could do inside until the forensics team had finished. One thing had suggested itself to him, though, when he had inspected the study.

There were three books missing from one of the shelves that lined three walls of the study.

Two books were found on the study table, presumably removed from the shelf. When his men had tried to see if the books fit the gap in the shelf they had realized that another book was possibly missing.

Kapoor didn't know if this was important to the case or not. All he knew was that the book seemed to be the only object missing from the house. He could not shake off the feeling that it had something to do with the murder. But what could it be?

His thoughts were interrupted by the forensic specialist assigned to the case, who joined him outside the house. 'Did you find the murder weapon, Suresh?' Kapoor enquired.

The forensic specialist looked at him. 'You know, that's the strange part about the case. This is just my first impression, but I'm pretty sure I am correct. We'll know more once we examine the body and I am sure that the autopsy will give us some more information, but ...' he paused, 'this is going to sound silly ....'

'Go on.' Kapoor was getting used to strange facts popping up in this case.

'Well, it is just that the body was ripped apart rather than hacked. It doesn't appear to me that any weapon was used for this. My examination of the tissue scattered ...'

Kapoor held up his hand, knowing where Suresh was going with his narrative. 'Spare me the gory details.' He pondered this new angle. 'No man is strong enough to tear another into pieces.'

Suresh nodded. 'I don't know what to make of it. This ... It just isn't physically possible. But it did happen.'

'Thanks, Suresh.' A thrill coursed through Kapoor. More questions. No answers. This case was getting more interesting by the day.

His phone rang. It was Constable Harish, the man shadowing Virendra Singh.

'Yes?' Kapoor was eager for news.

Sir, they have just pulled over to the side of the expressway and stopped. I can't be sure, but I think Virendra Singh is on the phone. This is the first stop they have made after the brief stop in Noida. They've been going at a pretty good speed until now.'

'Stick with them. He is even more important to this case now. The only surviving link. Keep us informed whenever you make a stop. We will connect you to the local police. You may need backup. Be careful. This could turn dangerous. If Virendra Singh and his family are attacked, you must call for backup and help them. I don't want to lose another key link in this case. Am I clear?'

'Yes, sir. Got it.'

Kapoor put his phone in his pocket. His brow furrowed.

Someone had killed Trivedi. Before his death, Trivedi had spoken to Upadhyay. Now he, too, was dead. Murdered.

And both men had died mysteriously.

With no witnesses.

His thoughts turned to the dead man's daughter. There was no news of her yet.

Where was she?

Chapter Fourteen

Hidden in Plain Sight

The Metro Station
New Delhi

Maya burst into the metro station, panting from having run all the way from Arjun's house.

She had fled without any thought to where she would go. But, as she ran, it was almost like her feet guided her back to the metro station. It was a good choice, full of people as it was. She felt safe here. At least she was not alone.

The short run back had seemed very long. At every step, she had kept imagining that she could hear footsteps pursuing her, hunting her down. The vision of those eerie creatures kept popping up in her head, chasing her down the street.

But nothing had happened and she had reached the station, safe, if out of breath.

She didn't have money to buy a ticket and, in any case, she had nowhere to go. Making her way to a corner where she could speak privately, without losing the comfort of being among people, she called Arjun again.

Where was he? Was he safe? What had happened to his uncle and mother? Why were there strange creatures in their house?

Her head spun.

This time, the call connected.

'Maya!' Arjun almost shouted.

Just the sound of his voice was so comforting that Maya broke down and sobbed her heart out into the phone. The trauma she had undergone, and the sheer relief of knowing that Arjun was safe was too much for her. Until now, somehow, she had managed to keep her fear, anxiety and panic suppressed. The dam finally burst now and she couldn't hold herself back.

'Hey, it's okay,' Arjun, under the impression that she was breaking down because of his sudden departure, tried to comfort her. In fact, he felt a little teary himself. 'We'll still see each other. I don't know where we are going, but it isn't too far away, I'm sure. And anyway, there's WhatsApp and Snapchat!'

'Where *are* you, AJ?' Maya pulled herself together. Something he had said had struck her. 'I don't understand … Where are you going?'

'You mean you didn't know?' she heard the surprise in Arjun's voice. 'I thought your Dad would have told you by now.'

Maya felt a pang of grief at the mention of her father. But the well within her had run dry now and there was just a numb sensation of pain and loss. No more tears.

'Dad …' she hesitated, unable to say the words. 'I think Dad is dead.' Her voice shook, despite her attempt to control herself.

'What?' The shock in Arjun's voice was palpable. Neither of them spoke for a while. Maya knew he was struggling for words.

'Someone came to see him,' she spoke tremulously, breaking the awkward silence. 'His name was Shukra. I think he killed Dad.' A dry sob escaped her as she said the words.

'Shukra?' Arjun echoed her. He was still at a loss for words.

'Arjun, give me the phone,' Maya heard Virendra's voice.

'Maya's dad … he has been killed,' she heard Arjun say as he probably passed the phone to his uncle.

Virendra came on the line immediately. Maya could sense the tension in his tone, the undercurrent of shock at hearing about the murder of his old friend. And a hint of anger.

'Tell me what happened, Maya. I want to know the details. Leave nothing out.'

Maya told him everything she had seen and heard after she had heard the raised voices and stepped out of her room.

'And you clearly heard your father call him Shukra?' Virendra asked.

'Yes, uncle. And Shukra called Dad Dhruv. I don't know why.'

There was a moment of silence.

Maya spoke first. She wanted to tell Virendra about her experience at his house too. Her voice shook as she recalled the sudden chill in the air and the foul stench that had accompanied the appearance of the creatures she had seen there.

Surprisingly Virendra didn't react much. Neither did he show any disbelief at their house being occupied by seemingly unearthly beings.

'Do you still have the amulet that your father gave you?' he enquired, instead.

'Y ... Yes, I do. I'm wearing it.' Maya was puzzled. How did Virendra know about the amulet? She was sure she hadn't mentioned it to him. And why was he asking about it? Wasn't he worried about what was happening at his house? Or about what had happened to her father?

'Good. Come what may, don't take it off. It is the only reason you are still alive.' There was no further word of explanation. 'Where are you now?'

'I'm at the metro station near our house.'

'Stay put. You were right to go there. It is the safest place for you right now. They won't attack you in the midst of so many people. And, whatever you do, don't even think about going back home.'

Maya wondered how Virendra sounded so sure or how he seemed to know so much. She wanted to ask him who 'they' were and why 'they' would attack her at all. But she knew that no explanation would be forthcoming. And, after all, her father had implied that Virendra would know what to do. She could trust him.

'You will come for me?' Maya's hopes rose.

'No.' Her heart sank at his reply. 'We're too far and we still have a long way to go. It'll take too much time. I am going to call someone who will come for you. Don't worry, he will find you. Just stay put.'

'But ... how will I recognize him?' Maya wondered. She was worried. Who was this new person Virendra was alluding to?

'He will be wearing an amulet identical to yours. Ask him to show it to you. Don't worry. Shukra and his gang will never wear that amulet. Trust me.'

Maya did trust Virendra. He was her father's closest friend.

'Be strong, child. You will be safe soon.' Virendra disconnected the call.

Maya stood there, hugging herself and wondering when her rescuer would come.

More importantly, what would happen next?

Chapter Fifteen

Kapoor Investigates

Arjun's House
New Delhi

SP Kapoor looked around the sitting room. They had arrived here a short while ago, to find the house in darkness and the curtains drawn tightly shut, with the front door open.

A quick search revealed that the house was empty. It seemed that, in their haste to flee the city, Virendra and his family had not even bothered to lock the house. It was a clear indication that they had no intention of returning.

Kapoor hadn't expected anything else. After all, he knew that Virendra Singh had driven away a couple of hours ago, along with his sister and nephew. He was now on his way to Agra. Kapoor was getting regular updates on his whereabouts.

He didn't really know what he had been hoping to find in this house. Maybe some clue to the mystery. Something, anything that might demonstrate the link between Virendra and the two murders that Kapoor was now investigating.

A theory had begun to form in his mind. The two men, Upadhyay and Singh, had come to Delhi from Allahabad. So had Trivedi. They had an interconnected past. What if they had all been involved in something there? Perhaps they had all come to Delhi to escape it. And these murders…. Maybe it was just their past catching up with them. If that were the case, Virendra Singh would be the next target.

From what the constable had told him, Upadhyay had seemed to know the mysterious stranger who had called on him and who was, at the moment, their prime suspect. That pointed to a possible link between the three men and the stranger.

This would explain why Singh had packed up and left after finding out the details of Trivedi's murder. He had known he was in danger. But then, why hadn't Upadhyay also fled?

Instead, he had welcomed the stranger into his house. That didn't make sense. If Singh had been scared enough to leave town immediately, then surely Upadhyay should also have been a worried man.

There had to be missing pieces. Until he figured them out nothing would make sense.

He sniffed the air. 'Can you smell something?' he asked one of his men.

The constable also sniffed and screwed up his nose. 'There is a smell sir. Very faint, but it is there.'

Kapoor nodded, relieved. He had thought that his mind was playing tricks on him. With all the mysterious happenings, he couldn't be sure. Was the smell important? He didn't think so and dismissed it from his mind.

Virendra Singh's words from that morning kept playing in his head. *It sounds like a case involving the supernatural.*

Had that man really believed his own words or was he trying to mislead the investigation? Kapoor compressed his lips with determination. He was going to find out. It was just a matter of time before Singh would reveal his hand. And Kapoor would be there when that happened.

The Agra-Gwalior highway

'What happened?' Arjun couldn't hold it in any more. 'Is she okay? What happened to Maya's dad? I want to talk to her.'

After Virendra had finished speaking to Maya, he had resumed the drive at a much higher speed. It was as if he was now in an even greater hurry to reach their destination.

Arjun was upset. He had been so stunned by Maya's words that he hadn't known how to react or what to say. It seemed scarcely believable that Naresh uncle was dead, killed by this Shukra dude. He had been in such a daze that he barely heard the conversation between Virendra and Maya.

Now that he had just about recovered, he wanted to speak to Maya. He wanted to be there for her, to console her and comfort her. Where would she go? What would she do?

'It won't help to talk to her at this moment,' Virendra replied. 'She is still in a state of shock and needs time to recover. You can speak to her all you want once we reach.'

'But she needs someone to look after her,' Arjun protested. 'Shouldn't we go back for her?'

'We're not going back to Delhi,' Virendra said, firmly. 'There is a reason we left and that reason has not changed. In fact, things have just gotten worse.'

'So you know this guy Shukra?' Arjun guessed. 'Is he the reason we left Delhi?'

Pramila turned around in her seat and gave him a reassuring look. 'Arjun, just give us some time. There is a good reason for everything that we are doing. I promise you that you will be told everything in due course.'

'But Maya?' Arjun persisted. 'She can't be left alone! If we're not going back for her, what is she going to do? Where will she go? She has no one else in Delhi who she can go to!'

'I've taken care of that.' Virendra's tone was sharp. Hadn't the boy been listening? He sighed. Arjun was already in a tizzy with their sudden departure, which must have been accentuated by the news from Maya. His tone softened. 'I've asked a friend to pick her up and take her to his house. He's a reliable guy. His wife and he will take good care of Maya. Don't worry about her. She'll be fine.'

Arjun wasn't satisfied, but he knew his uncle. There was no way he would sway from a course of action once he had set his mind to it. There was nothing Arjun could do but accept things as they were and hope for the best. He sulkily settled down in the backseat of the car and gazed out of the window. The familiar feeling of being stifled surged within him. It was almost as if he lived in a gilded prison. Protected but unable to either assert himself or leave.

Not that he had an unhappy life. But he wished he had more independence now that he was fifteen years old. Children younger than him had more freedom. Whereas in his family, neither Pramila nor Virendra seemed to realize that he was practically a grown up!

Virendra sighed inwardly as he drove. He realized how Arjun was feeling. And he wished that things could be different.

For now, though, Arjun's feelings were not uppermost in his mind.

He thought of his friend. Upadhyay and Virendra had discussed at length the circumstances behind Trivedi's murder and everything had pointed to one possibility.

Upadhyay's death had only proved one thing. They had been right in their conclusions.

How long could he keep the danger at bay?

Chapter Sixteen

The Rescuer Arrives

The Metro Station
New Delhi

Maya looked at her watch and shivered. It wasn't really cold — winter was still a few months away and the evening was pleasant. But she had been waiting here all alone for over half an hour now and she wondered when her rescuer would turn up.

She tried to reassure herself that it would take time for someone to respond to Virendra's call and make his way to the metro station. She had no way of knowing from which part of Delhi he would come. If the man was travelling from a distance, it would take quite some time to navigate the traffic on the city's roads before he got here.

She looked around at the people. There was a steady stream going in and coming out of the station. People catching their trains to go home. Or people arriving together in hordes at the station, before dissipating, and making their way home. Weary faces, tired bodies, sullen spirits jostled with eager anticipation, dreamy looks and expressions of happiness.

Which one of them would come for her?

Her eyes settled upon a short, stout man, in a tee shirt and jeans, wearing a baseball cap, who was walking rapidly towards her. Dismissing him from her mind, she allowed her gaze to wander over the faces in the crowd. But no one she could see appeared to be a likely candidate.

'Maya?' A soft voice at her side made her jump.

It was the stout man she had just observed.

The last person she would have expected.

He smiled at her. 'I'm Ratan Tiwari. Virendra called me and asked me to come for you. Don't be nervous. You are safe now.'

She stared doubtfully at him.

He seemed to understand the look on her face. Reaching inside his tee shirt collar, he pulled out a gold chain to which an amulet was attached. He extended it as far as possible for her to see.

'Here,' Tiwari said. 'Virendra asked me to show you this as proof of my identity.'

Maya studied the amulet. It seemed to be identical to hers.

She smiled back at him. 'Thank you, Tiwari*ji*.'

'Call me Ratan,' Tiwari beamed at her. 'I hate the "uncle" and the "*ji*". Makes me feel much older than I really am. I really am not *that* old, you know,' he said with a guffaw.

Maya's spirits rose. It was difficult not to be cheerful around this man. His smile and his jovial demeanour were contagious. There was also something very reassuring about him. He hadn't referred to her father or her recent traumatic experiences, even though it was hardly likely that he didn't know about them. Virendra would have been sure to have told him. Maya was grateful for this reprieve; her memories were all she could cope with for now, without another person stirring them up all over again.

'Come on, then,' Tiwari continued. 'Let's go.' He motioned towards the exit from the station.

Maya began walking with Tiwari by her side. 'Where are we going?'

Tiwari smiled at her. 'My wife is preparing dinner for you. You will spend the night at our house. Tomorrow morning ... well, tomorrow's another day and we can worry about it then. Here we are, now, here's my car.'

Maya slid into the front passenger seat, while Tiwari chattered away.

'Fasten your seat belt. And away we go!'

As Tiwari kept talking, one thought bothered Maya. Why had Tiwari hedged about what was going to happen tomorrow? She hoped there was a plan to follow. After all, she couldn't stay with Tiwari and his wife for the rest of her life.

What lay in store for her in the morning?

Somewhere on the highway beyond Agra

'Sir, they didn't stop at Agra,' Constable Harish reported to Kapoor.

'They didn't? Then where are they going?'

'I'm not sure, but if I had to guess, probably Gwalior, sir.'

Kapoor quickly googled the distance between Agra and Gwalior. 'You could be right,' he agreed. 'Gwalior is just a shade over two hours from Agra by road. Let me know when you reach.'

'Okay, sir.' Harish yawned and frowned to concentrate on the road. The car he was following had not stopped even for its occupants to have dinner. Clearly, they planned to eat in Gwalior.

He wondered what he would discover when they arrived at their destination.

Chapter Seventeen

The Diary

Ratan Tiwari's house
New Delhi

Maya sat on the bed and pored over the handwritten diary that she had retrieved from her father's study.

They had reached Tiwari's house and his wife had fussed over Maya, making her hot chocolate, served with cookies, and then cooking up a scrumptious dinner comprising dal, rotis, fried okra and potatoes in a delicious curry.

All through dinner, Tiwari had regaled Maya with jokes and witty anecdotes. They had even exchanged views on some stories from the Mahabharata. Tiwari was a PhD in Sanskrit and taught at Delhi University, in a South Campus college. He was chuffed to know that Maya, too, was fluent in Sanskrit and had read the ancient texts.

It was only after she had eaten that the exhaustion kicked in. Maya had not realized how drained she was — physically, mentally and emotionally. All the thoughts and emotions that she had brutally suppressed until now came flooding back, threatening to pull her under, drown her with their intensity.

Tiwari and his wife, sensing that Maya was tottering on a precipice, suggested that she retire and try and get some sleep.

As she said goodnight, Maya heard Tiwari mutter something under his breath. His careful intonation indicated to her that he was chanting some sort of a mantra, but her tired mind was too foggy for her to make out the words, which he was mumbling softly, almost to himself.

As Maya entered her bedroom for the night, a surprising sense of peace, calm and quietude settled over her like a cloud of sweet fragrance. She immersed herself in it, allowing her tired mind and body to surrender to its caress.

But Maya could not fall asleep. There was something she had to do first. Fighting back her drowsiness, she picked up the diary. Ever since she had fled her house, she had clung to that diary without a thought. But now, she finally had time to be curious. What did the diary contain? Why was it so important that her father had insisted she retrieve it before she escape? If he had considered it to be important enough for her to risk being observed by Shukra, why hadn't he told her what to do with it?

She replayed her father's words again and again in her mind, trying to remember exactly what he had said. Had she missed something? Was there a crucial clue that she had not picked up?

Her father's words were etched into her mind. He had told her to pick up the diary and run. She was to call Virendra and tell him what had happened. That was all.

Nothing about what was to be done with the diary.

Then what was its importance? Why had he asked her to secure it in the first place?

Clearly her father hadn't wanted it to fall into Shukra's hands. That possibility gave rise to another set of questions.

A thought came to her. Could this be the reason Shukra had come to their house? Had he been searching for the diary and discovered that her father had it in his possession? And had Shukra killed her father because he had refused to disclose where it was?

Maya opened the diary. Perhaps there were answers within.

She flipped through page after page of neat handwriting. When she had taken a quick look at the diary earlier, she had thought the handwritten entries were in Hindi, since the script used was Devanagari. Now, however, she realized that some of the writing was in Sanskrit, though many pages were covered with writing in a strange, unfamiliar language, which she did not understand.

A verse caught her eye as she scanned the pages. It was a mantra. She looked at the title. It was called the Narsimha mantra.

She frowned.

Narsimha.

Where had she heard that word before?

Then it came back to her. The story of the avatar of Vishnu — the half man, half lion called Narsimha — who had killed Hiranyakasipu, the son of Diti. Hiranyakasipu had been granted a boon by Brahma that he could be killed by neither man nor beast. Vishnu had then taken the form of Narsimha — neither man nor animal, but a hybrid of both — and ripped the Asura apart, putting an end to his tyranny of the three worlds.

Was this mantra somehow connected to that story? Despite her long held belief that mantras were for the gullible, she was curious. The tale of Hiranyakasipu, who had made several futile attempts to kill his son Prahlad, only because Prahlad was a staunch devotee and believer of Vishnu, had ended with the appearance of the Narsimha avatar. But what did that have to do with this mantra?

Maya read the mantra out loud.

'उग्रं वीरं महाविष्णुं ज्वलन्तं सर्वतोमुखं ।
नरसिम्हम भीषणं भद्रं मृत्योर्र् मृत्युं नमाम्यहम् ॥'

'Ugram viram maha vishnum
Jvalantum sarvato mukham
Narsingam bhishanam bhadram
Mrityur mrtyum namami aham'

She sat back after reciting it. What would happen now? When nothing happened, she yawned and flipped through some more pages of the diary. More pages with verses in the unknown language she had encountered in the earlier pages. Her eye fell on some diagrams and hand drawn sketches. What were these? Each diagram or sketch had a caption. But the captions were all in the same strange language that half the diary seemed to be written in.

She couldn't make head or tail of it. What had her father intended her to do with this book when she couldn't even read it?

She yawned again. This time, she didn't attempt to repel the onslaught of sleep. Keeping the diary aside, she switched off the light and lay down, surrendering finally to the welcoming arms of slumber.

Chapter Eighteen

The Dream

Ratan Tiwari's house
New Delhi

Maya's body jerked violently and she sat up with a start.

For a few moments, she was hopelessly disoriented, unable to figure out where she was.

Gradually, Maya recognized her surroundings. She was in the guest bedroom in Ratan Tiwari's flat. She had been reading the diary. And then, she had fallen asleep.

Until she had rudely been awoken by something. She was puzzled. What had disturbed her sleep? She had distinctly felt her body jerk violently.

Through the foggy recesses of her mind, the memories crept back. The dream.

She remembered now.

Slowly, like an ink stain spreading through fine fabric, the memory of the dream strengthened and became more vivid as the images of what she had dreamt of grew clearer.

And what a dream it had been! A dream that was as baffling as it was staggering, as terrifying as it was amazing.

Maya had dreamt that she had floated out of bed, out through the window, and into the sky teeming with stars. It was an amazing feeling, the sensation of lightness, almost weightlessness, and the ability not just to fly but also to look down on the world from above.

The dream had shifted from one location to another as quickly as her thoughts changed. One moment, she was hovering over Tiwari's house; the next, she was inside the sitting room of her house — the room where her father had been brutally murdered a few hours ago. To her amazement, she had been able to pass through the walls of the house.

Her wonder had swiftly turned to sadness as she saw the blood spattered carpet and couch. There were blood stains on the walls too. Unable to take any more of this sight, her thoughts had unwittingly changed to focus on Arjun's house. In the twinkling of an eye, she was in the same room where she had seen the two terrifying creatures earlier that evening. But now, in her dream, the room was empty, and seemed just like it had always been, all these years.

Maya had found herself thinking about Arjun, and was instantly transported to another place, a location which she did not recognize. She saw the Land Cruiser that belonged to Virendra, driving along a narrow, single lane road, hemmed in by fields on either side. In the distance, the horizon was an uneven stretch of black — like dark clouds amassing, preparing to unleash havoc on the countryside around.

The thought of dark clouds triggered the memory of the man, Shukra. Who was he? How did her father know him? What unknown power did he have that had enabled him to torment her father in the way he did?

Almost instantly, at the very thought of Shukra, she was transported away from the scene with the Land Cruiser, to a place that was darker than night, where even the glow of the stars could not be seen.

A vast multitude was gathered here. Maya hovered over them, unable to comprehend the scene below her. A distinct sense of unease had crept into the dream now. She wanted to tear herself away from this place, from the hordes below, but she could not.

In the distance, she saw a figure. The leader of this gathering. She wondered who he was, and floated closer to get a better look.

In the light of the torches that lit the rocky platform on which he stood, addressing his followers, she recognized him with a jolt.

It was Shukra! She couldn't mistake that eyepatch, that face, and that single eye that had fixed her with a gaze so piercing that it could melt steel, back in the study at her house.

The torches threw a flickering light on the people in the front of the crowd gathered before Shukra. Maya shrank in horror as she saw them.

They weren't people. Not normal human beings.

It was a motley group. Some of them were replicas of the creatures she had encountered at Arjun's house. But there were others, more frightful in appearance, with eyes that were bloodshot; nameless creatures, some with spittle dribbling down their mouths, others with teeth that were sharp and protruding. It was like the population of hell had descended on this place.

Or was this hell itself?

Maya tried screaming but couldn't. She frantically searched for a way out, anything that would get her away from here.

Shukra was bellowing something to his eager audience. Maya couldn't make out what it was. She didn't *want* to know what he was saying. All she wanted was to get out of there!

But it seemed that, even in her dream, she was trapped in this infernal place. She wanted to cry out for help, but no sound came out. Maya despaired. She knew she was dreaming, yet she could not bring herself to wake up. How long would this nightmare last?

Tiwari's smiling, round face suddenly came to her mind, the comfort and security of his pleasant company providing a welcome distraction from the horrifying scene below her.

In a flash she was whisked away from the horrifying scene below her and was back to the warmth and comfort of her bed in Tiwari's guest room.

It was then that she had woken up with a jerk, wondering where she was.

The scenes from her dream were all too real, etched in vivid colours. Even though she knew it had been a dream, she found herself trembling. The last part of it, especially, had been a nightmare, nothing less.

Finally, her exhaustion once more got the better of her. She gave up trying to understand what the dream had meant or why she had dreamed about these things at all, and floated off into a dreamless sleep.

Chapter Nineteen

Panna

Day Four

Near Panna National Park
Madhya Pradesh

'Where are we?' Arjun mumbled, waking up as the Land Cruiser jolted over yet another bump. The road for the last hour or so had been patchy and bumpy yet Arjun had managed to sleep through most of the last couple of hours. The fatigue of the long drive had caught up with him.

They had driven almost non-stop for around 12 hours now, halting only for a quick dinner at Gwalior. After that, they had resumed the journey, passing Orchha and Jhansi in the dead of night, the only souls seemingly awake while the towns and villages they passed through lay deep in slumber.

Virendra did not appear to be tired in the least. He had handed the wheel to Pramila for a couple of hours, after the call with Maya, while driving from Agra to Gwalior. But he had not napped in that time. Instead, he had been lost in deep thought.

Arjun had kept himself occupied through the journey with the playlist on his phone, but even he was beginning to get tired of listening to the same songs over and over again.

'Almost there,' Virendra said grimly, as alert as when they had left Delhi. 'Just a few minutes to go.'

He had still not disclosed their destination to Arjun. If Pramila knew, she had also chosen to keep mum except for asking Arjun at regular intervals if he was hungry or thirsty. She had tried to keep things normal, talking about the last time she had been in Gwalior, which had been several years ago. Arjun knew she was trying to make things easy for him, but he just couldn't pretend along. He wanted answers.

The SUV rumbled past a large signboard that proclaimed 'Panna National Park'. Arjun gazed at the signboard, and at the gates to the park, which were locked, and looked at his watch.

Before long, the first fingers of light would creep over the horizon, signalling the advent of dawn and heralding the start of a new day.

They passed a small village. A goat tied to a post outside one of the huts bleated indignantly at the vehicle disturbing the peace of the early morning hours. An insomniac goat, Arjun thought to himself and grinned.

Through the windows of the Land Cruiser, he stared curiously as the village they passed gave way to forest on either side.

What wonders did the forest hide? Arjun mused. He had never been to Panna but looking at the dense foliage around, he was sure that the park would be wonderful to explore. He remembered one of his geography teachers mentioning it in class when he was in the seventh grade. Arjun wished that he had paid more attention then. It had been with reference to some geological formation, but now he didn't remember.

He was jolted out of his reverie by the abrupt halt of the Land Cruiser.

Virendra had edged the car to the side and parked on the rough, unpaved shoulder of the road, which was wide enough to accommodate the vehicle.

'Right,' Virendra announced. 'Here we are.'

The three of them got off the car, stretching their limbs, which were stiff from the long drive.

'What now?' Arjun wondered aloud.

For the first time since they had left Delhi, Virendra allowed himself the shadow of a smile.

'You are going to see something really amazing,' he told Arjun. 'Come on.'

Chapter Twenty

The Pandava Falls

Near Panna National Park
Madhya Pradesh

The sky was beginning to lighten in the east, and they could just about make out a path that led down from the road, between the trees where the car was parked.

The three of them started down the path, and soon arrived at a stairway built of rocks, probably quarried from the nearby hills. Virendra switched on the torch on his mobile phone.

'Careful now,' he cautioned them as he brought up the rear so that Pramila and Arjun could see their way down in the beam from his mobile phone. 'There's a sharp drop ahead. You'll see a railing on your left. Stay away from it. Just in case.'

Arjun held Pramila's hand protectively as they descended the stairway. As Virendra had forewarned there was, indeed, a railing to their left. It was painted green and beyond it, Arjun could see a massive black gap in the trees that were packed densely all around it. While he could clearly discern the outlines of the gap and the extent of its spread, in the slowly advancing dawn, he could not see any features of the yawning chasm or what it contained.

Arjun sensed that his uncle had been here before. And probably more than once.

'Keep going,' Virendra urged. 'We're almost there.'

The path now led down the slope, the railing continuing along the flanks of the path. Finally, they reached level ground.

'Be cautious, everybody,' Virendra warned. 'Keep going straight. If you go left, you will land in the water.'

Dawn had progressed and in the dim light, Arjun could now make out a few details.

Behind him was the path leading down from the Land Cruiser parked far above at the side of the road, now hidden from view. They were now standing at the bottom and at the fringe of the chasm he had observed from the vantage point at the foot of the stairs. To his right and before him was dense forest — trees packed tightly together as if huddling close to each other to keep warm through the night. On his left he could just about make out a large body of water, a lake? And beyond it, a steep slope rising almost perpendicular to the ground, soaring into the air.

'What's that?' Arjun asked Virendra, pointing to an indistinct, dark blot some way up the sharply inclined cliff.

'Those, my boy, are the Pandava caves,' Virendra told him, 'and just over there,' he pointed to the slowly lifting gloom to the side of the lake that was opposite to where they stood, 'are the Pandava falls. It is said that the Pandavas came here during their exile. But it's not where we are headed.'

In the half light of the dawn, Arjun felt, rather than saw, the majestic beauty of this place. While the colours were subdued and there was hardly any light there was a strange, yet welcome sense of peace. The silence was comforting, rather than eerie.

But he was still left wondering.

What were they doing here in this godforsaken place at this odd time of the day?

Chapter Twenty-one

At the Cliff Wall

Pandava Falls
Madhya Pradesh

Arjun followed his uncle, still holding Pramila's hand, even though they were now walking on level ground. They were following a concrete path between the trees that skirted the lake, heading straight for the perpendicular cliff at the far end.

As they walked, the features of the lake that lay at the bottom of the chasm were slowly revealed in the early morning light. The lake and the chasm, bereft of any forest cover, were lit up by the first rays of the sun that were emerging from the horizon, escaping the prison of night.

Arjun could now see the deep emerald hue of the lake. The trickle of water at the far end, which was all that was left of the falls in this season; the deep grey, black and brown colours of the cliff they were walking towards, which was draped in a profusion of plants that seemed to hang like sheer curtains that covered the side of the cliff, yet allowed its natural beauty to shine through, all combined to make his surroundings magical.

Directly in front of them were what appeared to be stone facades for caves at ground level that were carved into the side of the cliff, either naturally or by human hand. Above this lower row of caves was a cave higher up, set in the wall of the cliff—the one that Arjun had seen earlier.

At that time, it had been indistinct but now its yellow interior was clearer and Arjun could see artefacts within, though he could not make out what they were.

But Virendra was not making his way towards the caves. Instead, he was walking *away* from them, off the concrete path and through a cluster of trees, towards another part of the cliff wall, which was bare, apart from the creepers that adorned it.

They reached the cliff face and stood there.

'Now what?' Arjun asked his uncle.

'Now, we wait.' Virendra struck the cliff wall thrice with the palm of his hand.

Arjun was baffled. What was wrong with his uncle? Virendra was acting mighty strangely and he couldn't understand why. He felt rather silly, standing here, in the middle of a forest, next to a lake, with his uncle slapping the wall of a cliff. His mother seemed unperturbed by her brother's strange behavior. Would someone tell him what was going on?

He didn't have to wait long to get his answer.

Pandava Falls
Madhya Pradesh

Harish, who had been following the three fugitives from Delhi, rubbed his eyes in disbelief.

He had watched as Virendra had parked the Land Cruiser and the three occupants had clambered out and made their way down the path to the lake at the bottom of the Pandava falls.

While he wondered what they planned to do, in this desolate wilderness, in the pre-dawn gloom, he had dutifully followed them down, keeping at a discreet distance, as instructed by his boss.

When Virendra had struck off the concrete path and headed for the cliff face, Harish had taken refuge in one of the caves, from where he stuck his head out and watched the trio, partly hidden by a creeper that dangled from the cliff above the cave and covered the cave entrance.

As the day advanced and the darkness began lifting over the lake,

Harish had had to move deeper into the cave, which meant that his line of sight was not as clear as it had been earlier, especially since the portion of the forest where Virendra, Pramila and Arjun stood was still shrouded in semi darkness, shaded by the densely packed trees through which the weak light of the dawn could not penetrate.

Harish thought he saw a fourth person join the trio. It looked like a woman but he couldn't be sure.

Where had she suddenly appeared from? And what was she doing here, all alone in the forest, at this unearthly hour?

Then, as he watched, the four of them seemed to vanish.

One moment, they were huddled together, speaking in soft tones that did not allow him to hear what they said.

The next moment, they were gone.

All he could see was the cliff face.

He poked his head out, throwing caution to the winds, to get a better view.

But there was no one to be seen.

He looked around wildly.

Nothing disturbed the peace of the forest.

Bewildered, he cautiously advanced to the spot where he had seen Virendra strike the rock with his hand. He couldn't be sure about the exact spot but he approximated the area and searched for traces of the trio he had stalked all the way from Delhi.

But there was no sign of them.

He returned to the rock and slapped it like he had observed Virendra do.

Nothing. Just hard rock.

Confused, he made his way back to where his car was parked, at a safe distance from the Land Cruiser, hidden from view by a bend in the road and a copse of trees that had strayed almost to the edge of the road.

He had to report this to his boss. Raman Kapoor would not be pleased.

How was he going to explain this?

Chapter Twenty-two

Maya leaves Delhi

Ratan Tiwari's house
New Delhi

Maya struggled to open her eyes. Her eyelids felt like they had been tied down by weights. She had barely slept a few hours. What had woken her up this time? Was it morning already?

There was a knock on the door.

That must be it. Someone was knocking on the door.

The curtains were drawn shut and the room was in darkness, so she couldn't make out.

Half groggy, she pulled herself out of bed and shuffled to the door. Ratan's wife, Megha stood outside, a big smile on her face.

'Good morning, Maya!' she beamed. 'Ratan asked me to wake you up. Both of you need to be on your way soon. You need an early start, there's a long way to go. I'm making breakfast. Do you like stuffed paranthas?'

Maya smiled back weakly, still feeling sleepy and disoriented. Last night's dream continued to weigh heavily on her mind and body. Not only had it been mentally draining but, surprisingly, she felt physically exhausted.

Not a dream. A nightmare.

'Be with you in a few minutes,' she mumbled back.

'Here,' Megha handed her a fresh tee shirt. 'It might be a bit big for you, since it is mine and, well, I'm not fifteen anymore,' she laughed. 'But you don't have fresh clothes so I thought I'd give you this.'

Maya accepted the garment gratefully and Megha disappeared to prepare breakfast.

In half an hour, Maya had showered and changed into Megha's tee shirt, paired with the same jeans she had on the previous day. The smell of paranthas wafted to her and she suddenly felt hungry. All thoughts of last night's nightmare were pushed aside for now.

'So, where are we going?' Maya asked at the breakfast table, in between mouthfuls of the most delicious paneer paranthas she had ever tasted in her life. Her father hadn't been a terribly good cook and breakfast was usually toast and a glass of milk. The sudden memory of her father, smiling at the breakfast table, caught Maya off guard. She swallowed a piece of her parantha quickly, to keep the tears at bay.

Strangely, though, Ratan was a bit subdued this morning. His trademark smile was missing and the non-stop chatter that had marked dinner was absent at breakfast. He was also clearly avoiding the subject of their destination. Maya wondered if something had brought him down or if he was just not a morning person.

She decided to take the bull by the horns. A lot had happened and she had been at the receiving end. She felt she deserved to know what was happening. Virendra's cryptic words on the call had not really helped, and in fact had made her feel more restless.

'What if Shukra comes after me?' she looked directly at Tiwari.

The effect of her words was instantaneous.

Tiwari dropped the piece of parantha he was about to put in his mouth. Megha, who was serving them both, froze in mid stride. It was as if time stood still for a few moments.

Tiwari returned Maya's gaze, looking her in the eye. 'If he had to come after you, he would have done that yesterday itself. But he didn't. There is a very good reason for that. *You* are not the one he is after.'

The rest of breakfast was spent in silence. Both Megha and Tiwari seemed disturbed by her question. What were they so worried about? How much did they know? Maya couldn't make out.

Not that the lack of conversation worried Maya. She was occupied with her own thoughts. Three questions gripped her mind.

Who was the unfortunate person Shukra was after?

And why did he kill her father?

Would she ever get the answers?

Chapter Twenty-three

The Valley of Music

Pandava Falls
Madhya Pradesh

Arjun's jaw dropped as a woman seemed to walk out of the rock face.
Was he imagining things?

She was the most beautiful woman he had ever seen. Attired in a silk
blouse and long silk skirt that reached her feet, a silk fabric was draped
across her blouse like a *dupatta*. Her jewellery — earrings, a nose ring
and a necklace — glittered with diamonds. And when she spoke, her
voice was soft and musical.

'Welcome back, Kanakpratap,' she smiled at Virendra, then turned
to Pramila. 'And we always have a special place for you, Yajnaseni.' She
turned to Arjun. 'And who is this?'

Arjun was too mesmerized by the woman's charisma to ask who
Kanakpratap and Yajnaseni were. The words barely registered as he
tried hard not to gawk.

Virendra smiled back at her. 'Good to see you, Varsha. It has been
a long time.' He gestured towards Arjun. 'This is my nephew Arjun.
Rudrapratap's son.'

Varsha smiled at Arjun. 'It is a pleasure to have you among us, Arjun.
Welcome to the land of the Gandharvas. Come with me.'

She turned around and walked through the rock face of the cliff that towered above them.

Pramila followed her, walking through the rock and vanishing.

'Come on, then,' Virendra gestured to Arjun to follow him and disappeared into the rock.

Arjun stood there, gaping, unsure of what to do next.

Virendra reappeared, walking back out of the rock. He pointed to the cliff wall.

'This is an illusion,' he explained. He held out his hand and pushed it through the rock. It disappeared halfway, as if it had been cut off at the elbow.

'Just walk through and you will be in the land of the Gandharvas,' Virendra informed Arjun. 'This is a device to prevent strangers who visit this place from finding their way in. Consider it a portal that leads from our world to theirs. Few humans are permitted to enter and, without a Gandharva companion, you would not be able to pass through unless you knew the mantra that allows you to enter,' he explained, noticing Arjun's bafflement.

He walked through the rock again and, hesitantly, Arjun followed.

To his surprise, as he touched the rock wall, it seemed to melt and become fluid, flowing around his body. As he walked deeper into the cliff, the fluid seemed to part before him and solidify behind him. He was walking straight through the rock, the stone visible on either side of him and behind him.

A few paces, and he was out of the rock, standing and staring at the sight that lay before him.

He blinked at first and then squinted as he emerged from the near darkness of the interior of the rock into daylight again. This place seemed to be in a different time zone. The sun was already high in the sky, which was clear, with not a trace of clouds.

He stood, with Varsha, Pramila and Virendra, upon the edge of a valley, lush and green, surrounded by a ring of hills that stretched on every side, as far as the eye could see. A narrow river ran through the valley near its eastern border and, on either side of the river, stretched green, tree-lined meadows. This was unreal!

On the southern side, the slope of the hills was gradual and the hillside was dotted with beautiful stone houses. In the distance, below the stone houses, were large buildings, built around squares, with the largest square before the biggest building.

The sound of music floated out to them as they stood there, gazing upon the beauty that lay before them.

The overall picture was serene and tranquil.

'They are waiting for you,' Varsha told Virendra.

She turned and gracefully made her way down the slope, into the valley. As they descended, Arjun glanced back at the way they had come but could see no sign of the magical entrance they had just used. There was only the rocky cliff that rose behind them, with no gap that could serve as an entry.

They reached the floor of the valley and walked towards the buildings they had seen from above.

The sound of music was all around them now. The voices singing were pure and melodious. The cheerful music and the harmony of the instruments instantly lifted their spirits. They felt unusually refreshed, despite the long, almost nonstop, more than twelve-hour long drive from Delhi.

Arjun still could not believe this was happening. Was he truly among the Gandharvas or was this some fantastic dream?

He had heard about them all his life, from Pramila, as she narrated stories to him from the epics. He knew they were celestial musicians. But he had always treated those stories as myths, never believing them to be real. He had never expected to one day find himself in their midst, listening to their music live.

As they approached the large buildings in the valley, a group of Gandharvas came out to meet them. They all smiled and bowed to the little group. The men among them came up to Virendra and hugged him, while the women did the same for Pramila.

Arjun noted that even the men among the Gandharvas were dressed in silk. They wore waist-length tunics, with short sleeves and elaborate collars, and loose fitting leggings that extended until their ankles, with a slit at the back of their calves that exposed their well-worked leather boots.

Clearly, both Virendra and Pramila were well known to these people. They were being greeted like old friends.

Arjun stood on the sidelines, fidgeting, feeling awkward and ignored. He was still trying to come to terms with the fact that these beautiful people, in gorgeous clothes, who were talking and laughing in front of him were Gandharvas—beings he had not even believed existed.

'Come,' Varsha said to Virendra after the warm welcome and exchange of greetings. 'Visvavasu awaits.'

'Visvavasu is the king of these Gandharvas,' Pramila whispered to Arjun, noticing that he was looking a little lost.

Arjun gave a casual nod, as if he had heard of Visvavasu before. He did not want his mother to know how ill at ease he felt. He did not want her constant protection. He fell in line behind the others as they made their way to the largest building in the valley.

Chapter Twenty-four

The Gandharva Council

The Gandharva valley

The group, led by Varsha, made its way towards the largest building that dominated the valley, with an enormous square before it. The sound of the music grew louder as they approached. It was coming from inside the building.

Arjun wondered if it was a theatre for musical performances. He had heard stories, from Pramila, about the musical prowess of the Gandharvas, and today he was experiencing it for himself. The music he heard was nothing short of divine.

They entered the building and walked through the imposing entrance, into a narrow corridor that suddenly opened up into a gigantic hall.

Arjun stared with wonder, at the ceiling that soared high above them, painted with murals in vivid colours. He was even more amazed by the absence of pillars in the hall, despite its magnificent size. Even the walls were painted in bright colours.

Virendra observed Arjun gaping and sidled up to him. 'It's breathtaking, isn't it? Arjun, be sure to pay your respects to the king. Also, remember, no questions. I'll answer any questions you have afterwards.'

Arjun nodded, still dumbfounded by the splendour of the hall. So the building was probably a palace where the king resided. He realized that this was some sort of *durbar*, a hall where the king met his subjects.

He looked straight ahead and, sure enough, sitting on a raised platform at the far end, on a gilded throne, studded with the biggest jewels he had ever seen in his life was a man, who had to be the king. Sitting in front of the grand figure of the king were the musicians, responsible for the mesmerizing melody that filled not just the hall but the entire building. Arjun figured that the music was resonating and amplifying through some architectural device.

As the group approached, the king held up his hand and the music abruptly ceased. He rose and descended from his throne and walked slowly towards them.

The king was a tall man, his youthful good looks belying his true age. His long dark hair flowed to his shoulders and his well-muscled physique was apparent even through the golden tunic he wore.

Virendra and Pramila bowed as they came up to the king. Arjun hesitated for a second, unsure, and then followed suit.

The king smiled. 'Welcome back, Kanakpratap,' he addressed Virendra, then turned to Pramila, 'and Yajnaseni.' He looked at Arjun. 'Your nephew?'

Arjun looked at his uncle, confused. *Kanakpratap?* This was the second time today he had heard his uncle being addressed in this manner.

Virendra nodded. 'It is always a pleasure to be among the Gandharvas, O Visvavasu,' he replied. 'This is my nephew, Arjun. Rudrapratap's son.'

'Welcome, Arjun,' Visvavasu smiled at him. He turned back to Virendra. 'Come, let us go into the private chamber. There is much to discuss.'

Visvavasu waved his hand and the musicians launched into their performance once more. Beautiful strains of the sitar filled the air as the king led the group towards a door set in the wall behind the throne.

Arjun guessed that there was a second, smaller, hall beyond that door—a room which not everyone was permitted to enter. His curiosity, and excitement, was increasing by leaps and bounds. His mother and uncle actually knew the Gandharva king? And what were they being ushered in to discuss? Would he finally get some answers, as Virendra had promised, or would there be even more mysteries?

Chapter Twenty-five

New Mysteries for Kapoor

SP Kapoor's residence
New Delhi

'What do you mean they disappeared?' SP Kapoor demanded. 'How can three human beings physically vanish?'

Harish had finally called SP Kapoor from Panna, with the disconcerting news. For a while, he had resisted, knowing there was no explanation for the report he was going to make and hoping that Virendra and his family would somehow show up. Finally, though, his sense of duty prevailed and he decided to face Kapoor's wrath rather than delay information.

'Are you sure you didn't slip up? This had better not be a cover up!' Kapoor thundered on.

Harish patiently listened to his boss vent his anger. He had expected Kapoor to be angry. Only, he thought, there was no way Kapoor's frustration could match his own. After following his quarry across half of North India and not letting them out of his sight for a moment, to have them disappear without a trace was the worst possible end to the cross country pursuit he had just been engaged in. He knew his boss well. Soon, he would stop raging and cool down.

True enough, Kapoor's fury was soon spent and, as logic took over, he realized that he was unjustly giving Harish a dressing down. He knew his man well. Come what may Harish would not have abandoned his duty.

But nothing — absolutely nothing — could explain what Harish was telling him. There had to be a rational explanation for this.

'Perhaps they disappeared into the forest,' Kapoor suggested, clutching at straws. 'Or they took a shortcut and went back to the road.'

Harish doggedly stuck to his story. 'No, sir. After I lost sight of them, I searched the forest around for a while. They weren't there. When I went back up, there was no one around, just the Land Cruiser, standing where it had been left. If they had indeed gone back, why would they leave the Land Cruiser there, with all their bags? For one they would need their car — public transport is hard to come by in these parts. And then, even if they did find some way to get away, they would surely take their bags!'

Kapoor had to agree with Harish's logic. But he still couldn't accept what seemed to have happened.

'Stay there,' he instructed. 'Don't move. Wait. If their bags are still in the car, they will be back.' He disconnected the call.

Almost immediately, his phone rang again.

It was Suresh, the forensic scientist who had visited the Upadhyay house on the previous evening.

'Sorry to disturb you early in the morning.'

'I hope you have a good reason to call so early.' Kapoor was still smarting at having lost his only lead in this case.

'I got the autopsy and forensic examinations expedited as you had requested,' Suresh responded, 'and I thought you would want to know what we've found.'

'Answers?'

'Well, not exactly,' Suresh admitted, 'but definitely more than we had last evening.'

'Go on. I'm listening.'

'First, the preliminary autopsy report. I had guessed correctly. There's no evidence of any kind of sharp bladed weapon or tool being used on the victim. The tears on the muscles and ligaments of ...'

'Spare me the gore,' Kapoor snapped. 'Tell me the conclusion.'

'Well, okay.' Suresh sounded wounded. 'Just thought you'd like to know on what basis we figured this out. Okay, the conclusion we reached is that the four limbs were pulled in different directions with extreme force, causing the body to rip apart.'

Kapoor frowned. 'It would take powerful forces to make that happen.'

'Absolutely,' Suresh agreed. 'You know, I've read that, in the olden days, this was one form of execution. A man's limbs would be tied to four horses and they would be goaded to gallop at full speed in four different directions. The victim would ...'

'Yes, yes, I get the picture,' Kapoor stopped him impatiently. He was a police officer and violence was a part of his job. But, while he could face mobs and had no compunction in shooting at criminals — he had actually killed a couple of them in encounters — he didn't really have the stomach for gore.

'Well, okay.' Suresh sounded disappointed. 'Anyway, that explains why there was no murder weapon found. None was used.'

'Hard to believe that one man could have accomplished that,' Kapoor snorted. 'We *know* that there was only one person there who could have killed Upadhyay — the suspect.'

'My job is to analyze the facts of our findings and give you a report. I'm not the investigator on this case,' Suresh retorted.

'And you called me at this time of the morning to tell me this? A riddle to which we have no answer?'

'There's more,' Suresh told him, indignation creeping into his voice. He felt Kapoor just wasn't showing enough gratitude for the favour he was doing him. He had no way of knowing that the call with Harish had soured Kapoor's mood for the day. 'We found fingerprints that are unidentified so far.'

'Ah!' Kapoor sounded upbeat for the first time since the conversation had begun.

'Well, that's mixed news, really. The bad news is that we found two sets of fingerprints. One set was on the front gate of the house, on the latch of the gate to be specific. The other was on the handle of the front door, which is on the *inside* of the door.' He paused, allowing the implication to sink in.

Kapoor was quick to catch on. 'So, what you're implying is that the person who opened the gate to enter was different from the person who opened the front door to leave the house. How is that possible?'

'Exactly. I know it doesn't make sense. But I'm just giving you the facts. We lifted prints from all over the house. The victim's, his daughter's plus two other sets of prints. Presumably the maid and some other friend. Of course, we can only verify that once your boys are able to find the maid and identify the "friend".'

'The facts can be easily explained. The fingerprints aren't date or time stamped. They could be from a visitor earlier in the day. We weren't shadowing Upadhyay then, so we wouldn't know.'

There was a pause. Then Suresh spoke up tentatively. 'Ajit said in his statement that he saw the suspect open the gate.'

'Correct.'

'Then we should have matching fingerprints on both the gate and the door handle. But we don't. The suspect should have left fingerprints on the gate as well. But he didn't. How do we explain that?'

'Ajit is positive that he saw *only* one person enter and leave the house: the suspect. Not two different people. Maybe the suspect used different hands to open the gate and the door? That could explain the difference in prints.'

'No, it wouldn't. Because that isn't the only difference in the two sets of prints.'

'What do you mean? Don't speak in riddles.'

'The size of the hands differ,' Suresh explained. 'The hands that made the prints on the gate are much smaller than the hands that made the prints on the door handle. They definitely belong to two different people.'

There was silence.

'Hello?' Suresh said, uncertainly.

'I'm still here,' Kapoor replied. 'Just thinking. Well, thanks a lot for letting me know.'

He cut the call and ran a hand through his hair, his brow creased, as he mused over what Suresh had just told him.

Nothing in this case seemed to make sense — people disappearing, a suspect with seemingly superhuman strength, fingerprints that couldn't be explained. And, of course, there was still the mystery of Trivedi's death.

Virendra Singh's words came back to him. *Supernatural*, he had said. As he considered the possibility for a split second, Kapoor shivered involuntarily. He quickly pushed the thought aside. He was not a believer in the paranormal. Neither was he superstitious.

There had to be a rational explanation for everything. And he was going to find it.

Chapter Twenty-six

Answers & Questions

Visvavasu's Private Chamber
The Gandharva Valley

The chamber had a long wooden table with a polished top and several chairs around it. At the head of the table was a gilded chair, now occupied by Visvavasu. The other Gandharvas — the three men and three women, including Varsha, who had greeted the newcomers from Delhi — along with Virendra, Pramila and Arjun, sat on the chairs on either side of Visvavasu.

The king fixed Virendra, who sat on his right, with a gaze. 'So, Kanak,' he began. 'Your presence here is a confirmation of what we believe to be true.'

Arjun flinched as Visvavasu addressed Virendra as 'Kanak' but, remembering his uncle's whispered words of warning, he checked himself.

But Visvavasu had already noticed Arjun's reaction, though he didn't say anything.

Virendra nodded, as if he was accustomed to being addressed in this manner. 'When we left Delhi, it was more as a precaution based on conjecture. It seemed to be the only logical way to explain what happened to Dhananjay. The three of us left Delhi only because we felt that, speculative or not, we could not be too careful. The best course of action was to leave. And, as we drove here we got news that confirmed our suspicion.'

'Dhruv,' Visvavasu murmured. 'I had wondered why he had not accompanied you.'

'He stayed back to check if our suspicion was correct,' Virendra said, bitterly. 'He said the *Sangha* would protect him if the search went awry. If I had had even an inkling ...' He shook his head and looked away.

Arjun could see that Virendra was deeply affected. It seemed to him that his uncle was on the verge of tears. But who was Dhruv? Who were they talking about? And who was Dhananjay? The only person by that name that Arjun knew was DJ sir. But there was no way his uncle would have known him. He was confused but he kept silent. There would be enough time later to quiz Virendra and get his answers.

'We had no idea that the tables would turn,' Virendra resumed. 'We thought that we were hunting Shukra. But, in reality, he was hunting us. Somehow, and I have no idea how, he knew what had happened in Allahabad. And he came for us. Fortunately, for the three of us — and, perhaps, for the entire world — we had left Delhi by then. But Dhruv had stayed back. I see it all now, I understand Shukra's ploy. Dhananjay's murder was just a smokescreen, a ruse to divert our attention. And it succeeded. While we were trying to figure out where Shukra could be hiding, he came at us. Poor Dhruv didn't stand a chance.'

Visvavasu shook his head, his face sombre, reflecting the pain he felt at hearing the news.

'Dhruv had a daughter, did he not?' the king asked, finally breaking the silence that had descended in a gloomy pall around the table. 'A *sadh.*'

'Yes,' Virendra affirmed. 'Her name is Maya. Dhruv somehow managed to warn her and gave her a *kavach*. She managed to escape from the house, with her life. It was she who called us and gave us the news.'

Arjun started visibly at these words. The 'Dhruv' they had been talking about was Maya's father? He didn't get it. How come everyone he knew suddenly had two sets of names? He had always known Maya's father as Naresh uncle. And what was a *sadh*?

Visvavasu's keen eyes observed Arjun's surprise again. 'You haven't told him,' he remarked to Virendra, indicating Arjun.

'No,' Virendra shook his head. 'Not yet.'

Visvavasu nodded. 'I think you were right not to.' He paused. 'And what about Maya?'

'I asked one of the *Sangha* to take care of her. He will bring her to us safely. In fact they are on their way right now.'

Maya was on her way to Panna? Arjun perked up visibly at this information. This was the best news he had heard since leaving Delhi.

'So you plan to take her to the Gurukul?' Visvavasu raised one eyebrow.

Once again, Arjun was at a loss to understand what he meant. But it seemed that, to his uncle, the implication was clear.

'Yes,' Virendra's voice was resolute. 'I will. Her father has died trying to ensure that the world does not enter its darkest moment in the history of humanity. We cannot abandon her. We owe him this much. And, after all, Dhruv was a Maharishi. Let's not forget that.'

'Descent is not important, Kanak,' Visvavasu countered. 'Who you are, where you were born, who your father was — these are all things that matter only to *sadhs*. Not to the *Sangha* or the *Gana*. You know the rules as well as I do. Only the ones chosen for the *Gana* are allowed in the Gurukul.' He shrugged. 'But who am I to stop you? I don't run the place.'

Virendra's expression hardened. 'She will stay there. I will ensure that. She has nowhere else to go.'

Arjun looked on in wonder, understanding not one word of what was being discussed. His head spun.

'So, Shukra has returned,' Visvavasu dismissed the subject of Maya and moved on. 'Where has he been these last fourteen years? And what does he plan now? We are ill prepared to deal with him.'

'True,' Virendra agreed. 'For a while, we thought we had seen the last of him. That we had enough time to prepare.' He looked at the Gandharva king. 'But there is the prophecy, you know.'

Visvavasu's face took on an amused expression. Clearly, he did not believe the prophecy, whatever it was.

'The prophecy,' he chuckled. 'Let's not waste our time trifling with verses which are so ancient now that they may no longer mean anything useful. Instead, I would advise you to prepare for war. We will support you in that. We have no choice. The three *loks* are in great peril. Don't forget, predictions are accurate only at the time that they are made. Even they can change over time, depending on the actions of the people involved. That is the law of Karma.'

'The prophecy came from the Saptarishis,' Virendra shot back, 'not from a minor astrologer. Predictions can certainly change if the assumptions on which they are made also change. But that hasn't happened. Not yet.'

The smile disappeared from Visvavasu's face. He shook his head. 'You put too much faith in the prophecy, Kanak. You forget that you have only part of the prophecy. Who knows what the other parts say?'

'Shukra certainly believes in the prophecy,' Virendra said, his voice gentle but firm. 'That's why he came to Allahabad fourteen years ago. And I do too. We have devoted our lives, sacrificed much, to enable the prophecy to come true. And it will!' He looked straight at Visvavasu. 'We'd better pray that it does. Nothing else is going to stop Shukra. Not you, not I, not the *Sangha*. Not even the Devas or the Saptarishis. And you know that better than I do.'

Chapter Twenty-seven

Shukra Reflects

Unknown location
India

Shukra sat in the cavern, lost in thought. He had stumbled upon this hideaway 5,000 years ago, after his confrontation with the Saptarishis. Defeated, and humiliated, he had fled their presence, searching for a refuge. And he had found it here. A chance discovery of the narrow gorge that led to the source of the river that carved out the gorge, had turned out to be providential. It had led him to the cave in the side of the mountains overlooking the gorge.

Something about the cave had struck him as being strangely familiar. He had explored it thoroughly, finally unearthing the narrow crevice at its rear that led through a steep upward sloping passage into this natural cavern hollowed out within the mountainside.

It was then that he understood why the place had seemed familiar. It was almost identical to another structure he had explored long ago; only that structure had been built by the Devas for a very specific purpose.

Shukra had decided, there and then, that this was the place where he would meditate for as long as it took to accomplish his purpose. He was clear about what he wanted — what he needed — and how it would help him. His defeat at the hands of the Saptarishis had actually given him a sense of purpose. He knew that his *tapas* would bear fruit. He knew that his devotion was appreciated. And now, it would go even further.

What frustrated him no end was his failure to get everything he wanted. And it had not been for lack of tapasya. Shukra had single-mindedly pursued his purpose. For 5,000 years he had meditated. His devotion and perseverance had resulted in powers that made him much stronger than he had ever been.

But then, his meditation had been rudely disturbed fifteen years ago. It was ironic. The same enhanced powers that had made him stronger had also made him more sensitive to external vibrations. And led to the disruption of his carefully planned tapasya.

The cosmic vibrations that had touched his inner consciousness while he was deep in meditation had conveyed one clear message to him.

A child had been born. And it was no ordinary child. It was the child of the prophecy. The child who was destined to stop him from achieving what he had started 5,000 years ago.

It would have been foolhardy to ignore the warning. Shukra had immediately set about looking for the child. While his meditation may have been disrupted and his careful plans foiled, there had still been a chance to reinforce his position and consolidate his power by eliminating the child.

The powers he had gained due to his tapasya had come in handy. The spirit world was now under his command and it was their help that he sought when looking for the child. After six months he had received the much awaited news—the child had been found. It was a boy and he was in Allahabad.

It had been simple after that. Shukra had killed the child, ensuring the elimination of the immediate threat. There were no descendants, no connections, no loose ends. The prophecy had been defeated.

Kaliyuga was here. The Saptarishis and Devas were helpless; their powers were weakened and their ability to influence the affairs of *Bhu-lok*, severely diminished. Shukra had been satisfied. He no longer needed to meditate to get additional powers, now that the main threat to his plans was out of the way.

Or so he had thought at that time.

Shukra had decided that the time was right for him to implement his plan. But he had not foreseen the multiple obstacles that would confront him.

To begin with, the face of *Bhu-lok* had changed in the 5,000 years that he had been away. The world was no longer what it had been when Kaliyuga began. Even Bharatvarsha was now a different place, with different people and a totally different geography. His confidence had quickly evaporated. What had seemed to be child's play had suddenly morphed into a difficult game of riddles.

And he was not good at solving riddles. If anything, he hated them.

Because of this, he had spent the last fourteen years searching for the key that would deliver to him the means to locate what he needed to achieve his goals.

And he had found it.

But it was during that quest, that he had made a startling discovery. One that had shocked him to his core and filled him with a fury that could make the three worlds tremble.

The child was alive.

He had been tricked. The boy he had killed was not the child of the prophecy. How this could have happened was beyond his understanding. But it was the truth. He had failed in his mission. And his entire plan was in grave peril.

As Shukra planned his next move, he had had a stroke of luck. He had found someone who could help him. Who *had* helped him. And he had been able to trace the boy of the prophecy. There he had learnt of the elaborate plan that had been hatched to defeat him and thwart his mission.

It had been easy for Shukra to decide on the fate of the people who stood in the way of him realizing his ambitions. He could not allow them to live.

Shukra had followed the trail to New Delhi.

But, once again, the boy had escaped.

Shukra rose and paced the length of the cavern thinking hard.

He was troubled. Something that he had thought impossible had happened at the Upadhyay house. Something that never should have happened.

At that time, in the heat of the moment, deeply focused on carrying out his planned actions, he had paid no heed to the aberration.

Now, with the luxury of time to reflect, it had come back to haunt him.

He now knew where the boy was; where he had been taken. Even as he sat and mused, the boy was in the company of the Gandharvas.

But that was not the thought that really bothered him and increased his frustration.

It was the recollection of what had happened at the Upadhyay house. He gnashed his teeth as he remembered the mantra he had used. And what had happened as a result. He had been shocked but unable to understand it.

And it was this episode that had inserted a niggling thought into his mind; one that had begun to grow with time, until it had exploded as a full-blown doubt.

Had he been correct about the child from the prophecy?

Chapter Twenty-eight

Some Answers

The Gandharva Valley

Arjun marvelled at the scenic beauty of the valley as he followed Virendra and Pramila along the path that led up the side of the mountains that guarded the southern flank of the valley. Led by Varsha, the trio from Delhi threaded their way through the Gandharva houses. Built at a fair distance from each other, with vast spaces between them, the houses lined the mountainside like bay windows protruding from a stone building.

He could not help but admire the well-tended gardens that adjoined the houses, each flaunting a profusion of flowers in myriad colours. Colourful, silken, curtains fluttered coyly in the cottage windows. Some of them were parted to reveal kitchens from where aromas wafted out — food being cooked for the midday meal.

Arjun suddenly realized he was hungry. After the halt for dinner at Gwalior, there had been no time for eating. They had driven straight, all the way to Panna. He hoped that the Gandharvas would serve them some food.

Presently, they arrived at a small house with blue chik blinds lining the windows. In front of the house was a garden — a patch of green grass and some bright seasonal flowers — blocked off by a wooden gate.

It looked really inviting to their tired eyes and they gratefully entered the sitting room and flopped down on the comfortable chairs there.

'I'm sure you must be hungry,' Varsha smiled at them. 'Food is on its way.'

After she left, there was an uncomfortable silence. For one thing, they were all tired, and welcomed the luxury of being able to sit down and rest for a while. For another, while Arjun was bursting with questions, he didn't know where to start or how to broach the subject.

But he knew this was his opportunity to find out just what was going on. Clearly, things were not as they seemed. He needed to know how deep these waters ran.

He looked at Virendra, who was slumped on a chair with his head thrown back and his eyes closed.

'What's all this about, uncle?' he asked. 'Why are we here? Why are these people calling you Kanakpratap? Who are you, really?'

He was shocked by his own directness.

Virendra opened his eyes. 'I guess we owe you an explanation,' he said, his tone contrite. 'But use that name with respect, Arjun. I will explain to you what it means.' He paused and then looked Arjun in the eye.

'You need to hear this story carefully.'

The Agra-Gwalior Highway

Maya woke up with a start and looked around to find herself in Tiwari's little car. He smiled at her. 'Had a good nap?' he asked. 'You were out for the count.'

She nodded, smiling a bit sheepishly. Somewhere along the way, sleep had overwhelmed her. After last night's terrifying nightmare, she had really needed to catch up on her sleep. The smooth road, the hum of the car engine and the pleasant weather had all contributed to lull her into a deep, dreamless sleep.

'Hungry?' Tiwari indicated the back seat of the car with a nod of his head. 'There are bananas at the back. And water.'

Maya wasn't feeling particularly hungry, but her mouth was a bit dry, so Tiwari pulled over to the side and they both slaked their thirst.

'Can I ask you something?' Maya turned to Tiwari after they had resumed the journey.

Tiwari looked at her curiously, then turned his attention back to the highway. 'Sure, Maya. I think I know what you want to ask. But go ahead. I'll answer you to the best of my ability.'

Maya hesitated for a moment. She had thought long and hard about her dream last night. She desperately wanted to understand what it had meant. However, despite Tiwari's good-naturedness and her trust in him, she couldn't bring herself to talk about the dream frankly. It had been just too bizarre.

But there were still questions to which she wanted answers.

Like, who was Shukra? Why had he come to her house? What had he wanted from her father?

And, the big question that had popped into her mind this morning at the breakfast table.

Who was Shukra really after?

Chapter Twenty-nine

The Story of the Past

The Gandharva Valley

'My real name is Kanakpratap Singh,' Virendra told Arjun. 'Rudrapratap Singh, my elder brother, was your father.'

'What?' Arjun couldn't believe his ears. All this time he had known Virendra to be his *mother's* brother. Why had Virendra and Pramila pretended to be brother and sister?

'And my real name is Yajnaseni,' Pramila added. 'The Dhruv you've been hearing about was Maya's father, who you know as Naresh uncle. He had also changed his name. I know this is confusing for you, Arjun, but there is a legitimate reason why we all had to change our names.' She looked at Virendra who nodded at her, asking her to continue.

'When you were just about one year old, Shukra turned up at our doorstep in Allahabad,' Pramila resumed. 'We had no idea who he was. Luckily for us, Dhruv had dropped in for a cup of tea and he figured out what Shukra was after. Your father and Dhruv decided to face Shukra, while Virendra and I managed to escape with you. We came to Delhi. Later, Dhruv joined us with Maya. He confirmed our fears. Shukra had proved to be too powerful for the two of them to tackle. He had killed your father and Dhruv just about escaped with his life. So the three of us changed our names – and our lives – in case Shukra came looking for us again. And we managed to outwit him for almost fourteen years, though we were always careful, always scared of him hunting us down. I don't know how he was able to find us after all this time.'

Arjun didn't understand.

'Who is Shukra?' he asked, seeking more clarity. 'And why is he after us? Why did he kill my father?'

Pramila sighed and looked at Virendra. It was clear that she expected him to take up the thread of the explanation.

Virendra nodded his acknowledgement. 'I will tell you. But whether you will believe me or not is a different matter.'

'Why should I disbelieve anything you tell me, uncle?' Arjun was baffled. 'I *need* to know. Please.'

'To understand what this is all about,' Virendra continued, 'we have to go back 5,000 years. Perhaps more. Shukracharya — or Shukra, as we refer to him — is the son of Bhrigu, a wise and great sage, who lived thousands of years ago. Unfortunately, the son turned out to be the opposite of the father. Shukra bonded with the Asuras and became their guru. Being a passionate devotee of Lord Shiva, he managed to obtain the *vidya* required to resurrect the dead, through sheer hard tapasya. A rare ability. Shukra is a great Rishi in his own right. If only he had turned his powers to the pursuit of good. Instead, he kept trying to find ways of helping the Asuras to gain control of the three worlds. 5,000 years ago, the Saptarishis decided to put an end to his machinations. They warned him of dire consequences if he continued his attempts to open the gates of *Pataala Lok*. Shukra disappeared. For 5,000 years, no one knew where he had gone or what had become of him. Then, without warning, he appeared fourteen years ago. In Allahabad.'

Arjun's head spun. He couldn't believe what he was hearing. This stuff was right out of mythology! How could something like this be real?

This tale brought back memories of his history class and how DJ sir had discussed the Mahabharata with them. He had liked narrating stories from the ancient epic and would always describe them with such animation that the stories appeared real. He had once told them the story of Shukra and Kacha, the son of Brihaspati — the guru of the Devas — who was the only person to have learned the science of resurrecting the dead from Shukra. Devayani, Shukra's daughter, had been in love with Kacha, and had wanted to marry him. He still remembered bits of that story.

But that was all mythology! Fantasy!

Yet, his uncle and mother were talking to him about the main character of these mythological stories as if the guy was real.

A thought struck him. 'So if Shukra is back, why can't the Saptarishis take care of him like they did 5,000 years ago?'

'It's not as simple as it seems, Arjun. It was the Dwapara Yuga, 5,000 years ago,' Pramila replied. 'That was around the time of the Mahabharata, when Lord Krishna still walked this earth.'

Arjun's bewilderment increased. His mother was speaking of Lord Krishna as if he had really existed. He knew a lot of people revered the epic but for him, the Mahabharata had been a story and nothing more.

'With the passing of Lord Krishna from this world,' Pramila resumed, 'Kaliyuga began. This is the fourth and final stage before the universe is destroyed and the cycle of creation begins again.' She looked at Arjun. 'I have told you about the four *yugas*, remember?'

Arjun remembered well.

'In Kaliyuga,' Pramila continued, 'the power of the Saptarishis and the Devas is diminished. All the stories of the Devas being visible in *Bhu-lok* — in our world — and intervening in the affairs of humans, is from before Kaliyuga. Once the fourth age began, they have had to retreat to their own worlds, which cannot be accessed by humans anymore.'

'Not all humans,' Virendra corrected her. 'Some humans can still, at least theoretically, visit Swargalok. But that is a very rare occurrence. Those worlds are generally out of bounds for us.'

'True,' Pramila agreed. 'It is the same with the Saptarishis. Their power is of little use in *Bhu-lok* though they do continue to ensure that the universe functions normally. But they cannot, and do not, interfere in the affairs of humans. They will not stop Shukra, because they cannot.'

'Apart from that,' Virendra interjected, 'we fear that Shukra has spent the last 5,000 years in tapasya. If he has sought and obtained more boons from Lord Shiva, who knows what powers he has acquired since then. For him, Kaliyuga is the perfect time to set his plans in motion.'

Despite his misgivings about what he was hearing, Arjun couldn't help but feel a chill creep up his spine and enter his heart.

'But why is he after us?' he asked plaintively.

Chapter Thirty

More Revelations

The Agra-Gwalior Highway
Madhya Pradesh

The car had just passed through the ravines of Central India, made notorious by the dacoits who had infested this region until just a few decades ago. Now peaceful, the ravines still looked ominous and threatening. Maya could just imagine the terror that the bandits would have once struck into the hearts of the villagers who lived in the region.

'So what does Shukra want?' Maya asked, looking away from the ravines and focusing on the answers that she wanted. 'Why did he kill my father?'

Tiwari looked at her, surprised.

Maya nodded, her lips compressed, trying to suppress her anguish. 'Yes, Ratan, I know. You don't have to keep it from me. My father is dead. I don't have evidence, but I feel it. Shukra murdered my father. I want to know why.'

'You know who Shukra is,' Tiwari told her, 'you just don't realize it yet. You've read quite a few ancient texts. Remember Shukracharya, the son of Bhrigu?'

Maya's eyes widened at this revelation. 'You can't be serious.' She stared at Tiwari in disbelief. His face was grim. Its usual cheeriness seemed to have drained away, replaced by a granite gloom that told her that, not only was he dead serious, but also that he was worried.

She sat back, trying to sort out her thoughts, which seemed caught in a whirlwind.

How was what Tiwari was saying even possible? The Shukracharya of Vedic tradition had lived thousands of years ago! He was just a character in stories that she had read in the Mahabharata and other ancient Sanskrit texts that her father had shared with her.

'You're right,' Tiwari affirmed, reading her thoughts. 'Shukra is indeed a character from those texts of thousands of years ago. But while many stories in the Vedas, Puranas and the epics may be allegorical in nature or have spiritual underpinnings, surely you didn't believe that there was absolutely no basis for them? That they were pure fiction? Did the possibility never cross your mind that some of the characters may have actually existed?'

Maya admitted that she had wondered as much, several times. 'But how can he still be alive today if he is the Shukracharya written about so many years ago?' she was still incredulous.

'He is a yogi,' Tiwari explained. 'A very powerful yogi. A Rishi of one of the highest orders. Remember, he is the grandson of Brahma himself.'

'I know,' Maya replied. 'I've read about the creation of Bhrigu, Shukra's father.'

'Just think about it then, and you'll realize that you knew it all along. You just never stopped to think about it, forget about accepting the reality of it.'

Against her will, her mind recalled the scene she had witnessed on stepping out of her room. Her father, floating in the air, struggling to communicate with her against the invisible grip that Shukra seemed to have over him.

The mantra that Shukra had been muttering!

It hit her like a lightning bolt.

It couldn't be.

Yet, there it was.

She had understood the mantra that Shukra was reciting. Her father had compelled her to learn Sanskrit from a very early age, even though it was never a part of the school curriculum. As a result, she had picked up the language quite easily and fairly quickly, and was proficient in reading, writing and even speaking Sanskrit. Despite not having been taught the mantras, she could understand their true meaning.

She knew from whatever she had read about Shukracharya, that he had the ability to get information from someone's mind. And that's exactly what he had been doing.

Shukra had used the mantra to read her father's mind!

But what had he been looking for? What did her father know that Shukra had to resort to forcing it out of him?

She turned to Tiwari. 'Fine. If that really was the Shukracharya from the ancient texts, then I don't give a damn about how he turned up thousands of years after he is supposed to have lived on earth. I suppose there are things here that I don't yet know of.' A bitterness crept into her voice. 'But I would still like to know why he killed my father. What did my dad have to do with any of this?'

There was silence for a few moments as Tiwari mulled over what he would say. He wanted to be honest with this girl, who was now orphaned. She had seen her father meet with a gruesome end, and Tiwari felt immense compassion in his heart, for her. But he was also bound by the rules of the *Sangha*. And he didn't know enough about Maya yet. He decided to probe first.

'Maya, Dhananjay Trivedi was your teacher, right? Did he ever speak to you about the *Gana*?'

'The *Gana*?' Maya's baffled expression spoke for itself. She also wondered how Ratan Tiwari knew Dhananjay Trivedi, but she didn't ask. There were too many new facts being revealed and Maya felt overwhelmed. For now, all that mattered to her was her father's death. She needed to gather as much information around it as possible.

Tiwari pondered some more. The girl had never heard of the *Gana*, which simply meant that she had never been approached for recruitment. Trivedi had been the designated recruiter for her school and clearly he had not thought her suitable. Yet, she was the daughter of Dhruv. But then, why did Virendra want her at the Gurukul if she wasn't a potential recruit? He couldn't reconcile the apparent contradictions.

'To answer your question,' he began, choosing his words carefully, not wanting to reveal too much, 'your Dad was a Maharishi.' He turned to her and their eyes met briefly before he turned his attention back to the road.

Maya let out an involuntary gasp. She knew what a Maharishi was. She had read enough about them. But this didn't make sense! Maharishis existed ... well, aeons ago. Not in this day and age! No one today had the powers that the Maharishis of the Mahabharata and the other Vedic texts had. Plus, this was her Dad they were talking about. Her mild-mannered academic, bookish father. How could he have been a Maharishi? Had she not known him at all … ?

Yet, she remembered how her father had communicated with her on that last day. Words that had been spoken straight to her mind.

Telepathy.

Like the ancient Maharishis.

Could it be true?

'His real name was Dhruv,' Tiwari added gently. 'He was one of the most powerful Maharishis alive. No one else could have fought Shukra the way he did.'

Maya nodded wordlessly. She realized that Virendra must have conveyed her description of what she had witnessed, to Tiwari.

'He said that he couldn't hold him off much longer,' she said softly, more to herself than to Tiwari, beginning to believe more and more in the amazing tale that was unfolding through Tiwari's words.

Another memory wafted through her mind. 'I think that Shukra had some kind of a hold on me. On my mind. A grip that I couldn't free myself from. But Dad broke it. He told me to run.' She looked at Tiwari. 'He was no match for Shukra, though. And now, I can see why.

The grandson of Brahma. The son of a Saptarishi. Who could stand against him?'

Tiwari continued to focus on the road ahead. 'Actually, I wasn't referring to what you saw. I was talking about what happened fourteen years ago. In Allahabad.'

Chapter Thirty-one

Arjun Learns the Truth

The Gandharva Valley

'Not us,' Virendra said slowly, emphasizing each word. 'It isn't *us* that Shukra is after.' He paused and took a deep breath, clearly intending to elaborate.

Before he could continue, Arjun jumped in. 'Then why did we leave Delhi?' he demanded. He sounded angry and distressed.

'Hear me out, Arjun,' Virendra calmed himself with an effort. It seemed like Arjun was going out of his way to be annoying. He knew he had to be patient with the boy. It must have been a huge disruption for him, being uprooted from Delhi, where he had spent all his childhood, and having to flee town at such short notice, leaving his school, his friends behind. And so far he had no idea what all of it was for.

Arjun folded his arms and tried not to glare at Virendra.

'We are Kshatriyas,' Virendra resumed. 'But not ordinary Kshatriyas. We are *Chandravanshis* — the Lunar dynasty, descended from Buddha, the son of Soma. We are direct descendants of Yayati, a king and a sage, venerated by history. The responsibility of leading the entire Kshatriya clan, to protect humanity, falls upon our shoulders. In my generation, your father, Rudrapratap, had that responsibility. As his son, that mantle passed down to you after his death.'

Pramila rose and went to Arjun. She stood behind him, one hand on his shoulder.

Virendra took another deep breath and continued. 'Shukra wanted to wipe out Yayati's lineage. That's why he killed your father. And he didn't stop there. He tried to kill you, too. It is only because of Dhruv that you escaped death.' He hesitated, then carried on. 'Dhruv helped us all escape from Allahabad. Without him, you wouldn't be alive. None of us would be alive.'

Arjun felt strange. He had never known his father but to hear a story about his death at the hands of an ancient Rishi who was the guru of the Asuras felt surreal. He was still trying to comprehend the revelation that he belonged to a line of kings that was famous in mythology for their deeds and valour.

Was all of this true? He couldn't believe that his own mother and uncle would cook up such a fantastic story. He had seen for himself the urgency with which Virendra had driven them all the way here from Delhi.

Things which had seemed odd earlier, began to make sense.

Virendra's non-stop driving with only a few halts along the way; brief and hurried, as if someone was pursuing them.

Because the risk of Shukra pursuing them had loomed large.

The call with Maya and Virendra's immediate reaction when Arjun had echoed Shukra's name. His uncle had almost snatched the phone from his hand. He hadn't understood why at the time but now he did.

Shukra was the biggest threat to all of their lives.

Maya's news about her father being killed by Shukra. Now he understood the motive behind the murder. *Of course! If Maya's father had helped them escape Allahabad, then surely Shukra would've been hell bent on extracting revenge for thwarting his plans.*

A cold fear took hold of him as he began connecting the dots.

Everything led to one inescapable fact. If Shukra had wanted to wipe out Yayati's lineage, and had failed to do so in Allahabad, then he would want to complete the job now.

His uncle's words rang true. Shukra was not after *them*.

Shukra was after *him*.

The Gwalior-Jhansi highway

Maya was silent. She sat shell-shocked.

Devastated.

She didn't know how she should feel after hearing what Tiwari had just told her. On the one hand, there was pride that welled up within her. Pride and respect for her father; for the manner in which he had battled Shukra in Allahabad.

On the other hand, though, there was the disturbing revelation of how Dhruv had ensured Arjun's safety. Her father had made Shukra believe that he had succeeded in killing Arjun and his mother, but to do that he had had to make a supreme sacrifice.

Her father's ploy had allowed Arjun to escape with his life and his family. But at what cost? She couldn't believe that her father had done the unthinkable. Or that she hadn't known his terrible secret; a secret that he had hidden away, never allowing even a hint to surface in all the years she was growing up.

Maya couldn't even begin to imagine how her father had spent the last fourteen years harbouring a secret so terrible.

She buried her face in her hands and wept, struggling with the conflicting emotions that coursed through her being.

Tiwari looked over at her, concerned, but said nothing. He understood what Maya was going through. It was best to let her vent her emotions.

Silence reigned in the car for the next few hours. Maya sat, lost in thought, sometimes with her eyes closed, at other times staring out of the window at the passing scenery.

They whizzed through Jhansi and Orchha and reached the narrow road leading to the Panna National Park. Darkness was falling now and Tiwari wanted to reach their destination before daylight disappeared. Maya had told him about her experience in Arjun's house and Tiwari knew what that meant.

Suddenly, Maya, who had been looking out of the window, gave a startled exclamation. She began looking around frantically, at the road that stretched before them, and the fields on either side.

'Um, looking for something?' Tiwari ventured.

Maya settled back in her seat, looking puzzled. 'Just checking something out,' came her terse reply.

'We're almost there,' Tiwari told her. 'Just a few more miles to go.'

Maya nodded absently. Tiwari was worried. When they had left Delhi, she had been insistent on knowing where they were going. He hadn't told her yet, but their destination didn't appear to interest her any more.

He could only hope that he had done the right thing by revealing the truth about her father. They had almost reached Panna. Soon she would meet Arjun and Virendra. He knew that Arjun and Maya were good friends.

But that was before she and Tiwari had had this chat.

How would Maya react when she met them?

Chapter Thirty-two

Unhappy Reunion

Pandava Falls
Madhya Pradesh

The little group stood outside the cliff face, the entrance to the Gandharva valley, in the growing dusk. The lake and the forest were deserted. As the sun had begun to set the few straggling tourists had also disappeared, and there was no one else around.

Arjun looked on dejectedly as Varsha and the other Gandharvas bade farewell to Virendra and Pramila.

He had been in a daze ever since his uncle and mother had revealed to him their true identities along with the history of his family and their lineage. It had all seemed so unreal.

Arjun had locked himself away in a room in the Gandharva cottage for the rest of the day, emerging only when food arrived for them from the king's kitchens. It seemed hard to believe that, just yesterday, he had been an ordinary schoolboy, preparing for a history test. Now, suddenly, he was the heir to an ancient line of kings who were among the most respected and heroic warriors of Indian mythology.

Only, this was no longer mythology. It was very, very real.

The immense protective shield that Virendra had thrown around him all this while, began to make sense. The many things that had stifled him and restricted his freedom— his uncle insisting on dropping him to school and picking him up every day; never being allowed, in his entire life, to leave the house without either Virendra or Pramila chaperoning him; not being allowed to attend birthday parties, school functions and melas alone, or go for movies with friends. There had never been an exception to this rule. He had always had either his uncle or his mother hovering around. He had never understood it and had often chafed at their constant presence in his life. Only now did he understand why it was so important for them to watch him all the time.

And it didn't make him any happier now that he knew.

Arjun also realized now the true purpose of the sword fighting lessons imparted to him by his uncle. He had, on occasion, wondered where his uncle had honed his own sword fighting skills, but it had never seemed important, so he had never asked. The answer lay in plain sight now. It was obvious that martial skills were passed down the generations in his family. His own father had not been around to teach him, so his uncle had.

Had his own father also been an ace swordsman? The thought flashed through Arjun's mind before the bigger implication hit him again.

He had to carry on his family's responsibility of protecting humanity.

Arjun felt vaguely inadequate. He was just a fifteen-year-old boy. How he was supposed to discharge this responsibility, was beyond him. Virendra had offered no word of explanation either. Just the statement that his father's responsibility had passed down to Arjun.

Great.

And now they were going to the Gurukul. Whatever *that* was. Again, Virendra and Pramila had been tightlipped about it. The only thing that Arjun had been able to figure out was that it seemed to be a place where they would be safe.

Where *he* would be safe.

Where Shukra would not be able to reach him.

Arjun was baffled. He had got the impression that Shukra was immensely powerful. Virendra had told him that the onset of Kaliyuga, along with Shukra's presumed 5,000 years of tapasya, had only increased his powers. If this was true, how could any place be so impregnable that it could keep Shukra at bay?

And there were still things that he did not understand. Questions that had been left unasked and unanswered.

Like, how had Maya's father saved Arjun's life? How had they been able to deceive Shukra and flee Allahabad? Surely a Rishi as powerful as Shukra would not be so easy to fool. Yet, somehow, Maya's father seemed to have done just that.

But if Shukra was pursuing them now, it obviously meant that he had discovered the deception. The question was, how? What had led him to learn that Arjun was still alive? And how had he known where to find Arjun? If both DJ sir and Maya's father were dead it was clear that Shukra was uncomfortably close to his target. But not on target yet.

Which meant that he was not omniscient. Or infallible. He had been defeated once, and could be defeated again, Arjun reminded himself.

Despite that realization, Arjun could not help the dread creeping up on him: Shukra was targeting *him*, specifically. If the Son of Bhrigu had tracked Arjun all the way from Allahabad to Delhi, what would stop him from pursuing Arjun to Panna, and then to the Gurukul?

For the first time in his life, Arjun was seriously terrified. If his uncle, who had protected him all these years, was worried enough to flee Delhi in order to evade Shukra, it meant that he feared that the threat was too big for him to handle.

And Arjun didn't like the thought of that at all.

Panna National Park
Madhya Pradesh

The sun had almost set and the gates of the park were shut. No one was around. The rangers had left for the night.

Tiwari parked his car in front of the gates, casting a worried glance at the setting sun, as he alighted. 'Maya, please stay in the car,' he instructed.

Maya nodded. She was curious to know why they had stopped here, but she said nothing. She watched Tiwari amble towards the park gates, which were secured by an iron chain that was looped several times around the bars of both gates, and held in place by a large padlock.

Tiwari stood before the gates, muttering something. Maya could hear his voice through the open windows of the little car, but she couldn't make out what he was saying or who he was speaking to.

She let out a gasp. Was she seeing things in the dim twilight? She squinted hard. No, she was not imagining this. It was really happening. The padlock which, until now, had firmly secured the gate, was now in Tiwari's hand.

As she looked on, the chain around the gates began unlooping, unwinding sinuously until it hung limply from only one of the gates. Tiwari reached out his hand and hung the padlock from one of the chain's links.

Maya gaped as Tiwari calmly walked back to the car.

What had just happened?

The question remained unasked. Just as Tiwari reached the car, a large vehicle drew up and came to a halt beside him.

Maya recognized Virendra's Land Cruiser. A weird, cold feeling coursed through her veins as she realized that Virendra, Pramila and Arjun were here.

She felt uncomfortable. Tiwari hadn't told her they would be meeting them.

'Maya!' Arjun sprang out of the SUV, beaming joyfully. This was the only bright spot in his day. He had been looking forward to this moment ever since Virendra had revealed that Maya was going to join them in Panna.

Maya closed her eyes and tried to get a grip on her emotions. This was Arjun. Her childhood friend. They had grown up together. Been a part of every significant moment in each other's lives. She should be happy and relieved to see him.

But something had changed. Something had died within her. Maya couldn't understand it. A part of her shrank back at this reunion.

She desperately wished she was somewhere else.

Chapter Thirty-three

Into the Park

Panna National Park
Madhya Pradesh

'Hey, AJ,' Maya smiled as Arjun ran up to Tiwari's car. She tried to sound enthusiastic but despite her best efforts, there was a listlessness in her voice that betrayed her state of mind.

Arjun did not miss the lack of enthusiasm in her voice. 'What's the matter, Maya?' A look of concern replaced the enormous smile of joy.

Almost immediately, he felt like kicking himself. What was wrong with him? Maya's father had been brutally murdered by Shukra, and he was asking her what the matter was. He couldn't have asked a stupider question if he tried. *Of course* she didn't reciprocate his sunny welcome.

'I'm sorry about your Dad, Maya,' he said, conscious that he had yet to express his condolences to her. 'I ...' words failed him again. Did Maya know about Shukra? About the background of her father's murder? Did she know what had happened in Allahabad?

'Ratan told me why you left Delhi.' Maya tried to change the topic quickly. She couldn't bear to think of her father, not just yet. She tried to calm her internal conflict. Whatever had happened in the past, Arjun's life was in very real danger. She wondered if he even knew the full extent of the danger at hand.

There was an uncomfortable, awkward silence as both of them grappled with their emotions.

Arjun nodded dolefully. 'Shukra's after me. I know. I was just told. I'm scared, Maya. What's going to happen if he finds me?' A shadow fell across his face.

Maya could see the terror in his eyes. She forgot her own thoughts. Before her, stood her oldest friend, scared and being hunted by a powerful Rishi whose ruthlessness she had witnessed. Her heart went out to him. She reached for his hand and pressed it comfortingly.

Arjun looked up at her gratefully. 'We're going to the Gurukul,' he said, now immersed completely in thoughts of his imminent fate. 'Uncle and Mom tell me we'll be safe there. *I'll* be safe there.' He shook his head. 'I am not so sure. God knows how anyone can stop Shukra.'

The bitterness swept through Maya again, without warning. The last time Shukra had tried to kill Arjun, her father had stopped him.

This time, her father was not there. He was dead. Killed by Shukra for protecting Arjun.

The emotions Maya had repressed briefly came flooding back. Tiwari's words still echoed in her head, explaining what Dhruv had done in Allahabad to ensure Arjun's safety. Maya had spent the entire journey trying to tell herself that Arjun himself was blameless. He was only a baby back then, unaware of what had been going on. It was her father with whom she was really angry, not Arjun. But try as she might, she couldn't get it out of her mind that Arjun was alive because of her father's sacrifice.

'Come on, you two, let's move it.' Virendra's voice, grim and hard-edged, floated out to them. Both he and Tiwari had stood with Pramila, to one side, conversing in low tones, glancing occasionally to the west, to where the sun was rapidly sinking below the horizon. 'We need to reach the Gurukul fast.'

Virendra pushed the gates open, while Maya and Arjun clambered into Tiwari's car.

'Right,' Tiwari said, slipping into the driver's seat and shifting gears, 'here we go.' He smiled at Maya and winked at Arjun in the rear view mirror.

Meanwhile, Virendra, too, had started the Land Cruiser, which took the lead and rumbled through the gates into the park. Tiwari, followed the bigger car inside, but stopped briefly to hop out and run to the gates. He was back in a couple of minutes.

'Can't leave the gates open,' he grinned at the children. 'Don't want the rangers to know that we went in after closing hours.'

The two cars sped through the park, on the narrow tarmac road that led into the forest from the entrance.

New Delhi

SP Raman Kapoor was in a foul mood. All the leads had dried up. Everyone connected with the case seemed to have disappeared without a trace—Upadhyay's daughter, Virendra and his family, the stranger who was the prime suspect. Not one of them had left any tracks. And he wasn't even counting the mysterious Vishwaraj, who Trivedi had met minutes prior to his murder, if Upadhyay was to be believed. Where could they all have disappeared?

As much as he hated it, Kapoor had to admit that he was stumped. And he didn't like it. It only strengthened his resolve to keep going, to find more leads. He had never given up before. And he wasn't about to make this his first unsolved case.

His phone rang, and he grabbed at it, a lifeline in the ocean of uncertainty that this case had rapidly developed into.

'Yes, Harish,' he barked into the phone as Harish greeted him. 'Tell me that you have some information.'

'Yes, sir.' Harish sounded tentative and strained. 'They re-appeared a short while ago. I followed them to the gates of Panna National Park. A second car was already standing there. A man and a girl got out of the other car. They stood talking for a short while and then got back into the cars and drove into the park. I don't know how they got in but they locked the gate after them. I am breaking open the lock and following them inside. Just wanted to report this to you.'

Kapoor nodded. 'Go ahead. I'll handle any objections. But be careful. It is going to be dark pretty soon. There won't be any lights in the park, and there are sure to be animals around. Tigers and stuff. Watch your back.'

'I will, sir.' Harish signed off.

Kapoor stared at the phone.

Just what was Virendra Singh up to?

And the girl in the second car …. Could it be Upadhyay's daughter? If she was, then how had she reached Panna? And who was the man with her? Had Virendra known about Upadhyay's death? Had he arranged for the girl to be brought to Panna by the other, unknown man? Or had Upadhyay's daughter been kidnapped? Somehow that was not the impression Harish's account gave him.

There was another possibility he had not considered. Was Virendra Singh behind all of this?

And what were all of them doing inside the park?

Chapter Thirty-four

Driving in the Park

Panna National Park
Madhya Pradesh

As they drove through the park, Arjun excitedly told Maya about the Gandharvas, the secret entrance into their valley and his meeting with Visvavasu. Maya listened quietly, not commenting or interrupting. Somehow, she just couldn't share his excitement and exuberance. She felt like this was Arjun's adventure and she had been dragged into it against her will. At this point, she just wanted to be alone with her thoughts.

'What's happened?' Arjun said to no one in particular, as Tiwari suddenly braked. The Land Cruiser in front of them had halted without warning.

Virendra alighted from the big SUV and strode towards their car. Tiwari looked up at him enquiringly.

'It's better if we all pile into one car,' Virendra told Tiwari. 'We'll move faster.'

Tiwari nodded and gestured to Maya and Arjun to change cars. Both of them complied, hurrying to the Land Cruiser, urged along by Virendra. From the back seat of the Land Cruiser, they watched curiously as Tiwari drove away, down a dirt path that led deeper into the forest, towards a rocky outcrop a short distance away.

Virendra drummed impatiently on the steering wheel of the SUV as they waited, casting occasional glances at the sinking sun as it hung over the treetops. Anxiety was writ large on his face.

Outside, the shadows began to deepen as the sun sank below the horizon. The last streaks of orange and pink against the blue canvas of the sky, put there as if by the random strokes of a broad brush, the last surge of brightness and colour to liven up the sky before darkness swallowed up the heavens, began to fade.

Tiwari came running out of the murky gloom within the forest and swung open the door, jumping into the car. Virendra accelerated even before Tiwari could slam the door shut and they sped away. Maya and Arjun looked at each other in wonder.

What was the rush?

'We're late,' Virendra grumbled.

'We have to take our chances,' Tiwari replied. 'There's no other way.'

Virendra grunted in response. Apparently he, too, realized that there was no choice but to go on, late or not.

The lights of the Land Cruiser came on, slicing through the darkness that enveloped the road ahead.

'Hang on tight,' Virendra warned them abruptly, a split second before the car lurched to the right as it turned off the tarmac road, and onto one of the dirt paths leading into the forest, without slowing down. The big SUV wobbled on its suspension, then stabilized and began dealing with the job of tackling the rough and bumpy forest path while racing ahead at top speed.

Trees, lining the path on either side, flashed past as they raced ahead, surrounded by huge plumes of dust thrown up by the wheels of the Land Cruiser. Dust particles danced in the twin beams of the headlights, but that did not deter Virendra, who kept the speed constant.

Inside the car, the occupants tried their best to hang onto anything they could to prevent being jolted around. It was clear that Virendra was going to keep up this pace until they reached the Gurukul.

'Is everyone wearing their amulets?' Tiwari asked suddenly, his voice breaking as he bounced around on the back seat, trying not to land on either of the children.

There was a chorus of confirmations.

'We stopped off at Noida,' Arjun told Maya, in jerks. 'Uncle picked them up from a friend who lives there.' He reached inside his shirt and pulled out a golden amulet, identical to the one given to Maya by her father.

Everyone seemed to think these amulets were a big deal, thought Maya. Even Virendra, whom she had always taken to be a logical and rational man, had asserted that she owed her life to the amulet she wore. She seemed to be the only one who had no faith in these amulets. Even now, while she wore the amulet her father had given her, she wasn't so sure. How could a little piece of metal protect them? Especially against someone as powerful as Shukra?

'Kanak!' Tiwari's voice was strained and thin. 'They're here! You were right!'

'Damn!' Virendra responded through gritted teeth. 'I was hoping to make it to the river before they showed up.'

Her thoughts interrupted, Maya looked out of the window, wondering what Tiwari was talking about.

But there was nothing outside.

Just the darkness. And the dust. The trees sprinting past them in the opposite direction.

What were they so worried about?

Then, without warning, it appeared at her window.

Maya screamed.

Chapter Thirty-five

Terror in the Park

Panna National Park
Madhya Pradesh

Maya screamed again.

The dull, lifeless eyes staring at her out of a desiccated face, the thin limbs, the frail-looking blackened trunk with ribs clearly visible, and the distended stomach — this was the same creature that she had encountered in Arjun's house in Delhi. Or, another one just like it.

The face at the window didn't move an inch after its sudden appearance. It was almost like it was stuck to the glass, even though Maya knew that wasn't possible. Somehow, the creature was keeping pace with the car, despite its speed.

But this was not all that horrified her. Beyond the creature, in the darkness that was momentarily lit up by the headlights of the car as they raced through the forest, Maya had caught a horrifying glimpse.

That fleeting glimpse had shown her hundreds of the same creatures swirling around in the darkness that surrounded the car. It was like the car was enveloped in a black shroud made up of the creatures.

'They're all around us!' Arjun shrieked, as terror-stricken as Maya. His face had gone white as he gazed into the stretch of the path before them, illuminated by the headlamps. 'What are they?' he cried.

'Arjun, get a grip on yourself.' Virendra's voice was curt. 'You are a

Kshatriya, a warrior. You cannot be afraid of immaterial beings like these. They have no substance. They lack the power to harm us.'

'What?' Arjun's disbelief was obvious. 'Can't you see? Shukra has sent them to kill me!'

'It's okay, Arjun. We are all here.' Pramila's comforting voice came from the passenger seat. 'Have faith.'

Arjun looked wild-eyed from one window to the next. He knew his mother wouldn't lie to him. But how could he overcome the terror that chilled him to his core?

'These are *pretas*,' Tiwari explained, gently. 'Spirits of people who have died a sudden, unnatural death. They have no material form.'

'Then why are they here?' Arjun demanded.

'Probably sent by Shukra,' Tiwari admitted. 'But they can't touch us.'

'They can't get inside the car?' Arjun asked hopefully.

'The car has no power to stop these creatures. They do not have a material body like ours, so no physical obstacle can stop them. They can very easily pass through the metal frame and glass windows and enter the car. What's holding them back are the amulets we are wearing. These amulets contain a very powerful mantra called the *Narsimha* mantra. As long as we wear the amulets, they cannot touch us. Don't worry, they will keep a safe distance from us.'

Maya did not look convinced. 'If we are safe from these ... *pretas*,' she shuddered at using the word for these disgusting creatures whom she had met before, 'then why are you guys so troubled to see them show up? Surely we can still make it to the river?'

Tiwari sighed. There was much that these children had to learn about. 'We aren't worried about the *pretas*,' he replied, patiently. 'Or, for that matter, the *bhutas* — spirits of the dead who have not yet been allowed to rebirth in another body — who are doubtless also circling around us in the darkness, unseen. Shukra would assume that we have some sort of protection against them. What we're afraid of is something else.'

Virendra took up the explanation, his eyes still firmly fixed on the dusty path ahead of them, ignoring the masses of spirits outside. 'These are pure spirits, unencumbered by a physical body. As a result, they are able to travel in an instant to wherever they wish to go. Nothing can come in their way. That makes them very useful as spies. By now, they would have reported back to Shukra and his minions that they have located and identified us.'

'How would they have identified us?' Arjun interrupted.

'That's difficult to explain,' Tiwari said. 'They would, just ... know.'

'You mean,' Maya said slowly, 'that Shukra now knows where we are? He is going to hunt us down?' Her mind fought back the terror that slowly crept back as the memory of Shukra pinning her father mid-air, and his agonized cries as she fled the house, came back to her.

A deathly silence descended in the cabin of the speeding SUV.

Maya's blood ran cold. Her worst fears were going to come true. She couldn't stand the thought of having to face that monster again. Involuntarily, she tightened her grasp on her father's diary, till her hands hurt.

Finally, Virendra spoke. 'We have to get to the Gurukul. We don't have too much time.'

Beside Maya, Arjun sniffed. She looked at her friend, worried. After all, it was him that Shukra was after and wanted dead. If Shukra turned up now, with a determination to complete what he had failed to do fourteen years ago in Allahabad, how could anyone protect Arjun?

Despite all her misgivings and resentment, Maya melted. Her heart went out to her friend. She reached out and clasped Arjun's hand. It was trembling. The boy was terrified. He gratefully held her hand, squeezing it, welcoming the comfort.

The car rushed on, cutting through the darkness and the ghouls floating around it.

Were they going to make it to the sanctuary of the Gurukul?

In another part of the park

Harish drove slowly, cautiously along the forest path. By the time he had broken the padlock that secured the chain around the park gates, both cars had disappeared. As the sun sank in the west, he fervently hoped that the cars had stayed on this road and that he would catch up with them somewhere ahead. If they had turned off the road into the forest, how was he going to track them down in the dark? He couldn't possibly switch on the headlights without giving himself away.

He had still not figured out where Virendra and the others had vanished to for the entire day, emerging only at sundown. He was just grateful for their reappearance. Now, though, he wondered if the timing of their reappearance and entry into the park was planned. At this time, there was no one around to watch them. And, though he doubted that they suspected his presence here, the growing darkness would make it nearly impossible for anyone to follow them to wherever they were headed.

Which raised the question — where *were* they headed?

He cursed as he suddenly noticed that he had passed a trail leading off the road and into the forest. He could not afford to get distracted. There was no point on focusing on questions which had no answers. He had to concentrate on the job at hand, which was following his quarry and finding out why they were here.

Harish reversed slowly until he reached the junction of the forest path and the road. He shook his head in frustration. It was quite dark now and there was no way to make out the tracks unless he switched the headlights on.

There was no way out. He had to do it.

With a tightening of his gut, he reversed the car a bit more and then got out to examine the road and the dirt path in the light of the car headlamps.

There were visible tracks here. But only one set, left by a single car, which had driven off the tarmac and onto the dirt path. He looked closely at the tracks and gathered that they belonged to the smaller car that he had seen at the gates along with the SUV. The one carrying the unidentified man and the young girl.

Had the two cars split up? If so, which one should he follow?

Harish arrived at a quick decision. The SUV was his primary quarry. He was not going to waste time searching for the smaller car.

There was no time to lose. The longer he took, the further away the SUV would get.

He got back into his car, switched the lights off, and drove ahead slowly.

Another dirt path came into sight, leading off the tarmac, to his right, into the forest.

Harish alighted once more and examined the road.

A car appeared to have turned into the path from the road at high speed. The tyre marks clearly belonged to the SUV.

He walked up the road, beyond the junction of the paths, and examined the ground carefully. The hard tarmac made it difficult to make out any tracks. It seemed to him that his conclusion was correct. The two cars had gone their separate ways. He couldn't understand why, but this was the only possibility he could think of.

It didn't matter. He had found the path his quarry had taken.

Harish decided to follow the tracks into the forest.

He switched off the headlights of the car as he drove off the tarmac and onto the dirt path, bumping and swaying on the rough track.

Immediately, the darkness deepened all around him. He could barely make out the outlines of the trees on either side, which melted into a dark, shapeless mass of foliage beyond, where the forest thickened. He squinted ahead as he drove on slowly. The others would have had to drive with their headlights on. There was no way anyone could take a chance in the dark, especially if they were driving fast. He hoped to see a pinprick of light that would indicate that he had not fallen too far behind.

But there was nothing ahead except the deep, dark gloom.

He switched the headlights on. The forest suddenly sprang to life. The trees lining the road glowed in the twin beams, deepening the shadows in the forest that stretched behind and beyond them.

Harish accelerated, jolting over the uneven path as the car sped through the forest. A feeling of elation was beginning to take hold of him. This was a forest. There were wild animals here, even tigers. Surely,

Virendra wasn't foolhardy enough to risk the lives of his companions by seeking refuge and a hideaway in the jungle?

No, Harish was quite sure that, sooner or later, he would come upon the three fugitives he had been tasked to follow. All he had to do was stay the course until that happened.

Chapter Thirty-six

Flight through the Forest

Panna National Park
Madhya Pradesh

'We won't reach the river in time,' Virendra said. 'We'll have to use the other entrance,' he added reluctantly.

Maya wondered what the 'other entrance' was and why Virendra seemed loath to use it to access the Gurukul.

Tiwari appeared to consider Virendra's words. 'I guess you're right, Kanak,' he said finally. 'I don't like the idea either, but ...'

'Do it,' Pramila spoke up sharply. She had been sitting quietly all along, seemingly indifferent to the ghostly shapes outside the car. 'We *have* to get Arjun to safety. That is all that matters right now. I don't care about anything else.'

Her commanding tone took both Arjun and Maya by surprise. Arjun had never heard his mother speak in this manner before to her uncle. She sounded ... imperious. It was very unlike her.

The Land Cruiser swayed once more on its suspension as Virendra flung it around a bend and down another, narrower forest path, without taking his foot off the accelerator.

'We're almost there,' Virendra said through gritted teeth. 'Get ready all of you. The moment the car stops, we run. Forget the suitcases. Just run as fast as you can. Stay together and follow my lead. Ratan, can you get the torches from my backpack?'

Wordlessly, Tiwari kneeled on his seat and pulled the backpack towards him, rummaging through it until he found two powerful torches. He handed one each to Maya and Arjun and sat down again, waiting.

'Right, torches on!' Virendra commanded. Maya and Arjun switched on their torches and light flooded the cabin of the Land Cruiser.

The SUV screeched to a halt. Maya hurriedly tucked the diary in the waistband of her jeans. She didn't want to risk losing it.

'Go!' Virendra ordered and they all spilled out of the car and onto the dirt path. The car's headlights were on, illuminating the path ahead of them. The eerie shapes of the *pretas* milled around them, floating in mid-air, clearly visible now, in the light of the car headlamps and the torches. A fetid, dank smell permeated the cold air.

Virendra led them off the path and into the forest, weaving through the trees clustered together on the right side of the track. Arjun was shepherded by Pramila into position behind Virendra and in front of her. Maya followed her, one hand constantly feeling the diary through her tee shirt to ensure it did not slip out of the waistband of her jeans. Tiwari brought up the rear.

'Don't stop. Keep moving. Hurry!' Virendra ordered.

Another path came into sight; a narrow one to be sure, and barely visible, but a path nevertheless, to be traversed only in single file.

The group hurried down the path, trying to avoid tripping over roots hidden by undergrowth, which could not be discerned in the light of the torches, and flapping their hands at low growing branches to keep them from slapping them in their faces. More than once, Maya and Arjun stumbled but were caught by Pramila or Tiwari.

No one looked back, but they didn't need to. They all knew that they were being followed by the ghostly cloud of spirits.

Presently, the trees began to thin out until they emerged in a large clearing where there was nothing but grass. A rocky hill rose up before them, at the far end of the clearing, maybe fifty feet from where the forest ended.

The trees lining the clearing, in a rough semi-circle, seemed to be conscious of an invisible border that they could not cross.

But to the five human beings who emerged from the cover of the forest and sprinted across the clearing, no such border mattered.

Nor did it seem to affect the mass of twisted, emaciated creatures that formed a roiling, dark cloud that ebbed and flowed above the refugees who were running like their lives depended on it.

Virendra reached the rock face and turned to see how the rest of the group was doing.

The other four were close on his heels.

Almost there.

Almost in.

Almost ...

'Kanak!' There was fear in Tiwari's voice as he panted his way across the last few yards between him and the hillside where the rest of the group now stood. He was out of breath, unable to say anything more.

Virendra looked around at the dark sky, at the mass of spirits above, desperately seeking to identify the source of Tiwari's alarm.

There was a scream. But not born of terror.

An agonized cry of pain.

To everyone's surprise, Maya fell to the ground, clutching her head, rolling around, screaming all the while.

Chapter Thirty-seven

Terror in the Clearing

In the clearing
Panna National Park

Virendra, Pramila and Arjun stared at Maya, wondering what had happened to her, and unsure of what to do.

Only Tiwari knew what had happened to the young girl. 'Something's coming,' he panted, and shook his head, closing his eyes to focus.

Pramila rushed to Maya and tried to calm her, but it was clear that something grave was afflicting the girl. Tears rolled down her face, her eyes were shut tight, and she pressed the palms of her hands tight against her head. She seemed to be in the throes of a fit or an attack.

'What's happened to Maya?' Arjun was distressed. The threat to his life was momentarily forgotten and a deep concern for the well-being of his friend had taken over instead. 'Do something! Help her!'

Pramila looked at Virendra, bewildered. He shook his head. He didn't have an answer either. Instead, he scanned the sky, mindful of Tiwari's warning, even as Pramila picked up the torch that Maya had dropped.

Tiwari stood to one side, his eyes shut tight as he muttered something under his breath. Virendra guessed he was reciting a mantra.

But for what?

Then, he saw it. His eyes widened with wonder.

What was happening?

Pramila and Arjun gazed in amazement.

Arjun's jaw dropped. Pramila rose from where she had been kneeling near Maya, who was lying on her side, curled up in a foetal position. The girl had stopped screaming. She now sobbed uncontrollably while her body shivered perceptibly. Something was happening to her, but no one knew what it was. She still held her head tight with both her hands.

As the little group watched, in the light of their torches, a spectacle that was as astonishing as it was terrifying was unfolding.

The dark mass of *pretas which* had followed them through the forest and sallied forth from the cover of the trees, now hovering above them at a safe distance like a dark, grey bellied cloud in a thunderstorm, had parted to create a gap through which a black fog now rolled into the clearing.

As it slowly wafted through the mass of spirits, the *pretas* seemed to shrink away from the fog, almost as if it was toxic enough to harm even the spirits of the dead.

The fog seemed to be made of the darkness itself; no, of a blackness that was even darker than the cloak of the night. As the cloud of *pretas* parted, the fog drifted through the opening, blotting out the stars that shone in the sky, hiding from sight the canopy of the night.

Tiwari's eyes snapped open. 'Kanak!' he urged, his voice tense.

Virendra whirled toward him.

'They're here.' Tiwari's voice was strained. He was the only one who appeared to understand what was happening. He was also making a Herculean effort to suppress the terror that was born of his knowledge. 'Kanak, I can sense their presence but I don't know what they are. Nothing like I've ever seen before – that's the only thing I can say for sure. We can't enter the Gurukul without knowing what we are up against. Too much of a risk. You need to make a stand. Here, in this clearing.'

Virendra nodded, not understanding fully, though he guessed that something was going to happen now that would require his skills as a Kshatriya. It was clear that Tiwari felt that the powers of a Rishi would not be enough to tackle whatever it was they were facing. The specialized powers of a warrior were needed.

'Swords.' Virendra's command was curt and urgent.

Arjun gave him a baffled look. Swords? They had left the wooden case, in which the swords were packed, back in the car. It was impossible to go back there to get it now!

He looked at his mother and his jaw dropped. There was a long, shiny sword in her hand, glinting in the light of the torch that she held in her other hand. His head spun. What was his mother doing with a sword? And where had she got it from?

Arjun turned to look at Virendra just in time to see two swords materialize, one in each hand, as if out of thin air.

What was happening here? Was he dreaming?

The next moment, Virendra turned to Arjun and nodded, tossing one of the swords to him. Arjun caught it deftly and drew it from the scabbard, in one smooth, swift motion. He quickly took up a position to attack, as taught by his uncle.

Virendra gave him an approving glance, as if to say, 'Good job. Good stance. First step.' As he would do back home when they were practicing.

As Arjun steeled himself and looked ahead, he was overcome with shock and horror at the scene that began unfolding before his eyes.

In another part of the park

There was no warning. No time for him to prepare.

One moment, Harish was racing along the dirt path, being jolted along in his seat, with nothing around him but the trees, the dust cloud thrown up by the car, and the darkness.

The next moment, he was surrounded by a scene out of a nightmare.

Hideous creatures appeared out of nowhere and descended upon his car. It was as if the darkness surrounding him had suddenly taken on a life of its own, manifesting itself in a multitude of horrific forms. They swirled around him, all emaciated limbs, incomplete bodies, fangs and claws.

A terror that he had never experienced before overcame him as he hurtled on, unable to do anything to stop them. His mind would not work. A dark sense of horror filled his senses, his blood running cold.

Through the open window a foul odour pervaded the air, making it difficult to breathe. It was as if all the open drains of the world had converged on this very path.

The stench snapped him out of the spell that had held him in its thrall. Still gripped by fear and terror, he slammed the brakes, bringing the car to an abrupt halt.

Sweating profusely and trying desperately to keep his already strained nerves from succumbing to the dark panic, lurking at the edges of his consciousness, he swung the car to his right, then reversed at top speed, turned again, and then reversed once more, until he was able to point the car in the direction from which he had just come.

Hanging onto consciousness by a thread, he pushed the accelerator to the floor. The car lurched forward, then raced back along the dirt track, retracing its journey.

The moments stretched like eternity. He thought there was no hope left for him. Surely, he was going to die here at the hands of these demons, or whatever they were.

Then, as abruptly as they had appeared, the shapes swirling around him vanished into thin air. Like they had been sucked back into the darkness from where they had come.

Harish was left on the rough path, with the trees and the darkness. The whirl of chaos that had swept him up in its wake was gone. A deathly stillness reigned.

But he didn't stop. Gripping the wheel with hands slippery with sweat, his clothes sticking to his body, beads of perspiration dripping down his forehead into his eyes, he could focus on only one thing.

He had to get out of this place.

Now.

Chapter Thirty-eight

Kapoor's Files

SP Kapoor's office
New Delhi

Raman Kapoor snatched up his phone from his desk the moment it rang. He was sitting late in office today, poring over some files that he had requested for.

He hoped that Harish had found at least some clue.

'Yes, Harish?'

For a few moments, there was no reply. Just heavy breathing on the line. Kapoor was baffled.

'Harish!' His tone was strident now.

'Sir,' Harish responded faintly, his voice quavering. 'Sir ...'

'Go on, Harish,' Kapoor interrupted impatiently. 'I'm listening. I can hear you. Are you inside the park?'

'Sir,' Harish stammered, unable to get the words out. 'Sir, the park ...'

There was silence once more.

'Good heavens, Harish, what's the matter with you, man? Get it out!'

The words finally tumbled out in a rush. 'Sir, the park is haunted. There are creatures there that I cannot describe. Terrifying things. They pursued me.' His voice broke.

Kapoor sat down, bewildered. What was Harish going on about?

This was one of his best men whom he trusted implicitly. What had happened?

'What do you mean haunted? Where are Virendra and the others?' he demanded.

'I don't know, sir.' Harish finally collected his wits about him and narrated his experience to Kapoor.

Kapoor was stunned into silence. He couldn't believe what he was hearing.

'Take a break, Harish,' he said finally, his tone more gentle now. 'I'll have someone arrange food and a bed for the night. I'll arrange for a team from Gwalior to reach Panna tomorrow and check out the forest with you. We'll coordinate with the park rangers as well so they can guide you around the park. Let's see if we can find a reasonable explanation for what you witnessed tonight. You need some rest. Check for clues to the whereabouts of our fugitives tomorrow.'

Kapoor sat back when the call ended and contemplated the discussion he had just had. It was unbelievable. Harish had sounded so utterly convinced that he had experienced supernatural creatures in the forest. Kapoor could feel his jitters through the phone. Yet, his own brain refused to entertain the possibility. What could have terrorized one of his best men almost to the extent of a breakdown? The investigation would throw up clues, he was sure of that. No point speculating until then.

He turned his attention to the files on his desk. Not wanting to leave any loose ends in this case, and also out of desperation in the absence of any concrete leads, he had asked for files on all cases of unnatural deaths for which there were no explanations forthcoming. A tall stack of files had duly arrived in his office and he had spent most of the day going through them.

Most of the files pertained to murders which were fairly nondescript but had remained unsolved for want of motives or suspects. Some of them were also unexplained suicides.

Kapoor sighed and rubbed his eyes wearily. He had to go through the lot.

Three hours later, Kapoor had finished going through all the files. He leaned back in his chair and stared at the two files that he had picked out of the stack.

He felt satisfied. His hunch had paid off. Going through the files had not been a futile exercise after all. Buried in the mass of paperwork were two cases that had confounded investigators but had been overlooked, despite the bewildering nature of the murders. They had been marked unsolved and had been put away to gather dust.

There seemed no end in sight to the mysteries in this case. He sat back and basked in the thrill of the mounting challenge that the case presented. The sensation was familiar. It had started as a simple murder that seemed impossible to explain. It had been interesting enough to begin with. Now, as he ploughed on, it was developing into something more complex, like a multi-headed monster that was impossible to kill; not very different from many of his past cases.

His expectation of finding new clues in the files had been belied. Oh, he had found something. But what he had read in these two files did not present any clues to solving the case.

Instead, true to the nature of this case, it only made the waters murkier.

The mystery continued to deepen with every step that he took.

Kapoor sat back and contemplated his next course of action.

Chapter Thirty-nine

Shukra's Army

In the clearing
Panna National Park

Out of the corner of his eye, Arjun saw Virendra glance at Tiwari, who nodded back in acknowledgement. A quiet signal had passed between the two men.

Tiwari turned and dashed towards the hillside and disappeared. It was as if he had run right into the rock.

Arjun figured that this was the 'entrance' Virendra had referred to earlier. He wasn't too surprised. Earlier today, they had entered the Gandharva valley in much the same manner.

A device to keep prying eyes out and conceal the entrance to the Gurukul.

But something more was transpiring in the clearing.

The black fog was now sinking to the ground like a fine black veil dropping over the forest beyond it.

As Arjun watched with a growing sense of alarm, the black fog started disintegrating into amorphous clouds of black, wispy, smoke, which began separating from the fog. As the individual wisps of smoke touched the ground, a remarkable transformation was taking place before his eyes.

The nebulous forms of the black clouds were stretching and elongating in all directions as they slowly morphed into physical bodies that looked remarkably human in shape. As each one touched down, its transformation was complete.

Yet, as he observed them more closely, the newly formed bodies were not really normal. They were very similar in appearance, yet quite different.

The overall shape and form was similar to that of a human being — a torso, two legs, two arms, and a head.

But that was where the resemblance ended.

For these creatures that were forming right in front of his eyes had no faces. No mouth, no nose and no ears. Just blood-red eyes glaring away, burning into the little group that cowered before them in the shadow of the hillside.

The monstrous beings created from the mist had pale skin, with a deep red hue. Even at this distance, he could see the sharp talons at the ends of their fingers and toes.

What were they?

A knot formed in Arjun's stomach. One question haunted him.

Was Shukra here?

As the clouds of black smoke continued to descend to the ground, the faceless creatures multiplied in number. Arjun watched, transfixed. What was happening right now was beyond his comprehension.

Silence had descended on the clearing. With a start, Arjun realized that Maya had stopped sobbing. She was still lying on the ground in a foetal position, her hands over her ears now. But no sound came from her.

Was she conscious? He took a step towards her.

Virendra frowned at him. 'Focus!' was the message in his glance.

Arjun hesitated, then made up his mind. He didn't want to disobey his uncle. But there was no way he was going to let any harm come to Maya. She was his childhood companion, his one true friend in the world. He needed to protect her. Surely, Virendra couldn't have a problem with that! With a decisive step Arjun moved towards Maya and stood protectively between her and the strange creatures that were now slowly advancing towards them.

The one thing he knew was that, at some point in time, he would have to join his uncle in attacking these creatures, along with his mother.

His mother.

He glanced at Pramila. She, too, was focused on the creatures. She stood with the sword in her hand, in a stance identical to that of Virendra's. Arjun had never seen her with a sword before, but here she was, acting like a seasoned warrior.

And, perhaps, she was one.

As Arjun wondered about what else he did not know about his mother, there was a commotion and all hell seemed to break loose.

The hillside behind him erupted and a mass of people came racing out into the clearing. Men and women, girls and boys, some dressed in white homespun robes, others in colourful leggings and tunics emerged from the rock, led by Tiwari, who immediately headed towards Maya and Arjun.

The younger children carried old fashioned torches whose flames licked the darkness around them, while the men and women and older children in the close-fitted coloured uniforms, carried bows and swords that glinted in the light of the torches.

The folks in the white robes were all chanting a mantra as they burst into the clearing from the rock face of the hillside.

'The Kshatriyas,' Virendra exclaimed in relief.

Who were these people? wondered Arjun.

But there was no time to think. Virendra was charging, with a bloodcurdling roar, towards the army of Shukra's creatures.

Pramila followed Virendra, brandishing her sword.

Arjun, startled out of his contemplation, hastened behind them, adding to the din with his own full-throated shriek. To his great surprise, the fear that had gripped him so far was replaced by a rush of adrenaline.

With yells and roars, the sword wielding people who had emerged from the rock, joined Virendra, Pramila and Arjun in their assault on Shukra's army.

On their part, the creatures, anticipating the attack, let out fearsome roars and charged, meeting the advancing humans half-way.

The air resonated with mantras, roars and chants as the two sides clashed in the clearing. Virendra and Pramila advanced through the ranks of the creatures, cutting them down with fierce strokes, their swords flashing in the light of scores of flaming torches as they swung their weapons in all directions.

Shukra's army was strong and fought back viciously. Cries of pain filled the air as the creatures overwhelmed some of their attackers. Their skin was tough and hard, like armour, and their sharp talons doubled up as weapons with which they tore at the men, women and children from the Gurukul. But, even as the Kshatriya army from the Gurukul fought fiercely — slashing and hacking, depleting the ranks of the creatures — the black fog continued to swirl overhead, a seemingly unlimited source to replenish the enemy forces.

Sooner or later, Arjun knew, the Kshatriyas would be overwhelmed. What would happen then?

Chapter Forty

The Battle of the Gurukul

**In the clearing
Panna National Park**

Maya's eyes fluttered open. There was an indistinct shape hovering over her. What was it?

As her eyes came into focus, the hazy shape sharpened into Tiwari's face. He was kneeling by her side and examining her, an anxious look on his face.

An enormous din surrounded her; a peculiar mix of chanting, screams, blood curdling roars, cries of pain and the sound of fighting came to her ears.

What was happening?

She struggled to rise but succeeded only in propping herself up on her elbow. What had happened to her? She felt drained and had no recollection of why she found herself lying on the ground now.

Her last memory was one of standing in the clearing, wondering if they were trapped between the forest and the hillside, with the *pretas* hovering above them ominously. Then, suddenly her head seemed to be on fire. The next thing she knew, she was lying on the ground, wondering what was going on around her.

'Maya! Thank goodness you are okay. Let me help you,' Tiwari said kindly, helping her to her feet and supporting her as she unsteadily stood up, leaning against the rocky hillside. Maya gazed at the battle that raged before her eyes.

A cold dread wrapped its icy fingers around her heart as she took in the scene. Warriors from the Gurukul had reached the scene and were now battling an army of strange creatures, which were mysteriously materializing out of a strange black mist.

The creatures were no match for the skill and weapons of the warriors, but their numbers kept increasing despite the onslaught, as the warriors began to tire in the face of fierce resistance.

All around her, a soft chanting filled the night air amid the sounds of battle. Tiwari, too, was chanting something, Maya noted.

A mantra.

Maya strained to make out the words.

|| उग्रं वीरं महाविष्णुं ज्वलन्तं सर्वतोमुखं |
नरसिम्हम भीषणं भद्रं मृत्योर् मृत्युं नमाम्यहम् ||

Ugram viram maha vishnum
Jvalantum sarvato mukham
Narsingam bhishanam bhadram
Mrityur mrtyum namami aham

Startled, she realized that he was reciting the *Narsimha* mantra. She had read it only last night in the diary. Her hand rose to feel the diary still safe under her tee shirt. Somehow, she remembered every word of the mantra, despite her drowsiness while reading it.

Maya had felt helpless until now. Something — she didn't know what — had deprived her of her senses. Whatever it was, she could still feel the after effects. It had drained her completely.

As she stood watching the warriors — men, women, children, including her childhood friend — fighting a losing battle with creatures whom she was sure Shukra had something to do with, she felt a fierce determination seize her.

Now, she saw an opening. A chance to do something. She was going to do what she could.

Maya assessed the situation. The only way they could win this battle was by destroying the mist from which the creatures kept emerging. Would the mantra succeed in doing that? She had no idea. But she had to try. There seemed no other way out. She closed her eyes and focused on the black fog that swirled overhead, at the centre of the cloud of *pretas*. This was her only hope, even if it meant nothing in the end.

Maya began reciting the mantra. Tiwari cast a surprised look at her, without breaking the rhythm of the mantra he was reciting.

While Maya took up the chant along with Tiwari and some of the other white-robed people from the Gurukul, Arjun continued the battle with the pale creatures. Following the lead of his mother and uncle, he had charged into their ranks and used his skills with the sword to good effect, cutting down the creatures as he advanced into their midst.

He could hear, all around him, the roars and shouts of the Kshatriyas from the Gurukul as they, too, slashed their way through the unearthly army that they confronted. Some of the Kshatriyas used their bows to devastating effect, plucking arrows from the quivers slung across their backs, drawing the bowstring and shooting in one fluid movement, at lightning speed. Others wielded swords, like Arjun, using a blend of swiftness, dexterity and sheer strength to cut down the monsters.

Arjun silently thanked his uncle for the training and for pushing him to keep at it even when he would tire of the constant practice.

It was those practice sessions, with unending repeats of different techniques and movements that stood Arjun in good stead now. He was light on his feet, nimbly ducking the clumsy attacking movements of the creatures while swiftly spotting opportunities to hack through their defences and strike them down.

Arjun had quickly gauged the main disadvantage the creatures suffered from. While they were larger and stronger than the humans battling them, the Kshatriyas were well trained in warfare. The creatures, on the other hand, probably because they were newly formed, seemed to be unaccustomed to their freshly generated physical bodies. Their movements were awkward and slow, as if they were still learning how to use their newly formed limbs. Despite their physical superiority, the unearthly beings were no match for the Kshatriyas.

They reminded Arjun of the rubber monsters in the old horror movies and in Star Trek, played either by men in rubber suits or mechanical frames that moved jerkily. He grinned at the thought, despite himself, then hurriedly skipped out of the way to avoid being shredded by the sharp claws of a giant creature who had shambled up to him and took a swipe at him.

'Oh crap,' he muttered to himself as he turned to face the creature. 'That was close. No more dreaming about rubber monsters, AJ.'

Arjun could feel himself beginning to tire. Shukra's army was being constantly replenished by the black mist. While the Kshatriyas hadn't suffered any casualties so far, they would be outnumbered soon.

He cast a worried glance at the mist swirling overhead, and rubbed his eyes. Was he imagining it? Or was the mist actually dissipating?

Seeing him distracted, one of the creatures came lumbering up to Arjun, and growled as it raised its arm in preparation to strike him.

Arjun, totally absorbed in watching the mist, failed to see the creature approach and became aware of the danger only when he heard it growl. He tried to jump out of the creature's way to avoid its blow but couldn't do it in time. A pale, muscled arm slammed into his sword arm like a sledgehammer, knocking it out of his grasp and sending it flying to the ground.

Knocked off balance by the blow, Arjun went careening back, crashing into another creature, which had its back to him and was busy battling a Kshatriya boy.

Surprised, the creature turned its head to look at Arjun, taking its eyes off its opponent. The boy saw his opportunity and swiftly cut down the creature with a few well directed blows of his sword.

Arjun had slumped to the ground after the collision, his eyes fixed on his own opponent who had plodded forward and was now preparing to rip him to shreds with its claws.

In a flash, the boy, whose opponent Arjun had just ploughed into, rushed at the monster, slicing off its hand as it charged. The creature bellowed with pain and anger as its hand, severed at the elbow, dropped straight on Arjun, taking the wind out of him.

Arjun stared in disgust at the severed hand lying on his stomach, oozing a sticky green substance that seemed to cling to his tee shirt.

'Thought you needed a hand,' the boy winked and grinned at Arjun, as he despatched the creature, attacking its knees and then decapitating it as it tottered before him.

The boy held out his hand and helped Arjun up. 'Thanks,' Arjun said, gratefully. 'You ...'

'Save it,' the boy said as he pointed to Arjun's sword, lying on the ground near them. 'There are two more coming your way.'

Arjun leaped at his sword and brandished it menacingly, flashing his saviour a grin as he prepared to face the two monsters lumbering towards him.

A shout suddenly went up. 'The mist! It's fading!'

The shout was echoed across the clearing by the others.

Arjun heard Virendra's voice. 'Cut them all down! Leave none of them standing!'

The children of the Gurukul attacked with a vengeance, bolstered by the knowledge that the source of the creatures was gone.

It didn't take long, after that, to cut down the remaining creatures and secure the clearing.

Chapter Forty-one

Gurukul

In the clearing
Panna National Park

Maya surveyed the clearing, strewn with the bodies of the creatures, many of which were missing arms, legs or even heads.

She had been chanting the mantra, her eyes tightly shut, focusing on the black mist, when a shout had startled her. Someone was screaming something about the mist having disappeared. She looked up, expecting to see the cloud of *pretas* surrounding the black mist, but there was nothing there.

The entire mass of spirits had vanished, along with the black mist. All that was visible was the night sky, which looked like a sheet of black paper with innumerable little holes in it through which a light shone, creating thousands of little diamonds in the sky.

The inhabitants of the Gurukul had made quick work of the remaining creatures from Shukra's army, until not one monster remained standing.

A solemn and grave silence descended on the clearing, as people got to work. A pit was hastily dug at one edge of the clearing and the dead creatures and their hacked off body parts swiftly buried. The injured warriors were carried through the rocky hillside, back into the Gurukul.

Maya scanned the clearing, searching for Arjun, Virendra and

Pramila, but with the mass of people milling around the clearing she couldn't spot them.

Once again, she checked to see if her father's diary was safe and was relieved to feel it pressing against her. As she looked up, she saw a movement in the trees beyond the circumference of the clearing. Was it an animal, disturbed by the noise and the fighting? It certainly couldn't be anyone from the Gurukul. She strained her eyes to make out the figure that was dimly visible in the light of the torches.

A voice at her elbow made her jump.

'How are you feeling now, Maya?' It was Tiwari, smiling at her. 'Sorry,' he said, realizing he had startled her. 'Didn't mean to scare you.'

'That's okay. I'm fine,' Maya smiled back at him, a bit sheepishly. She was relieved that the ordeal was finally over. 'What happened to me?'

'You blacked out.'

'I don't know what came over me. But I'm okay now.' She gestured at the clearing, at the remains of the creatures. 'Those were Shukra's creatures, weren't they?'

Tiwari nodded, his face serious now.

'I've read about Shukra in the ancient texts,' Maya continued, 'but I've never read about anything like this.'

Tiwari looked at her. 'There is much we have to learn about Shukra that the scriptures do not mention. They talk of the Shukra who lived 5,000 years ago. The Shukra we confront now is different. Vastly more powerful. And we have no idea what powers he may have acquired since he disappeared from the ancient texts.'

'But what made the black fog disappear?' Maya had to know. 'Something happened. Both the mist and the *pretas* disappeared.'

'The power of the *Narasimha* mantra,' Tiwari said, 'is immense. With so many of us chanting the mantra together, it may have countered and weakened Shukra's power to sustain the fog he had created.' He gestured towards the rock face they were standing next to. 'But let's enter the Gurukul now. There will be time to talk later.'

Maya was not satisfied with his explanation. She felt that Tiwari was holding back something, but she allowed him to lead her through the hillside. The walk through the rock was a novel experience for Maya, who had not experienced the entry into the Gandharva valley. She realized that the rock was supposed to camouflage the entrance into the Gurukul and ensure that only those who knew how to gain access could enter.

As she emerged from the rock, an amazing sight greeted her. Children her age and a bit older, sat cross-legged in meditative postures around what she guessed was the boundary of the Gurukul. The power of the mantra they were chanting together, coursed through her. She strained to catch the words and, to her surprise, was able to make them out quite clearly.

ॐ ॥ ॐ त्र्यम्बकं यजामहे
सुगन्धिं पुष्टिवर्धनम्
उर्वारुकमिव बन्धनान्
मृत्योर्मुक्षीय मामृतात् ॥

OM triyambakam yajāmahe sugandhim pushtivardhanam,
urvārukamiva bandhanān mrrityormokshiya māmrritāt.

Tiwari noticed her silently enunciating the mantra and smiled. He fell back a step and whispered to her, 'The mantra protects the Gurukul and keeps evil out of it. It is chanted twenty-four hours a day, every day of the year, non stop.'

Maya nodded, overcome with wonder. She looked around and took in the serene tranquility and the beauty of the Gurukul.

In front of her stretched a forest, with a thick carpet of grass, sparsely populated by trees. Unlike the forest on the other side of the rock, the trees here were well spaced out; not so close that they would appear dense, but close enough to provide shelter and comfort. Gently glowing orbs of light floated in the air at regular intervals providing sufficient light without hurting the eyes.

Cottages stretched on either side of her in a straight line, creating a kind of central avenue starting from the hillside. Each cottage had a

thatched roof and small windows through which lights shone out. To her surprise, these lights seemed to be electric lights.

Directly ahead of her at some distance, stood a large wooden structure with a thatched roof. It was the only building shrouded in darkness. The central avenue led straight between the parallel lines of cottages to the stairs leading into this structure.

As Maya looked around, she noticed that the injured were carried away to one of the cottages behind the ones that lined the avenue, which appeared to be a small hospital. Tiwari led her towards another cottage down a path that led off the central avenue. It turned out to be the guesthouse. Maya discovered it was a small cottage with six little bedrooms and a larger room that doubled as a dining room and a sitting room.

'You'd better get some rest,' Tiwari told Maya, kindly but firmly, his tone indicating that this wasn't a request. 'The *Mahamati* Council may want to see you.'

Maya nodded. She was too tired to ask who or what the *Mahamati* Council was. The cross country journey from Delhi to Panna, followed by the unexpected events of the evening had left her exhausted. She was only too happy to be able to retire somewhere she could relax and think. There were too many thoughts jostling for attention in her mind.

But before she could do that she had to tell Tiwari about what she had seen in the clearing outside the Gurukul.

Tiwari listened attentively to her. 'You are sure about this?' he asked her when she had finished.

Maya looked doubtful. 'I can't be very sure. The light from the torches didn't exactly reach the edge of the clearing.'

'Well, there's nothing to be done at the moment,' Tiwari said, conclusively. 'Whoever or whatever it was would have left by now. Don't think about it too much and get some rest.'

A girl who seemed to be just slightly younger than Maya, led her to one of the bedrooms in the guesthouse and left. Alone in her room, Maya tried to come to terms with the rush of events in the last two days. She still couldn't believe all that she had experienced in this short period of time. Just yesterday, she had happily returned from school with Arjun, blissfully unaware of the events that would unfold, which would change her life forever.

There were still a lot of things that she didn't understand. To begin with, what was she doing here? What was this place—the Gurukul? She had never heard of it. Even Tiwari had never really explained where he was taking her.

Then, there was the big surprise of the evening: the mantra. Had it really worked? Was it the power of all those white-robed people, chanting the Narsimha mantra along with Tiwari and Maya, that had ultimately defeated Shukra's army? A part of her didn't want to believe it, wanted to cling on to her long-held beliefs that mantras and charms were merely symbolic — artificial crutches for people who couldn't do things on their own and required the comfort of something that was more powerful than them.

Yet, she couldn't dismiss what she had seen with her own eyes. And she had actually felt an inexplicable power course strongly through her while the mantra was being chanted. Could she have been wrong in being dismissive about mantras all her life? She didn't know what to think anymore. She desperately wanted someone to explain things to her. She needed to know more. Once again, the memories of her father that she had suppressed with difficulty, rose to the surface. Maya brushed them aside. She had to seek some answers here, at the Gurukul.

Deep in the recesses of her mind, something tugged at her. A distant memory? A forgotten dream? An old friend? It seemed like a mix of all of these.

Then, it was gone, leaving Maya bewildered. Was she imagining things?

Her thoughts turned to Arjun. She hadn't seen him among the injured who were carried off to the Gurukul sick bay for treatment. But a worry, a deep concern for him bubbled within her. She knew she wouldn't be able to quell that sensation until she finally saw him with her own eyes and satisfied herself that he was okay.

Maya was surprised. Despite the fact that they had grown up together, practically living in each other's house, she had never really thought about what he meant to her. It was only now that it dawned on her that she and Arjun shared some kind of a special connection, a bond forged by their years of togetherness, sharing each other's secrets, having each other's shoulders to lean on, cry on. She had never known her mother and Arjun had never known his father. But they had always had each other.

She thought of how aloof she had been with him when they had reunited near the gates of the park. She had felt anger and resentment in that moment that she saw him, but now all she felt was regret. It was not fair, she reflected, to throw away the years of togetherness, the special bond they shared, all for something that she knew Arjun had nothing to do with, and which had been no fault of his. A wave of guilt washed over her, increasing her apprehensions about his fate in the battle and her eagerness to see him again, safe and sound.

How was she going to find out if Arjun had survived the battle unscathed or not?

As Maya sat, lost in deep thought, a knock on the door made her jump.

Chapter Forty-two

The Mahamati Council

The clearing outside the Gurukul
Panna National Park

The last of the creatures had been dumped into the pit that had been excavated by a team of warriors who had escaped relatively unscathed after the battle. Arjun had helped, turning up his nose in disgust at the sight of the sticky, green slime that greeted his eyes everywhere — on the severed limbs and mangled trunks of the creatures and across the carpet of grass that lined the floor of the clearing.

He wiped his hands on his tee shirt and shuddered. Not that it helped, since his tee shirt, too, was fairly soaked in the slime.

The boy who had helped Arjun in the battle came up to him, a big grin plastered on his face.

'Good work, eh?' the boy remarked, oblivious to the damage done to his uniform — which was rent in several places — and to the sticky green ooze that clung to the silk fabric. 'They never had a chance. The dim-wits of the spirit world against the finest Kshatriyas this side of the Narmada. By the way, my name is Varun.'

'Arjun.'

Varun looked at Arjun appraisingly. 'So you're the scion of Yayati, huh?'

Arjun flushed. He didn't know how to react. He didn't even know if Varun was making fun of him or not.

'I guess I am,' he responded tentatively.

'Did you enjoy it?'

'Huh?'

'The battle, dude.' Varun sounded exasperated. 'The fighting, the killing. Well, in a manner of speaking. You can't really kill something that is already dead, right?'

Arjun didn't have a clue as to what Varun was going on about. 'Who were these creatures?' he asked Varun.

'Not "who", but "what". You have a lot to learn, my friend. Which Gurukul were you in before this?'

Arjun shrugged. 'Never been to a Gurukul before.'

'Seriously?' Varun guffawed. 'You're kidding me, right?' He saw the look on Arjun's face and raised his eyebrows. 'You aren't kidding me. Wow. You mean this was the first time you encountered creatures like this?'

Arjun wanted to say that he didn't even know creatures like this existed until tonight. But he thought it wise to keep his ignorance to himself. He simply shook his head.

'Shoot me.' Varun's tone suddenly changed. 'I would never have guessed. You handled that sword like you've been in battle a million times before.'

'I did enjoy it. For the first time in my life, I was actually fighting a real battle. It wasn't a practice session. It was real. I could smell the danger. And it gave me a high,' Arjun admitted. He looked at Varun. 'Is that wrong? To feel good about killing someone?'

Varun made a face. 'It's complicated. For starters, those weren't "someone". Okay, fine, I don't really know what they were either. I haven't seen them before today, but I do know this. They were spirits in a physical form. And spirits are dead. We can't do a thing to spirits with our swords and fancy fighting techniques. We can only attack their physical forms. Material objects can't touch immaterial beings. That's what the Rishis are there for. They can do stuff to the spirits that doesn't need material objects. So you weren't really killing them, you know.' He grinned. 'But if you enjoyed the fighting, well, then, you are a Kshatriya alright. If you were squeamish about fighting them or about getting their blood on your clothes, or whatever this thing is, since spirits don't have blood,' he indicated the green ooze on his uniform, 'then you're in the wrong place.' He slapped Arjun on the back. 'But that swordplay ...' He shook his head. 'Man, that was good. Really good.'

'Thanks.' Arjun liked Varun. 'I had a good trainer. My uncle.'

'Really? You've been training out there without setting foot in a Gurukul? Is that even allowed?'

'Okay everyone, back to the Gurukul and to your dorms!' One of the uniformed adult Kshatriyas called out and the younger lot, who were still in the clearing, dutifully began trooping through the rock and into the Gurukul.

The Gurukul Guesthouse
Panna National Park

Virendra, Pramila and Tiwari sat facing a group of five individuals who sat in a semi-circle in the sitting room of the guesthouse.

The three men and two women were clearly from the Gurukul. Two of the men and one woman were dressed in white robes, while the other two were dressed in the raiment of Kshatriyas — colourful, well-fitting silk tunics and leggings with knee-length boots.

Virendra and Pramila knew the five well. These were the members of the *Mahamati* Council. The *Mahamatis* were the men and women — Maharishis, Rishis and Kshatriyas — who trained the children studying in the Gurukul. The Council comprised the *Mahamatis* who ran the Gurukul on behalf of the Saptarishis, overseeing all the other *Mahamatis*. The head of the Gurukul was Maharishi Mahesh, who sat in the centre of the group, flanked by the other two Maharishis — Jignesh and Usha. The two Kshatriyas — Amba and Parth — sat at opposite ends of the semi-circle.

The Council had just been briefed by Virendra, Pramila and Tiwari on the developments that had led to their presence here, tonight, at the Gurukul.

'Vishwaraj!' Jignesh was the first to react to Virendra's news that Dhananjay Trivedi had been accosted by the young man shortly before his death. He shook his head in disbelief. 'Are you sure that Dhruv heard the right name?'

'Dhruv and I had the same reaction as you,' Virendra said grimly. 'I don't know Vishwaraj personally, but Dhruv had taught the lad in Allahabad. We were aware of his standing in the *Gana*, his exceptional yogic powers, and the fact that the *Sangha* was grooming him to be Arjun's Rishi partner once Arjun had completed his Kshatriya training. It was difficult for us to believe that Vishwaraj could be involved in Dhananjay's murder. Especially once we established that Shukra was behind it all.'

'We cannot imagine that Vishwaraj would assist Shukra,' Usha joined in. 'I know the boy. Not only is he strong in the *siddhis*, but he also has an exceptional value system. I cannot comprehend what would compel him to deviate from his own values.'

'Nevertheless,' Amba spoke up, 'if he is indeed a traitor to the *Sangha*, then he must be found and stopped. It is entirely possible that Vishwaraj could have been co-opted to lead the *Vikritis*. A young Rishi, on the cusp of being inducted into the *Sangha*, would suit Shukra's plans very well. If that be the case, then it may be necessary to obtain permission from the *Sangha* Council to destroy him.'

'We don't know that for sure yet,' Usha protested. 'I agree that we should find Vishwaraj. But we cannot pass a death sentence on the boy without giving him a fair trial. He is not so powerful yet that he cannot be subdued by us and brought to trial.'

'I agree with Usha,' Virendra said. Amba and Parth looked at him, surprised. 'The *Vikritis* have been around for thousands of years now. For all these centuries, they have found a way to choose their leaders without poaching Rishis from the *Sangha*. Why should they start now? It doesn't make sense. We must consider the possibility that the

Vishwaraj who accosted Dhananjay was not the boy at all. It may have been Shukra himself, in the guise of an illusion.'

There was silence as they all pondered this possibility.

'Very well, then,' Mahesh said finally. 'Let us bring him in and the *Sangha* Council will try him. If he is innocent of our charges, then let him prove it. I think that is fair.' He looked around. 'Any disagreement?'

Nobody disagreed. Amba and Parth, too, seemed to have accepted the decision.

Now, let's talk about tonight. What happened, is definitely worrisome.' Mahesh shook his head gravely. 'Shukra's army at our doorstep ... This was something that was totally unexpected. We were woefully unprepared for it. This will not be the first time that Shukra's actions will not fit into our plans to restrain him. It is critical that we understand the lessons we can draw from what happened tonight.'

Chapter Forty-three

The Council Debates

The Guesthouse
The Gurukul

'His power has certainly increased,' Parth observed. 'All these years we've been trying to guess what he achieved through 5,000 years of meditation. What we saw tonight, I think, was just a glimpse of his powers.'

'One thing is for sure,' Usha stated, 'he has definitely asked Lord Shiva for the command of the *Bhuta gana*, and it has been given to him. That's the only explanation for his ability to command the spirits of the dead.'

Mahesh nodded. 'Earlier, he had only the power to bring the dead back to life. Tonight, we have seen him cloak the spirits of the dead in material bodies; physical forms that he has crafted and designed.' He looked at Amba. 'What did you think? You fought those creatures.'

'They are tough as nails,' Amba replied. 'Their bodies have a natural armour that protects them. Even our consecrated swords had difficulty cutting through their armour. If the black mist, their source, had not been tackled in time, funeral pyres would have lit up the Gurukul tonight. We would have been overwhelmed without a doubt.'

'They have talons that can equal any sword that we possess,' Parth added. 'We didn't have time to prepare for the battle, so none of us wore armour. We had to make do with our protective mantras. But I am not sure if even our armour would be able to withstand a sustained onslaught by those creatures. We were lucky.'

'Lucky!' Jignesh snorted. 'Luck had no part to play in what happened tonight. It was the force of the mantra that stopped the process of the creation of the creatures.'

'Not really,' Usha sounded a note of dissent. 'I agree that our numbers helped to reinforce the power of the Narsimha mantra and that would have definitely been a factor in stopping the growth of Shukra's army. But I think there was something else that contributed to our cause tonight.'

Jignesh turned to her and raised his eyebrows. 'And what was that?'

Usha shrugged. 'I really don't know,' she admitted. 'But I believe something happened tonight, that I cannot explain. Something which stopped the black fog from creating more of those creatures.' She looked at Mahesh and Jignesh. 'Didn't you feel it, too?'

Mahesh nodded.

'Well,' Jignesh conceded reluctantly, 'there was this point just before the fog disappeared. I did feel something, but I really can't describe what the sensation was or what caused it. I thought I had imagined it but if all three of us felt it, then it couldn't have been imaginary.'

'We should meditate on this,' Mahesh declared. 'There are many things in this world that we do not understand. Many of our powers were gifted to us by the Devas and the Saptarishis before they retreated, in the face of Kaliyuga. The human race never had the powers we, the chosen ones, have now. If something happened tonight that we do not understand, we must reflect and seek to understand it. If it helped us today, who knows of what use it could be in the future.'

Tiwari opened his mouth to speak, then hesitated and kept quiet. He wrestled with an inner conflict, torn between sharing his thoughts with the group and keeping them to himself. Perhaps it was too soon, he reflected.

'What I want to know,' Jignesh turned to Virendra, his eyes narrowing and growing hard, 'is how Shukra's ghoul army knew that you were here. Surely they didn't follow you all the way from Delhi!'

Virendra shrugged. 'Beats me. I've been mystified by that myself. We told no one that we were coming here.'

'The girl,' Jignesh pressed. 'What about her?'

'She's Dhruv's daughter, for god's sake!' Virendra bristled. 'She was witness to her father's murder at the hands of Shukra. She didn't even know that the spirits existed. Are you trying to insinuate that she told Shukra about our location while he was trying to kill her father?'

'Easy, Kanakpratap, easy,' Amba tried to calm Virendra. 'No one is accusing anyone. Jignesh does have a valid point. You, too, wondered about Shukra trailing you all the way here. He's just puzzled about it, that's all.'

Virendra gave Jignesh a sullen look.

'She didn't know where we were going, anyway,' Tiwari chimed in. 'I drove her here and I didn't disclose the location to her until we reached the gates of the park.' Tiwari hesitated once, before deciding to contine. 'There could be another explanation for their knowledge of our location,' he said.

'What?' Jignesh's eyes bored into him.

'There was someone else here tonight.'

Chapter Forty-four

More Questions for the Council

The Guesthouse
The Gurukul

'Someone who is not a part of the Gurukul,' Tiwari continued. 'A young man, who was skulking in the shadows beyond the edge of the clearing.'

'Who was he?' Mahesh wondered aloud. 'Did you get a look at his face?'

Tiwari shook his head. 'I didn't see him. Maya did. She said she couldn't see his face, but even if she had, it is highly unlikely she would know him. But it does seem to be a remarkable coincidence that someone was lurking in the shadows exactly when the *pretas* appeared and Shukra's army descended on us.'

Jignesh threw up his hands. 'She didn't see his face! Ludicrous. Are we now supposed to take the word of a stripling who has no clue of what we are all about? I mean who in the fourteen *lokas* would be hanging around here, following you from Delhi and whom we can connect in some way to Shukra?'

There was silence as the same thought crossed everyone's minds.

Amba voiced it for them all. 'It could have been Vishwaraj. That would explain everything.'

'Fine,' Jignesh barked. 'We'll bring him in and find out once and for all what his involvement is in all of this.'

Parth nodded. 'We'll spread the word right away. If he really is involved with Shukra, then we'll have to hunt for him. I'm sure he wouldn't stay with the *Gana*, unless he thinks no one from the *Sangha* suspects him. But if he was here tonight, it won't take long to find him.'

'What's the girl doing here anyway?' Jignesh didn't seem very pleased about Maya's presence. 'Does she have the power?'

Virendra shook his head, his face hard. He knew what was coming next. He had broken the rules by bringing Maya here. 'No. She is a *sadh*.'

'Then why ... ?' Jignesh was interrupted by Tiwari before he could complete his question.

'Um, I have an observation,' Tiwari said hesitantly, looking around at the group. 'We all believe that she is a *sadh*. But she knows the Narsimha mantra.'

'Lots of *sadhs* know the Narsimha mantra!' Jignesh snorted. 'What is so special about that?'

'I mean ... she knows it instinctively,' Tiwari replied. 'While we were driving here, I asked her if she knew any mantras. She said that Dhruv had not taught her any.'

'Rubbish!' Jignesh declared. 'She couldn't have been born knowing the mantra!'

Tiwari shook his head. 'I believe she didn't know the mantra before coming here. But she heard me chanting it and joined in immediately. And her enunciation of the mantra was perfect. As good as any of our Rishis, including some of our younger *Mahamatis*. I don't believe anyone can pick up a mantra that perfectly, just by listening to it being chanted a couple of times.' He looked straight at Jignesh. 'You know how much training these children go through before they perfect their enunciation.'

'You mean that she may have some powers?' Mahesh looked thoughtful. 'But how would they have gone undetected for so many years? She should have been recruited by now if there was any indication that she wasn't a *sadh*.'

'I don't have an answer,' Tiwari held up his hands. 'All I can tell you is what I observed. If she does have some powers, any powers, we should not turn her away. The least we should do is explore and find out.'

'I agree,' Usha spoke up. 'Maybe Ratan is wrong and she is just a *sadh* after all. But we should run a check and find out for sure.'

'Very well,' Mahesh said, his tone indicating that this was the last word on the subject. 'She stays here. For now. We will enroll her for six months. But if we find that there is nothing that justifies her staying on for more training,' he looked from Virendra to Pramila and then to Tiwari, 'she goes back.'

'Why didn't Shukra come himself?' Pramila suddenly spoke up, her soft voice drawing everyone's attention immediately. 'Why did he send an army of creatures instead?'

Virendra looked at her. He knew what Pramila was thinking. Her face was hard now, accepting the reality and questioning what had happened tonight.

'We all know,' Pramila continued, 'that Shukra wants my son dead. He tried to kill him fourteen years ago and almost succeeded. I lost my husband but, thanks to Dhruv, my son and I escaped. What I want to know is this: why has he deviated from that single-minded focus?'

'We cannot understand how Shukra's mind works,' Mahesh began, but he wasn't allowed to complete.

'I'm not asking for that.' Pramila's voice could have sliced through steel as she cut short Mahesh's response. 'This is not just about Arjun. This is much bigger. Can't you see?'

The room fell silent.

Pramila sighed. 'Look, we all know that Shukra's meditation was interrupted when Arjun was born. It was motivation enough for him to forego the fruits of his 5,000-year tapasya and come hunting my son with the single-minded intention of killing him. We also know that Shukra is a mystic yogi. He has the power of the *siddhis*. He can travel at will. Nothing could have — would have — stopped him from arriving at the Gurukul tonight, once he knew that Arjun was here. So, why didn't he?'

Once again, there was silence. No one seemed to have an answer to her questions.

'Isn't it possible that Shukra has some other game plan in mind?' Pramila went on, seeing that the others hadn't considered the possibility that had occurred to her. 'Remember, Shukra is the son of Bhrigu. He has always been well known for his intelligence and his far sightedness. Even Lord Krishna endorsed these attributes of Shukra. Is it not possible that he is planning something bigger?'

'You mean the Gurukul?' Usha looked thoughtful. 'You could be right. For thousands of years, our Gurukuls have been hidden away, both by the Saptarishis and the changes that time has wrought on the topography of *Bhu-lok* over the centuries. Now he knows where this Gurukul is.'

Pramila nodded, satisfied that her train of thought was finally being followed by at least one member of the Council. 'That's one possibility. Here's another one. Could tonight have simply been a test of both, the functionality of his army and our abilities to fight them?'

Parth's eyes widened with realization. 'The creatures we fought were clumsy and slow footed. Definitely not battle trained. Shukra could have simply been testing his creations in a real battle scenario!'

'If that supposition is correct, then we are in trouble.' Amba looked grim. 'Shukra would have learnt from tonight's encounter that his creatures may not be the best warriors, but they can overrun our forces if there are enough of them. Our fighters are human and they tire. In the face of superior numbers, I don't think we can stand against them for too long.'

'Well, then,' Mahesh said, with a tone of finality, 'we need to start preparing. I will get the word out to the *Sangha* Council. The other Gurukuls need to know. There's no telling when and where Shukra will strike next.' He looked at Amba and Usha. 'We need to modify our plan to stop Shukra that we set in motion fourteen years ago. We must develop a solution to destroy these creatures. Weapon upgrades, more powerful mantras.... Whatever it takes. We can't leave anything to chance. The future depends on our success.'

Amba and Usha nodded. The war had begun.

'Let's get the children in,' Jignesh said, signalling the end of the discussion.

'I'll get them.' Tiwari volunteered.

Virendra leaned over and whispered something in Tiwari's ear.

Tiwari nodded, then rose and left the room. As he walked away, lost in thought, he felt immensely guilty about holding back information from the Council, but he had had no choice. If he had disclosed what he had observed, Maya could get in deep trouble. And he didn't believe that it was any fault of hers. She probably didn't even know. He had decided to keep mum until he had got to the bottom of the mystery. He couldn't put her life in jeopardy based on a suspicion. He didn't know if he was doing the right thing. But he couldn't throw her to the lions without being sure. He could only hope that his decision to withhold information from the council would not cost them dearly.

It was baffling. He knew why Maya had fallen to the ground clutching her head. It had happened just seconds before the black fog had appeared. He, too, had felt the fog approach. But he was a Maharishi, with years of yogic discipline and powers that had been passed down from his earlier births.

Maya was just a child. Yet, the approach of the black fog, even before it was visually discernible, had affected her. Was it possible that there was some connection between *her* and the black fog?

The very thought chilled him to the bone.

Chapter Forty-five

Exchanging Notes

The Guesthouse
The Gurukul

Maya opened the door to find Arjun standing there, a broad grin on his face. She squealed in delight and rushed forward to hug him.

To her surprise, he backed away hurriedly, holding his hands out before him to ward her off.

She stopped and frowned. 'What's the matter?'

'This.' Arjun stepped into the room, where the light was brighter and Maya got a good look at what he was showing her. Green, slimy ooze stuck to his clothes, which were ripped in places, no doubt at the hands of the monsters he had faced off in the clearing.

'Yuck! Is that what I think it is?' Maya wrinkled her nose in disgust.

'From the creatures,' Arjun grinned, then added with a mischievous twinkle in his eyes, 'Here, you wanna take a closer look?' He dipped his fingertip into the ooze on his t-shirt and held it out to Maya, who shrank back involuntarily. The slime smelled foul and reminded her of the stench at Arjun's house moments before she had encountered the *pretas*.

'Stop it, AJ! Ugh! You're disgusting. Boys!' She flounced onto the bed and sat there, her arms folded.

Arjun chuckled and wiped the green slime on his clothes. They were dirty anyway. 'Sorry, couldn't restrain myself. I think I smell like crap.'

'You do. But, goodness, I'm so happy to see you, AJ! I was worried sick about you.'

Arjun shut the door and sat down in the lone chair in the room. 'Hey, I was worried sick about myself. But it all worked out in the end, didn't it?'

'It did.' Maya's face became serious. 'But I'm still worried. I can't figure out why Shukra was missing from the scene.'

'Who cares? We won, didn't we?'

'You think he's given up on hunting you down?' Maya couldn't stop a touch of asperity from creeping into her voice. She was irritated at Arjun's carelessness when his life was still in danger.

Arjun sat up straight in his chair and looked at her. 'I'm not worried about Shukra anymore. I'm with people who can protect me. I'm safe here.'

Maya shook her head. 'I'm not convinced, AJ. They're hiding something from us. You're supposed to be the leader of the Kshatriyas. A direct descendant of Yayati. What's that supposed to mean? Are you expected to lead the entire lot against Shukra? Are you supposed to be the guy who stops him?'

'Of course not. I don't think any individual can stand up to Shukra. We all have to do it together.'

'That's just the problem, AJ. I don't think anyone has the means to defeat Shukra.' Tears welled up in her eyes. 'Believe me, I've seen what he can do. You're the closest thing to family for me. I don't want anything to happen to you.'

'Hey …' Arjun was concerned for Maya. 'It's okay. Nothing is going to happen to me. I'm sure the folks running the Gurukul have a plan.'

'Sorry.' Maya wiped her tears. 'I guess the last two days have just been too much for me.'

'I understand. But you know what makes me confident?'

'What?'

'Did you see what happened just before the mist disappeared?'

Maya shook her head. 'My eyes were closed. I was focused on chanting the mantra.'

'Seriously? You were chanting the mantra? That's so cool! Where did you learn it from?'

'I didn't learn it. It was in this diary.' Maya indicated her father's diary. 'I read it last night while I was flipping through it. Then, when I heard it being chanted, it just came back to me. So I thought that I would join the others since there was nothing else I could do. And I hadn't been very useful until then anyway.'

'What happened to you out there?' said Arjun, with a tinge of guilt. He had totally forgotten about Maya rolling on the ground in pain, holding her head. 'I got busy fighting the creatures, and just couldn't help you.'

Maya shrugged. 'Ratan told me that I passed out. I don't know why. But I'm fine now.' She smiled. 'See? But what is it that you were going to say? What happened just before the mist disappeared?'

As Arjun opened his mouth to reply, there was a knock on the door. 'Come in!' Maya cried. The door opened and Tiwari entered.

'I thought I'd find you two together,' he smiled. 'Come on. The Council wants to see you both. It won't do to keep them waiting.'

Chapter Forty-six

Welcome to the Gurukul

The Guesthouse
The Gurukul

Arjun and Maya were seated before the five members of the *Mahamati* Council. Virendra, Pramila and Tiwari were seated to the side.

After the greetings and introductions, there was a moment of silence as the two groups surveyed each other; Arjun and Maya with apprehension and the five Council members with interest and curiosity.

It was clear that the Council was thinking of the prophecy. It had said that a child would be born in the line of Yayati, who would be the chosen one to lead the fight. Arjun's date of birth had matched with the prophecy. Their hopes and plans, so painfully drawn up and executed over the last fourteen years, all rested on the frail shoulders of this fifteen-year-old boy.

Finally, Mahesh spoke up. 'Welcome to the Gurukul, Arjun and Maya. You have both gone through a lot in the last few hours. But you don't need to worry any more. You are both safe here.'

Arjun and Maya nodded, tongue-tied.

Jignesh nodded to Arjun. 'You acquitted yourself well on the battlefield today.'

'Indeed,' Parth joined in. 'I have never seen anyone who has not been through the training at any Gurukul, fight the way you fought.'

'Thank you,' Arjun murmured, a little uncomfortable with all the attention.

'Would you like to brief them, Usha?' Mahesh looked at the Maharishi who sat on his right.

Usha nodded and smiled at Arjun and Maya. 'Both of you start training tomorrow. Your circumstances are unusual, and so will your training be. Until we decide what level you are at, we will not assign you to any group. Instead, you will both have your own individual instructors.' She fixed her gaze on Arjun and addressed him. 'Kanak will continue training you. And Amba will be your sparring partner for the training sessions, under the supervision of Kanak.'

'Not just Amba,' Virendra interjected. 'I will request that Parth also be a sparring partner for Arjun.'

Parth gave Virendra a quizzical look. 'Isn't one of us enough?'

'Not when his training sessions will revolve around fighting multiple opponents. He will need the practice.'

Amba raised an eyebrow. 'Your confidence in the boy is amazing, Kanak. This will be interesting.' She looked at Parth. 'What do you say?'

'Fine by me.' Parth shrugged, but still looked doubtful. 'There isn't a Kshatriya in the *Gana* who can pull that off.'

'Not yet,' Virendra agreed. 'But there's always a first one. Remember, this is the scion of Yayati. He has the blood of great kings, illustrious Kshatriyas, running through his veins.'

'Very well,' Mahesh sealed the agreement. 'It will be done.'

Usha turned her attention to Maya. 'And you will be trained by Jignesh, who has volunteered for the task. As Dhruv's daughter, we think you may have latent powers, which need to be developed. Mind you, this will be more than just training to become a Rishi. It will simultaneously be an evaluation of your powers, if you have any.'

Maya's heart leapt with delight as she heard this. So far, she had been unsure of her future in the Gurukul. But now, she was to be given the opportunity to become a Rishi! Like the other white-robed children who she had seen in the clearing! The words Usha spoke next did little to dampen her excitement.

'But there is something you must be aware of right away,' Usha continued. 'If Jignesh's evaluation concludes that you do not have yogic powers or that they are not adequately developed, you will have to leave the Gurukul. Is that clear?'

Maya nodded, her eyes shining. Arjun glanced at her, bewildered, wondering if she had really heard what Usha had said.

'Mahesh will train both of you in the fundamentals of meditation,' Usha carried on. 'You will both need this ability to master the powers that may lie dormant within you. That's all for now.'

There was a moment of silence.

'Is that the diary you mentioned?' Virendra gestured to the leather notebook that Maya was carrying. He had instructed Tiwari to ask Maya to bring it with her to the Council meeting.

Maya nodded. 'Dad asked me to pick this up from the study and run.' She held up the notebook and looked at it wistfully.

'Can I see it, please?' Mahesh held out his hand and Maya handed over the book to him.

He began leafing through the pages of the diary, a look of great interest on his face. Gradually, the look changed to one of astonishment. He began flipping the pages faster, then looked up at Maya. 'Did your father ever mention this diary to you before?'

Maya shook her head. 'Never.'

Mahesh looked at Virendra. 'Did Dhruv talk to you about this diary? Did he say something? Anything?' His voice seemed to have taken on a tone of desperation.

'Why? What's in the diary?' Virendra countered. 'The first I heard about it was when Maya mentioned it.' He was annoyed that he had not thought of looking at the diary when he had had the chance. He had been so completely occupied with his own thoughts and the things he needed to get done that the diary had slipped his mind.

Mahesh closed the notebook with a snap. 'Dhruv was onto something. We know he had spent many years, after Shukra's reappearance in Allahabad, searching for the weapons that would thwart Shukra's plans. It seems, from the entries in this notebook, that he had found something significant. Whether it concerned the weapons or not, I cannot say. But it had to be significant.'

Jignesh held out his hand for the book and leafed through it.

'I don't get it,' Parth said. 'If you know it is significant, why can't you say if it concerns the weapons or not?'

'Because much of the diary is in *Brahmabhasha*,' Jignesh said, slowly. 'Dhruv mentions this quite clearly. He certainly found something that was important enough to copy and record. I don't know where he could have come across any text in *Brahmabhasha*, but here it is. And I don't know how he planned to translate these verses he had copied, but knowing Dhruv, he must have had a plan.'

'Surely, someone can translate it.' Virendra reached for the book.

'No human can,' Mahesh said sorrowfully. 'This is the language of the *Devas*, the mother of Sanskrit. A language as ancient as Satya Yuga, not meant for humans to learn. We have no way of knowing what these words mean.'

'Damn!' exclaimed Virendra, having leafed through the book. 'Why didn't Dhruv tell me about this? And what's the rest of the book about? The parts that you can read?' His annoyance had changed to resentment that Dhruv had not bothered to share something as important as this with him.

'Mantras,' Jignesh replied. 'All kinds of mantras. Looks like Dhruv was collecting them all in one place. It's like a fairly comprehensive manual for mantras.'

'What about the Gandharvas? Can they not help with deciphering the bits in Brahmabhasha?' Maya spoke up and immediately regretted it. The forbidding look directed at her by Jignesh plainly said that this was a matter to be discussed only by the Council and she should keep out of it. She shivered inwardly and decided to keep her thoughts to herself.

'The Gandharvas won't help,' Mahesh replied, kindly. 'Only the *Devas* could have. And we cannot contact them any longer. Whatever Dhruv found, whatever he was trying to do, it's lost without him. We can do nothing with this diary. It is useless to us.'

'Can I please have it back then?' Maya requested. She didn't like what Mahesh had said. Her father had clearly laboured over this. To copy out verses in an unknown language, while ensuring that there were no inaccuracies, was hard work. She didn't like it being dismissed as useless. If they didn't value it, she wanted it back.

Virendra held out the book. 'Here you go,' he told Maya. 'Keep it carefully. It may not be of much use now, but you never know ...'

After the two children had left, Jignesh looked at the other members of the *Mahamati* Council. 'We don't have much time,' his face bore a troubled expression. 'Even as we speak, Shukra must be amassing his forces and getting ready for a fresh onslaught. Kanak, you say that the boy does not need too much training. That he is almost ready. I hope you are right.'

'I know that I am,' Virendra said grimly. 'You will see for yourself. I have not spent the last fourteen years in vain. I have done everything in my power to prepare the boy. He will be ready to face Shukra! That is my promise to you. But where are his weapons — the ones mentioned in the prophecy? We have spent fourteen years looking for them and what do we have to show for it?'

'Finding weapons that disappeared over 5,000 years ago is no child's play,' Amba gently chastised Virendra. 'And it is even more difficult when we don't know what it is we are looking for. We have only been able to go through a few lakh ancient texts in these fourteen years. There are millions left. There just aren't enough of us to search any faster. It is like looking for a needle in a haystack, only in this case, we don't even know if it's a needle we are looking for. Dhruv seems to be the only one who had made any progress, going by his notebook. And now, even that is of no help.'

'Kanak speaks the truth,' Mahesh said grimly, countering Amba. 'The fragment of the prophecy that we possess does not tell us what will happen when the boy confronts Shukra. We have to equip him to be fully prepared when the time comes. No matter how skillful he is as a warrior, without the right weapons he will be ineffectual against Shukra's powers. The boy needs weapons that are powerful enough to destroy Shukra. If we cannot find them, then the world is in terrible jeopardy. And we can do little to stop what is certainly coming.'

Chapter Forty-seven

Maya Reflects

Maya's bedroom
The Guesthouse

Maya lay awake in bed, staring at the ceiling in the darkness.

After leaving the Council meeting, she and Arjun had eaten dinner in silence and then parted company. Both of them were weighed down and preoccupied after the discussion with the Mahamatis.

Maya could guess what was on Arjun's mind. It was all very well to talk about him being the heir to one of the most respected Kshatriya lineages in Indian history. But to live it was quite another thing. She realized that the responsibility and burden of it was just beginning to sink in for Arjun. It was a scary thought. He was just a fifteen-year-old boy. Her heart went out to him.

She, too, had her own demons to confront. While she had been ecstatic about her prospects of becoming a Rishi, during the meeting with the Council, she really hadn't realized the import of Usha's words. She had been so swept away by the prospect of being welcomed into the Gurukul that nothing else had mattered. Now, as she reflected with a cooler mind, the realization dawned.

Nothing in her fifteen years upon this Earth had ever indicated that she had the ability to become a Rishi. What if she didn't have the yogic powers that were needed to make the cut? It was clear that there was no place for her in the Gurukul if she didn't prove herself. Where would she go if she failed? What would she do? None of this had occurred to her at that time. It hit her now. Her future was as uncertain as ever.

It also occurred to her that perhaps the Council had taken her on out of pity. An orphan, who had recently lost her father. The daughter of an important member of the *Sangha*. They were giving her a chance, not because they saw anything special in her, but because of who her father had been.

And she resented that.

She didn't want pity. She didn't need sympathy. What she really wanted was to prove herself. But the uncertainty, the fear of failure nagged at her.

Added to that was the callous treatment, in her eyes, of her father's diary. It had been dismissed as being useless. Maya bristled at the memory.

But that discussion hadn't been entirely fruitless, she had to admit. She had learned something new. The existence of a language not accessible to humans. The possibility that there was knowledge that even the *Sangha*, with their human limitations, did not know about.

Before retiring for the night, she had spent two hours reading the diary. She had gone through it seriously for the first time, spending time on its pages, attempting to understand what it was trying to tell her. The last time she had looked at it, in Tiwari's house, she had merely flipped through it in curiosity. Tonight, she had studied it. She wanted to know more about its contents, at least the bits she could understand. She had lingered for a while on the pages with the diagrams and sketches, trying to make sense of them, to no avail.

She had examined every Sanskrit shloka. Every mantra.

Her father had specifically asked her to take the diary with her. Why had he been so insistent? There had to be a reason. She tried recalling his exact words. His last words. What had he asked her to do with the diary?

Try as she might, she couldn't remember her father telling her to give the diary to Virendra or anyone else. He had simply asked her to take it and run. Of course, he *had* instructed her to call Virendra. 'Call

Virendra. Tell him.' That's what her father had said. At that time, she had assumed that what he meant was that she was to tell him about the diary.

And she had. It was the first thing that she had mentioned to Virendra when she finally got to speak to him.

Now, it struck her that perhaps she had been mistaken. Virendra had shown no recognition of the diary when it was mentioned. He hadn't even acknowledged it on the call. Even tonight, he had admitted that he knew nothing of what was in the diary. It was obvious, now, that her father had never mentioned it to him. He definitely had not intended her to give the diary to him.

Then what had he wanted?

Had her father expected her to be able to figure out, by herself, what the notebook contained and why it was significant? That thought seemed preposterous to her. Until tonight, she had no idea that a language called *Brahmabhasha* even existed. And even now that she had found out about it, there was no way to translate the sections of the diary that were inscribed in that language.

Was it possible that her father had not told anyone about the existence of this diary? That seemed illogical. Why would he want his hard work to be consigned to the dustbin of ignorance? If he had worked so hard to put together these inscriptions, there had to be a reason. And there had to be someone he had shared this with, who could decipher it all.

But who could that be? And how could Maya find out?

Or was there another way of figuring out how to translate the contents of the diary?

The maelstrom of thoughts in her mind kept sleep at bay. She sat in the darkness, unseeing, thinking, sorting out the strands in her mind. And she came to a conclusion. The only thing she didn't know yet was how she would put it into motion. But she knew she would find a way. She would just have to keep trying.

Now, as she tried to sleep, another thought troubled her. A thought that wouldn't go away, however hard she tried. She didn't know why it nagged her so much, but it clung to her mind, not letting go.

Why had Shukra not appeared tonight? This would have been his big chance to achieve his objective. She had seen a demonstration of his power against her own father who, she now knew, was a powerful Maharishi. It would have been child's play for Shukra to eliminate Arjun tonight, especially with the backing of his army of monsters.

So why had he stayed away when his prey had been vulnerable and within reach?

Was it possible that everyone was mistaken about his keen desire to kill Arjun?

Was there something that everyone was missing?

Chapter Forty-eight

Gurukul Day 1

Day Five
The Gurukul

'You have to understand,' Jignesh said, 'that this is a rather unusual teaching assignment for me.'

Maya looked at him and nodded in acknowledgement. She knew what he meant. Arjun and she were the only students in the Gurukul who were not sitting in one of the classrooms, where all the other students got their instruction. At least for the foreseeable future, this anomaly would stand.

In the morning, she had been woken up at 5.30 a.m. by one of the girls, a novice, who accompanied her to the Assembly Hall, where Mahesh was waiting to instruct Arjun and Maya in the science of meditation. The Assembly Hall had turned out to be the large, mysterious wooden building that had been shrouded in darkness, last night. The building consisted of a large subterranean hall, in which all members of the Gurukul would gather each morning to pray, meditate and chant mantras for a positive mindset through the day. There was also a smaller hall on the ground floor of the building.

After the morning assembly, the students had dispersed to their respective classrooms, while Arjun and Maya had climbed the stairs to the hall on the ground floor, where Mahesh began their meditation classes.

Both of them had been provided with special clothes — Maya, the white robes of the Rishis and Arjun, the silk uniform of the Kshatriyas.

'Someone got all my stuff from the car last night,' Arjun had whispered to Maya at the first opportunity they got to talk. 'I wonder what they did with the Land Cruiser, though. I'm sure they wouldn't have left it there to be found by the park rangers in the morning!'

After their session with Mahesh, Arjun had left to join Virendra, for his first training session at the Gurukul, while Maya was led to one of the classrooms where Jignesh awaited her.

'Let us walk around the Gurukul,' Jignesh suggested after emerging from the classroom where he had just completed a class on mantras. 'Have you had a chance to look around yet?'

Maya was wary. Though Jignesh seemed quite warm and friendly, in contrast to the stone and steel exterior that he had exhibited last night, she wasn't sure of him. Something in Jignesh's tone last night had indicated to her that he didn't approve of the idea of Maya enrolling at the Gurukul. Why he should have displayed such animosity was beyond her understanding, but she was quite sure that her feeling about him was correct. She decided to be careful and not get on his wrong side. He seemed to be the kind of person who would harbour a grudge.

'Just a bit,' she replied. It was only in the daytime that the true size of the campus had become apparent to her. Last night, all that Maya could see were the cottages lining the central avenue that terminated at the Assembly Hall. Today, she had learned that these brick and thatch cottages, quaintly rounded in shape, housed the dormitories for the students.

Behind and beyond the dormitories were the residential cottages for the teachers, the communal dining room where all the students had their meals, the sick bay and the guesthouse, where the group from Delhi was housed.

All the buildings had been cleverly woven into the tapestry of the forest that sprawled on this side of the hill. Except for the central avenue, which was bereft of trees, the entire Gurukul was a mass of foliage. Another reminder that they were in the middle of a forest — an impression that was easily dispelled by the artificial lights and the density of humans that she had witnessed last night — was the presence of sambar, chital and nilgai, wandering around with no fear of the humans who lived here. It was an amazing sight.

Maya had caught just a glimpse of the campus that lay beyond the Assembly Hall, as she walked down to meet Jignesh. The previous night, it had seemed that the campus ended at the Assembly Hall. In the morning light, she was amazed to see how it stretched out, beyond and away from the Hall, though her view was restricted by the cottages housing the classrooms that were lined up along a second central avenue; a mirror image to the layout on the other side of the Assembly Hall.

'Well, then, we'll just saunter around and talk,' Jignesh replied.

So, here they were, walking down the central avenue with the classrooms on either side. Through the closed glass windows, Maya could see the students sitting inside attentively listening to their instructors.

'The cottages are air-conditioned,' Maya noted with surprise. It hadn't occurred to her last night when she had slept in an air-conditioned room. This was the last thing she had expected to find here, especially in the middle of a forest.

'We live in the 21st century,' Jignesh smiled, 'not the Vedic Age. As you will see shortly, one section of the campus is dedicated to an array of solar panels, which powers most of the electricity requirements of the Gurukul. And, in case you haven't noticed, every cottage has its own solar power generator.'

They came to the end of the central avenue. Maya gasped at the view that greeted her eyes. It was breathtaking. This was where the heart of the Gurukul lay.

On one side, the river Ken flowed past the campus, hidden from her eyes by a border of trees thickly closeted together, forming a natural barrier that stretched from the hill behind the Assembly Hall to the point where the river curved away from the Gurukul. The border of trees hid the cottages from anyone cruising down the river, though she could see the river through gaps in the trees, the sunlight twinkling off the swiftly flowing water.

Maya realized that this was the entrance that Virendra had been aiming for, before the appearance of the spirits forced him to change his plans.

In the shadow of the forest that lined the river was a vast, open field that served as the training grounds for the physical exercises of the Kshatriyas. At the moment, there were only two figures in the grounds — Maya guessed it was Arjun and Virendra, engaged in their training session.

On the opposite side, was another vast stretch of open space, bereft of trees.

'That's where the Rishis practice the application of their powers,' Jignesh told her. Maya wondered what kind of application was practiced in the open, but didn't ask.

Beyond the practice field of the Rishis, lay another vast, dark, forest that seemed to stretch until the horizon, its trees tightly packed together, making the forest look like it was shrouded in a blanket of darkness even in the daytime.

'And that's the Dandaka forest,' Jignesh pointed out. 'Or what's left of it.'

Maya recognized the name. This was the forest mentioned in the Mahabharata, and referred to in more detail in the Ramayana. It was in this forest that Lord Rama, with Sita and Lakshmana, had spent most of his years of exile. It was from this forest that Sita had been abducted by Ravana. And it was in this forest that Lord Rama had killed Rakshasas. She remembered reading that it was a vast forest that had spread across most of central and south India. From Jignesh's words, she concluded that the forest had shrunk over the centuries and diminished until this was all that was left of it.

'The forest is out of bounds for students from the Gurukul,' Jignesh informed her sternly, emphasizing the restriction. 'No one can go in there. But if any student even attempts to enter the forest, we will get to know immediately. And there will be consequences.'

Maya wondered why he was being so emphatic in his warning. Had students transgressed before this? Or did Jignesh suspect that Maya would try and enter the forest? On her part, she had no desire to go into the forest, which looked decidedly uninviting.

It was then that she remembered one more thing about the Dandaka forest. She had read about it in one of the ancient texts. The thought chilled her.

It had been created by Shukracharya.

Chapter Forty-nine

About the Sangha

The Gurukul

'Now that you are here in the Gurukul,' Jignesh said, 'let me start by telling you about the *Sangha* and the *Gana*.'

They had walked down from the central avenue between the classrooms, past the Kshatriya training field, where Virendra was putting Arjun through his paces, and were now strolling in the shade of the trees lining the river.

Maya recalled that Tiwari had mentioned the *Gana* during their drive to Panna. He had also mentioned that her father was a member of the *Sangha*, but had not elaborated. The story of what had happened in Allahabad had taken over her thoughts and she had not wanted to discuss anything else after that. She now listened attentively as Jignesh spoke.

'You know, of course, about Shukra and the Saptarishis,' Jignesh began.

'I know about Shukracharya,' Maya replied. 'Ratan told me. And I have read about the Saptarishis in the Mahabharata and other ancient texts.'

'Very well. Let me tell you about what happened at the start of Kaliyuga, 5,000 years ago. You know that there are seven levels of the lower planets, or the netherworlds. You would have read about them in the scriptures.'

Maya nodded. Atala, Vitala, Sutala, Talatala, Mahatala, Rasatala and Patala. These were the seven levels of the netherworlds, each one inhabited by a different set of beings.

'Good. If you know this, then you also know that, of the seven levels, Vitala is where Lord Shiva resides as *Hathakesvara*, and Sutala is occupied by the son of Virocana — Bali — whom the *Vamana* avatar of Lord Vishnu had pushed into the netherworld. Bali had always been a pious man and a devotee of Lord Vishnu. The only reason he was relegated to Sutala was because Indra feared that his own kingship of the Devas was threatened. The other five levels are occupied by the Daityas, Danavas and the Nagas. When Kaliyuga began, the Devas and the Saptarishis withdrew from this world. It was then that Shukracharya decided to take advantage of the change of ages and open the gates of the five levels of the netherworlds where the Asuras and Nagas live. His plan was to release them upon our world, *Bhu-lok*, which they would rule along with the netherworlds.' Jignesh looked at Maya to see if she was following the story so far.

Satisfied that her entire attention was focused on him, he continued. 'It was then that the Saptarishis warned Shukra against going through with his plans. Faced with their collective powers, Shukra had to admit defeat. He disappeared for 5,000 years. Fourteen years ago, he reappeared in Allahabad. You know what happened next.'

Maya nodded, Tiwari's narration of the unpleasant events in Allahabad resurfacing in her mind. She pushed them away with an effort.

'Is that when the *Sangha* was created?' she asked. 'When Shukra disappeared 5,000 years ago? To ensure that Shukra never followed up on his plans?'

'Indeed, that was when the *Sangha* was created,' Jignesh agreed, 'but not just to keep Shukra in check. The Saptarishis wanted to ensure that the world would remain safe, even during Kaliyuga, when the worst manifestations of evil would materialize. When Kaliyuga began, they chose a group of men and women to be their representatives and handed over the responsibility of protecting humanity from evil to them. Some of these chosen ones had yogic powers and others were Kshatriyas. The Maharishis and the Kshatriyas have worked together ever since, as members of the *Sangha*, to form a protective shield around humanity. Those spirits you encountered last night,' Jignesh gestured in the direction of the hill beyond which the clearing lay, 'they didn't just appear out of nowhere. They are around us all the time, mostly invisible, sometimes wreaking havoc, sometimes benevolent. But they are there, nevertheless. Who do you think keeps humanity from seeing them?'

'The *Sangha*,' breathed Maya. The presence of an invisible, secret Order, thousands of years old, protecting humanity without anyone knowing of its existence was an amazing revelation.

'The Maharishis and Kshatriyas of the *Sangha* have three responsibilities,' Jignesh continued. 'The first one is to protect humanity from evil spirits and demons. Many members of the *Sangha* work as teachers in schools and universities across the country, discharging this responsibility with the help of the youngsters who pass out of Gurukuls like this one, graduating to become members of the *Gana*. Together, the *Sangha* and the *Gana* extend a protective shield over humanity, keeping evil away. Your father, your late history teacher, Dhananjay, and Ratan are all examples of *Sangha* members engaged in this task.'

'You mean some of our teachers in school were — I mean are — actually members of the *Sangha*?' Maya was astonished. She would never have believed it.

'Correct. The second responsibility of the *Sangha* is to train the sons and daughters of *Sangha* members, who are born with the necessary abilities and powers to grow into either Rishis or Kshatriyas; future members of the *Gana*. Many of us work in the Gurukuls scattered around India, training these youngsters. And, the third responsibility is to actively seek out children, born in *sadh* families, who have the potential to be trained to be either future Rishis or Kshatriyas. The children who are thus chosen are sent to one of the Gurukuls, where they undergo training, after receiving permission from their parents and an undertaking that the existence of the *Sangha* and *Gana* will not be revealed by them, ever.'

'Who are the *sadh* families?' Maya wanted to know.

'Normal humans,' Jignesh replied, 'who do not possess the powers that either the Rishis or the Kshatriyas command. I will tell you more about *sadhs* later.'

'But why keep the existence of the *Sangha* a secret?' Maya was curious.

'It is important to remain unknown,' Jignesh explained. 'With our powers and our numbers, we would not be welcome in the *sadh* world. Not in Kaliyuga, where everyone is suspicious of things they do not understand. Some *sadhs* would consider us gods with our superior powers and abilities and worship us instead of meditating on the true Supreme Consciousness. And there would be others who would fear us, doubt us, and worry that we are a threat to humanity. It is better to serve humanity and fulfil our destinies by remaining unobserved and unknown. The Saptarishis set this down as a guiding principle of the *Sangha* when they created it, 5,000 years ago. The *Sangha* has rules and we all abide by them.'

Maya silently contemplated the immensity of the scale of the *Sangha*. Just how many youngsters were out there in schools all over the country, keeping humanity safe? Her mind boggled.

She felt honoured to have the opportunity to become a part of this Order. A fierce determination rose within her. They had said that they weren't sure she was going to make it.

Well, she *was*. Whatever it took.

Chapter Fifty

First lesson

The Gurukul

As Maya and Jignesh stood talking, the sound of a motorboat came to their ears. The sun had risen higher in the sky now and tourists would have entered the park, hiring jeeps for safaris along the trails within the forest, or taking motorboat rides down the river. Maya could imagine just how amazing that experience would be, motoring down the river, watching its placid surface being broken by the occasional fish, looking for crocodiles.

Meera, the girl who had woken her up this morning, had helpfully told her to avoid swimming in the river because it had crocodiles. What a brilliant place to get away from the bustle of city life!

'Tourists.' Jignesh turned up his nose.

They passed a student who was sitting cross-legged, her eyes closed, chanting the same mantra that Maya had heard when she first entered the Gurukul last night. Tiwari had told her it was chanted non-stop.

'Do tourists ever venture into the Gurukul?' Maya wanted to know.

'Of course not.' Jignesh sounded most indignant. 'A powerful mantra has been used to create an illusion of impenetrability along the riverside. This has ensured that no one will even contemplate pushing through the forest that goes down all the way to the river's edge.' He indicated the bank of trees along which they were walking. 'The Gurukul is well and truly isolated from the rest of humanity, in keeping with our principle of invisibility. And, as you have seen, all along the boundary of the Gurukul, there are students posted, in rotational shifts, whose sole responsibility is to create a second protective shield that ensures that intruders of the non-human kind are also kept out. The mantra that they chant is for this purpose.'

Maya now realized why Virendra had brought Arjun here. It was the safest place on Earth.

Was it possible that Shukra had not appeared last night because he knew this? Or was there another reason?

Maya brushed her thoughts aside. Jignesh was speaking again.

'Time for your first lesson,' he was saying. 'What is your understanding of yogic powers — the *siddhis*?'

Maya was flummoxed by this unexpected question. At first, she wanted to blurt out that she had no clue. How was she to know anything about yogic powers? Then, she remembered that she had read a lot about the Rishis of old who had meditated, often for hundreds of years, to acquire special powers. She expressed her thoughts to Jignesh.

'Quite correct,' Jignesh sounded impressed. 'That was possible in the previous yugas, when the lifespan of humans was longer by multiples of our current lifespan. In Kaliyuga, it would be impossible to attain the *siddhis* through pure tapasya. So, how do you think youngsters like yourself have acquired powers that would have taken yogis hundreds, if not thousands, of years to attain through meditation in the ancient past?'

Once again, Maya didn't have an answer. But she ventured a guess. 'Genes?' she suggested. 'As you said just a few minutes ago, the sons and daughters of the members of the *Sangha* are also members of the *Gana*. They must have inherited their powers from their parents, and their ancestors, including those who lived thousands of years ago.'

Jignesh nodded. 'That's the logical answer. Logical and scientific. And adequate for *sadhs*. But not for us. Genes are important, there's no doubt about that. Because there is a reason why each of us is born into the lineages that we come from. And if you are going to be a Rishi, you need to know the truth.' He gave her an appraising look. 'You seem to be quite familiar with the ancient texts.'

'Dad made me read them,' Maya admitted reluctantly, remembering how much she had resented the lessons. 'He taught me Sanskrit and then made sure that I read all the books he gave me. The Mahabharata, the Ramayana, the Puranas and the Vedas. All original Sanskrit texts.'

Jignesh raised an eyebrow. 'You must have hated it,' he commiserated with her.

Maya was taken aback. It was the first time Jignesh had really understood anything about her.

'I did,' she agreed. 'I didn't understand half of what I was reading. I never knew why Dad insisted on it. It was the only thing I can remember that he imposed on me.'

'Well then,' Jignesh resumed, 'a lot of what I am about to tell you might sound familiar, since it is straight from the texts that you have mentioned. If you didn't understand what you read earlier, you will now, since I will explain it to you.'

Maya eyed him doubtfully. This was beginning to sound ominous. Her Dad had also promised to help her understand the texts. 'Read them first,' he had told her, 'get acquainted with the stories and the verses. I will explain everything at the right time.'

It had never happened. Perhaps he would have followed up on his promise, had he lived ...

But her concern now was that this lesson might turn out to be as boring as it had been back when she had read the texts for the first time. It was like being back in one of Sumitra's classes, where she would simply read out extracts from the text book. It was guaranteed to make any teenager go to sleep. Only, there she was one in a class of thirty. Here, she was alone with Jignesh.

She tried to look interested and attentive.

'To begin with,' Jignesh continued, oblivious to Maya's apprehensions, 'you have to understand that we don't look down upon *sadhs*. Truthfully, there is no real difference between them and us. We are not superior to them in any way just because we have powers that they don't. We are human beings just like them. And every single human being on the face of the earth has the ability to attain the *siddhis*. It is just that most people are too caught up in this material world, too busy with their little attachments, their myriad distractions, to be able to focus on the means to acquire the *siddhis*. In ancient times, it required *tapasya*, a complete focus and commitment. In today's age of short attention spans, how many people have the ability to focus on non-material things? That's why we have the Gurukuls. We choose youngsters who have the potential to be groomed, who we know we can teach and who will willingly learn to focus on the truth without allowing distractions and attachments to divert their focus. And, sadly, we have found that those who do not have the powers are almost always those who are not interested in making the effort to acquire them. We call them *sadhs*, to distinguish them from those who enter the Gurukuls.'

Jignesh looked at Maya to see if this was getting too heavy for her.

From the expression on her face, it was.

'There's another factor that plays a major role in the acquisition of yogic powers in Kaliyuga, and differentiates *sadhs* from *Sangha* and *Gana* members, but we'll talk about that some other time,' he said, hurriedly changing the theme. 'Let's move on to mantras.'

Interest flickered on Maya's face. Jignesh was encouraged.

'Did your father teach you any mantras?' he enquired.

Maya shook her head. 'Never.'

'Then, how did you know the *Narsimha* mantra last night?'

'I read it in the diary that I showed the Council. The one I picked up from Dad's study table.'

'I didn't mean just the words. You know Sanskrit, so the words and their meanings would be clear to you. I meant the intonation, the articulation of the syllables, the exact pronunciation. How did you know that?'

'I heard Ratan reciting the mantra and simply followed his lead.'

Jignesh took a deep breath. He could see that Maya wasn't getting his point. 'Let me explain,' he said. 'Do you remember the story of the creation of Vritrasura?'

Maya nodded, eager to display her knowledge. 'When Indra killed Visvarupa, his father, Tvasta decided to create a demon to kill Indra. But he ended up creating Vritrasura, who was destined to be killed by Indra.' It suddenly dawned on her. 'Oh, I understand now. It was Tvasta's mispronunciation of the name "Indra" that led to the mistake.'

'Very good.' Jignesh was impressed. The girl was sharp. 'So you see,' he concluded, 'the correct articulation of every word is the key to the success of any mantra.'

He showed her a book he was carrying. 'There are six categories of mantras which the *Sangha* and *Gana* members use.' He counted them off on his fingers. 'Mantras to remove anxiety and instill peace, defensive mantras for protection, offensive mantras to destroy or chase evil away, mantras for creating an illusion, mantras for manipulating matter and, finally, mantras to activate the *siddhis*. The mantras for peace of mind are the simplest and require the least amount of yogic power. The mantras to activate the *siddhis* are the most powerful and require the highest level of yogic power.' He handed the book to her.

'Now,' he said. 'Let us practice some of the mantras to remove anxiety and create peace of mind.'

Chapter Fifty-one

Kapoor's Investigations

Dr. Gupta's Institute of Mental Health & Behavioural Sciences
New Delhi

Raman Kapoor strode into the lobby of the psychiatric hospital and headed for the reception.

The young girl behind the counter looked up, a terrified expression on her face as she noticed his uniform.

Kapoor smiled at her, trying to be affable. 'I wanted to meet one of your patients,' he told the receptionist. 'A man by the name of Rakesh Saini. He was brought here for treatment two weeks ago.'

'Yes, sir,' the receptionist stammered. 'I'll have to call Dr. Gupta first and request his permission.'

Kapoor nodded. 'Certainly. I'll be happy to meet Dr. Gupta in person and speak to him.'

The girl made a quick call as Kapoor made himself comfortable on one of the faux leather single seaters in the lobby. 'Dr. Gupta will see you now,' the receptionist called to Kapoor as she put down the phone.

A white uniformed attendant approached Kapoor and motioned to him to follow her. Kapoor rose and accompanied her to the lift, which took them to the second floor. The attendant led him down a corridor to a room at the end and knocked on the door.

'Come in,' a muffled voice floated out from inside the room.

The attendant pushed the door open and gestured for Kapoor to enter.

'SP Raman Kapoor?' Dr. Gupta looked up from his desk as Kapoor walked into the room. The attendant disappeared, shutting the door behind her.

Gupta was a medium-sized man with a slight paunch and thinning white hair. Kapoor guessed he would be in his late fifties, perhaps pushing sixty. The psychiatrist had quite a reputation in the city and was well known for the work he had done in helping people with depression and other psychological conditions. His hospital was famous for treating not just celebrities and the rich but also offering treatment to people who couldn't afford it.

'What can I do for you?' Gupta came to the point after the initial greetings.

'I wanted to see one of your patients,' Kapoor told him, as both men sat down. 'Rakesh Saini. He was admitted here two weeks ago.'

'Saini.' Gupta's forehead furrowed. 'Oh, yes, of course. He was suffering from delusions.'

'That's what the police report said,' Kapoor agreed. 'Is that common, doctor? I mean do you get a lot of cases like that?'

'Not many. But that doesn't mean anything. Depression, itself, is a huge problem in India. It is estimated that one in five Indians suffers from it. Yet, very few people who are affected actually visit a psychiatrist for treatment. It is a condition that can be managed, but the social stigma of undergoing psychiatric treatment holds back many young people from seeking professional help. It is unfortunate.'

'Yes, it is. So, this guy, Saini,' Kapoor tried to bring the conversation back to the reason he was there. 'Can I please see him?'

'I'll need to check with the psychiatrist in charge of the case.' Gupta picked up the intercom receiver lying on a small side table next to the sofa and dialled a two-digit number. 'Dr. Kumar, can you come to my office please. It is urgent. A police case.'

He put the receiver down and looked at Kapoor. 'Is there any progress in the case? I mean, any clues to the identity of the murderer?'

'That's the reason I'm here. I want to know exactly what happened. I'm hoping Saini can give us some clue. The investigating officer tells me that they haven't made much headway in the case.'

Gupta nodded sympathetically. 'We'll see if Saini is in a condition to give you information.'

There was a knock on the door. 'Come in!' Gupta called out.

The door opened and a young man wearing a white lab coat entered.

'SP Kapoor, meet Dr. Kumar,' Gupta introduced the two men. 'SP Kapoor wants to meet Rakesh Saini,' he told Kumar, 'and I thought I'd check with you if that would be possible.'

Kumar shook his head. 'I'm afraid not. Mr. Saini's condition has not changed despite our treatment.' He frowned. 'It really is an unusual case. The delusion is so strong that it appears to have taken hold of his mind in a remarkable manner, unlike anything I have ever seen before.' He looked at Kapoor. 'I am sorry, but I cannot allow him to meet you. Seeing a police officer may agitate him and it could possibly lead to a deterioration of his condition.'

'You mean,' Kapoor said, 'that he has not changed his belief about what he saw that day? He still believes that his delusion is reality?'

Kumar nodded. 'Correct. I am only hoping that there has not been a permanent change in his brain that will preserve the delusion as a real memory for the rest of his life.'

'I understand,' Kapoor said, trying to hide his disappointment. 'In that case, I don't think he would be able to add to what there is in the police report anyway. Thank you both for your time.'

As Kapoor left Gupta's office and made his way down the stairs to the lobby, he mused that it may not be long before *he* might require Dr. Gupta's services. The way this case was proceeding — or, to be accurate, not moving forward at all — was feeding a feeling of frustration and anxiety that was building up within him. He had been searching for that elusive clue that would help him crack the case, for a while now. But even this route had reached a dead end. The specialists here seemed to be helpless in the face of Saini's stubbornness in clinging on to a belief that seemed preposterous to anyone else except Saini.

The police report on this case was one of the two that he had chanced upon last night from the pile he had diligently been going through. Both reports pertained to mysterious murders which were almost identical to each other, and to a third murder.

The death of Dhananjay Trivedi.

All three murders involved the death of a school or college teacher. In all three cases, the victim's insides had been subjected to fifth degree burns, while their skin and clothes had been untouched by fire.

Kapoor's hopes had lifted when he read that one of the murders had an eye witness. Rakesh Saini. He was also a teacher and a close friend of the victim. Both men had been together when the victim had died.

Saini's testimony had supported the cause of death as described in the preliminary autopsy report. But it had gone beyond that.

Saini had claimed that he had *seen* his friend burst into flames without warning. One moment, the two men were talking; the next, the victim was on fire. Saini had claimed that he had not only seen the fire but also felt its heat. He had also stated that there was, amazingly, no smoke emanating from the fire.

But it was the final statement in his testimony that bordered on the ludicrous. It had clearly been a delusion.

Saini had refused to believe that his friend's body had been untouched by the flames. He had insisted that the flames had been so strong that his friend's body had been reduced to a pile of ashes. Even when the victim's corpse was being removed from the murder site, all Saini could see were the ashes being carried away.

Kapoor sighed. He had hoped his meeting with Saini would shed some light on the case and perhaps even his bizarre statement to the police. Alas, he had discovered nothing that could alter what Saini said he had seen with his own eyes.

Chapter Fifty-two

Tracks and Tricks

Day 6

SP Kapoor's Office
New Delhi

Raman Kapoor's face fell as he listened to the report from Panna. The police team from Gwalior had duly arrived yesterday at the national park and, with the cooperation of the park rangers, had spent two entire days combing the area where Harish had, purportedly, undergone his supernatural experiences.

Naturally, Kapoor had not briefed the search party on the exact nature of Harish's report; and Harish himself had no reason to be forthcoming about the terror he had experienced. In fact, he was beginning to feel a bit sheepish now, doubting himself as he walked through the forest with the other men in the daytime. Had he been seeing things? Hallucinating?

He had had a long, tiring drive from Delhi, constantly on tenterhooks, uncertain about when he would get his next meal or the next toilet break. A policeman's job is never easy and this particular assignment had been especially taxing. Was it possible that the exhaustion from the drive and tension had caused his mind to see things that were not really there? After all, nothing had happened to him. He was safe and sound, if a bit traumatized by the whole experience.

Meanwhile, the search party was going in blind. They really didn't know what they were looking for. All that they had been told was that three fugitives from Delhi had entered the park in the dead of night and had not come back out. Harish had, quite truthfully, sworn to that. He had spent the rest of the night camped outside the park in his Gypsy, shivering and terrified. He would not set foot inside the park, but he would not abandon his post either.

The befuddled search party found nothing of consequence. They had gone down the trail where Harish had encountered the spirits and had turned back to flee the park. It was difficult to follow tracks because, by the time the team from Gwalior reached Panna, countless tourists had driven down the forest path in their hired jeeps, seeking encounters with wildlife, especially the famed tigers of Panna. It was impossible to distinguish one set of tracks from the other now.

Still, the party had fanned out across the jungle, trying to cover as much ground as possible on both days before it grew too dark to see anything. Harish, especially, was keen to leave the park before the sun went down. Whatever it may have been, he did not want a repeat of that night.

Kapoor put the phone down and sat, staring into space for a while. His brain was whirring with thoughts and ideas, trying to work out his next step. It didn't take him too long, though, to reach a decision.

He rose from his desk, picked up his cap and settled it on his head. 'Ready my car,' he told a constable. 'And call Suresh. Yes, the forensics guy. I want him to meet me at Upadhyay's house in half an hour. Tell him to be there on time.'

Exactly thirty minutes later, Kapoor arrived at Maya's house. The sun had set by now and the street lamps cast a dismal glow on the deserted street. There was no sign of Suresh yet.

Kapoor shook his head. *Bloody forensics. They were never on time.* 'Keys.'

The constable accompanying Kapoor handed him the keys to the house. Kapoor walked up to the front door and unlocked it.

The door opened with a slight creak. The sitting room was a cavern of darkness.

Undeterred, Kapoor strode into the house. He knew where the light switches were.

The house had been untouched since Upadhyay's death. As the lights flickered on, the first thing he noticed were the bloodstains on the walls, the sofas and the carpet.

He quickly walked past the living room. This was not what he had come for. He entered the study. There was dust everywhere. On the books, on the desk, on the books that lay on the desk.

Kapoor smirked. This was Delhi. The dust capital of the world. Heat and dust. Just a couple of days without dusting and even the space vacated by the three missing books from the shelf was covered in a fine layer of dust. A few weeks and no one would be able to guess that three books had recently been taken off the shelf. It would have almost seemed like they had never been there.

Illusions. They could change things so dramatically. Alter evidence. Hide tracks. Distract the mind so that it would appear that magic had happened.

Kapoor didn't believe in magic. He was here to see if he had missed anything on his earlier visit. At that time, with all those people milling about, it was possible he may have been distracted. Just like in a magic show. He could have missed the real trick. *That* was what he was here to find out.

What was that trick?

Chapter Fifty-three

Kapoor's Discovery

The Upadhyay House
New Delhi

Kapoor stared in disbelief. He had come here, fully prepared to accept that he may have missed something on his earlier, and only, visit. Now, he was angry with himself. Apparently, he was not fully prepared to accept that he had made a mistake.

He *had* missed something.

And so had the rest of his team.

That didn't bother him much. They were not all that competent and it didn't surprise him that they had missed something. He would have been more surprised if they had actually found it. But he prided himself on his own perspicacity and powers of observation. It was difficult for him to accept that he had actually overlooked a vital clue.

For there it was, out of sight, yet in plain sight.

The desk in the study was an old-fashioned one. It was designed in an antique style, with two sets of drawers on either side of an open space beneath the desktop, which was open from both sides, with carvings decorating the length and breadth of the desk.

On the carpet of the study, in the narrow sliver of space under the drawers on the left side of the desk, was a single sheet of paper. Kapoor didn't know yet, if it was important or not, but it didn't change the fact that it was remiss of him not to have been thorough enough in his examination of the study earlier. It was obvious that it had been there before the murder.

Could it be important?

Kapoor sat on his haunches. Slowly, gingerly, he reached out for the sheet of paper.

'Boss?'

Kapoor jumped and whirled around, an instinctive reaction.

Damn Suresh. Bloody forensics.

'You asked for me?' Suresh was oblivious to Kapoor's reaction.

'I did. You were supposed to be here ten minutes ago, goddamnit!'

'Sorry, boss. Got caught up with a new case.' Suresh warmed to his subject. 'A corpse without a head. The body ...'

'Zip it. Not my case.'

'Sorry, boss.'

'Just wait in the sitting room, will you?'

'Sure, boss.' Suresh turned around and returned to the sitting room, painfully aware now that Kapoor was upset with him.

With Suresh gone, Kapoor returned to the task of retrieving the sheet of paper. He picked it up and studied it.

The first thing to catch his eye was a drawing. A rough impression by someone who was not terribly artistic. But, despite the lack of sketching skills, the object that was represented in the drawing was quite clear.

It was a sword.

But not an ordinary sword.

The shape of the sword was quite clear. But for some reason, the sword was depicted as being engulfed in flames.

It was a burning sword.

Chapter Fifty-four

The Archives

The Upadhyay House
New Delhi

Kapoor stared unbelievingly at the sheet of paper in his hands. Was this a child's drawing? This was getting farcical now. He had thought he had found a vital clue to the murders and all he had in his hands was a drawing of a flaming sword.

Kapoor would have dismissed the crude drawing had it not been for the inscriptions below the sketch, which he could not understand. The script was Devanagari, but the language, quite obviously, was not Hindi.

Far from getting closer to resolving the mystery, it had just deepened further.

He would have to look at this later. Suresh was here. Time to get cracking on the other stuff.

He folded the sheet with the drawing of the sword and put it into his pocket. Repressing his instinctive urge to steer clear of the living room, he slowly walked into it.

Suresh stood there, looking enquiringly at him.

Kapoor took a deep breath. 'I want you to reconstruct what happened here.'

This was the last thing he wanted. He knew Suresh would revel in the graphic details. For him it was akin to torture.

But he needed this. He needed to know.

Suresh beamed. He enjoyed this kind of thing. 'Sure, boss. I had tried to tell you on the day of the murder, but you weren't interested,' he said with a cheeky smirk.

'I know, I know.' Kapoor was resigned to the task. He steeled himself for what he knew would inevitably follow.

The Gurukul
Panna National Park

'Hey AJ! Got time for a chat?' On a break from the tomes of homework Jignesh had assigned her, Maya had been searching for Arjun. But she hadn't been able to find him anywhere. She had finally spotted him returning to the guesthouse and decided to corner him before he disappeared again.

Arjun looked wearily at her. 'I don't know, Maya. I need to shower and change and then go to my dorm.'

'You've been assigned a dorm?'

'Yeah.'

'How come I haven't?'

Arjun looked surprised. 'You haven't?' He shrugged. 'I have no clue how these people think.'

'I'll ask Mahamati Jignesh,' Maya pouted. 'You look tired, AJ.'

'I'm exhausted,' Arjun sighed. 'I've never had to practice for more than an hour or so in a day, back home.' He shook his head, still unable to get over his day. 'All I've done yesterday and today is practice my sword-fighting and work out at the gym. If you don't count the time I spent in learning mantras for various purposes. And I don't even know Sanskrit, so that wasn't the easiest part of my day. *And* I still have homework to do.'

'I know what you mean. I've spent the day drowning in mantras myself and I've lots more to cover. Hey, you'd better carry on then. You have to pack and transfer your stuff to the dorm.'

Arjun nodded and hurried away while Maya made her way to the Gurukul's archives, which were housed in one of the cottages behind the dormitories. She tried not to be upset that she had not been assigned a dormitory yet. In fact, she could guess the reason. Unlike Arjun, who had demonstrated his qualification for the Gurukul, she was still under evaluation. She would probably have to stay at the guesthouse until Jignesh approved of her admission to the Gurukul. Only then would she be allotted a dormitory. It didn't matter, she thought. She would wait. But she would get there.

Maya had been amazed when she entered the cottage that housed the archives for the first time this afternoon. Jignesh had assigned her some homework on the mantras for which she had to refer to some books he had suggested. Her jaw had dropped at the fabulous collection within the cottage. The archives were a treasure trove of manuscripts, some of which were patently ancient, written on parchment centuries ago and preserved carefully in glass cases. The most fragile texts were not accessible, but their copies were available for students to read.

She finished her homework, then sat at one of the laptops in the reading room which provided a listing of all the documents by title, subject and authorship. After seeing the collection of manuscripts earlier today, an idea had crept into her mind, which she wanted to put into action now. She performed a few quick searches of the database and soon found what she was looking for.

The book she wanted was on the second floor of the cottage, in one of the darkest corners. Clearly, this was not a very sought after text. Locating the book, she returned to the reading room on the ground floor and began studying the text, making notes in a small notebook that had been given to her as part of her student kit.

'We're closing in five minutes,' the Keeper of the Archives, an elderly Maharishi named Gurumurthy came up to Maya and intoned softly.

He glanced at the book that Maya was studying. 'Interested in ancient languages, are we?' A friendly smiled crossed his face.

'Yes,' Maya looked up at him as he stood over the desk where she sat, hesitating as she turned a thought over in her mind. 'Actually,' she decided to risk it, 'I'm looking for references to *Brahmabhasha*.'

Gurumurthy pursed his lips thoughtfully. He tapped the book Maya was reading. 'This book is probably the best one that we have here.' He looked at her sagely. 'But you won't get too much from any book, you know. *Brahmabhasha* was the mother of Sanskrit. The language of the Devas. Its grammar was defined by Indra, Soma and Mahesha himself, or so they say. It wasn't meant for us humans. We got Sanskrit — *Devabhasha* — a sub-dialect, if you will, of *Brahmabhasha*. No one knew much about it even then. I'm afraid that the knowledge, scant as it was thousands of years ago, has not really survived in our books today.'

Maya was crestfallen. She had been making notes from the book she was studying, of references to other books, hoping that she would find something somewhere that would help her make sense of her father's diary.

She shut the book, disappointed.

'Don't worry about putting it back,' Gurumurthy said, gently, seeing the disappointment on her face. 'I'll do it for you.'

'Thank you.' Maya tried to smile through her disappointment and walked towards the door.

'Oh, wait a minute.'

Maya turned to see Gurumurthy looking thoughtful. 'There is one possibility that I hadn't thought of. It just occurred to me.'

'A possibility of translating *Brahmabhasha*?'

'No, no.' Gurumurthy spread his hands before him. 'No one on Earth can do that in this day and age. But if you want to know more about that ancient language, then there is only one man alive in India who can help you.' He paused. 'Well, hopefully, he is still alive. No one has heard from him in decades.'

Maya approached Gurumurthy, a hopeful look on her face. 'Who is he?'

'His name is Satyavachana. A Maharishi. Possibly the most powerful

Maharishi alive today. Maybe even the most powerful Maharishi to have ever lived since Kaliyuga began.'

Maya's hopes soared. This sounded promising. 'And where can I find him?'

Gurumurthy looked troubled. He realized he had raised Maya's expectations. And he was about to disappoint her.

'I don't know,' he said. 'No one does.'

Chapter Fifty-five

Maya Dreams Again

The Guesthouse
The Gurukul

That night, Maya sat up late, studying her father's notebook, going through the shlokas and mantras all over again. She knew some of them by heart already and could recite them with her eyes closed. She studied the diagrams and sketches over and over again, trying to make sense of them, but to no avail.

Finally, she put the diary aside. There *had* to be a way of deciphering the verses in the notebook.

It was logical.

From everything she had heard so far, no one could read or understand *Brahmabhasha*.

Even the mysterious Satyavachana who Gurumurthy had told her about, could only give her more information about the language, according to the Keeper of the Archives. And that was logical too. If *Brahmabhasha* was a language used by the *Devas*, then no human would have been taught the language.

So where had her father got these verses from? If *Brahmabhasha* was a language that no human knew, how had her father been able to lay his hands on it and inscribe it in his diary?

He had to have had a source.

Maya remembered reading the Mahabharata. The cryptic verses in the Adi Parva came to her mind.

षष्टिं शतसहस्राणि चकारान्यां स संहिताम्
त्रिंशच्छतसहस्रं च देवलोके प्रतिष्ठितम् ।
पित्र्ये पञ्चदश प्रोक्तं गन्धर्वेषु चतुर्दश:
एकं शतसहस्रं तु मानुषेषु प्रतिष्ठितम् ।

He then completed another compilation consisting of sixty hundred thousand shlokas. Of these, thirty hundred thousand are known in the world of Devas. Fifteen hundred thousand in the world of Pitris, fourteen hundred thousand in the world of Gandharvas and one hundred thousand in the world of mankind.

Was it possible that the Mahabharata was, in its own cryptic way, referring to verses in *Brahmabhasha*, that were not accessible to humans? Were the 'thirty hundred thousand' verses, referred to in these shlokas, composed in *Brahmabhasha*? Was that why only one hundred thousand verses were shared with humans? And if this was true, who knew what those missing verses from the human version contained? There were still many mysteries in the Mahabharata; many verses that were undecipherable or which didn't make sense. Could it be that these missing verses also hid a secret?

Was it possible that her father had found a source for these missing verses? Or verses like these written in *Brahmabhasha*?

There was only one way to find out. She had to meet Satyavachana. She didn't know how, but she was determined to find him.

Maya turned the lights out. It had been a long day and she was tired.

She decided to recite one of the mantras she had learned today. A mantra for peace of mind and relaxation. A mantra to calm her. She needed it with all the thinking she had been doing; the myriad thoughts still swirling around within her mind.

It didn't take her long to fall asleep after reciting the mantra.

She dreamed.

For the second time in four nights, she dreamed that she was free of her body, floating in the air, an invisible, imperceptible breeze of some kind whisking her out of the room, this time through the wall of the cottage and into the open air beneath the canopy of trees that shaded the Gurukul.

Then, she soared higher, above the treetops. The night sky blazed with a profusion of white lights, twinkling as if in time to some unheard music. It was the most beautiful sight she had ever seen.

Below her, the Ken river flowed peacefully, the light of a million stars crashing against its waters and breaking up into shards and slivers until the river seemed to be lit up by an unseen source.

She was filled with an unusual sense of peace.

A name floated into her consciousness. Called up from some distant memory, it hovered for a while, indistinct, as she ignored it. The sense of calmness, of eternal peace, was something she didn't want to let go of.

The name became visible.

With a start, she found herself transported in the twinkling of an eye to another forest.

Maya looked around bewildered and lost. To one side, a river flowed in serpentine curves, bordered by a forest that stretched all the way until and over low hills that continued right up to the horizon.

She hovered over the hills, noticing a track that weaved among the trees. She followed it, amazed at her own dream. All it needed was a thought and she was moving along the track, as weightless as a feather. After a while, the track disappeared among the trees and she could see, through the treetops, the roof of a building.

Was it a cottage? It was difficult to make out in the light of the stars.

What was this place? This was not Panna. It was not the Gurukul. She had never seen this location before.

At the thought of the Gurukul and Panna, the landscape below her disappeared and she found herself disappearing into a black, borderless void ....

Maya sat up in bed with a jerk, fully awake.

Where was she?

The rustle of the bedsheet under her hands, the soft whisper of the air conditioner in her room brought her back to her senses. She was in her room in the guesthouse. She was perspiring for some reason, despite it being fairly cool.

It was just a dream. She hadn't gone anywhere.

Just a dream ...

Chapter Fifty-six

Maya Shares her Troubles

Day Seven

The Guesthouse
The Gurukul

Tiwari studied Maya as he waited for her to speak. The girl seemed troubled, conflicted even. That much was clear from her expression and he could sense her hesitation and ... was it fear? Possibly. But fear of what?

He didn't want to push her. Maya had come to him in the morning, seeking a private meeting.

'I ... I have something to talk about which I can't share with anyone else,' she had told him. 'Something that is confidential.'

He had agreed to meet her in the evening in the sitting room of the guesthouse, ensuring that the door to the room was shut, to give them privacy.

Tiwari was concerned as he watched Maya struggle with her thoughts, with what she wanted to do and what she thought was the right thing to do.

Perhaps that was the root of her fear, he thought.

So, he waited. Maya had chosen to speak to him over Arjun, Virendra or Pramila—the people she knew well. It was clear the girl trusted him. He didn't want to let her down. And above all, he wanted to help her.

'Ratan,' Maya began, cautiously, 'swear to me that you will not tell anyone else what I am about to tell you.'

'If you don't want me to tell anyone, I won't. I promise.'

Maya nodded but said nothing more.

What was troubling her so much? Tiwari wondered if it had to do with the misgivings he had entertained on the night when Shukra's army of monsters had materialized at the Gurukul.

'I'm scared,' Maya confessed after a while, finally appearing to overcome her hesitation and misgivings. 'I don't understand it and I'm afraid. I'm scared of talking about this to anyone else. The only person I can trust is you.' She looked at him pleadingly. 'Please help me.'

'Tell me what it is,' Tiwari said gently, in a reassuring tone.

'I ... I don't know if something is wrong with me ... my mind ... I don't know. I'm scared,' Maya reiterated.

'What is scaring you?'

'I've been having these dreams,' Maya's words came out in a rush, almost as if she was scared that she might change her mind and hold something back if she didn't get them out in a hurry. 'Weird dreams. Sometimes nightmares.' She lowered her voice as if afraid someone might overhear. 'The first one was in your house. The night when you rescued me at the Metro station.'

It was Tiwari's turn to hesitate. He was almost afraid to ask. 'What was it that you dreamed about?' he finally questioned.

'That is what terrifies me. I dreamt about places I've never been to. Things I haven't seen. I don't know why or how.'

'Tell me what you saw in your dreams,' he goaded her on gently.

Maya told him. She narrated everything she had seen in her dream, as she slept in Tiwari's guest bedroom. The blood spattered scene at her house, the lonely, winding, narrow road that she had seen the Land Cruiser traversing, the nightmare that involved Shukra and his motley monsters. She described her second dream from last night, the sensation of weightlessness that she hadn't noticed in her first dream, the instant change of scenes and the forest on the hills that she had seen.

Tiwari was silent when she finished. He had his own struggles to deal with now.

Maya mistook his silence as encouragement to elaborate and explain further. She carried on, oblivious.

'The dreams are not what scare me. It's the fact that what I'm seeing seems like real stuff.' Her voice became animated. 'You remember when we were driving to Panna and you asked me if I was looking for something? Well, I was looking around frantically because I had seen that very road in my dream at your house. It was the same road that the Land Cruiser was driving on, in my dream. I couldn't believe my eyes when we drove down that stretch of road because it was exactly the same as what I had seen! I didn't understand it then. But I later realized that I had also seen, in the same dream, the monsters whom we fought in the clearing outside the Gurukul. They were among the creatures that Shukra was speaking to. I can't remember what he was saying to them, but I remember the creatures vividly. I could almost feel them in the dream, it was so realistic.'

Maya stopped talking and looked at Tiwari, her hands in her lap. 'What's happening to me, Ratan? Why am I dreaming of things like this? It scares me. Am I seeing things in my dream that somehow come true?'

Tiwari took a deep breath. 'You are absolutely sure about all that you just said?'

Maya nodded.

'You were right not to tell anyone else about this.' Tiwari hesitated. 'People might misunderstand.'

'Misunderstand?' Maya was confused.

'Yes. You see, all your life, you have never displayed any signs of yogic power. No one has ever detected any potential in you to become a Rishi. That is why you were never approached for recruitment to any of the Gurukuls. If your dreams, however, are an indication, then people would be disposed to think that there was something amiss.'

'Like what?' Maya didn't understand.

'Like you being an agent of Shukra,' Tiwari said in a grim voice.

Chapter Fifty-seven

Tiwari Explains

The Guesthouse
The Gurukul

Maya was horrified. 'An agent of Shukra! Why would anyone think that?'

'There's no other way to explain this.' Tiwari paused. 'Let's start with the concept of the *atma*. You know what that is, right?'

'The spirit. The soul. It is eternal and lives on beyond the body.'

'Correct. Actually, we have three bodies, in a manner of speaking. Like the layers of an onion, each body is wrapped within the other. The innermost body is the *atma* — the soul, which you can call our spiritual body. The *atma* is enveloped by what is called the *sukshma sharir* — the subtle or imperceptible body, which consists of the mind, intelligence and false ego. The outermost layer is our physical body, the *sthula sharir* — the gross body which determines our physical appearance and constitution.'

Maya listened wide-eyed, and more than a bit confused. What did this have to do with her dreams? And how would this make anyone think that she was an agent of Shukra?

'We will get to it,' Tiwari reassured her, seeing the doubtful expression on her face. 'But first you need to understand the concept of the *atma*. You see, when we die, the soul leaves the gross body, carrying the *sukshma sharir* or the subtle body with it. The gross body dies but the *atma* and subtle body live on, until we eventually leave the material world and our soul returns to the spiritual realm, leaving the subtle body behind. Are you with me so far?'

Maya nodded.

'Now, here's the thing,' Tiwari resumed. 'It is possible, with highly developed yogic powers, for the *atma* to leave the physical body even while the person is alive. The physical body does not die, it is simply bereft of the soul for as long as it is outside the body.' He paused, allowing the thought to sink in.

Maya contemplated this.

'You mean,' she said slowly, 'that my dreams weren't really dreams. They were *real*. I wasn't dreaming that I was flying around the countryside seeing things. I was *actually* doing it. Or, at least, my *atma* was.' She looked at Tiwari for validation. 'Am I correct?'

'Yes, Maya. The *atma* has the capability of moving at the speed of thought. Because it has no physical constraints, it can go anywhere, guided just by a thought and nothing else. Were you thinking of specific locations or specific people while you thought you were dreaming?'

Maya's eyes widened. 'Yes, I was.' She reflected back on her dream that first night in Tiwari's house. 'When I thought about Arjun, I saw the Land Cruiser driving along the road to Panna. Then, somehow, the thought of Shukra came into my mind and I saw him with his army of creatures. And I went to sleep thinking of Dad. That's why ...'

Her voice quavered. 'Does that mean that the bloodstains on the wall, the blood on the carpet of the living room was actually my father's? Is that how ... ?' She wiped a tear from her eye.

Tiwari stayed silent, allowing her to recover her composure.

'So how was I able to do this without yogic powers?' Maya queried finally, bringing her emotions under control. 'You said this needed highly developed yogic powers. I don't have yogic powers.'

'That's just the problem,' Tiwari said, quietly. 'If you don't have yogic powers, then how can anyone explain what you have experienced, and what you have done? There are Maharishis in the *Sangha* who are not capable of performing this feat, despite all their powers. Yet you, a fifteen-year-old girl, have done it.'

'But that doesn't connect me to Shukra in any way!'

'Not directly, no,' Tiwari admitted. 'But there is another strange thing that happened, which cannot be easily explained.'

Maya looked askance at him. What more could there be?

'You remember that you passed out in the clearing that night?'

She nodded, recalling suddenly waking up and finding herself in the midst of a battle, with people chanting the Narsimha mantra all around her.

'Well, you didn't really pass out. I didn't tell you about it earlier because I wasn't sure if my observation was correct. But what you have just told me seems to add up.'

'What had happened to me?' Maya demanded, tearfully. She was even more scared than she had been earlier.

Tiwari felt sorry for her. He didn't want to go on with this explanation, but this was the best thing to do. She had to know.

'When the black fog appeared,' he explained, 'in fact, even before it appeared — probably seconds prior to its appearance — you collapsed on the ground, holding your head, screaming in pain and, probably, delirium. You were sobbing. Then, as suddenly as you had started, you stopped screaming and went completely silent. That was when the fog began producing the monsters.'

Maya couldn't believe what she was hearing. 'Are you telling me that there was a connection between what I felt, and the fog, and the appearance of those creatures? How can you believe that, Ratan?'

Tiwari shook his head. 'I don't believe that, Maya. But the coincidence is too great, don't you think? Someone who doesn't know you might point out ...' He hesitated. This was going to be difficult. But he wanted the girl to know what she might be up against if someone got to know about her experiences. '... That you were also present when Shukra killed your Dad. You have been present every time something associated with Shukra happens. The *pretas* in the forest are just another example.'

'That doesn't mean anything!' Maya remonstrated, tears running down her cheeks now. 'I *loved* my Dad. I still love him! And I have nothing to do with Shukra! I hate him! I ...' Words failed her.

'I know, Maya. And I believe you. But this is exactly why you should keep quiet about everything you have told me. I have told no one about what I observed in the clearing. You have to ensure that you never, ever, tell anyone either. Not even Arjun.'

Maya nodded tearfully.

'There's one more thing,' she said, wiping the tears from her face. 'I don't know if it has anything to do with my dreams ... my *atma* leaving my body at night, but it is a common factor.'

Tiwari listened attentively.

'Last night, before this happened,' she gestured ambiguously, not wanting to say the words again, 'I recited a mantra. Could that have something to do with my out of body experience?'

'Which mantra was it?'

Maya began reciting.

'Shaanta-kaaram bhujaga-shayanam padma-naabham suresham
vishwa-dhaaram gagana-sadrisham megha-varanam shubhaangam.
lakshmi-kaantam kamala-nayanam yogi-bhi-dhyaana-agamyam
vande vishnum bhava-bhaya-haram sarva-lokaika-naatham'

Tiwari was impressed. Maya's intonation was perfect and he could feel the power of the mantra coursing through his body, the resonance of the vowels and consonants melting into a current that ran through his muscles, his blood and his brain, caressing and relaxing them. An instant feeling of peace and calm settled over him and he basked in the effect of the mantra for a few moments, enjoying the invigorating sense of peace.

Finally, almost reluctantly, he spoke. 'That's interesting. You could be onto something here. That's exactly the same mantra that I recited for you just before you went to sleep in my house. You were tired, scared, and your mind was filled with all kinds of unpleasant thoughts, so I recited this mantra — the *shantaa-kaaram* mantra to help you relax.'

'It isn't Shukra,' Maya absently insisted.

'I know. Now, tell me one thing. What were you thinking of when you had your out of body experience last night?'

Chapter Fifty-eight

Maya's Plan

The Guesthouse
The Gurukul

Maya stood on the balcony attached to her room and savoured the fresh night air. It was such a refreshing change from the city. The quiet stillness of the forest around them, the rustling of the leaves on the trees that shaded the Gurukul during the day, the transparent darkness that settled over the cottages once the artificial lights were switched off, and the canopy of stars far above — glowing orbs, millions of miles away scattering their light; this was a world far removed from life in a big city where the dust, pollution, noise and bright lights overshadowed and overwhelmed the quiet beauty of nature.

It was true, she reflected, that humans, in their endeavour to conquer the earth, had only managed to distance themselves from it.

She had begun to realize why this location had been chosen for the Gurukul. She was certain that the other Gurukuls, too, were located in similar spots. It was the perfect place for youngsters like her, and the other children in the Gurukul, to discover themselves in the solitude that the place offered, while staying connected to other human beings. If they had to discover their inner power, as Jignesh continued to exhort her to do, there was no better place to do it — with no distractions or temptations of any kind.

But Maya was distracted. She knew it and she was aware that Jignesh was not blind to it either. The meditation classes with Mahesh were helping — they enabled her to centre herself and focus on her inner energies. They had helped to soothe the trauma she had undergone just a few days back. But even meditation was not sufficient to quell a strange restlessness within her. She didn't know where it came from or why it was there, but it tugged at her continuously, like a dull, nagging headache; only in this case, there was no pain, just a need for action.

But what that action was, she didn't know.

She did have her suspicions about the source of her restlessness. Maya felt that the diary may have something to do with it. While the pain caused by the loss of her father had been dulled somewhat by the meditation, the mystery of the diary had not been solved. Her father's last words echoed repeatedly in her ears. He had wanted her to do something. But he had not managed to tell her what it was that she was supposed to do.

And that disturbed her. She felt responsible, somehow, for completing what her father had started but had not been able to conclude. She wanted closure; she wanted her father to achieve closure.

Tonight's chat with Ratan had given her an idea; a possible means to accomplish this. Despite what the Council had said, she still believed that the Gandharvas might hold the key to translating the undecipherable pages in her father's diary. She had no way of getting to them, however. At least, no traditional way. But, if Tiwari was right, then she did have a way of reaching the Gandharvas.

And she planned to try it tonight.

Wistfully, she took a long deep breath of the forest air and entered her room, shutting and bolting the balcony door behind her.

It was time.

She switched off the lights, determined to do this properly. It had to work and she was taking no chances.

Settling herself on the bed in a meditative stance, she closed her eyes and began reciting the *shantaa-kaaram* mantra. The instant sense of calm that she was by now accustomed to, every time she chanted the mantra, penetrated every fibre of her being and her breathing slowed as she relaxed in mind and body.

The mantra completed, she lay down, prepared to sleep.

Tonight, she knew where she was going.

Within moments, she was asleep.

Maya began dreaming. To her astonishment, this time she *knew* that it was not a dream. She was fully aware, as she rose out of her body and looked down upon it from the ceiling of her room, that this was real. It was actually happening.

Recalling her conversation, earlier that evening with Tiwari, she guided her thoughts, with some difficulty, towards the Gandharvas. It didn't happen automatically as she had thought it would.

The Gandharva valley.

It was difficult to stay focused. Satyavachana, her home in Delhi, her school, the forest outside, the river Ken, and myriad other thoughts jostled with the thought of the Gandharvas. Maya fought to maintain her concentration.

But nothing happened.

She remained suspended above her bed, staring down at her physical body, deep in slumber.

Or was it dead? She couldn't make out the difference. After all, if her *atma* was the essence of her being and it was now out of her body, didn't that mean that her physical body was dead?

Another thought to wrestle with. She pushed it aside.

The Gandharva valley.

Again, nothing happened.

Maya tried again and again, to no avail. She couldn't understand it. Ratan had said that the *atma* could travel at the speed of thought, guided by thought. And that had been her experience on earlier occasions. Just the thought of a person or a location and she had been transported away.

Why was it not happening tonight?

Finally, unable to comprehend what was happening, and overwhelmed by a feeling of being drained of energy, she gave up and returned to her body. For some reason, tonight she did not wake up with a jerk.

Maya slept peacefully.

Chapter Fifty-nine

Looking for Answers

Day Eight

The Gurukul

Maya spent a restless day, despite having slept soundly last night. She was distracted and unable to resolve the conundrum of why she had failed to guide her own spirit using her thoughts. She had managed easily enough when she didn't know what she was doing, so why was it suddenly difficult? It wasn't possible that Ratan was wrong or that he had misled her in any way.

It was clear to her that she was missing something vital that was a prerequisite to achieve what she had been trying to do. Somehow, she had been able to do it unconsciously — though why that should happen was a mystery to her — but not when she was fully aware. It didn't make sense that she had to be unconscious of where she wanted to go to be able to travel at the speed of thought. That would be of no use at all. And Ratan, in his explanation to her, had implied that thoughts could guide the *atma*.

So why had it not happened last night?

Her distraction earned her reprimands through the day. First, during meditation class. Just yesterday, Mahesh had complimented her on her powers of concentration.

'For someone who has just entered the Gurukul, you show tremendous focus,' he had told her. 'You will be able to tap into your innermost consciousness with practice. Few people are able to achieve that.'

Arjun had rolled his eyes at Mahesh's compliments, but Maya had been thrilled to bits. She was, after all, still an outsider, unlike Arjun. Her powers and her very presence here were constantly being questioned. To be complimented in this manner was a privilege and she relished it.

But today was completely different. Her preoccupation with her failed attempt at *atma* travel the night before interfered with her concentration and focus.

And Mahesh had noticed.

'If you do not clear your mind of all the clutter, all the attachments, all the thoughts that are flowing through it,' he admonished her, 'how will you achieve perfect focus? You are not trying hard enough, Maya!'

Maya had sulked, even though she knew, deep in her heart, that Mahesh was correct.

'You okay?' Arjun had enquired, looking concerned, before leaving for his training sessions with Virendra.

Maya had simply nodded, angry with herself for allowing the distraction to get the better of her, and for having failed last night. A nagging doubt had crept into her mind.

Had the Council been correct in their doubts regarding her?

Her frustration and self-doubt persisted through the day, earning her more reprimands from Jignesh. His scathing remarks didn't help in improving her mood either.

By evening, Maya's mood was positively black. To make things worse, she didn't see Arjun in the Gurukul mess at dinnertime. It was the only time of the day when they would meet and she looked forward to their brief interaction over dinner, as they exchanged notes and cribbed about the rigour at the Gurukul.

As Maya sat down for dinner by herself, a novice just slightly younger than her came up to her table.

'Can I sit with you?' the novice asked shyly.

Maya recognized her as the girl who had led her to her room in the guesthouse on the night of her arrival at the Gurukul. She suppressed her black mood and put on a smile for the girl.

'Sure, why not?'

'My name's Amyra. I know yours.'

Maya smiled at Amyra. 'So you're a Rishi?' she asked, a bit pointlessly. Amyra wore white robes; quite clearly she was a Rishi. But Maya couldn't think of anything else to say to her.

'Yes,' Amyra giggled. She looked around furtively and lowered her voice to a whisper. 'Still a novice, though. And I have a special gift.'

'And what's that?' Maya was genuinely interested now.

'I'm a psychic,' came the whispered response.

'Oh, you can see the future?'

'No, not that type of psychic. I can't see the future. But I can see the past.'

Maya was puzzled. 'How is that a gift?'

Amyra shrugged. 'I don't know. I was told, when I was enrolled, that it is a gift.'

'Wait a minute, do you mean that you can see the past even if you weren't there?'

'Yes, of course.' Amyra sounded surprised that Maya hadn't understood the first time. 'Though I can only see back into the past up to a certain limit. I still haven't worked out how far back into the past I can see.'

'Mmmm.' Maya couldn't really see how that was terribly useful, but she refrained from saying so. Clearly, Amyra was proud of her gift and she didn't want to dampen her spirits.

'Are you a novice, too?' Amyra was curious.

'I'm not sure.' Maya tried to keep the tension out of her voice. Amyra had touched a raw nerve, which was accentuated by her already bleak mood. 'They haven't told me.'

'I was wondering why you are still at the guesthouse. Only guests stay there. Students are assigned a dormitory on the first day. Will you be leaving us soon?'

'I hope not. Now, if you will excuse me, I have some work to do.' Maya rose without waiting for an answer and left the mess hall, blinking back her tears and suppressing the feelings of anger and hurt, accentuated by self-doubt, that were bubbling up inside.

She made her way to the archives. Gurumurthy was there, his usual smiling self. Maya nodded at him in greeting and rushed past so that he wouldn't notice her half-hearted attempt to smile at him. Heading for the database laptops, she sat at one and began searching. Presently, she found the location of a couple of books that she felt would help her.

Retrieving the books, she returned to Gurumurthy. 'I know it is late, but I need to read these tonight,' she told him, a pleading look in her eyes. 'Can I please borrow these just for tonight? I promise I will return them tomorrow.'

Gurumurthy regarded her sagely, then took the books from her and studied them. 'Hmmm,' he said thoughtfully. 'A bit advanced for you, don't you think?' He looked up at her. 'Whatever you are planning, my dear, be careful.'

His eyes were learned and wise, and in their depths, Maya could see a host of questions.

Maya nodded numbly, chastened by his warning. Without a word, Gurumurthy stamped the books and handed them back to her.

'Goodnight.'

'Goodnight,' Maya mumbled in reply and stumbled out of the cottage housing the archives.

Back in her room, Maya opened the books with trembling hands and began reading.

Time flew past as she sat immersed in the books. There was so much to learn, so much she didn't know. So much that the world outside the Gurukul didn't know. Gurumurthy's warning made sense to her. If she was not careful, she could do herself serious harm.

But, she reflected, she didn't intend anything complicated. All she was looking for were answers.

After a couple of hours of unbroken research, she found what she was looking for.

When she finally shut the books, her eyes were shining.

She knew why she had failed to guide her *atma* to the Gandharva valley last night by means of her thoughts.

Chapter Sixty

Arjun Reflects

Day Ten

The Gurukul

The last few days had gone by in a rush for Arjun. Virendra had pushed him hard with several hours of practice and hard exercise in the gym every day.

'There's no point in getting your technique right if you don't have the strength and stamina to last out on the battlefield,' Arjun's uncle told him. Virendra's own physique and stamina, at his age, was testimony to the fact that he walked the talk. The man didn't have an ounce of fat on him. He was all rippling muscles. There were times when Arjun was glad that Virendra was his uncle. He would have hated to come up against him in a battle. Or, even in a fight on the street.

Arjun had gamely slaved on, uncomplaining, though he cribbed about it to Maya, every evening when they met briefly, for dinner in the Gurukul mess. That was the only time he ever got to see her these days. And she, too, was exhausted by the time she arrived at the mess. Arjun had heard from her about the rigorous mental exercises that Jignesh was making her undergo in an attempt to develop her yogic powers and also understand how much of them Maya really possessed. However tired they may be, Arjun and Maya both looked forward to their chat over dinner — it seemed to be the only thread binding them now.

Life had changed so much for them. From being carefree ninth graders — with no board exams to look forward to, thanks to the CBSE board — to this hard life of struggle. Arjun had the additional burden of knowing that he was being groomed for a much larger responsibility. His father, whom he had never known, had been the leader of the Kshatriyas and that mantle now rested on his shoulders.

The problem was that he hadn't the foggiest notion of what that meant. Or what he was supposed to do.

There were times when he really missed being back at school. He even managed to feel nostalgic about Sumitra's dreary classes. He and Maya had chuckled over a few jokes about her one night at dinner.

'I'm going to find a mantra,' Maya had said determinedly, 'that will make Sumitra disappear.'

She grinned at the thought, picturing Sumitra disappearing in a puff of smoke.

'The school will thank you,' Arjun had chuckled. 'They'll put up a statue of you and hang a garland around you once a year at annual day. Heh!'

'Right. And for the rest of the year, pigeons would do their bit on my head — I mean, my statue's head. Thanks a lot, AJ!'

However, such lighthearted moments were few and far in between. Mostly, he was too tired to even think.

In his heart, he suspected that his uncle had a solid reason for driving him so hard. He had never been such a tough taskmaster earlier. Ever. At times he wondered what his uncle had in mind. And at times he didn't want to know. He had a nasty feeling it would turn out to be a surprise he didn't want.

It was strange, Arjun thought, that his life and Maya's had changed so much in just a week. And yet, in many ways, nothing had changed. The environment had changed, the people who set the rules were different and the context was no longer the same.

But, on the ground, he — and Maya, too, he reflected — had no more independence over their lives than they had had back in Delhi when they were at school.

In Delhi, they were bound by school rules. Here, it was the rules of the Gurukul. His uncle and mother had made all the decisions in Delhi. *That* hadn't changed. If anything, they were stricter now. There had been a couple of days, when he had faced the wrath of his uncle because had not felt like practicing.

'I just don't feel like working out,' Arjun had complained. 'I'm not in the mood.'

'Do you think Arjuna from the Mahabharata had the luxury of saying that?' his uncle had thundered, his face black with anger. 'He probably had his off days; we all do. But, when you are a Kshatriya, your Dharma comes first. You have a responsibility. Nothing else matters.'

'Well, I'm not Arjuna,' Arjun had retorted, 'I mean, I am Arjun, but not the dude in the Mahabharata. He was Indra's son. I'm not.' His retort had riled his uncle even more.

But the earful he got from Virendra only made it all seem even more unfair. No one had asked him if he wanted the responsibility. It had been thrust upon him whether he liked it or not. And there were times — many occasions — when he didn't like it. He didn't want to be the leader of the Kshatriyas. He just wanted to curl up in the shade of the trees by the river and read a book.

Well, that wasn't going to happen today. Or anytime soon.

Chapter Sixty-one

Arjun Gets a Shock

The Kshatriya Practice Field
The Gurukul

Arjun stared in sheer disbelief. Following his uncle's instructions, he had arrived at the practice field on his own. The entire morning, prior to lunch, had been spent on practising the two techniques that his uncle had taught him on his first day in the Gurukul and which he had been practising ad nauseam since then.

Both were complex manoeuvres, and Arjun could see why only advanced sword-fighters were taught these. The time he spent in the gym only helped in getting him accustomed to the techniques and ensuring that he didn't tire soon with the complicated moves.

But *this*, he felt, was uncalled for.

When they broke for lunch, his uncle had given him a heads up about what the second half of the day held in store.

'Live combat practice today, Arjun,' Virendra had called out to him. 'Be prepared.'

Arjun had nodded. He knew what that meant.

He would have to face Amba and Parth during a live combat session. His uncle had given him five days to learn, train and practise. Today would be the first live combat session.

Arjun was nervous but still confident. He had trained well and the longer hours at the gym here had only done him good. He felt strong. While he had no doubts that Amba and Parth were not going to be walkovers, he thought he would be able to hold his own. At least for a while.

But he hadn't reckoned for what his uncle had planned for him.

Not only were Virendra, Amba and Parth trooping into the Kshatriya field, each carrying what looked like a large, flat, black rectangular metal case, but behind them Arjun could see Varun and Tanveer entering the field. They, too, were carrying the same flat, rectangular cases.

What were the boys doing here?

Varun and Tanveer were two Kshatriyas who shared the dormitory with Arjun, along with Agastya, a Rishi. Arjun had met Varun during the battle with Shukra's army, and, by sheer coincidence — though Varun insisted it was destiny — Arjun had been assigned the same dormitory as Varun.

Arjun was aware that the three boys he shared the dorm with were highly regarded. Varun and Tanveer were probably the most accomplished Kshatriyas in the Gurukul — and possibly even in the entire *Gana* — and Agastya was already considered to be one of the most powerful Rishis on campus.

'He can do stuff that will make your eyes pop out,' Varun had said as he had introduced Agastya to Arjun.

Arjun had, therefore, been chuffed no end when he realized that the *Mahamati* Council had considered him good enough to be equated with Varun, Agastya and Tanveer. It was a rule in the Gurukul that dorms were shared only by students who were at the same level of accomplishment. The novices, newly enrolled in the Gurukul, had a separate cottage all to themselves.

The four boys had got along like a house on fire from the first day and had become fast friends in the few days that Arjun had been with them.

Virendra gave Arjun a sly grin, relishing the lad's amazement and confusion.

'Ready, my boy?' he asked.

'Ready for what?' Arjun pointed to Varun and Tanveer. 'What are they doing here?'

'Combat practice,' came the cryptic reply. Virendra looked at his four companions. 'Let's set up and roll.'

'Hey, AJ.' Varun and Tanveer wore sheepish grins.

Arjun frowned. Then it struck him. It had been so obvious that he hadn't even bothered to consider it a possibility.

'No way!' he walked over to where Virendra was in the process of opening his sword case. 'This is pure suicide, uncle. I'm not doing it.'

'What do you mean?' Virendra stood up, hands on his hips, and glared at Arjun. 'I haven't trained you for so many years only for you to back away from a fight when the chips are down. You will damn well fight all four of them.'

'Not at the same time.'

'At the same time. And no arguments.'

'They'll kill me. I'm too young to die. I haven't even had a girlfriend yet.'

'I'm not in the mood for jokes, young man. You are a Kshatriya. Your dharma is to fight. And fight you will.'

'And what if I say no?' Arjun knew he was pushing it, but the alternative was to go up against the four most competent warriors in the Gurukul.

'Then you will have to fight five of us, not four. I'll join them. Do you want that?'

Arjun knew when he was defeated. He knew that Virendra was probably equal to all four of his current opponents. And Virendra would be as good as his word. Arjun didn't want to end up fighting the equivalent of eight supreme warriors. A sullen look crossed his face.

'Here,' Virendra opened the metal case. 'You are all going to be wearing armour. And the swords will be blunt. You aren't going to die. The worst that will happen is that you will get some pretty bad bruises.' He grinned wickedly. 'You've got to learn someday.'

Arjun rolled his eyes.

'Don't you roll your eyes at me, young man,' Virendra said sharply.

Varun and Tanveer hid broad grins, which only increased Arjun's irritation.

Virendra's face grew serious. 'Let me explain, Arjun. You haven't seen the worst of it yet. Those creatures you fought the other night were bumbling buffoons compared to what we may be up against. The day you come up against the *Vikritis*, you will know. They are deadly and have no compunctions. No morals or ethics while fighting. Everything goes. I will tell you more about them someday. For now, all you need to know is that you have to be prepared for them. And your preparation starts today. And don't forget, we don't know what Shukra has in store for us. We need to be prepared for the worst.'

Arjun had no clue what Virendra was going on about. All he knew was that he didn't have a choice. He was going kamikaze and he could do nothing about it.

He began donning the pieces of armour that were packed in the suitcase.

Chapter Sixty-two

Combat Practice

The Kshatriya Practice Field
The Gurukul

Arjun hefted his sword and stretched and wiggled to adjust his body armour. It wasn't very comfortable, but Virendra had told him that he would get used to it after a few sessions.

'Everyone does,' Virendra had assured Arjun. 'And the armour is strong but light and flexible. It is designed to enable even older Kshatriyas to fight should the need arise.'

At least Virendra had been right about the weight of the armour. Arjun marvelled at its lightness; it didn't seem to slow him down and, despite his fears, didn't restrict his movements at all.

His four opponents for the combat session were positioned randomly at four points around him. But Arjun knew that they would begin moving around as soon as the session began.

Strangely, though, they were all unarmed. Tanveer's bow and quiver were missing, as were the swords of the other three. Arjun wondered where their weapons were. They had all marched onto the field carrying only the cases in which the armour was packed.

Were they going to fight him with their bare hands?

He frowned. That didn't seem quite right.

It didn't matter. He had to take advantage of the situation.

He decided to make the first move. Quickly sizing up his adversaries, he decided that Amba was the one he should take out first. She was the nimblest and the fastest of the four, with a fearsome reputation for out-battling most of the male Kshatriyas on campus, making up in speed and technique for the brute strength that Parth and Varun had.

He would go for Parth next, followed by Varun, leaving Tanveer for the end. The archer, while dangerous with a bow in his hand, was no danger for him at the moment, since he was weaponless.

Arjun charged towards Amba, brandishing his sword. To his great surprise, she met his charge head on, sprinting towards him with a grace and speed that he didn't believe was possible.

But that was not the only surprise in store for Arjun.

When the two were barely five feet away from each other, Amba reached out into empty space and, magically, a sword appeared in her hand.

Arjun was taken aback. Where did that sword come from? It had materialized out of thin air!

A quick glance around and he saw that his other three opponents were also closing in on him and they, too, were armed now.

What had happened? Where had their weapons appeared from? His mind boggled, Arjun strained to keep his focus.

Before he knew it, Amba was upon him, attacking him with a level of swordplay that he had only been told about by Virendra during their practice sessions. She was lightning quick and it was all he could do to fend her off. Attack was out of the question.

Arjun realized his mistake. He had underestimated his opponents. He felt thoroughly under prepared.

Now, armed with his bow and arrows, Tanveer was the most dangerous of the four — he didn't even need to get close to Arjun to strike him.

Arjun thought swiftly, while parrying Amba's blows. She was quick and her technique was much superior to his own, but her sword strokes — while deadly — depended on agility and skill rather than strength.

He quickly decided on a new strategy. It was now or never. If he delayed any further, Tanveer would strike, and the session would be over.

Arjun angled to Amba's right so that Tanveer came into view from the corner of his eye. The archer was fitting an arrow to his longbow. Arjun had just seconds to execute his plan, and Varun was also now dangerously close. Where was Parth? Never mind. He would tackle that problem as soon as he got rid of the immediate one.

He had to time this well.

He heard the twang of the bowstring as Tanveer shot his arrow.

Several things happened in the milliseconds after the arrow left the bow.

The years of training with Virendra kicked in. It was almost as if Arjun was on auto pilot, defending himself against Amba, using the swordplay techniques that had, over the years, become part of his subconscious. He focused on the arrow that had just been released from behind him. It would strike him in microseconds.

'Udnayate!' he intoned softly, simultaneously jumping up and somersaulting in mid-air. The power of the mantra reinforced the action of his muscles, lifting him higher than he could have jumped on his own, until he was turning in mid-air above Amba's head, just as the arrow sailed past underneath him, striking Amba in the chest.

The momentum of the arrow lifted Amba off her feet and propelled her backwards as she fell heavily to the ground. She lay there, supine. The arrow tips were blunt and the armour would have protected her from harm, but she was out of the combat session for now.

One opponent down.

As his feet touched the ground, Arjun raced towards Tanveer. He had to take the archer out before he could shoot again.

Tanveer was already fitting a second arrow to his bow.

Varun was two feet away.

Where was Parth?

'Vegita Vriddhi!' A powerful, invisible, force suddenly gave additional strength to Arjun's muscles as he uttered the mantra, exponentially increasing his speed as he raced towards Tanveer.

Arjun reached Tanveer just as the archer let loose his second arrow.

It was too late to escape the arrow now. Instead of using a mantra, Arjun leveraged his own momentum, sharply tilting to the left, skidding as he tried to duck the arrow instead of trying to jump over it as he had done the first time.

He wasn't successful. Even as he went down, losing his balance in the process, the arrow struck his right shoulder and bounced off the armour harmlessly.

Arjun grimaced. He wasn't hurt. But the impact of the arrow would leave a painful bruise.

And the damage was done. Arjun hit the ground heavily, crashing into Tanveer who also went down.

Arjun recovered first, springing to his feet, planting his sword on Tanveer's armour.

Two down.

But the fall had robbed him of time. He felt a hard blow across his back.

Varun had caught up, no doubt using the same mantra for speed, and was now attacking him.

Arjun turned around swiftly and defended himself. The two boys were locked in combat for a few moments, thrusting and parrying, landing powerful strokes on each other's armours. In a real battle with swords that had not been blunted, both would have been wounded or worse. Even now, the blows would hurt and leave bruises.

Varun was strong, his blows potent and well-aimed, and Arjun struggled to get the upper hand.

Suddenly, there was movement at his side and Arjun saw Parth descend to the ground.

Had he been in the air? How ... ?

Now Arjun had two men to fight, both accomplished swordsmen. But he had only one sword.

The sound of swords clashing filled the air as the three Kshatriyas fought fiercely, Arjun switching his attention from Parth to Varun and back, trying his best to focus on both his opponents, ensuring that he didn't make any mistakes that would allow them to prevail over him.

Suddenly, Parth disappeared again.

Arjun was bewildered. What on earth was happening?

He attacked Varun with renewed vigour, driving his dorm-mate back with the ferocity of his blows.

Without warning, Arjun felt a stinging knock on his helmet from behind him, jarring his brains despite the protective armour absorbing the shock of the blow from the blunt sword.

He groaned. Parth!

It was a signal that the combat was over. Arjun had been 'killed' in battle. The blow to the head was a fatal one.

Arjun turned to see Parth standing behind him, helmet in hand, grinning.

Virendra strode up to them, clapping, as Amba and Tanveer rose from their supine positions and joined the others.

'Well done, Arjun,' Amba said warmly. 'Those were some good moves. And you put the mantras to good use, considering that you have had less than a week to practise.'

'Yes, well fought,' Parth agreed. 'Considering this was your first multi-player combat session, you were very impressive.'

Arjun bowed in acknowledgement and waited for Virendra's comments.

'You were good,' Virendra said. 'All the years of training showed up in your moves today.'

'But I got killed in the end,' Arjun said, looking dejected.

'Don't worry about that too much,' Virendra told him. 'You can't be perfect with just a week's practice. Remember that there is no Kshatriya in the Gana, as yet, who has excelled at multi-player combat. You need to work on the areas where you made mistakes, both strategic and tactical. We'll work on them together. With enough practice, a day will come when you will defeat the same four opponents who overcame you today. I know it will.'

Chapter Sixty-three

More Secrets

The Kshatriya Practice Field
The Gurukul

'So you see,' Virendra concluded, 'the two key pieces that were missing from your strategy pertained to your inability to expect the unexpected. Your assumptions didn't factor in the uncertainties of battle. If you had not assumed that your opponents were unarmed, you would have approached the battle differently. And if you had been able to keep an eye on Parth, you would have been better placed to counter his attack at the end. You underestimated your opponents; which, in turn, lowered your own performance and your ability to respond appropriately to the challenges you faced. Let that be the biggest lesson for you today.'

For the last hour, Virendra had been pointing out the weaknesses in Arjun's strategy and tactics during the combat and explaining how he could have done better. The two *Mahamatis* had left the field along with Varun and Tanveer immediately after the combat session concluded.

Arjun had listened attentively, realizing, for the first time, the importance of this training. The implications of his position were beginning to sink in. These were no longer sporting games — good exercise and fun to do. At home, at the end of each sparring or training session with his uncle, he would simply wash away the sweat from the sessions with a good shower. It didn't matter whether he did well or not, whether he won or lost the bout. Once the session was over Arjun would move on to other things that mattered—his schoolwork, tests and friends.

Things were no longer the same. Today it had finally dawned on him that his uncle had not spent the last six years in futile games. Unknown to Arjun, Virendra had been preparing him for this day; when he would slip into the shoes that his father had left behind. The scion of Yayati, leader of the Kshatriyas. These were not mere words. They were going to define his life from hereon.

And the combat session had driven home the realization that he was not yet ready for this role. If today's combat had been a real battle, he would have been dead. If there were warriors on Shukra's side who were even a tenth as accomplished as the four Kshatriyas he had faced today, it would be enough. If he was to be a leader like his father, he knew that he would have to prove himself to be worthy of that role, of that title.

Of his bloodline.

And he was determined to prove his mettle. So he listened carefully, taking notes where required, his burning desire to master the destiny that had been thrust upon him honing his focus to a fine point, so that no distraction could affect him.

But he wanted answers to his questions. His entire strategy for the practice session had depended on the two mysteries that had foxed him and caught him off guard. Arjun knew it was not by accident that he had been placed in the situation in which he had found himself during the combat. And he knew that his uncle had the answers to his questions.

'Now let's tackle the two big questions that have been on your mind,' Virendra smiled at him, as they sat in the shade of the trees that lined the boundary of the Kshatriya practice field that ran parallel to the river. 'Your first question is about the weapons of your opponents, isn't it?'

'Yes. If I had known they had weapons when we started, my strategy would've been different. I would have gone for Tanveer first, not Amba. What happened there? How did they suddenly get their weapons?' Arjun paused, suddenly remembering something that had slipped out of his memory in the rush of activities over the last week. He had seen exactly the same thing happen on the night of the battle with Shukra's monsters. Both his mother and Virendra were unarmed when they had left the SUV, but when the black fog appeared, their weapons, too, had appeared out of nowhere. In fact, Virendra had possessed two swords, one of which he had given to Arjun that night.

'There's a simple answer to that question,' Virendra told him. 'And it is time I taught you about carrying weapons. Or, rather, not carrying them. I will start by reiterating the basic principles of Kshatriya mantras, which you already know, but which bear repeating. And don't roll your eyes.'

'I'm not rolling my eyes,' Arjun protested.

Virendra studied his nephew for a moment. He had fully expected Arjun to groan and complain, as he usually did when Virendra repeated things too often for Arjun's liking. But Virendra saw something in Arjun's face that he had not seen before. He couldn't put his finger on it, but for just that fleeting instant, Arjun had reminded Virendra of his brother, Rudrapratap.

Something inside Virendra stirred. Was the prophecy finally coming to fruition? When he had stated to the *Mahamati* Council that Arjun would be ready very soon, he hadn't felt as confident as he had sounded. Virendra had not wanted to dampen the hopes of the *Mahamatis*; not when so much was at stake. Of course, he believed in Arjun's potential, but not in his readiness to take on the responsibilities that would be his as Yayati's true heir.

But now, as he gazed upon his nephew, he couldn't help feeling hopeful. Maybe the boy would be ready sooner than anyone expected.

Which was good. It would only strengthen the plan.

'Sorry.' The hint of a smile crossed Virendra's face. 'It's just that I've got accustomed to you protesting when I repeat basic principles which you already know.' His face grew serious as he resumed his explanation. 'As you learnt in your first lesson at the Gurukul, it is not only the Rishis who use mantras. Every Kshatriya who is accepted into the Gurukul also has the power to use mantras, though the mantras we use are very different from theirs. Now, tell me, what are the three main categories of Kshatriya mantras that I have taught you?'

Arjun's face was a study in seriousness as he replied, remembering
the theory class at the start of his first lesson with Virendra at the
Gurukul. 'The first category comprises mantras that are used to activate
weapons. These are not in use today but were actively used in ancient
times, especially while deploying celestial weapons — the weapons of
the Devas. These weapons were operated by the sound of the mantras.'

'Very good. The second category?'

'Mantras used in battle as an aid to increase speed, strength, stamina
and other physical actions that can reinforce our physical attributes.'

'Correct. As all five of you did today. Your application was especially
brilliant since you had just a few days to practice the use of the mantras.
Though I did notice that Amba held back on using any mantra that
could have helped her increase the impact of her blows. I guess she was
going easy on you today. Expect more trouble in future sessions with
her. And the third category?'

'Mantras that are used to consecrate our weapons to reinforce their
strength, accuracy and effectiveness.'

'Brilliant. And today you saw the application of theory in practice.'

Arjun nodded. He had learned today that the theory that Virendra
had been teaching him over the last week was not just academic in
nature. Everything had real, practical applications and could mean the
difference between life and death in a real combat situation.

'There is a fourth category that I didn't tell you about earlier, because
it is not associated with the use of weapons or in providing aid in battle.
It pertains to the storage of our weapons. Every Kshatriya who is capable
of using the three categories of mantras that you have already learned
about, is also capable of creating their own, personal, storage space for
their weapons. There is a mantra for that which I will teach you. Every
weapon that we possess has a mantra to recall it from the storage space;
to summon it into our grasp, quite literally. It is like having your own
code or password to open a locker in which your weapon is stored.'

Understanding dawned on Arjun. He remembered a story from the
Mahabharata which DJ sir had narrated to them. It concerned his own
namesake from the epic, the supreme archer, Arjuna, who had been

tasked with the protection of the women and children of the Vrishnis, after the departure of Lord Krishna from *Bhu-lok*. The group he was supposed to protect had been attacked by dacoits. At the most critical juncture, however, Arjuna failed to remember the mantras that would summon his weapons to him, as the result of an earlier curse.

Arjun had always wondered what that meant. How could Arjuna summon weapons using a mantra anyway? DJ sir had never explained. Now, however, he understood what the Mahabharata had referred to. Arjuna could not summon his weapons because he had forgotten the mantras to open the 'locker', as Virendra had described it, where the weapons were stored.

'And your second question,' Virendra continued, 'is regarding Parth and his disappearance during the fight.'

Arjun nodded, trying to focus on what Virendra was about to say now, even as the revelation about mantras used to summon weapons continued to occupy his thoughts.

'It is quite simple,' Virendra explained. 'Let me show you.'

Chapter Sixty-four

Secret Plans

That night

The Gurukul

Arjun opened the door of the cottage, which housed his dormitory, and looked around cautiously.

It was past eleven o'clock and the Gurukul was draped in a cloak of darkness, slumber and silence. Nothing stirred. Even the glowing orbs of light that usually lit up the central avenue and public areas had been extinguished.

He stood there for a few moments, making sure that no one was around, then looked back and nodded to Varun, Agastya and Tanveer, who were standing behind him, waiting.

'Let's go,' Arjun whispered to them and the three boys slipped out, shutting the door silently, and made their way down the central avenue to another cottage on the opposite side of the avenue.

They stopped in front of it.

Arjun frowned. 'This is not a good idea.'

'Then you can tell her yourself.' Varun rapped lightly on the door. It flew open immediately and a girl came out. She was Varun's twin and, though they were not identical twins, the resemblance was obvious.

She beamed at the three boys as she shut the door of the cottage behind her. 'This is so exciting!' she whispered.

'Go ahead,' Varun grinned at Arjun. 'Tell her.'

'Tell me what?' the girl looked enquiringly at Arjun.

Arjun shook his head in exasperation. 'Nothing, Adira. It's just that I didn't think I had the right to ask you to join us tonight.'

'Oooh, good one,' Varun chuckled.

Adira put her hands on her hips. 'I get it. You don't want me to come along with you. Because it's too dangerous? Because I'm a girl?'

Varun chuckled again, clearly tickled by this exchange.

'Zip it!' Arjun told him, then turned to Adira. 'Look, you're one of the best fighters in the Gurukul. I'm sure you could whip Varun's butt any day.'

'Hey!' Varun was indignant.

Arjun ignored him and carried on. 'So I'm not worried about your safety or anything like that. In fact, it's great to have you come along. I'll feel safer. Honestly. But it is also true that I really don't have the right to ask you to come along with us tonight. This is my mission, not yours. I really shouldn't be involving you at all.'

'And what about these low life guys?' Adira gestured to Arjun's three dormitory mates. 'How come you can involve them and not me?'

Tanveer muttered something under his breath, but Adira ignored him.

'I didn't have a choice,' Arjun grinned. 'You know how they are. Pile-ons.'

'Well, if it helps ease your conscience, you really didn't ask me to come along. When Varun told me what you guys were planning tonight, I told him I'd be a part of it. I didn't ask.'

'That's true,' Varun agreed. 'She virtually arm-twisted me into being included. She wanted ...'

'Shut up, Varun.' Adira shot him a glance that made him grimace, even in the darkness.

'Okay, enough talk,' Arjun said. 'Maya must be waiting for us. Let's go.'

The five youngsters made their way down the central avenue, heading towards the rock that barred the way in and out of the Gurukul.

Maya was indeed standing there, waiting. She looked surprised when she saw that Arjun was not alone.

'I had to tell Varun, Agastya and Tanveer about our plan,' Arjun confessed to Maya. 'They're my dorm-mates. They had to know.'

'And we decided that this was too great an adventure to let you both carry on by yourselves,' Varun chipped in.

'And when Varun mentioned it to me, I wanted to come along too,' Adira added.

Arjun shrugged. 'Well, there you are. Anyway, Varun and Agastya are two of the few guys who know the mantra that will allow us to walk through this rock here.'

Maya looked doubtful. 'AJ, there is a reason I am doing this in secret and didn't want to involve too many people. I don't know if I'm right or wrong. I'm just acting on a hunch. We could all get into trouble.'

Arjun looked around at the others. 'There's still time to go back. Varun, you can help us get out and then return.'

'I'm not going back.' Varun sounded determined. 'And if I do, who is going to let you back in?'

'I'm not leaving either,' Tanveer chimed in.

'Wild horses et cetera,' Adira said, apparently bored with the drama.

'You need a Rishi along,' Agastya added, grinning wickedly. 'You can't depend only on Kshatriyas to protect you if you encounter the *bhutagana*.'

Varun snorted in response.

'Well, then,' Arjun looked at Maya. 'It's settled. Let's go.'

'*Vikurute vyapaniya!*' Varun intoned, then gestured for Arjun to lead the way.

They walked through the hillside and into the clearing where they had battled Shukra's monsters just a few days ago.

A full moon lit up the sky above them and its silver light bathed the clearing in a soft glow, enhanced by the soft light from the millions of stars that twinkled in the sky beside it.

With Arjun in the lead, they crossed the clearing and entered the forest beyond, which was in pitch black darkness on this side of the hill.

Unlike the forest in which the Gurukul was built, the trees here densely crowded together, blocking out all light.

'How are we going to find our way through the forest in the dark?' Maya asked in dismay.

'Like I said. What would you do without me?' Agastya chuckled. '*Vidyutate*,' he intoned, with a flourish. A softly glowing sphere of light appeared before them, hovering in the air, floating before them as they walked, lighting their path and a few feet of the forest before them.

'What was that?' Maya was curious. It hadn't sounded like a mantra.

'*Laghu* mantras,' Agastya replied. 'You wouldn't have learned them yet. They teach them to you at a pretty advanced level. And a mantra like this is one of the higher mantras. It isn't magic, you know. Really more a manipulation of matter, just like the mantra that allows us to pass through the rock. Only, in this case, the mantra energizes matter and it is the excitation of the particles of matter that the mantra touches through sound that produces the light you see,' Agastya finished, enjoying his little lecture.

Maya remembered what Jignesh had told her in the lessons she had had over the last few days.

'There is no such thing as magic,' he had assured her. 'No one can make something out of nothing. Not even the Devas. There are always ingredients that are consumed, a process that consumes the ingredients in some form, and an output, which is a physical manifestation of the process. Mantras are the trigger for the process. You could say they are the switch that needs to be flipped in order to start the process. Mantras are not magic. Every mantra has a process by which it achieves what it is designed to do. Anyone can use mantras. But, in the hands of a powerful yogi, they can be used to accomplish anything.'

Maya understood. 'You mean *laghu* mantras are really shortened versions of full mantras?'

Agastya nodded. 'Like mantras on speed dial.'

'I'd like to try them,' Maya said.

'If Jignesh hasn't taught you *laghu* mantras yet, then you aren't ready for it,' Agastya said, sounding doubtful. 'You've only been here a few days, after all.'

'Still,' Maya insisted. 'I want to have a go at it. Tell me the mantra again.'

Agastya shrugged. 'Sure. *Vidyutate.*'

Maya stopped walking. She wanted to be able to concentrate. In her second session with Jignesh, he had told her that concentration was the key to harness the power of mantras.

'You have learnt the importance of sound, of correct articulation of the mantras. That is the foundation to recite an effective mantra. But the key to making a mantra work is the application of the mind while reciting the mantra. That is why some people use mantras more effectively than others. Your thoughts need to be focused completely on what the mantra needs to achieve. Without that, the mantra will not be completely effective. And that is why, even *sadhs* can recite mantras and obtain some benefits from them — peace of mind, calmness, protection from evil spirits. But only a yogi can effectively use the other five classes of mantras.'

The others stopped and watched as Maya closed her eyes and tried to empty her mind of clutter, as she had learned to do in the meditation classes. She tried to focus on the light that she wanted the mantra to produce. Agastya had said that the excitation of the particles of matter produced the light. That was what she needed to focus on. The sound of the mantra energizing matter. But it was hard. It was like trying to hold onto a slippery rubber ball.

'*Vidyutate!*' she intoned, ensuring that her articulation matched Agastya's.

She opened her eyes. The ball of light that Agastya had created still illuminated the forest around them. There should have been a second ball of light. But it wasn't there.

'What happened?' she asked. 'Did anything happen?'

'There was a flicker of light,' Varun told her. 'But just for a moment.'

'Maya, that was pretty good!' Agastya sounded impressed. 'Your enunciation of the mantra was perfect. But it isn't easy to manipulate matter. You need practice. Try again.'

Maya closed her eyes and tried a few more times, but it was the same result every time. The others reported a brief flicker of light that lasted for barely a second before it went out.

Only on the final try did she make some progress. When she opened her eyes, a ragged ball of light hung before her eyes for a fleeting instant, before winking out.

'I did it!' Maya was exultant.

'Yes, you did,' Varun agreed. 'Look, I'd love to stand around and watch you create one of those glowing thingummys, but we don't really have all night, you know. We need to be back before anyone discovers we're gone or else we'll be in hot water. And as good as Ags is at making mantras work, there's no mantra in the three *loks* that will save us if that happens.'

'Oh yeah, sure, sorry,' Maya couldn't disguise the delight in her voice. One thing was clear to her now. She would not be leaving the Gurukul. A question bothered her, though.

'If you guys can create light, then why were flaming torches being carried when you battled Shukra's monsters? Wouldn't it have been easier to have lights like this one all over the place — they would have been brighter and would have lit up a larger area.'

Agastya smiled. 'You know, that's a good question. The answer is pretty simple. When we were told by Maharishi Ratan about what was happening in the clearing, we all rushed out chanting the Narsimha mantra. We couldn't possibly chant any other mantra at that time, and our priority was protecting the Gurukul. Yet, we needed light to be able to see what we were up against. So the novices were told to carry torches while the advanced Rishis chanted the Narsimha mantra.'

Maya nodded and the group continued on their way. In the light thrown off by the glowing orb that hung before them, Arjun tried to read the expression on Maya's face. It was a mix of hope, fear and apprehension. He knew what she was trying to accomplish. He didn't understand her reasons, and when she had come to him earlier that day, after dinner, and told him of her plan, he had initially tried to dissuade her. When she had remained obstinate, he had decided that he would accompany her. There was no way he was going to allow her to carry out her crazy plan on her own. Now, as they all walked together, he was grateful for the company of his friends. He realized that Maya hadn't really made any friends in the Gurukul. She wasn't a part of any classes, remaining confined with Jignesh for all of her training. Her free time was spent in homework and preparation, so she never had an opportunity to mix with the other students. Hanging out with the others would be good for her, thought Arjun, even if it was on a risky mission like this one.

'Okay,' Maya took a deep breath, as they reached the forest path where Virendra had parked the Land Cruiser a few nights ago; from where they had made their dash towards the clearing and the Gurukul. 'Here we go. Let's see what lies in store for us.'

The six of them began the long walk through the jungle, down the forest track.

Chapter Sixty-five

Back to the Gandharva Valley

The Pandava Falls
Madhya Pradesh

Arjun gave Maya an enquiring look. 'You said you knew how to get in.'

They had walked all the way from the Gurukul, through the national park, vaulted over the locked gate of the park and then trudged down the narrow road, past the sleeping village, until they had reached the Pandava falls. They were now in front of the grey cliff face where Arjun had stood with his mother and uncle just a week ago, at the very spot where they had entered the valley of the Gandharvas.

'I do,' Maya said bravely, sounding more confident than she felt. 'I know the mantra that will do the trick.'

Agastya looked startled as he heard her words. He immediately shook his head. 'It won't work.'

'It will.' Deep in her heart, Maya hoped against hope that it would. It was one of the mantras she had come across in her father's diary. 'Why are you so sceptical anyway?' she snapped at Agastya.

Agastya threw up his hands and, ignoring her question, looked accusingly at Arjun. 'You didn't tell us this was part of the plan. I thought you had a way to get in. If I had known earlier that you were depending on a novice using the *Gandharvalok* mantra to get us in, I would have saved us all the trouble. That is, if the mantra she knows really is the one that can open the entrance to the land of the Gandharvas. But knowing the mantra isn't enough; none of us have been trained to use it. How do you expect it to work?'

'Well, you can go back,' Maya said sharply. 'I didn't ask any of you to come along.'

'Okay, okay,' Arjun interjected. 'Let's all keep calm and give it a try, shall we? Maya, why don't you go ahead?'

Agastya shrugged indifferently.

'*Gandharva krpaya vishto!*' Maya intoned in a low voice.

Even as she spoke the words, the other five felt something in the darkness swirl around them as goose bumps ran up their arms. Something did seem to be happening. But what was it?

Maya finished and looked at the cliff face. Nothing seemed to have changed. Nothing appeared to have happened.

She was disappointed. Had the mantra not worked after all?

Agastya snorted. 'I'm telling you ...' He broke off as Arjun extended his hand towards the rock face, and into the rock.

'It worked!' Arjun's face shone in the light thrown off by the ball of light that Agastya had created.

A sense of elation gripped Maya. This was just further proof that whatever was in her father's diary was important. Until now, she had not been very confident of her plan to visit the Gandharvas, especially since the *Mahamati* Council had refused to entertain the possibility of asking them for help. But now, she knew that her instincts had been correct. Surely there was something that the Gandharvas would know.

'I don't believe it.' Agastya's bewilderment showed on his face. 'It isn't possible. You are a novice. You can't even create a ball of light! How on earth did you ... ?' Words failed him and he shook his head again, this time in disbelief.

'Good work, Maya,' Arjun beamed at her. He turned to Agastya. 'Ags, will your lamp follow us through the rock?'

'No. The Gandharva valley is on another plane. We are stepping through a portal that will take us out of *Bhu-lok* and into *Gandharva-lok*.'

'It doesn't matter,' Maya said, suddenly. 'It isn't night time on the other side of the rock.'

'How do you know?' Adira wondered.

'I am not sure but I ... I just know.' Maya was as surprised as the others at her own words. She couldn't explain it, but she almost felt the warm sunshine of the Gandharva valley on her skin.

'Arjun gestured to the others. 'Follow me. Let's find out.'

Maya watched as Arjun walked through the rock, followed by Adira, Tanveer, and Varun. As Agastya passed her, she saw wonder and confusion in his eyes. She understood his bewilderment. The way the Gurukul functioned was simple. The children who came to study there had some power or the other but not the ability to use these effectively. It was only through careful training at the Gurukul, under the watchful eyes of the *Mahamatis*, that each student learned their powers, understood their strengths and developed their ability to use their powers to the maximum. This process took years. Even Arjun, she knew, had trained for the last six years with Virendra, even though he had not known at that time what he was being prepared for.

It was natural, therefore, for Agastya to expect that Maya, who had not even been officially accepted into the Gurukul as a novice, should not be able to use the mantras, especially the ones as powerful as this. Her lack of experience and expertise had been clearly demonstrated in her failure to do something as simple as create a ball of light by using mantras to manipulate matter. Opening a portal to another world was on a vastly different scale and a much higher level.

As Agastya disappeared within the rock, Maya followed, not quite relishing the feeling of fluid rock flowing around her body, touching her without quite providing the sensation of touch.

She emerged from the rock into blinding sunshine and a brilliant, azure sky, just as she had predicted when she was on the other side of the portal.

And froze in her tracks.

The four young Kshatriyas stood, weapons in hand, along with

Agastya, in defensive postures. Surrounding them on three sides, were
Gandharvas, armed to the teeth and brandishing their weapons.

It seemed that the six youngsters were intruding and the Gandharvas
weren't too happy about it.

Chapter Sixty-six

Audience with Visvavasu

The Gandharva Valley

Visvavasu glared at the four boys and two girls who stood before him. His face was grim.

When the Gandharva guards had accosted the group from the Gurukul, Arjun had demanded to see Visvavasu. Whether it was in response to that demand or a matter of protocol, they had been brought into Visvavasu's presence immediately, after being marched through the valley as prisoners of the guards.

They now stood in the great hall where Arjun had first met the Gandharva king.

'How dare you!' Visvavasu thundered. 'Entry into our world is possible only with our permission.' He looked at Arjun. 'When you came here earlier, your uncle had sent word to us that he wished to see us and consult with us. We agreed because Kanak is an old friend. Your father, Rudra, was also a dear friend. But even they would not enter our world without our permission. But what you have done today ...' He stopped and fixed the group before him with a steely eye.

'How did you activate the portal?' he demanded. 'Who taught you the mantra? Who, at the Gurukul, is responsible for this intrusion?'

'No one taught us the mantra,' Arjun sounded defiant. He was rebellious by nature and Visvavasu's proclamation of rules that were not meant to be broken had stirred his naturally defiant spirit. 'No one at the Gurukul even knows we are here.'

Visvavasu glared at him. 'That is not possible. A Gandharva spell protects the portal. No human can break the spell without the mantra. Especially not children. Only one of the Maharishis at the Gurukul would be capable of this.'

'But I'm telling you the truth,' Arjun insisted, his voice quiet but firm. 'We came on our own. And we used the mantra without anyone from the Gurukul teaching it to us. I am the scion of Yayati. I would not lie about this. We come with a purpose that is all our own.'

A thoughtful look crossed the Gandharva king's face. He surveyed the group, looking carefully at each of the faces before him.

Agastya's face was white with fear. Varun and Tanveer were visibly nervous, trying to hide their trembling hands behind their backs. Adira fidgeted and Maya's face betrayed her apprehension — it was she who had brought them here, after all. Only Arjun seemed calm — he had been in the presence of the Gandharvas before and he held Visvavasu's gaze as it settled on him. The other five seemed overawed to be in the presence of beings they had only heard or read about. Everything they knew about the Gandharvas indicated that the demi-gods, while friendly in general, made terrible enemies and were ruthless when disturbed. Even the Pandavas had not been spared their wrath on more than one occasion.

'If I am to believe you,' Visvavasu said finally, 'I must know where you obtained the mantra from. It is not something that is freely shared. Only a select few have access to it. Someone must have given it to you. Who was it?'

Arjun was silent. He didn't want to expose Maya. There was no telling what retribution the Gandharva king would bring upon her for this intrusion.

Visvavasu took his silence to mean a reluctance to tell the truth about who was behind their visit. His face grew dark.

'I don't care about your lineage, boy,' he snarled at Arjun. 'If you do not reveal who is behind this transgression ...'

'It was me,' an urgent voice spoke up. Maya couldn't take it anymore. She stepped forward, her face pale, her voice tremulous. 'Our visit to your valley was planned by me. It was my idea. I was the one who wanted to come here. They only accompanied me out of concern for my safety. If you have to hold someone responsible, it is I.'

Visvavasu was clearly taken aback. His face registered his surprise. Then, he frowned. 'What trick is this, now? Out with the truth, I have no time for games. You are only testing my patience!'

Maya's voice shook with emotion and fear as she responded. She had never spoken to a king before, let alone a Gandharva king. 'My name is Maya. I am the daughter of ...' she hesitated for a moment. If her father had truly been a great Maharishi, as everyone had told her, the Gandharva king would have heard of him. But what if he had not?

'I am the daughter of Maharishi Dhruv,' Maya completed her introduction.

She saw recognition in Visvavasu's face and continued hurriedly, trying to get in her explanation before the king could take off again. 'My father was killed by Shukracharya, a week ago, and I was brought to the Gurukul, after having escaped from Shukra. Before I fled, my father had asked me to take his diary with me. It contained his notes. I learned the mantra to enter your valley from this diary.'

There was silence when she finished. Visvavasu studied her face as he considered her explanation. Varun, Adira, Tanveer and Agastya looked at each other, plainly surprised. They had not known Maya's background or what had led to her arrival in the Gurukul. All that they, and the other students at the Gurukul, had been told was that Maya was a friend of Arjun's and she had accompanied him in his flight from Delhi.

'So,' Visvavasu said finally, '*you* are the daughter of Dhruv.'

Maya caught the emphasis but didn't understand what it meant.

'Let's say I believe your story,' Visvavasu continued. 'There are still unanswered questions. Let's start with this one. How were you able to recite the mantra correctly and access the entrance to our valley?'

'I don't know,' Maya admitted, truthfully.

'You do know that it takes a high level of yogic power to open the portal?' There was curiosity in the Gandharva king's eyes now.

'Y-yes,' Maya stammered. 'I really don't know how I did it, but I just had a feeling that I would be able to.'

'Hmmm.' Visvavasu pondered her reply. 'And how were you so confident that you could gain access to our world using a mantra that you have not been trained to use, if I am to believe you?'

'I-I don't know,' Maya's voice grew stronger as she realized that the king was partially convinced by her explanation. 'I guess I just thought it was a simple enough mantra. I've been pretty good at my lessons so far. Even *Mahamati* Jignesh has complimented me on my ability to pick up mantras and recite them well.'

Visvavasu's eyes did not leave Maya's face. He continued to study her as he spoke. 'And why did you want to come here? What did you hope to accomplish?'

Maya's hopes rose. Finally, she was going to get her chance to ask the question she had wanted to get an answer to, ever since she got here.

Chapter Sixty-seven

More on Brahmabhasha

The Gandharva Valley

Visvavasu was incredulous. 'You want help to read *Brahmabhasha?*'

'Yes,' Maya affirmed. 'There are several entries in my father's diary in an unfamiliar language. The *Mahamatis* believe it is *Brahmabhasha*. I thought the Gandharvas would know more about it than us.'

'Where is this diary?'

Maya reached into the folds of her white robes and pulled out the diary, placing it in Visvavasu's outstretched hand.

Silence reigned as the Gandharva king flipped through the pages of the notebook.

Finally, he looked up.

'Come with me.' Visvavasu gestured to Maya to follow him, then addressed the others. 'Wait here for us.'

Visvavasu took Maya inside the chamber where he had met with Arjun and his folks a week ago. The Gandharva king took the gilded chair at the head of the long wooden table that occupied the centre of the room and gestured to Maya to sit in the chair to his right.

Maya sat down, wondering what was going to happen next.

For a few moments, the king said nothing, but stared into the distance, collecting his thoughts.

Maya waited. She didn't know why she had been singled out from the group. It should have been clear to Visvavasu that Arjun was their leader. And he had also been pre-ordained to lead the fight against Shukra, as Yayati's heir.

'I wouldn't have believed it,' the Gandharva king said at length, 'if you hadn't been able to enter our world so easily, and if you had not mentioned *Brahmabhasha*. And you are the daughter of Dhruv — of a Maharishi — wielding powers that even I cannot understand. When I first heard that they were bringing you to the Gurukul, I was surprised. *Sadhs* are not permitted access to the Gurukul. And everyone who knew Dhruv knew that you are a *sadh*, or else you would have been enrolled in a Gurukul many years ago. But if you were able, without training, to recite a mantra as powerful as the one that guards the doors to our world, then I have to admit that we were wrong about you. Yet, how could everyone have made such a grievous error? To overlook a power like yours?'

'I don't really have that kind of power,' Maya said slowly, a little embarrassed. Visvavasu was overestimating her abilities. 'Truthfully, I have no idea how or why the mantra worked, when I can barely use any but the simplest mantras to achieve anything,' she said, thinking about the mantra that Agastya had taught her in the forest and her failure to create even a small ball of light. 'Perhaps it was a fluke,' she concluded.

Visvavasu shook his head. 'Nothing in this world happens by chance. There is no such thing as luck. Only karma. You create your luck by your own actions, both in this life and your previous life. But it is not my intention to give you a lecture on karma.' He looked at her. 'Have you heard of the prophecy?'

Maya shook her head.

'So they haven't told you.' Visvavasu's brow furrowed with thought. After a few moments, he continued. 'Well, I will. When the Saptarishis commanded Shukra to desist from his plan to open up the gates to the netherworlds, 5,000 years ago, they also created a prophecy. At least some people believe it was a prophecy. Others believe it was a set of instructions on how to stop Shukra if he ever disregarded the Saptarishis and made another attempt to unleash the inhabitants of the netherworlds onto *Bhu-lok*. It was divided into three parts and hidden away in different places. It is believed that one part of the prophecy was kept in *Bhu-lok* — your world; another part was hidden in *Devalok*; and the third piece was hidden in *Gandharvalok*.'

'Why was it divided into three parts and hidden away?' Maya wondered.

'Because the Saptarishis wanted to ensure that Shukra never got his hands on it. They never quite trusted him. They believed he might risk another attempt, especially in Kaliyuga when the Devas and the Saptarishis would not be around to stop him. If Shukra knew what the prophecy contained, then he would ensure that all the assumptions that the prophecy was based on, would never become reality.'

Maya's eyes widened. 'And the prophecy mentions Arjun. Is that why everyone believes that Shukra wants to kill him?'

Visvavasu nodded. 'The first part of the prophecy was guarded by the Sangha. Somehow — and no one has ever found out how — Shukra got to know what it contained. The prophecy itself doesn't mention Arjun by name. But it does mention two very specific details that clearly point to Arjun as being the One who will be responsible for defeating Shukra. First, the prophecy says that it is Yayati's heir who is the One. Second, the details of the birth of Yayati's heir exactly match the circumstances of Arjun's birth. It is not difficult to believe that a powerful Rishi like Shukra, too, would have put two and two together and identified Arjun as the One.'

He paused, before resuming. 'But it is not that part of the prophecy that I wanted to tell you about today. It is the part that is hidden in our world — the second part of the prophecy. Fortunately, that has remained concealed and undiscovered by Shukra but I have heard that it contains a few elements that I always believed to be impossible. Quite frankly, I never believed in the prophecy. Until today.'

Maya waited for him to tell her what had made him change his views. She could guess that it was for this purpose that he had brought her into this chamber, though it still didn't explain why he had singled her out.

'You see,' Visvavasu leaned forward and looked her in the eye, 'the prophecy mentions some of the weapons that will be used against Shukra. And it also talks about an ancient tongue rising again and revealing secrets.'

Maya understood. 'Brahmabhasha!'

'Exactly. I always scoffed at the idea of Brahmabhasha returning. With the Devas locked away in their own world it just didn't seem likely. Yet, here you are today, carrying a notebook which has inscriptions in that ancient tongue.'

'You mean that the verses that I cannot read in the diary are really in Brahmabhasha?'

'Yes. We Gandharvas cannot read the language, but we do recognize the words.'

Maya despaired. 'If the prophecy says Brahmabhasha will reveal secrets, then there must be some way of deciphering the inscriptions!'

'No doubt,' Visvavasu agreed. 'But I cannot help you there. What I can tell you, though, is that you must find the other two parts of the prophecy if you wish to stop Shukra. Without these parts you will be shooting in the dark, trying to figure out what will work and what won't. If the prophecy has been accurate so far, perhaps it really is more than just a prediction of events based on assumptions. Maybe those who say that it is a set of instructions are correct. If that is indeed the case, you will need those instructions.'

'But how do we find the parts of the prophecy hidden in your world and in Devalok? That sounds like an impossible task!'

Visvavasu shrugged. 'You will have to find a way.'

'And how do we get the verses in the diary deciphered?'

'There's only one person who can help you with that.'

'And who is that?'

'Satyavachana.'

Chapter Sixty-eight

Hot Water

Day 11

The Guesthouse
The Gurukul

The six children gathered in the sitting room of the guesthouse, their faces glum. After Maya's private audience with Visvavasu, the Gandharva king had arranged for word to be sent to the Gurukul about their presence in the Gandharva valley.

Virendra, Pramila and Tiwari had duly arrived at the Gandharva valley, in the Land Cruiser, and picked up the children from the Pandava falls. The journey back to the Gurukul had been completed in deathly silence. Neither the children nor the adults spoke. The group was keenly aware that they were in trouble and the adults, presumably, were going to address the situation only when they were back at the Gurukul.

Maya was deeply troubled. This entire expedition had been her idea. And the trip to meet the Gandharvas had turned out to be futile. They were as clueless about Brahmabhasha as everyone else. Now, the other five were also in hot water because of her.

The drive to the Gurukul had been uneventful. When they reached, Tiwari disappeared with the SUV, to park it wherever it had been hidden all these days, while Virendra and Pramila deposited the children at the guesthouse and left without a word.

'Guys,' Maya was the first to speak after the two left, 'I'm sorry.'

'For what?' Adira sounded surprised. 'I was just waiting for the grown-ups to leave before I could thank you for the experience. I don't think I would have ever got to meet the Gandharvas if you hadn't cooked up this plan.'

The others nodded, everyone but Agastya. 'It's all very well to be excited about the Gandharvas,' he said, his face surly, 'but the *Mahamatis* are not going to take this well. God only knows what punishment is in store for us. I don't know about you guys but if this stupid misadventure affects our final assessment, I'm going to be really ... '

'Ever the pessimist,' Varun broke in. He looked at Agastya. 'Can't you think happy thoughts for a change?'

'I'm only being realistic,' Agastya glared at him. 'We aren't supposed to go out of the Gurukul without a *Mahamati* accompanying us. That is the rule. We all know the rule and we all broke it. Now we will face the consequences. That is the rule of Karma.'

'Sure,' Adira agreed with him. 'That is Karma alright. But no one compelled us to accompany Maya. Least of all Maya herself. Each one of us is completely responsible for our own actions and decisions. We all volunteered. We made a choice. Whatever the consequences, we should be ready to face it.'

'Never mind the law of Karma,' Tanveer broke in. 'I want to know what you were talking about with the Gandharva king, Maya. Why did he want to speak to you in private?'

Maya recounted her conversation with Visvavasu to the others.

'Wow!' Varun commented when she had finished. 'So there really *is* a prophecy!'

'You mean you didn't know for sure?' Maya didn't understand.

'Well we've always heard about the prophecy,' Adira explained, 'but we never knew what it said. It is so closely guarded by the Sangha that only the *Mahamatis* know what the prophecy contains. And I think that even among them, only a few really know. For us students, it has always been a fantastic legend. Like the return of Shukra.'

'That's no legend,' Maya assured her. 'Shukra is very real. He killed my father. And he will stop at nothing to achieve his plans now that the Saptarishis and the Devas are no longer around to stop him.'

'The Sangha must have a plan,' Agastya said. 'They will not sit around and watch while Shukra opens the gates of *Pataala*.'

'They do,' Arjun agreed. He looked at Maya. 'Your dad was a part of it. Don't you remember? The night we first met the *Mahamatis*? When they first saw the diary, they said something about your dad searching for many years for weapons to defeat Shukra? They even said that the inscriptions in the diary, written in *Brahmabhasha*, could have something to do with whatever he may have discovered. Maybe that's why your dad used to travel so often. Perhaps he was out searching for something?'

Maya frowned, thinking hard. 'Dad did travel often,' she said slowly. 'Perhaps far too often for a schoolteacher. I never really thought about it then. It didn't seem important. And since he always left me at your house, I never lacked for company. You could be right, Arjun.'

'But if there is a prophecy,' Adira interjected, addressing Arjun, 'and it clearly identifies you as the one who will lead the *Sangha* and *Gana* against Shukra, then perhaps you should be the one looking for those weapons, whatever they are.'

Arjun looked at her in surprise. 'You're kidding, right? I mean, how can *I* find the weapons? I don't even know what they are!'

'Adira may have a point, AJ,' Maya responded. 'There are three parts to the prophecy. While only the *Sangha* — and Shukra — know what the first part of it contains, no one knows what is concealed in the other two parts. Even the Gandharvas don't, from what Visvavasu told me. All he could confirm was that the Gandharva prophecy actually mentions the weapons. It can tell us what we should be searching for! Who knows what else it contains? And what more could be hidden in the *Devalok* prophecy?'

Varun understood where Maya was going with this. 'You're saying that Arjun should be looking for the other two parts of the prophecy.'

'Are you nuts?' Arjun exploded. 'We're already in trouble for a short visit to *Gandharvalok*. And you're suggesting that I go traipsing in the world of the Gandharvas looking for the prophecy, when I don't even know where to start. Not to mention that the third part of the prophecy is effectively out of bounds for us, hidden as it is in *Devalok*, which I can't enter even if I were allowed to!'

'Not "I",' Maya smiled at him. '*We*. I'll help you.'

'Hey,' Varun protested. 'Don't leave me out. I'll also help.'

'Me, too,' Adira said, excitedly.

'I'm not staying back when you guys are having fun,' Tanveer grinned. 'Count me in.'

They all looked at Agastya, who sat there, sullen and silent.

'Come on, Ags,' Adira cajoled him. 'We need a strong Rishi with us. Wasn't it you who said that we Kshatriyas can't handle trouble on our own?'

'Fine,' came the surly reply. 'I'll come along. But I'm warning you now. You guys are going on a wild goose chase. And when the *Mahamatis* come to know, there will be hell to pay.'

Arjun looked at Maya. 'He is right, you know. We should get permission from the *Mahamatis*.'

'And what if they refuse?'

'It won't come to that,' Agastya said, perking up slightly. 'Whether the *Mahamatis* permit us or not is secondary. As Arjun just said, we don't even know where to start.'

They all pondered the dilemma.

'I have an idea,' Maya said finally. 'But you have to promise not to tell anyone.'

Chapter Sixty-nine

The Council Debates

The Assembly Hall
Gurukul

Mahesh fixed the six children standing before the *Mahamati* Council with a stern eye. He was flanked on either side by the other four members of the council — Parth, Jignesh, Usha and Amba. Virendra, Pramila and Tiwari sat to one side, silent observers.

'We have debated amongst ourselves,' Mahesh began, looking from one anxious face to the next, 'but we have been unable to come to a conclusion. One thing is clear to us and should be clear to you: you have transgressed. A cardinal rule of the Gurukul has been broken. No member of the *Gana* can move around outside a Gurukul without the presence of a member of the *Sangha*. Yet, here, we have a case where the six of you, not even full members of the *Gana*, ventured outside the Gurukul by yourselves.' He paused to allow the import of his words to sink in.

Maya wondered why the *Mahamatis* had been unable to come to a conclusion. Surely their transgression was clear and serious enough?

Jignesh's voice was hard and cold as he took over from Mahesh. 'We couldn't decide if you were being just plain foolish or overconfident in your abilities.' He spoke quietly, but the undercurrents of disapproval were perceptible in his tone.

'You,' he addressed Agastya. 'Have you become so powerful now that you fancy your chances against the *pisachas* and spirits that wander the world outside the Gurukul? I know you have worked on projects where you demonstrated your powers against creatures like these quite impressively. So you think you can handle them on your own now?'

He turned to Varun and Tanveer, addressing them both. 'And you two. Great warriors, acquitting yourselves well in the skirmishes that you have had with the *pisachas* on every mission that you have undertaken. But did you forget that the three of you have always had a *Mahamati* with you to ensure that you were protected? If you were ready for the outside world, we would have sent you to join the *Gana.*' He paused. 'What were you all thinking?'

Maya couldn't take it anymore. Despite everything that her companions had said to her, she still believed that she was responsible for the entire misadventure.

'It was my fault,' she spoke up in a small voice. 'It was my idea to go to the Gandharva valley. I thought the Gandharvas could help us decipher the inscriptions in my father's diary. I was the one who approached Arjun and asked him to accompany me.'

Mahesh turned to gaze at her. 'That doesn't matter,' he told Maya. 'They went with you. And, for that, they are responsible, not you. All six of you have broken the same rule.'

Jignesh regarded Maya with interest. 'Is it true,' he asked, 'that you recited the mantra to enter the valley of the Gandharvas?'

Maya nodded. She knew what was coming.

'And you got this mantra from your father's diary?'

'Yes, *Mahamati.*'

'Yet, no one taught you to recite this mantra. At least no one from the Gurukul.' Jignesh paused. 'Is there something you are hiding from us?'

Maya looked at him confused. 'Hiding? *Mahamati,* I don't understand what you mean.'

'You have barely mastered two classes of the simplest mantras. I have not seen any exceptional powers in you that would enable you to master the higher classes of mantras — creating illusions or manipulating matter — leave alone recite a mantra that opens a portal to another world.' His eyes bored into Maya. 'Who taught you how to do it?'

Maya stared back at him, her eyes wide, confused. Tiwari's words from a few days ago came back to her. She, too, had been wondering at her sudden, inexplicable, ability to recite the mantra that had allowed them to pass through the rock and into the world of the Gandharvas that lay beyond it, when she couldn't even utter the mantra that allowed them access to the Gurukul. Tiwari had talked of coincidences. Was it possible that those were not coincidences after all? That there was some sort of connection between her and Shukra which she was not aware of? And which she could not explain?

Tears came into her eyes as she thought about the implications of this possibility, and she blinked them away, trying to suppress the unpleasant thought.

Arjun realized what she was thinking; the same thought had occurred to him when Maya had confided in him about her dreams and Tiwari's explanation about her *atma* wandering at night. He slipped his hand into hers and squeezed it gently. Maya was grateful for the comforting gesture.

Jignesh opened his mouth to say more, but Mahesh, noticing Maya's distress, gently placed a hand on his arm.

'The upshot of all of this,' Mahesh said, 'is that you have made a serious mistake. What we were unable to decide is whether we should let this mistake pass, and let you all go with a warning never to repeat what you have done today: or if we should punish you for the transgression. Don't for a minute think this is because your error is insignificant. You have risked not just your own but the entire Gurukul's safety. But it is also true that you have helped us obtain some important information from the Gandharvas today; information that was not forthcoming earlier, and may not have been available at all had it not been for your unexpected intrusion into their world.'

Maya realized that Visvavasu would have shared with Virendra and Pramila the same information he had shared with her and they, in turn, would have informed the *Mahamatis*. Had the *Mahamatis* been able to figure out what the children hadn't?

Mahesh looked around at the other members of the council. An unspoken agreement seemed to pass between them.

'We have decided,' Mahesh said finally, 'to overlook your transgression tonight as a mistake born of either naivety or ignorance. We do not believe that you would have deliberately engaged in an act of defiance. But hear this and be clear: we will not permit the same mistake to be repeated. The next time, we shall not be as understanding or forgiving.' He nodded to dismiss the children.

Tiwari rose and led them away and out of the hall.

As they left, Jignesh's words kept haunting Maya. One thought in particular haunted her.

Had she had an implicit hand in the death of her own father?

Chapter Seventy

Maya Travels Again

That night

The Gurukul

Maya finished reciting the *shantaa-kaaram* mantra. Her body relaxed, her breathing slowed as she lay in bed awaiting the onset of sleep.

She knew where she was going tonight. She had been there once before, though she hadn't realized it at the time. She had been blissfully unaware of how close she had been to achieving her goal that night. Tonight, she was determined to complete what she had then left unfinished.

Presently, sleep overcame her, her eyelids drooped shut and Maya slumbered peacefully.

Before long, her *atma* emerged from her body and floated out of the guesthouse, flying straight through the walls as if the physical barrier did not exist.

Tonight, she didn't even need to focus hard to think of the name. It seemed to be embedded in her subconscious.

After her failure to visit the Gandharva valley in her spirit form, Maya had figured that there was a method to spirit travel; it was not a random process guided by thought. Her research in the archives had revealed the guidelines to *atma* travel. While sketchy, they had explained why she had been unable to visit the Gandharva valley in her spirit form. The portal that protected the Gandharva valley and the mantra to access the portal were one of the reasons for her failure, a fact that she had not known at the time of her first attempt. But that was not the only reason she had failed to enter the valley on that night. The books from the archives had provided more information on what she had missed by way of preparation for *atma* travel.

Tonight, she had prepared herself, using the knowledge she had gained from the texts in the archives.

And it had worked.

Without even consciously thinking about it, she was now floating over the river and the forest, which she had seen a few days ago. She found the same track she had seen on the earlier occasion and followed it to a small cottage nestled among the trees. It was the same building she had seen, from above, on her previous visit here in her spirit form.

Was this it?

She approached the cottage slowly, wondering what she would find. The trees were thickly clustered together, as if huddling against some unknown, unseen threat that lurked in the darkness of the forest.

A deep growl sounded from somewhere near the cottage.

A dog.

Or was it a wolf?

Startled, she stopped, hovering between the trees, unsure of whether she should proceed.

Surely a dog, or even a wolf, couldn't harm a spirit?

Gathering her nerves, she proceeded to advance cautiously towards the cottage.

There was movement in the darkness and a large black shape came hurtling out of nowhere until it stood before her, barking its head off.

An enormous dog; or perhaps a cross between a dog and a wolf. Its hackles were raised, and spit flew from its huge maw, as it stared directly at her and continued to bark.

Something told her the dog could *see* her.

Maya wasn't sure if the beast could actually stop her from proceeding, but she didn't want to find out. She stayed put, not moving, waiting.

What next?

A light came on within the cottage, its soft, lambent glow flowing out through one of the windows and bathing the trees around in an eerie, yellow hue. She heard the creak of door hinges, from the direction of the cottage, and an old man came into view, accompanied by a soft, yellow haze of light that hovered at his shoulder. He was tall and surprisingly erect, considering his apparent age. He walked slowly towards Maya.

She stared with fascination at his long, pure white hair, his flowing white beard, and the deep lines etched on his face.

'What's the matter then?' the old man asked the dog, who stopped barking and whined instead, as his tail wagged non-stop, happy to see his master who bent and scratched the dog's throat before straightening up and shining his lantern on Maya.

It had to be. Finally, she was face to face with the man who could give her the answers she was seeking.

Satyavachana.

Chapter Seventy-one

Conversation with a Maharishi

The Cottage

Satyavachana's first words came as a surprise to Maya.

'Yes, I am Satyavachana. I have been waiting for you,' he said, looking straight at her, though Maya was unsure if he could actually see her. 'Sooner or later you would come. I knew it. There is still hope, then,' he half mumbled to himself.

'Come on.' Satyavachana turned around and headed back to the cottage. Maya followed him. It appeared that the great Maharishi could see her.

Inside the cottage, he sat down, cross-legged, on a low wooden platform, roughly built from planks of wood that had been crudely hammered together, placed on the dirt floor.

'Make yourself comfortable,' Satyavachana said.

Maya looked around the room. It was bare, except for the wooden platform, on which the Maharishi now sat, and a second, larger and longer, wooden platform in another corner of the room, which she guessed was his bed. She wondered if there were other rooms in this cottage and what they held.

Satyavachana gazed directly at Maya. He seemed to divine her thoughts. 'Yes, I can see you,' he said, waving his hands. 'My yogic powers allow me to, both, see you and hear you even in your *atmic* form. Now, tell me, who are you?'

Maya struggled to answer the question. In her spirit form, she didn't possess vocal chords or a tongue to be able to create sounds to speak.

'A novice,' Satyavachana sighed, then looked at Maya curiously.'That's interesting. You haven't been tutored in *atma* travel. You're doing this all by yourself.'

Maya was shocked. This man seemed to be able to read her thoughts.

'No, I can't read your thoughts,' Satyavachana said, apparently oblivious to the fact that he was responding to Maya's unspoken thought. 'As an *atma*, you communicate using your thoughts. So right now, your thoughts are as loud and clear as words to me. Only a powerful yogi would be able to receive your communication, though. And, if you had been trained in spirit travel, then you would know how to filter your thoughts, which would allow you to communicate only certain thoughts, while keeping the others to yourself. You obviously don't know how to do that at the moment. Now, who are you? Definitely not the One.'

'My name is Maya. I am the daughter of Maharishi Dhruv.'

'Very good. You catch on quick. I knew Dhruv. I was sorry to hear about his passing on.'

Maya was taken aback.'You know he is dead?' How did this man get his news, living in a forest by himself?

'Yes, I do.' There was no further explanation forthcoming.'And you are here to seek my help, are you not? Where is the One?'

'The One?'

'Yes, the One,' Satyavachana said, impatiently, 'who will lead the Sangha against Shukra.'

'Oh, Arjun. He's back at the Gurukul.'

'Hmmm. And where are the other five?'

'The other five?' Maya was puzzled.

'Don't behave like an echo,' Satyavachana said, crossly.'The One. You. That makes two. Where are the other five?'

'I don't know what you are talking about,' Maya said, bewildered. The thought that Satyavachana was too senile to help her came to her mind. She pushed it away instantly, as she remembered that she was communicating through her thoughts. She really had to work on this bit, if she were to truly master *atma* travel.

'No, I am not senile,' Satyavachana chuckled. 'Old, yes. But I have my wits about me. And yes, you really do need to learn how to control your thoughts during spirit travel.'

He thought for a moment. 'So you don't know. No one has told you yet. Hmmm. You said you wanted me to help you with something. What was it?'

'I was told that you can help me translate some verses.'

'That depends. I am a Maharishi, not a linguist, you know.'

'They are in *Brahmabhasha*.'

The Maharishi's eyebrows shot up in surprise. '*Brahmabhasha!*'

'Yes.'

'How did you come by verses in *Brahmabhasha?* It is a dead language.'

'Yes. I was told by the *Mahamatis* and the Gandharvas that it was the language of the Devas, no longer in use. These verses are in a diary that belonged to my father, Maharishi Dhruv. I need to be able to decipher them. I think they may conceal clues that will help us find the missing parts of the prophecy and maybe even the weapons we need to defeat Shukra.'

'So Dhruv did find the verses,' Satyavachana mused. He perked up visibly and beamed at Maya. 'Forgive me for doubting you, Maya,' he said contritely, 'but I was beginning to wonder if you had any connection with the prophecy at all. You didn't seem to know anything about it and you seemed to have accidentally stumbled upon the secret of *atma* travel. But what you have just told me makes things very different.'

Maya didn't understand what he meant or how things were any different. As far as she was concerned, nothing had changed since the beginning of this very strange conversation.

'I will explain later. And, yes, I can help you with the verses, though

I cannot translate them myself. But first, there are things that we need to do.'

'What things?'

'Hang on a moment.' Satyavachana rose and walked over to the wooden platform that Maya had identified as his bed. He lay down and closed his eyes.

Suddenly, Maya sensed another presence next to her. Startled, she instinctively thought of the Gurukul and the safety it afforded and in an instant, she was back again in bed, in her room in the guesthouse, jerking awake as her *atma* re-entered her body.

There was a knock on her balcony door.

She sat up in bed, a sense of terror gripping her.

Who could it be, on her balcony, at this time of night?

Chapter Seventy-two

Satyavachana's Advice

The Guesthouse
Gurukul

'Open the door, Maya.'

Maya's eyes widened in surprise. It was Satyavachana's voice. But hadn't she left him in his cottage in the woods?

'It is I, Satyavachana.'

Maya sat, frozen in bed, unable to bring herself to open the balcony door. How could she be so sure that it was, indeed, the Maharishi? She had read and heard enough about Shukra's powers of illusion. What if it was the son of Bhrigu?

The memory of the chanting of mantras at the boundaries of the Gurukul came to her and cleared the fog of panic and fear. The mantra was aimed at keeping the Gurukul safe. She remembered Jignesh's assurance that even Shukra would be unable to penetrate the security offered by the mantra to the Gurukul.

But, if it was Satyavachana, how had he reached here? If he was able to knock on the door, he certainly wasn't here in his *atmic* form.

The knock persisted. Maya had read enough stories in the ancient texts about the curses that Maharishis were prone to dispensing, if someone offended them. She didn't want to be at the receiving end of a curse by someone who was supposed to be the most powerful Maharishi to have been born since the start of Kaliyuga. She sprang out of bed, afraid to keep the Maharishi waiting any longer, and flung open the balcony door.

Satyavachana stood there, his eyes twinkling in the soft light, to Maya's great surprise.

'I'm sorry I startled you back at my ashram,' he chuckled. 'I will not enter your room. Come on out onto the balcony. We need to talk.'

Maya stepped out into the balcony, enjoying the feel of the soft night breeze in her hair and on her skin. She realized what he was talking about.

'It was you.' She felt sheepish. 'The presence I felt at your ashram. It was your *atma*. You startled me out of my skin!'

An almost mischievous smile played on Satyavachana's lips. 'Actually, I startled you back *into* your skin, didn't I? You aren't the only one who is capable of spirit travel, you know.' His face grew serious. 'I want to show you something. If you are, indeed, one of the *Saptas*, then it is up to you, and the others, to stop what Shukra has already set in motion. I can only hope that it is not too late. The *Sangha*, as usual, are navel gazing, and have no idea what is happening.

The *Saptas*? Was the old Maharishi rambling again? What was he alluding to?

'I will return to my ashram now,' Satyavachana told her. 'Come back there in your *atmic* form as soon as you can. Do not tarry longer than necessary.'

Maya nodded, but the Maharishi had already vanished. She looked around openmouthed. How had he done that? Had he even really been here?

The urgency in Satyavachana's tone had not been lost on her. She returned to her room, locked the balcony door and sat on her bed, reciting the *shantaa-kaaram* mantra, which she now knew, was the gateway to her ability to travel using her *atma*.

Before long, she had dropped into a deep sleep and her *atma* was on its way to Satyavachana's ashram, even though she still didn't know exactly where it was located.

Maya reached the little cottage and sensed, rather than saw Satyavachana's *atma*.

'It's okay,' Satyavachana assured her, hearing her thoughts. 'You really can't see an *atma*. You can sense it, if your yogic powers are sufficiently developed.'

'But I don't have any powers,' Maya said, despondently. 'I don't even know if I am a *sadh* or not.'

'Oh, you're a *sadh* alright,' Satyavachana said, cheerfully. 'Everyone is. We are all born as *sadhs*. It is then up to us to become yogis or not. Or, as in the case of the *Sangha*, to become Rishis, Maharishis or Kshatriyas. True, our past lives do have a bearing on our circumstances of birth in our current life. But that doesn't mean that our past lives determine the course of our present lives. It is our actions in this life that determine what we will achieve in this life itself. That is the law of Karma. A *sadh* can become a Rishi. Or even a Maharishi. Look at Visvamitra. He was a Kshatriya to start with. But a *sadh*, nevertheless. He never had the powers the Kshatriyas of the *Sangha* have. Yet, he became a Maharishi. And not just any Maharishi. He became a Saptarishi. He is a member of the current Saptarishi Mandal.'

'But I can't use any of the higher mantras,' Maya responded. 'I've tried and failed.' As soon as this thought occurred to her, another thought flashed through her consciousness at the same time — the mantra that had enabled her to enter the Gandharva valley.

'There you are,' Satyavachana corrected her. 'You were able to use one of the highest classes of mantras. One that can only be used by the most powerful Maharishis. There are just a handful of people in the Sangha who have the capability to do what you did.'

Maya said nothing. She didn't know what to think.

'Give it time,' Satyavachana urged. 'If you failed to use a mantra, it wasn't because you cannot. It was because you could not focus your mind properly. That is a *sadh* trait, the inability to remove all material distractions from the mind. When you used the mantra to enter the Gandharva valley, your mind was clear of clutter and free of distraction.

Your entire being, your consciousness was focused on the mantra and what you wished to achieve. That is why you succeeded.'

Maya thought back and realized that he was right. In the forest at Panna, when she had attempted to create a ball of light, her mind had struggled to focus. At the Pandava falls, however, her concentration had been single-minded and she had focused on entering the valley. She had *wanted* to enter the valley. She also remembered Jignesh's words during her first lesson, about the difference between *sadhs* and the students at the Gurukuls. He had said exactly the same thing that Satyavachana was telling her now.

'But there will be time to talk about this later,' Satyavachana said, firmly but gently. 'For now, we need to act, if all is not to be lost. I am now going to bind your *atma* to mine, so that you can follow me wherever I go, even if you don't know where I intend to travel. I don't want you getting lost in the spirit world. You probably haven't realized, but Shukra now controls the spirit world. All spirits bow to his command as a result of a boon from Lord Shiva, who is the real master of the *Bhuta gana*. You have to be careful otherwise you will find your *atma* trapped, even while your body is alive, and you will become a vassal of Shukra, like the other spirits.'

Before Maya could respond, she found herself being whisked away in a blur of motion. She had no idea of time or space, just a sense of being connected in some way to Satyavachana as he drifted at high speed to an unknown destination.

It took just a few moments before the strange movement stopped. They had arrived at their destination. Maya steadied herself and looked around. She found herself gazing down on a sight that horrified her.

Chapter Seventy-three

The Search for Vishwaraj

Day 12

The Gurukul

The day dawned with a surprise for the students of the Gurukul.

'No meditation classes for a while,' everyone was informed.

Maya and Arjun had been the first to know, when they started for the Assembly Hall for their meditation classes. Jignesh had informed them, meeting them at the doorway of the subterranean assembly hall. '*Mahamati* Mahesh will not be in the Gurukul for a few days. Your classes will resume when he is back.'

He had then led Maya away to begin his classes with her while Arjun left to join his uncle in the practice field for his own training sessions.

As the day progressed and the news of *Mahamati* Mahesh's absence spread among the students, everyone agreed that this was highly unusual. Added to that was the unexplained absence of Usha and Amba. Today, only Parth appeared for the combat practice session with Arjun. There was no sign of Amba.

Not only was she missing from Arjun's training sessions but her classes with the other Kshatriyas had also been suspended, as were Usha's classes.

The students were quick to connect the dots. With Mahesh, Amba and Usha missing, all at the same time, it seemed apparent that the three of them had left the Gurukul together.

But that was not all. At lunchtime, Arjun searched for his mother, as was his usual practice, but he couldn't find her.

'Where's Mom?' he asked Virendra finally.

Virendra mumbled something that Arjun couldn't understand.

'Come on, uncle, please tell me. I haven't even seen her today.'

Virendra took Arjun by the arm and led him aside to a corner of the mess hall. 'She's gone with the other *Mahamatis*,' he informed Arjun, his voice low.

Arjun was mystified. The three *Mahamatis* leaving the Gurukul together was understandable. They could all be headed for a meeting of the *Sangha* Council. But his mother?

'Where have they gone?' he asked, keeping his voice low. From Virendra's attitude, he could gauge that this news was to be kept confidential.

'We received information last night that Vishwaraj has been located,' Virendra told him. 'They've gone to bring him in. They needed two Kshatriyas and two Maharishis. I would have gone, but your mother insisted on going instead.'

'Who is Vishwaraj?'

Virendra told him about Vishwaraj and Trivedi and how it was possible that Vishwaraj had a hand in the attack by Shukra's monsters on the night of their arrival at the Gurukul.

Arjun's heart sank. If Vishwaraj was in league with Shukra, as the *Mahamatis* believed was possible, then he could be dangerous. Arjun corrected himself immediately. Vishwaraj *would* be dangerous. The danger of the mission was implicit in the fact that the group that had gone to fetch him had to include two Maharishis and two Kshatriyas. It was an acknowledgement of either Vishwaraj's power or the possibility that he had reinforcements that would need to be subdued in order to capture the fugitive Rishi.

And his mother was part of the mission. She had voluntarily put herself in great danger. A part of him swelled with pride. But he couldn't push away the feeling of dread that had suddenly overcome him either.

He had lost his father to Shukra. He didn't want to lose his mother now.

Chapter Seventy-four

Satyavachana's Arrival

That evening

The Guesthouse
The Gurukul

Tiwari studied Maya's face as he mused on what she had just told him. They were both sitting in the living room of the guesthouse after Maya had requested a private word with the Maharishi.

Maya had been restless the entire day, earning a rebuke from Jignesh for not concentrating enough on her mantras. But how was she to focus on articulation and concentrate on the purpose of the mantras when her mind was driven to distraction by what she had seen the night before?

The scenes of the roiling mass of dark shapes as they emerged from the immense hole in the ground, the light of the moon and the stars glinting off their black-vermilion hued scales, goaded on by none other than Shukra himself, were burnt into her memory. She had spent the rest of the night shivering in her bed, notwithstanding the fact that Satyavachana had spoken to her at length about what needed to be done to counter them, trying to calm her down.

For, amid the general roar of Shukra's words, one phrase had stood out. As Maya huddled in her bed, post her *atma* travel, shrinking from the thought of the monstrous creatures she had seen, the words echoed in her head, chilling her to the bone.

'Destroy the Gurukul.'

Maya didn't have to guess very hard to figure out which Gurukul Shukra was alluding to. There was only one Gurukul where, according to the prophecy, his nemesis was being sheltered. It was clear that an attack on the Gurukul at Panna was imminent.

'What you say is serious, Maya,' Tiwari said, at length. 'Why did you wait so long to tell me?'

'I was afraid,' Maya said, plaintively. 'How could I reveal how I had come by this information without giving away the secret of my out of body experiences? And you had told me yourself that I should keep this secret to myself lest people suspect me of being linked in some way to Shukra. Besides, I thought that the Gurukul is protected by our mantra and cannot be overwhelmed by any of Shukra's creations. So I can't understand how Shukra could penetrate our security.'

'I understand your dilemma,' Tiwari said gently. 'But any information that concerns the safety of the Gurukul, needs to be flagged to the Council immediately. You should have come to me at once. I would have worked out a way to tell them without revealing your secret.' He paused before continuing.

'And what you saw last night were not creations of Shukra,' Tiwari assured her. 'They are beings as old as creation itself. True, they cannot overrun the Gurukul — even entering would be difficult for them, though not impossible — but they can certainly lay siege to the Gurukul and choke us out of our shelter and protective cover. That is what you heard Shukra say to them. That is what he plans. It is a masterstroke on his part. To release ...'

'There you are.' Tiwari was cut off abruptly by Virendra who had just entered the room. 'We've been looking all over for you.' He looked from Tiwari to Maya and back again, realizing he had interrupted a serious discussion. 'Sorry to barge in, but it is urgent. The Council has summoned both of you.'

Maya froze. The first thought that came to her mind was that the Council had somehow got to know of her atma travel with Satyavachana last night. Why else would they summon her?

Virendra did not explain and she walked briskly to keep pace with the Kshatriya's long strides as they trudged from the guesthouse to the Assembly Hall.

There was a palpable sense of excitement in the air; a buzz that Maya couldn't quite explain. Groups of students stood clustered around the central avenue leading to the Assembly Hall, talking in low voices.

Maya spotted Varun, Tanveer and Arjun. Varun silently mouthed something as she passed and Arjun gave her a surreptitious thumbs up sign.

What was going on?

The trio reached the Assembly Hall and mounted the steps to the meditation area where *Mahamati* Mahesh held his classes. The doors were shut. Maya knew what that meant. A session of the *Mahamati* Council was in progress.

A feeling of trepidation took hold of her. Why did the Council want her to be present at one of their sessions?

Virendra pushed the door open and they entered.

There were three people in the room. Jignesh and Parth from the *Mahamati* Council sat on chairs facing the door.

Maya sucked in her breath sharply as she saw the person who occupied the third chair.

Satyavachana!

No wonder ripples of excitement had spread through the campus. Satyavachana was notoriously reclusive, shunning the company of his fellow Maharishis. Most of the students and even some of the teachers had never laid eyes on him. When Gurumurthy had first told Maya about the reclusive Maharishi, he had mentioned that Satyavachana was on a self-imposed exile from the Sangha, for reasons that no one could remember — so far back in time had this incident occurred.

Yet, here he was, sitting with the *Mahamatis.*

What was he doing here?

Even as she asked herself the question, the answer came to Maya. Her worst fears were about to come true.

Satyavachana had come to Panna to warn the Council about the impending attack on the Gurukul.

Had he told them about Maya's *atma* travelling to his ashram? About how Maya and he had together witnessed the preparations for the attack?

She struggled with her dilemma. Should she acknowledge Satyavachana or pretend not to recognize him? If he had told the *Mahamatis* about her *atma* travelling and she pretended not to know him, she would look like a fool. But if he hadn't told them and she showed that she recognized him, that would land her in serious trouble and lead to the very revelation that she sought to avoid.

Maya stood there, confused, unable to take a decision.

Chapter Seventy-five

Maya's Secret

The Assembly Hall
The Gurukul

Satyavachana solved the problem for her. 'Good to see you again, Maya,' he greeted her in the deep voice that she had heard last night in his cottage.

Maya bowed in acknowledgement but said nothing in response.

Jignesh fixed Maya with a stern eye. 'Maharishi Satyavachana has enlightened us about your little adventure last night. You never told us that you were capable of *atma* travel.'

It wasn't a question, so Maya was unsure of how to respond. Was Jignesh looking for an apology?

Tiwari stepped in to her rescue. 'She had told me,' he admitted. 'I thought it best not to talk about it right now.'

Jignesh raised an eyebrow. 'It seems you and I need to speak in private about that, Maharishi Ratan.' He turned his attention back to Maya. 'You are quite a bundle of surprises. First the mantra to open the portal to *Gandharvalok*. And now using your *atma* to travel. Yet, you have not displayed any signs during your lessons so far, that would indicate your capability for either of these feats. What are we to make of this?'

'It is possible that she has not been taught to develop her powers,' Satyavachana said, quietly. 'She may have karmic reserves that she is unaware of. She needs help to tap into those reserves. What we have seen so far could be instances where she didn't need to be conscious of her karmic powers, but was able to use them at a subliminal level.'

Maya saw a flash of anger cross Jignesh's face. It was there only for a fleeting instant, disappearing almost immediately, but it was unmistakable.

'Maharishi Satyavachana has just informed us that Shukra has opened the gates to Mahatal,' Jignesh resumed. 'But of course, you already know this because you accompanied the Maharishi and witnessed this sight.' His tone was disapproving.

Instantly the memory from last night flooded back, and a wave of nausea washed over Maya.

'I did not tell you about the release of the descendants of Kadru so that you could castigate the child,' Satyavachana murmured to Jignesh but not so softly that Maya could not hear.

Jignesh flushed at the reprimand. 'She should have told us earlier,' he remonstrated. 'I had a class with her in the morning. Had we been informed then ...'

'You could still have done nothing about it.' Satyavachana's piercing gaze was now directed at Jignesh. His tone was sharp. 'Whether Maya informed you in time or not is not of the utmost importance. The events of the past week should have been enough of an indication of what was going to come. The Sangha has been sleeping! Action is what is needed now, not endless discussion. We need to prepare for what we know awaits us. I came here today, breaking my own vow, only because the world is in peril and I knew that Maya might hesitate to tell you what she saw for fear of being punished. I am glad I came for I see that I was right.'

Maya wondered what vow Satyavachana was referring to. She watched the two Maharishis with fascination. The tension in the room was palpable. Jignesh was clearly uncomfortable with Satyavachana's open admonitions, but it was also clear that he had to defer to the older Maharishi. She had no idea why Satyavachana was taking her side, but she was glad that he was. Ever since she had come to the Gurukul she had felt isolated and picked on. She had soldiered on, determined to master the mantras, in response to Jignesh's barbs, trying her best to cope with the anxiety and frustration that his continuous criticism would arouse. Maybe, she reflected, Satyavachana was not really taking her side. He was only being fair.

'She told me,' Tiwari interjected once again. 'We were about to come to you when we were summoned to the Council.'

'It doesn't matter,' Satyavachana repeated, now looking at Tiwari. 'You can strengthen your defences and try to stop them from getting in, but you cannot fight them. And you cannot hold them off forever. Your forces are already severely depleted with four of your most powerful Sangha members being away from the Gurukul. I can only hope that the news about Vishwaraj was not a ruse by Shukra to draw them away and leave the Gurukul thinly protected. But even if Mahesh and the others were here, you would not have the means to defeat the Nagas. It is only a matter of time before the Gurukul is besieged by them. You cannot stop it. There is only one course of action available to you, if you wish to be able to break the siege, once it starts. And I have told you what that is.'

Silence settled on the little group.

Maya knew exactly what Satyavachana was talking about. Last night, after they had returned from witnessing the hordes of Nagas pouring out of the now open gates of Mahatal, Maya had been increasingly worried. That was when Satyavachana had proposed a course of action. She had been planning to execute the plan herself, with the help of Arjun and his friends, if the Council was unable or unwilling to do it.

What Satyavachana had not told her was that he would arrive in person to ensure that the plan was implemented.

'This is the reason you were asked to join us in this Council, Maya,' Satyavachana turned his attention to her. 'Only you can do this.'

'I still think that one of the *Mahamatis* can carry out the plan better,' Jignesh said, stubbornly. 'It is too big a risk to send someone who isn't even a novice. What if she fails?'

'We've gone over this before,' Satyavachana replied. 'Every member of the Sangha, including me, is needed here to protect the Gurukul. We cannot afford to deplete our ranks any further. We do not know if Shukra has been able to conceive and develop a mantra or a weapon that is capable of piercing the protective shield and countering the mantra that you use to protect the Gurukul. We cannot send any of the Kshatriyas — that would take too much time. And none of your other students are capable of spirit travel. Only she is.' He pointed to Maya.

'Very well, then.' Jignesh conceded defeat, but didn't look happy in the least.

'Treat it as yet another test for her,' Satyavachana urged. 'If she succeeds, as I believe she will, then I will take her under my wing and teach her myself, for she will have then demonstrated that she is, indeed, a Rishi in the making.'

Jignesh said nothing but only nodded his assent.

Maya couldn't contain her excitement. The most powerful Maharishi since Kaliyuga began had not only vouched for her but also just offered to be her own personal *Mahamati*! It was something she would never have even dreamed of.

But, before that could happen, she had a task to complete.

The fate, not just of the Gurukul, but also of the world now rested on her shoulders.

Chapter Seventy-six

Time for Travel

The Guesthouse
The Gurukul

Maya smiled at Amyra as the two girls walked up to Maya's bedroom on the first floor of the cottage. Over the last few days, despite Maya's brusque treatment of her at dinner time four days ago, Amyra had made several attempts to be friendly.

Preoccupied and struggling with troubles of her own, and with the single-minded objective of getting the mysterious verses in her father's diary deciphered, Maya had paid the novice little attention. But she had realized that the girl meant well, and had been polite to her. It was just that making friends was not Maya's priority at this point in time. But Amyra was pleasantly persistent and Maya found herself growing fond of the girl.

Today, when the Council had agreed with Satyavachana on the plan to prepare for the imminent onslaught of the Nagas, it was Amyra who had volunteered to watch over Maya as she embarked on the most important journey of her life so far. Arjun had wanted to take on the role first, but the Council had overridden his bid to protect Maya.

'Your place is here, in the Gurukul,' Virendra had told him. 'If we have to fight the Nagas, you must be a part of the battle. We cannot afford to waste your mettle on a sentry's job.'

The other Council members had emphatically agreed with Virendra and Arjun had found himself without a choice. Much as he wanted to stay by Maya's side and ensure that she came to no harm, he had to back down.

It was then that Amyra had volunteered for a job which no one really wanted. And Maya was grateful. While everyone seemed to dismiss it as an unimportant role, Maya knew how critical it was. Not only was Amyra tasked with ensuring that no one disturbed Maya, but she also had to ensure that, until Maya completed her mission, she would be safe from harm. No one knew how long it would take Maya to find what she would be searching for. If something had to happen in that period, she would be unable to defend herself.

For Maya was going to embark on her search using her new-found talent for *atma* travel.

She held Amyra's hand as they stood at the door to her room. 'Thank you,' she said to the novice. She meant it sincerely.

Amyra smiled back cheerfully. 'I am happy that I could be of service. And come back soon with our deliverance.'

Amyra latched the door to the room from the inside and double-checked the balcony door and windows, then quietly sat on the floor in one corner of the room, as Maya lay down on the bed and chanted the *shantaa-kaaram* mantra.

She wasn't sure if sleep would come to her so early in the evening, but the mantra had its desired effect and the now familiar sensation of calm pervaded her entire being. Soon, she grew drowsy and slipped into a deep sleep.

As Maya, in her *atma* form, floated out of her body, she saw herself lying on the bed, immersed in slumber. Amyra sat in one corner, her eyes fixed on the door. She was evidently taking her duties very seriously. If Maya could smile to herself, she would have.

But it was time to leave. She flew out of the cottage, her *atma* passing effortlessly through the wall, and into the night air. Darkness had fallen and the lights of the cottages in the Gurukul, and the glowing orbs outside them, lit up the forest, looking like fireflies dotting the trees as Maya rose higher in the air.

The calm before the storm, she thought to herself.

She had prepared well for this journey, post her talk with Satyavachana the previous night. After classes, earlier in the day, she had spent all her free time in the archives, poring over books and maps that would help her triangulate the exact location where Satyavachana had said she would find what she sought. At that time, she had planned to employ the help of Arjun and his friends to undertake the journey. Now, of course, the plans had been altered.

Satyavachana had been extremely confident of her success, but Maya was plagued by a series of doubts.

First, would she really be able to locate a place as ancient as the location she was searching for? The city she had to find had vanished 5,000 years ago and there remained no trace of it today. There were geographical references in the ancient texts, and there had been recent archaeological discoveries in the region indicated by those texts, but nothing conclusive had been found.

Second, even if she did find the lost city, what she was searching for was not *in* the city. It was somewhere near it. That was all that Satyavachana could tell her.

'On an island hidden to the world,' he had told her. He had also given her the mantra that would help reveal the island. If she found it, that is.

That was her third fear. Would the mantra work?

And there was a fourth doubt, but she didn't want to think of it right now. If she did, then the entire exercise would be futile and her mission was destined to end in failure. She placed her faith in Satyavachana. If he had said it was possible, then he must be right.

Too many ifs. Too many possibilities for failure. And she was just a fifteen-year-old who wasn't even a member of the *Gana* yet.

It was time to leave the Gurukul, but something made Maya stop. She hovered over the forest, looking all around her.

She had felt something.

Sensed something.

What was it?

She scanned the forest below in all directions. Nothing moved.

She sensed it again.

Like gentle ripples in the air, caressing her. It was a strange sensation. Even though she did not possess a body, she could still feel the ripples. She didn't know how.

Only, this was no delicate caress of soft breeze against skin. There was an emotion in the ripples. The caress seemed to possess a hatred, a longing for destruction, a foul anger.

She shrank back but the sensation grew stronger.

A ripple through the air.

Of course! The air!

She scanned the sky, rising higher in order to get a better view.

Then, she saw it.

Against the darkness of the night, a darker mass.

It was blotting out the stars, drowning the night in its shadow.

And it was moving towards her.

Was it the black fog she had seen on that night when they had arrived in the Gurukul? The fog, which had produced Shukra's monsters?

Something told her this was not that black fog. It was something more deadly. More dangerous.

A horrible premonition flashed through her mind. A premonition based on a past memory.

The Nagas had arrived.

Chapter Seventy-seven

The Siege of the Gurukul

In the sky above the Gurukul

The black cloud was travelling at an amazing speed. Maya hurriedly floated higher. She didn't want to be in the way of the cloud, or be engulfed by it.

Maya used her consciousness to carry her at the speed of thought high above the forest.

Just in time.

Moments after she floated up, the black, roiling cloud sped past below her and descended around the Gurukul, surrounding it on all sides. From her vantage point, she could see the individual Nagas descending to the ground, taking up positions around the Gurukul.

Satyavachana had been right. The Nagas were unable to land directly within the Gurukul, but they were surrounding every inch of it. The siege of the Gurukul would be complete and thorough. Nothing could now get in. Or out.

Unless they travelled through the air.

Maya had seen enough. It was time for her to leave.

With a last look at the heart-rending scene below her, she vanished.

Inside the Gurukul

Mahamatis and students alike gazed in awe and dread at the scene unfolding above them.

The black cloud, which was visibly composed of dark, shiny, writhing shapes, had rolled in at a high speed from the west, taking them all by surprise, even though the Gurukul had been placed on alert for the arrival of the Nagas.

'They can fly?' Arjun was surprised.

'Read the Mahabharata,' Agastya replied through clenched teeth. 'After killing Parikshit, Takshaka fled through the air. He was seen by the ministers of the king, flying through the air. Mahatal is inhabited by Nagas like Takshaka. Who knows, Takshaka himself may be among the Nagas here.'

As they watched, the cloud disintegrated into individual shapes, which began descending along the boundaries of the Gurukul.

The chants of the mantra, around the Gurukul's boundaries, were doubled to reinforce their strength. If the Nagas were able to secure entry into the Gurukul, they were all doomed. Satyavachana had spoken truly. They had no means to vanquish the Nagas.

Their only hope, now, was Maya.

Chapter Seventy-eight

The Lost City

In the sky above Western India

Maya hovered in mid-air and stared at the vast, black, expanse that stretched below her as far as the eye could see. Far below her, the light of the stars danced on the waves, the only indication of where she was.

If she had done her homework correctly, then this was approximately the spot where the lost city was discovered in 2003. Based on the news reports and a few articles she had researched, she had identified a large swathe of the ocean, west of Hazira in Gujarat. She was now directly above that very stretch. In order to ensure that she reached the correct location, she had used Google Earth to find out the exact longitudinal and latitudinal details, which she had then memorized. It was these coordinates that had helped her arrive at this spot.

The team which had made the discovery in 2003 had not found anything substantial apart from a range of artefacts recovered from the site, though they had claimed to have found remains of the foundations of the ancient city. According to the reports, the scanning technology used at that time had found that the foundations of the city extended deep below the ocean bed.

Maya had, once again, reviewed the verses from the Mahabharata, which had described how the ocean had claimed this city for its own;

how the sea waters had flooded it bit by bit until it was fully submerged beneath the waves.

नियति तु जने तस्मिन् सागरो मकरालय: ।
द्वारकां रत्नसम्पूर्णो जलेनाप्लावयत् तदा ॥

After all the people had started, the ocean, the home of sharks, and alligators, flooded Dwarka, which still teemed with riches of every kind, with its waters.

यद् यद्धि पुरुषव्याघ्रो भूमेस्तस्या व्यमुञ्चत ।
तत् तत् सम्प्लावयामास सलिलेन स सागर: ॥

Whatever portion of the ground was passed over, the ocean immediately flooded over with his waters.

तदद्भुतमभिप्रेक्ष्य द्वारकावासिनो जना: ।
तूर्णात् तूर्णतरं जग्मुरहो दैवमिति ब्रुवन् ॥

Seeing this wonderful spectacle, the inhabitants of Dwarka walked faster and faster, saying 'Wonderful is the course of fate.'

Satyavachana's words came back to her. 'Find the lost, ancient, city of Dwarka; the city that was devoured by the ocean when Krishna passed from this world. It was foretold that this would happen.' He had given her a knowing look. 'Just like the prophecy which you and your friends will fulfil. What you seek is on an island, hidden from the world, which cannot be too far from Dwarka. Find Dwarka and you will find the solution, albeit temporary, to the siege of the Gurukul.'

Maya had found the city. But her curiosity was aroused. What did the city look like, drowned and ruined? She knew she would never get the opportunity to dive below the waves and see the underwater ruins.

For one thing, she didn't know how to dive; and even if she did, she was quite sure that she would never get permission to explore the lost city of Dwarka. For some strange reason, research and archaeological excavations had never been carried out at the reported site of the underwater ruins. Even the news articles, some of them by international agencies like the BBC, had a sceptical slant, implicitly questioning the authenticity of the find in the absence of any archaeological evidence.

She made up her mind. Surely a few minutes more wouldn't hurt?

Maya hurtled towards the black waters that lay below her, like a stone dropping from the sky, and cleaved through the water as she headed for the ocean floor. She didn't feel anything when she hit the water, and the density of the ocean didn't seem to matter. As she had done several times before, she took a moment to marvel at the *atma* and the feats it was capable of. Even though she did not possess the sensory organs in this form, having left them behind in her physical body in the Gurukul, she could still see and hear and feel — things that she would have thought impossible in her *atmic* form; yet it was very different from the physical sensation of sight, hearing and touch.

She saw the ruins come up below her. Stone structures, not more than a foot in height, rising from the seabed and stretching out in all directions as far as she could make out. Were these really the fabled walls of the ancient city?

Recalling the description of the sub bottom profiling images that the research team had reported, which revealed the massive foundations of the city, she decided to burrow under the seabed and see them for herself. She was quite enjoying herself now and appreciating the power that she possessed which gave her the ability to do things that *sadhs* would only dream about.

Maya shot below the sand strewn ocean floor and was immediately surrounded by a mass of rocks that formed the structure of the seabed. Among the rocks, she could see massive pillars sunk in between — the foundations of buildings that would have stood overhead when the city was still above the waves. A sense of wonder came over her at the amount of effort and the nature of the technology that would have been used to drill the enormous holes in the underlying rocks to hold the massive foundation pillars that she could see.

She stayed for a while, exploring the underside of the city, weaving through the hundreds of pillars that still held their ground, despite the passage of thousands of years, even as the buildings they had supported had crumbled and disappeared with time.

Finally, she wistfully decided to leave. She had a job to do and, while she had enjoyed her exploration, her mission was more important.

As she emerged from the sea, she turned her thoughts to finding the island. It had to be nearby, hidden from the prying eyes of humanity, the refuge of a solitary being.

The one whom she had come to find.

The only one who could save the Gurukul from the Nagas.

Chapter Seventy-nine

Doubts

The Gurukul

Jignesh, Parth, Virendra and Tiwari had worried looks on their faces.
Satyavachana had gone with one of the students to circumambulate
the perimeter of the Gurukul and ensure that the defences were solid.
The Council had a plan to keep the Nagas engaged while they waited
for Maya to return with help. In order for their plan to succeed their
defences needed to hold.

Jignesh, who was the head of the *Mahamati* Council while Mahesh
was away, had outlined his plan to keep the Nagas at bay while they
waited for Maya's return.

'They will want to wear us down,' was his analysis. 'Grind our
determination and resilience into dust, make us easy prey. We need to
pre-empt them, keep them engaged.' And so the plan had been hatched.

And, true to expectations, the Nagas had not been idle. Reports
had just come from the river that the Nagas on that front had begun
destroying the forest buffer that stood between the Gurukul and the
river. The stretch of forest along the riverbank had gone up in flames,
forcing the defenders of the boundary to retreat within the Gurukul,
effectively allowing the Nagas to advance.

Once the trees were gone, there would be no physical barrier between the Gurukul and the Nagas. What would happen then was anybody's guess.

'Their poison,' Jignesh said, bitterly, 'has lost none of its potency.'

'I don't understand,' Virendra said. 'How can their poison affect the trees?'

'The Nagas do not possess ordinary poison,' Tiwari explained. 'We don't know what it is, since no one alive today has witnessed the effect of the poison of a Naga. But it is unlike the poison of the ordinary snakes that roam *Bhu-lok*. In the Mahabharata, for example, there is reference to a confrontation between Saptarishi Kasyapa and Takshaka, when the latter is on his way to kill Parikshit, the son of the Pandava Arjuna. Takshaka boasts of his ability to kill any living being and challenges Kasyapa to revive a banyan tree, which he has reduced to ashes through his poison. They've probably done the same thing here to our forest buffer.'

'Satyavachana would have seen the conflagration,' Jignesh said grimly, 'and he must be engaged in countering their attack. That is the only explanation for his absence. He should have been back by now, otherwise.'

'If that is the case,' Virendra said, 'then the riverbank is our weak spot.'

'Yes,' Parth agreed. 'We had placed the maximum reinforcements there, knowing this. The other three sides are reasonably well protected by natural barriers — the Dandaka forest on two sides and the hill on the third.'

'They would never cut through the Dandaka,' Jignesh said, forcefully.

'No, they wouldn't,' Parth agreed.

'Once Satyavachana returns,' Jignesh said, pacing the chamber, 'we will launch our counter offensive.' He looked at Virendra. 'Are we ready?'

Virendra smiled grimly, a smile devoid of humour. 'We are ready to attack at a moment's notice.'

'Good. We need to be.' Jignesh lapsed into silence as they waited for the return of the great Maharishi.

In the sky over Dwarka

A pang of self-doubt assailed Maya as she considered her options. She had managed to find the lost city of Dwarka. One doubt had been laid to rest. But others remained. She still didn't know where the island was. She didn't know if the mantra to help her find the island would work. And, worst of all, even if the mantra worked, would it have the effect that she desired?

After all, hadn't Jignesh told her that mantras operated through the use of sound, which was why articulation was so important? But here, as an *atma* without a body, there was no way she could recite the mantra and produce the sound that was required to activate the power hidden within it. What good would just applying her mind and focusing on the objective of the mantra be, if it couldn't be heard?

This was the fourth doubt that she had kept at bay until now. Having come so close to attaining her goal, however, she had to confront it.

Why had Satyavachana insisted on this mission being entrusted to her when there was so much that she could not control?

A sense of hopelessness flooded over her. This was just not going to work. Her mission was going to fail.

And the Gurukul was doomed.

Chapter Eighty

The Hidden Island

The Gurukul

'The news is not good.' Virendra's face looked like it had been carved out of granite. His teeth were clenched and his entire body was tense and stiff, like a freshly strung bow.

He gave his report. 'We launched our guerrilla attack, going at the Nagas through the hillside, hoping to create a diversion. The attack was successful to the extent that we created a bit of chaos in the ranks of the Nagas camped there, and there were no casualties on our side. But the ploy didn't work. There are just too many of them encircling the camp for any kind of diversionary tactics to be effective. Instead, in retaliation, the Nagas on the riverside have advanced and taken over the Kshatriya practice field. The Nagas have scorched both the forest and the field. Our Kshatriyas and Rishis have had to withdraw; they cannot withstand the heat from the blaze created by the poison of the Nagas. Whatever their cursed poison is, it is too powerful for us to withstand.'

Jignesh nodded. 'Then let us defend that boundary vigorously and aggressively.'

'Time is running out,' Virendra said, sounding despondent. 'If Maya doesn't return soon ...' He left his sentence incomplete, but everyone knew what was running through his mind.

In the sky over Dwarka

Maya struggled with her dilemma. A part of her desperately wanted to prove herself, while another part had given up and was ready to return to the Gurukul. The familiar doubts rose up again, trying to convince her that she was never meant to be a Rishi, that she didn't have the powers that were required for a member of the *Gana*. Hadn't Jignesh implied as much even if he had not explicitly said so?

On the other hand, her father had entrusted her with the diary. He had not given her any specific instructions on whom to go to for help to decipher the verses in the diary. Surely he would have indicated something to her if that was his intention? Or was he relying on Maya to figure out how to decipher the verses by herself? That didn't seem logical, unless ...

A thought struck her.

Why hadn't it occurred to her before?

A new resolve took hold of her.

She would do it.

Maya fought against the multiple thoughts that were distracting her, diluting her focus, pulling her towards the Gurukul, towards the Nagas, away from Dwarka. She gathered her concentration until she could feel a tight knot form somewhere in her being, and focused on what she had come here to achieve.

Slowly, the mantra that Satyavachana had given her began unfolding in her consciousness.

Maya was surprised at the power of the mantra, which coursed through her entire being, making it pulse with energy as she recited the mantra in her thoughts.

'*Om namo bhagawate garudaya trayambakaya sadhsttvastu swaha.*'

As she repeated the mantra, the power she could sense seemed to grow in strength.

Something tugged at her *atma*.

What was it? Certainly not a physical force.

There it was again. A perceptible pull.

Maya continued to focus on the mantra and allowed herself to be led away by the unseen, unfelt, force that was exerting a pull on her.

Slowly but surely, it came into view. A dim, hazy shape, like something viewed through a fog, its silhouette barely distinguishable at first, then coming into focus gradually, until it lay before her, its outlines clearly visible and the colours vivid despite the darkness of the night.

It was like being able to see in the dark, as if a powerful light had suddenly been turned on; a light that could not be seen but which illuminated all that lay in the path of its beam.

Maya had found it. The hidden island was hidden no more.

Chapter Eighty-one

Last stand

The Gurukul

A host of pale, anxious faces gazed in the direction of the river Ken. More than half the Gurukul was assembled here — students and *Mahamatis* — including Jignesh, Parth, Virendra and Tiwari.

Several hours had passed since Maya had left to begin her search for Dwarka.

Glowing orbs of light floated in the air, lighting up the night sky and illuminating the scene on the ground.

The sight was terrifying. Not because the band of trees that stretched beyond the Kshatriya practice field had disappeared, leaving blackened stumps and ashes in its place. Nor because the field itself was scorched and blackened in most places, mute testimony to the rage of the Nagas who had destroyed everything in their path.

But because of the sight of the Nagas themselves. With all physical barriers destroyed, the Nagas were now in plain sight. They were enormous creatures, rising over ten feet in height when fully erect. Most of the time, though, they were bent, hunched up as they moved around, the light from the orbs glinting off their scaled bodies. They wore very little armour, confident in their ability to withstand any kind of attack and any weapon that the humans may wield.

Arjun noticed that they bore some similarities to humans. They had two sets of forelimbs and walked upright on two legs, though with a marked hunch.

Their faces bore human features, with broad noses, prominent chins and cheekbones and a jaw that jutted out slightly, more like those of apes than snakes, though their facial skin was reptilian like the rest of their bodies. Their eyes were yellow slits beneath fearsome eyebrows and some of them had wavy horned structures rising from the back of their heads. None of them appeared to carry any weapons. Perhaps they didn't need them. Their poison, whatever it was, seemed to be potent enough to destroy anything that stood in their way.

From time to time, the Nagas would set up a roar, and the denizens of the Gurukul would see more Nagas pour in from the river and cluster in groups.

All that stopped them from overwhelming the Gurukul was the constant chant of the protective mantra and the continuous shouts of 'Garudaya Trayambakaya' that were hurled by the Rishis of the Gurukul at the Nagas. Nothing else stood between the reptilians and the humans.

The power of the attacking mantra that the Rishis were hurling at the Nagas was perceptible. It was keeping them on their toes, constantly churning the hordes gathered there, not allowing them to combine into a formation that would let them attack the Gurukul.

Satyavachana had stayed back at the Assembly Hall, meditating on a mantra, which he claimed would reinforce the efforts of the Gurukul forces in keeping the Nagas at bay.

As Arjun looked on, he saw a slight commotion in the ranks of the Nagas. A section of them seemed to part and a young boy, just a few years older than Arjun, walked through the gap created by the fearsome creatures.

'Vishwaraj!' Arjun heard Jignesh mutter, the surprise in his voice apparent.

Arjun's blood ran cold. His mother had gone to hunt and capture

Vishwaraj with the other *Mahamatis*. What had happened? If they had succeeded in their mission, then Vishwaraj shouldn't be here.

And if Vishwaraj was here, then ...

Words failed him as his worst fears appeared to have come true.

But there was no time to ponder on what had befallen Pramila and the *Mahamatis*.

All hell broke loose.

'Get Satyavachana!' Jignesh roared. 'We need him here, now!'

Arjun sidled up to Tiwari, not understanding the reason for the commotion. 'What ... what is happening?' he asked tremulously, struggling to focus and make sense of it all.

Tiwari's face was grim. 'I can't be sure, but I think — and it seems Jignesh does, too — that Vishwaraj is reciting a counter mantra.'

'A mantra to destroy the effect of our mantras?'

Tiwari shook his head. 'No. The power of positive mantras cannot be destroyed. But it is possible that Shukra has developed a shield of some sort, using mantras. After all, mantras can be used for anything, as you know. It is just that no one has ever come up with the idea or the means to use the power of mantras to achieve evil ends. If Vishwaraj succeeds in shielding the Nagas from the power of our mantras, then nothing will stop them from overrunning the Gurukul.'

With these ominous words, Tiwari lapsed into silence.

Arjun looked on as Vishwaraj stood there, apparently doing nothing. What was he waiting for?

Suddenly, as Arjun watched, Vishwaraj started speaking in a loud voice. Arjun couldn't make out the words over the chant of the mantras being recited in the Gurukul, but it was clear that Vishwaraj was attempting something.

The Nagas seemed to be regrouping, as Vishwaraj continued to speak. Clearly, he was intoning some sort of mantra that was helping the Nagas. Despite the constant chanting of the mantras, that protected the Gurukul from the Nagas, it was clear that the reptilian army was slowly re-organising itself.

How long would it be before the Gurukul would falter?

Where was Maya?

Was she going to return in time? And would she bring help with her?

Arjun stared at the dark sky above and at the Nagas, a well of fear rising in his heart.

A student ran up to Jignesh. '*Mahamati*, Maharishi Satyavachana is not in the Assembly Hall.'

'Then search for him!' Jignesh thundered above the clamour of the mantras, Vishwaraj's intonation and the roars of the Nagas. 'Find him fast! We need him here more than ever!'

Arjun's heart sank. If Satyavachana could not be found, what were their chances against an assault by the Nagas? An assault, which looked more and more imminent.

Time was not on their side.

Chapter Eighty-two

Too late

The Gurukul

Arjun watched, terrified, as the Nagas advanced, finally breaking through the invisible barrier that had held them at bay until now. Vishwaraj had fallen silent and stood staring at his opponents, as the Nagas marched past him, on either side, toward the Gurukul. Whatever he had done had worked. The mantras that the Rishis from the Gurukul continued to hurl at the Nagas seemed to have no effect.

Full of trepidation, Arjun looked at his uncle and braced himself, waiting for the command to attack. The Rishis had held back the Nagas for as long as they could. It would be up to the Kshatriyas now to stave off the savage assault that he knew would come.

This was different from the battle with Shukra's army on the first night they arrived at the Gurukul. Those were blundering, clumsy creatures who only held the advantage of superior numbers. Tonight was different. The Nagas were a well oiled fighting machine – it was obvious from the way they organized themselves. And their prowess as warriors was legendary. Despite himself, despite his efforts to keep his spirits up, Arjun realized that this was a battle that they could not win.

He saw Parth, Virendra and Jignesh hurriedly confer. Words passed between the three men that Arjun could not hear.

What were they discussing?

To his surprise, Parth suddenly turned around and yelled, 'Retreat!'

While Virendra marched through the ranks around him, echoing the cry of 'Retreat!' Jignesh, Parth and Usha disappeared, no doubt to spread the word among the other defenders of the Gurukul.

Virendra came up to Arjun who looked at his uncle questioningly.

'We're too sparsely spread out,' Virendra told him, understanding his unspoken question. 'The area to defend is too large and we're thin on the ground. We will have massive casualties if we stay here and make a stand. We've decided to retreat to the Assembly Hall. It will be easier to defend. Our forces will be concentrated. We can hold out there for a while longer and hopefully buy some time. But not for too long. We can only hope that Maya comes back soon. Otherwise ... '

Arjun looked at his uncle's grim face and nodded. Though his heart was terrified, he knew that if they had to make a stand, the Assembly Hall was their best bet. The novices had already been shepherded into the subterranean hall, to keep them safe, when the siege had begun. With the fighting forces of the Gurukul concentrated around the Hall, they still stood a chance.

The defenders of the Gurukul slowly retreated, converging on the Assembly Hall and leaving the rest of the Gurukul, adjacent to the field of the Kshatriyas, unguarded and undefended.

A tight ring began to form around the Assembly Hall amid the chanting of mantras and the roar of the Nagas, which grew progressively louder and menacing as they drew closer.

'Maya!' Arjun suddenly remembered that Maya was asleep in the guesthouse, with only Amyra to guard her. With the entire Gurukul army gathered around the Assembly Hall, the guesthouse was among the cottages that had been left undefended. Somehow, with Satyavachana suddenly disappearing, and the Nagas advancing, it seemed that everyone had forgotten that Maya's physical body was still in the Gurukul.

Arjun broke away from the rest of the defenders and ran towards the guesthouse.

'Arjun, wait!' Virendra called, realizing what his nephew was planning to do. 'You can't go alone!' He looked around desperately, torn between following his nephew and staying with the defending forces.

'*Mahamati* Kanakpratap.' Virendra looked around in surprise. It was Varun. Behind him were Tanveer, Agastya and Adira. Varun spoke again. 'We will go after Arjun.'

There was no time to lose. Virendra nodded at them, gratefully, and the four children sprinted off in the direction of the guesthouse.

In the sky above the Gurukul

Maya gazed in horror at the scene that was unfolding on the ground below. She had decided to return, not to the confines of her room in the guesthouse, but to the sky over the Gurukul, before finally returning to her body. She had wanted to see how the siege was progressing.

She saw that things were going badly for the inhabitants of the Gurukul, who were losing ground to the Nagas.

In the light of the glowing orbs that danced over the Gurukul, she saw the Nagas begin to cross the Kshatriya practice field and advance towards the cottages that housed the classrooms and dormitories. Beyond the classrooms, she could see the students and *Mahamatis* of the Gurukul form a knot around the Assembly Hall.

Fear gripped her as she realized that she may have been too late in returning. The Gurukul was almost overrun. How long could they defend the Assembly Hall without the weapons to strike against the Nagas?

A sense of guilt washed over her. She had spent too long indulging herself, exploring the ruins and the foundations of Dwarka. Had she not deviated from the plan, she would have accomplished her mission and returned sooner.

She corrected herself immediately. It wasn't her return that was important to their cause. She had travelled here at the speed of thought. But *he* couldn't do that. It would take time to cover the distance from the Gulf of Cambay to Panna.

As she looked on, the Nagas reached the first set of cottages and began tearing them apart with their bare forelimbs, slashing, pounding and kicking at the walls and roofs until the cottages disintegrated.

A terrifying thought flashed through her consciousness as she saw half the Naga forces break away. They were unable to advance beyond the classrooms to the Assembly Hall. That was a good sign. It meant that the defences still held.

What it also meant was that the Nagas, seemingly intent on the destruction of the Gurukul, bypassed the Assembly Hall and began wrecking the dormitories that lay between the Assembly Hall and the hillside that served as the alternate entrance to the Gurukul. The guesthouse lay in the same direction, Maya recalled with rising panic. It was just a matter of time before the Nagas reached and made short work of the guesthouse as well.

Amyra!

Maya's first thought was for the novice who was guarding her while she slept. It was supposed to be a simple job, not requiring any specialized skills. Which was why Amyra had been accepted as a sentry, without a fuss or debate, when she had volunteered. No one had imagined then that the Nagas would ever penetrate the defenses of the Gurukul, leave alone reach as far as the guesthouse. The novice stood no chance against the Nagas when even the *Mahamatis* were helpless in the face of their onslaught.

Maya watched, frozen with terror, as the Nagas began demolishing the dormitories, heading slowly but surely towards the guesthouse.

Chapter Eighty-three

Assault on the Guesthouse

The Guesthouse

Arjun reached the guesthouse and clattered up the stairs to Maya's room. He tried the door but it was locked. He pounded at it.

'Let me in!' he cried.

But there was no response.

Inside Maya's room, Amyra stared, wide-eyed at the door. Someone was clamouring to get in. Who could it be? She had instructions to let no one in, to allow no one to disturb Maya's sleep. Maya's mission was critical to the survival of the Gurukul. If her sleep was disturbed, the entire mission could be jeopardized.

Amyra sat, huddled on the floor, curled up in the corner as the pounding on the door continued. She was not going to open the door.

Not if *Mahamati* Mahesh himself asked her to.

Not until Maya woke up on her own.

Amyra glanced nervously at Maya, who was still slumbering peacefully, her breathing slow and regular. The noise at the door didn't seem to affect her.

Outside the room, Varun, Tanveer, Agastya and Adira joined Arjun.

'Door's locked,' Arjun said tersely.

'Break it open.' Varun looked at the others. 'Let's do it together.'

The roars of the Nagas were getting closer. It was only a matter of moments before they reached this cottage and began tearing it down.

Outside the Guesthouse

The Nagas demolished the last of the dormitories and advanced, with a roar, on the guesthouse. It was among the last few cottages standing between them and the hillside.

Maya, looking on, snapped out of her paralysis. If the Nagas reached the guesthouse before her *atma* re-entered her body …

The thought instantly whisked her away.

Inside the Guesthouse

Maya awoke with a jerk and sat up in bed, the horror of the scene outside still playing out in her mind.

Amyra sprang to her feet. 'Maya! Are you okay?'

Maya nodded and got out of bed slowly. The first few minutes after her *atma* travel were always disorienting. She always carried a sensation of being drained, of a physical and mental weakness that would instantly put her back to sleep.

But tonight, she did not have that luxury.

The two girls shrank against a wall in horror as the cottage shuddered and the noise of glass shattering and walls collapsing, amid the roars of the Nagas, came to their ears.

Outside the Guesthouse

The first group of Nagas reached the guesthouse and began attacking it. Two balconies were torn down along with half of the thatched roof, in an instant. Windows shattered and window frames were jerked out of their sockets and flung away as the powerful arms of the Nagas battered the cottage, the roars of the reptilians filling the night.

Inside the Guesthouse

The door to the room flew open under the combined assault of Arjun and his friends, as the lock gave way.

Maya and Amyra looked up in surprise as five bodies tumbled into the room.

'Quick,' Arjun hissed. 'We have to get out of here now!'

But it was too late.

The section of the wall in which the door leading to the balcony was set, was abruptly ripped away, and disappeared, leaving a gaping hole.

Through the ragged gap, three enormous Nagas came into view.

Before anyone could blink, Tanveer fitted his bow with an arrow and let it fly. A second arrow followed almost instantly, and a third and a fourth.

Maya was amazed. She had never seen Tanveer in action with a bow before and had no idea of his skills, though she had heard a lot from Arjun about how Tanveer had displayed his prowess in the practice combat sessions.

The archer's hands were a blur as he launched a barrage of arrows at the Nagas. While the arrows could not cause serious harm to the Nagas, they definitely acted as an irritant. The three Nagas, apparently frustrated by the continuous arrow pricks, disappeared from view.

'We need to move now,' Arjun urged. He could tell that the relief from the Nagas wouldn't last long. This was the only opening they had to escape. 'The Nagas will be ...' he began.

'Look!' Amyra interrupted him, pointing through the hole in the wall.

They all stared.

The six children, despite their misgivings, drew closer to the hole in the wall to get a better look.

Maya heaved a sigh of relief.

Their deliverance was at hand.

Chapter Eighty-four

The Final Battle

The Assembly Hall
The Gurukul

Jignesh stared, stunned, at the sudden appearance of Satyavachana.

'Maharishi,' he began, trying to keep his anger in check, 'we were searching for you.'

Satyavachana nodded, understanding. 'I had not forsaken you. Look.' He pointed towards the sky.

A strange sound came to the ears of everyone on the ground.

A sound of wings flapping.

But these were no ordinary wings. To make a sound that could be heard over the din of battle, they had to be enormous wings.

Almost with one accord, hundreds of eyes, both human and Naga, turned to the sky.

Inside the Guesthouse

The six children watched in rapt fascination as a gigantic shape swooped down from the sky, revealing its form as it approached the hundreds of orbs of light floating in the air above the Gurukul.

It was a being as strange as it was awe-inspiring. With the face of an eagle and the body of a human — two immensely muscular arms jutting out from a well-muscled, golden torso, and legs that looked like tree trunks — the being had a pair of enormous wings attached to its shoulder blades that gently beat the night air, as he flew over the battlefield that had been the Gurukul.

Garuda.

The bane of the Nagas.

The Assembly Hall

A loud cheer broke out among the forces of the Gurukul at the sight of Garuda. Jignesh smiled at Satyavachana, a tight, tired smile.

Maya had done it. She had brought back help. She had managed to find the only one who could save them tonight from the wrath of the Nagas.

The effect on the Nagas was electrifying. For a few moments, they, too, stood frozen, unbelieving, gazing at the sight of their nemesis circling above them.

Then, with roars, now tinged with fear, the ranks that had been organized just a while ago, disintegrated as the Naga troops scattered in all directions.

Almost simultaneously, the massive form of Garuda emitted a loud roar and swooped in, diving at lightning speed into the hordes of Nagas amassed below, tearing into their ranks and ripping, clawing, slashing at them.

Virendra looked at Jignesh. 'This is our chance to destroy as many Nagas as we can. Garuda doesn't need our help, but if we pitch in, we can cause serious damage to their army before they retreat.' He swiftly outlined his plan to the Maharishi.

Jignesh nodded, seeing the wisdom in the Kshatriya's words.

Shouts filled the air, jostling with the roars and screams of the Nagas, as the *Mahamatis*, led by Virendra and Jignesh, rallied their student troops for one final attack. With Garuda spreading mayhem among the Nagas, there was no fear of defeat.

Virendra's voice cut through the din. 'Attack!'

In response to his command, the mass of children huddled around the Assembly Hall began separating into three different strands, which drifted away from the main body of the students, only to coalesce again in different locations.

In the Guesthouse

'You did it!' Arjun exulted, beaming broadly.

The seven cheered, their voices joining the chorus outside the Assembly Hall.

'What's happening now?' Maya wondered, as she saw the group of students begin to break up into smaller segments, moving in different directions.

They watched as the students from the Gurukul, along with their *Mahamatis*, came together for a final onslaught on the army of Nagas.

Slowly, the plan of attack became clear to the seven children in the guesthouse.

The Gurukul army had split up into three groups. Two of the groups, consisting of the majority of the students, were moving swiftly to outflank the Nagas, while the third, smaller, group was going to engage head on with the Nagas.

'What are they doing?' Adira couldn't understand. None of the others responded. They were as baffled as she was.

Only Agastya could figure out what was happening. 'Look carefully. The group in the centre, rushing headlong towards the Nagas, are the most advanced students; the ones who have mastered the higher classes of mantras. Mantras for attack, for creating illusions, and for manipulating matter.' He couldn't resist a word of self-praise. 'Like me.'

Varun snorted, but remained glued to the action that was unfolding before their eyes.

'They are the only ones who can inflict any sort of harm on the Nagas,' Agastya continued, ignoring Varun. 'None of the weapons the Kshatriyas carry can really destroy the Nagas, but they can be used defensively.' He pointed to the other two groups of students, who had by now almost encircled the milling mass of Nagas and were taking up a defensive position on either side of the Naga army.

'Those two groups are going to use defensive mantras and their weapons to repel the Nagas and hem them in,' Agastya concluded.

The strategy behind the formations became clearer to Arjun. 'I get it. The group in the centre will attack the Nagas, reinforcing Garuda's onslaught. The Nagas will be flanked on two sides by our defensive troops and on one side by the river. They will have nowhere to run, making them an easier target for Garuda. Brilliant strategy. I wonder who thought of it.'

Shrill cries from the Gurukul army came to their ears as the assault on the Nagas began.

Garuda continued his aerial offensive against the Nagas even as the Gurukul army began their attack. The celestial bird dived again and again into the mass of Nagas below him, his gargantuan form a blur even in the light of the orbs.

Repeatedly, Garuda scooped up armfuls of the Nagas, seizing even more of them using his clawed feet and then shot back up into the sky, where he, then, let go of the creatures, not stopping to watch them plummet to their deaths, but diving once again to rip through their ranks, using his claws to deadly effect.

As Arjun had predicted, the fresh assault from the direction of the Gurukul only added to the turmoil among the Nagas, who were in a wild state of disarray by now. On three sides, they were being prodded and poked at close quarters and from above them, a deadly death rained down in the form of Garuda.

The seven children watched with a new found glee as the monstrous reptiles who, until a short while ago, had seemed invincible, now ran helter-skelter, trying to find a place to hide.

But there was none.

The Nagas who had attacked the dormitories and the guesthouse also made off, leaving their work of destruction incomplete, focused only on escaping the wrath of Garuda.

The reptiles had amassed in such large numbers to exploit the weakness they had discovered in the boundary of the Gurukul, that they became easy pickings for the celestial bird.

A few of the luckier Nagas were able to beat a hasty retreat towards the river and across it, managing, somehow, to escape into the darkness. But many of them did not make it.

Only Vishwaraj stood his ground, balefully glaring at the Gurukul.

Maya stared at the lone, unmoving, figure of the boy. She was sure that she had seen him once before, on the night they had arrived at Panna. His face had not been visible that night. Tonight, too, she couldn't distinguish his features. But something told her it had been the same person she looked upon tonight. Until tonight, she hadn't even known who he was. Arjun had just told her. The only time she had heard of Vishwaraj before tonight was when his name was mentioned in the Assembly Hall, after Satyavachana had arrived at the Gurukul.

As Maya watched him Vishwaraj suddenly turned and walked away, disappearing into the night. He didn't seem to be afraid of Garuda at all, to Maya's surprise.

Maya stared at the retreating figure of the boy who was supposed to have gone over to Shukra. This was the boy who had met DJ sir just before the history teacher had died. There was a connection between this boy and her father's murder, since she now knew that Trivedi had called her father minutes before his death.

What was that connection?

Chapter Eighty-five

The Saptas

The Guesthouse
Gurukul

Peals of laughter echoed round the sitting room of the ruined guesthouse. The ground floor had survived, more or less intact, though the upper floors had been either completely or partially destroyed by the Nagas.

'The Nagas were coming in through the balcony, and she refused to open the door for us!' Agastya chuckled, eliciting another round of laughter.

The seven children — Arjun, Maya, Varun, Adira, Tanveer, Agastya and Amyra — had been permitted to stay up late tonight, after a session with the *Mahamati* Council, where their courage and resolve had been feted by Satyavachana, among others. It was during the session that Arjun had been informed that the Council had received word from Mahamati Mahesh and the others who had left to apprehend Vishwaraj.

'We don't know if the news about locating Vishwaraj was a ruse by Shukra to get them to leave the Gurukul,' Parth had said, 'but we have managed to confirm that all four of them are safe. They are on their way back, now that we know that Vishwaraj was last seen here, at the Gurukul, with the Nagas. Who knows where he must be by now.'

This piece of news had left Arjun in considerably higher spirits than he had been in all evening.

After the Council session, Arjun had requested permission for the group to spend time together.

'*Mahamatis*, in a way all seven of us worked as a team in whatever we did,' he had told the Council. What he had left unsaid was that all of them had lots of questions, which were unanswered, and they were all keen to hear about Maya's journey to seek the help of Garuda.

They were sitting together and laughing now, but they could all remember the terror they had felt moments ago. Amyra's refusal to open the door, which was now a joke, had seemed a matter of life and death, then.

Amyra had taken the jokes sportingly. For a novice, to be accepted as a part of an elite group in the Gurukul was enough reward for her dogged protection of Maya.

'Hey,' Arjun said, finally, 'enough jokes here. She was doing her job and I respect that. Her instructions were very clear. Maya was not to be disturbed.' He flashed a smile at Amyra, who smiled back awkwardly. A compliment from Yayati's scion, mentioned in the prophecy as the One, was high praise indeed.

'I never knew Maharishis could travel physically from one place to another,' Maya said, changing the subject. 'I knew the *atma* could travel, but what Satyavachana did was new to me.'

During the Council session, Satyavachana had disclosed the reason for his disappearance. He had realized that while Maya could return from Dwarka in an instant in her *atma* form, Garuda would take some time to fly from his island to Panna, his enormous wings and speed notwithstanding. So he had decided to help Maya and had used his *siddhis* to travel to Dwarka and bring Garuda back with him.

'I have heard stories of powerful Maharishis using their *siddhis* to travel long distances physically, in a short span of time,' Agastya admitted. 'But I don't know how they did it or how Maharishi Satyavachana did it. Did he tell you how?'

Maya pursed her lips. 'No, he didn't. He did the same thing last night, when I visited his ashram as an *atma*. I accidentally came back to the Gurukul and within moments, he was on my balcony, knocking at the door. I never asked him how he did it and he never offered an explanation either.'

'Well, you'll get to know, I'm sure,' Agastya said, sounding a bit envious. 'After all, he has said he's going to teach you himself.'

'I'm nervous about that,' Maya said, truthfully. Tonight had been a red letter day for her. The Council, albeit in the absence of three members, had decided to enroll Maya officially in the Gurukul. Her exploits had saved the Gurukul and its inhabitants from annihilation. Satyavachana had initiated the idea and Jignesh and Parth had readily agreed.

'So,' Arjun looked around at the group. 'I've been thinking about it ... are we the *Saptas* mentioned in the prophecy?'

Adira shrugged. 'I would think so. I think the seven of us have come together for a reason. If you look back, you can see that each of us made a choice. A decision. And the actions we took as a result of that decision led us here. I don't believe that was a coincidence.'

'If that's true,' Tanveer said, thoughtfully, 'then it is up to us to fulfil the rest of the prophecy.'

Tonight, for the first time, the seven children in the room had heard the prophecy. Or at least the part that had been left in *Bhu-lok*.

> *Shukra's eclipse shall fade one day*
> *In Kaliyuga will his power grow*
> *Seven weapons, sharp and swift*
> *Will be the means to counter him*
> *The One will come, born on the day*
> *The solstice that will be the sign*
> *Yayati's scion shall be the One*
> *To lead the Seven into war.*

'Yes,' Varun agreed. 'If we are the Seven mentioned in the prophecy, then we need to find the seven weapons the prophecy refers to.'

'Before we do that,' Arjun said, 'we need to find the other two parts of the prophecy. Until we know the complete prophecy, we will not have the means to defeat Shukra. If the Saptarishis thought it better to divide up the prophecy and hide each part away, then there must be something in the prophecy that will give us the power to go up against Shukra. My gut feel is the same as Maya's. I think we both believe that the weapons mentioned in the prophecy are not going to be sufficient to defeat Shukra.'

And the key to finding the rest of the prophecy may just be found in the diary.

Maya sat quietly, listening to Arjun. She had not forgotten Satyavachana's words — he could help her with deciphering the verses in her father's diary. She had resolved that she would ensure that Satyavachana did help her to find out just why her father had believed the diary to be so important. But she kept her thoughts to herself. She wanted to be sure before she told the others anything.

There was a knock on the door of the sitting room and Virendra entered.

'Time to wind up, guys,' he smiled at them. 'Tomorrow, we start rebuilding the Gurukul.'

'What do we do about the destruction of the trees by the river?' Maya wanted to know. 'Won't the *sadhs* notice that they've been burned down?'

Virendra shook his head. 'Mantras have already been chanted to create the illusion of the forest along the river exactly the way it was before tonight. The *sadhs* will not notice the difference. You will see for yourself in the morning. Now, guys, wrap up. Adira, Maya's in your dorm now, right?'

As a result of the destruction of the guesthouse, and also Maya's formal induction into the Gurukul, she had been assigned to a dorm where she had to sleep from tonight. Virendra, too, had to move out to share a cottage with one of the *Mahamatis*. All the dorms that had been destroyed were the ones in which the boys were accommodated. They would spend their nights in the Assembly Hall until the cottages were reconstructed, which wouldn't take too much time since mantras would speed up the process.

Adira beamed and nodded. 'I'm glad she's been assigned to our dorm. I'll help her settle in.'

'Great,' Virendra rubbed his hands together. 'See you all tomorrow, then. We have a lot of work to do to get the Gurukul back to normal.'

Epilogue

Day 13

SP Kapoor's Office
New Delhi

Raman Kapoor sat at his desk and stared at the sheet of paper he had retrieved from Upadhyay's study. He studied the crudely drawn sword that had been sketched on the page. A long, broad sword, with a hefty looking hilt.

A two-edged sword whose blade was engulfed in flames.

What in heaven's name was this drawing about? Was it a clue to some angle of the case that had not yet been revealed? Or was it insignificant?

He studied the rows of inscriptions above and below the drawing. The script was definitely Devanagari, but the language was not Hindi. Neither was it Sanskrit. Kapoor had sent a scanned copy of the inscriptions for translation and it had been confirmed that the language was an unknown one.

A new language? Or an old, forgotten one?

In either case, how did Upadhyay know of it? He was a history teacher. Was it possible that he had come across the inscriptions somewhere? Perhaps on some ancient monument or stele? There were thousands of inscriptions in monuments and temples scattered all over India. Where was Kapoor to start looking in order to connect the dots?

So many questions.

It had been a whole week since he had found the drawing of the sword and nothing new had turned up in the last seven days to shed light on the mysterious case.

And then, there was the fire that had been reported to have broken out in Panna National Park last night. A man from one of the villages bordering the park had claimed to have seen flames in a section of the forest that was fairly remote and barely frequented, bordered by the river Ken. The villager had also reported hearing noises of some sort, though he couldn't make out what was causing the uproar.

The park rangers had immediately set out to investigate. Three rangers had taken a motorboat and cruised along the Ken, searching for the fire, or traces of it. Helicopters had been placed on standby to help put out the forest fire if, indeed, there was still a conflagration going in the jungle.

But the rangers had seen nothing untoward. They had cruised up and down the river a few times, without coming across any indication of a forest fire. A subsequent helicopter survey of that part of the forest had also drawn a blank.

The park rangers had dismissed the case and put it down to either hallucination or the effect of alcohol.

But Kapoor could not dismiss the matter so easily. There were too many coincidences. Panna was where Virendra had fled with his family. It was also where Upadhyay's daughter had possibly landed up, an unexpected twist to the case. It was this very forest where one of his best men claimed to have been chased by evil spirits. There was still no sign of Virendra or his family; or Upadhyay's daughter — if it had indeed been her — for that matter. They had all seemed to disappear into thin air after reaching Panna.

Was there a connection between his case and the mysterious forest fire?

Kapoor didn't know. But he had some ideas on how he wanted to proceed with the investigation. And he believed strongly that Virendra would not — could not — remain hidden forever.

Sooner or later, the man had to surface.

Kapoor would be waiting and watching.

Until then, his investigations would continue.

Raman Kapoor was not going to rest until he had got to the bottom of this mystery.

Author's Note

While this is a fantasy story and, therefore, completely fictional, there is much in the book that is based on real verses in the Mahabharata, the Srimad Bhagavatam, the Bhagavad Gita, and the Puranas. I thought I should help readers understand which parts of the story are products of my imagination, and provide references for the parts which are based on or sourced from the texts mentioned above. The list below is organised by order of appearance in the story, as far as possible.

Louis Alexandre Berthier: is a historical figure and was, as described, the Chief of Staff under Napoleon. For more information, see https://en.wikipedia.org/wiki/Louis-Alexandre_Berthier

The Rosetta Stone: was, indeed, discovered by Captain Pierre Bouchard in August 1799. However, it wasn't until much later that it became the means to decipher the Egyptian hieroglyphics. I have taken the liberty of compressing several years into the shorter space of a month, purely for dramatic effect. For more information on the Stone which is housed today in the British Museum, in London, please log in to The Quest Club to read the complete history of the Stone as published by the British Museum, along with photographs taken by me of the Rosetta Stone.

Napoleon's night in the Great Pyramid: there is no historical record of this, though there are several references to the episode I have described in the prologue, some narrated by respected writers. It is true, however, that Al-Mamoun first tunnelled into the pyramid in 820 AD, and Alexander and Caesar couldn't possibly have entered it before then. For more information on this, and photographs, please log in to The Quest Club. According to most accounts, Napoleon carried the secret of what happened that night to his death and the words 'You will never believe me if I told you' were supposedly uttered by Napoleon on his deathbed when he was asked to describe his experience on that night. I have taken the liberty of altering the story, and, in the Prologue, Napoleon says these words to Berthier immediately after he emerges from the pyramid.

Bhrigu: is a Brahmarishi — created by Brahma. In Book 4 (Pauloma Parva) of the Adi Parva (Book 1 of the Mahabharata), Chapter 5, Verse 6, Bhrigu is described as having been begotten by Brahma. Bhrigu's birth is also described in Book 7 (Sambhava Parva) of the Adi Parva, Chapter 66.

Shukracharya: was the son of Bhrigu and, therefore, a grandson of Brahma as mentioned in Chapter 30. Shukra has been described in several places in the Mahabharata as a very powerful Rishi, an 'ascetic of ascetics'. He was the Guru of the Asuras, and possessed the ability to resurrect the dead as the result of a boon from Lord Shiva, whose devotee he was. Interestingly, one of his wives was Jayanti, Indra's daughter. How he lost one eye is described in the story of the Vamana avatar of Lord Vishnu and Bali. You can read more about it in Puranic Cosmology, Page 760 (point 8) and Page 103 (Point 6).

Saptarishis : the story about their power diminishing during Kaliyuga is fictional. So is it with the Devas.

Narsimha mantra: this is a real mantra and has been reproduced in its exact form wherever it is quoted in the book. The mantra used in the book is also referred to as the Narsimha Maha Mantra.

Hiranyakasipu and Prahlad: the story can be found in the Vishnu Purana, Chapter 3, Section 1, Verses 11-14. It can also be found in the Srimad Bhagavatam, Canto 7, Chapters 2-10.

Visvavasu: in the Mahabharata, Visvavasu is described as the King of the Gandharvas in the Adi Parva: Book 4: Pauloma Parva, Chapter 8, Verse 5.

Sadh: short form for *sadharan*, which means 'ordinary' in Hindi. Used to refer to people who are not members of either the *Sangha* or the *Gana* for reasons explained in Chapter 50.

Kacha and Shukra: the story of Kacha and Shukra, as narrated in Chapter 29, can be found in the Mahabharata, in the Adi Parva: Book 7: Sambhava Parva, Chapter 76.

The Chandravanshis: Yayati's history is described in the Mahabharata, Adi Parva: Book 7: Sambhava Parva, Chapter 75.

Lord Shiva and the Bhutagana: the references in the book to Lord Shiva's command of the Bhutagana is based on the descriptions in the Srimad Bhagavatam, Canto 4, Chapter 2, verses 14-15, 32; Chapter 3, verse 7; Chapter 4, verse 34; Chapter 5, verses 4, 13, 25-26. However, the passing of the command to Shukra is purely fictional.

Vikritis: are fictional. Who are they? You will find out as the series progresses.

Brahmabhasha: my description and interpretation of Brahmabhasha as a predecessor of Sanskrit and the language of the Devas was inspired by a similar line of thought expressed by Akshoy K. Majumdar in his book *The Hindu History*, Chapter 6, page 68 :'Their tongue at "Indralaya" was Brahmabhasha, often mentioned in the Upanishadas. That tongue, gradually refined by the Devas, became Sanskrit.'

Ancient texts: according to David Pingree, who conducted a research study on ancient manuscripts in India, there are over 30 million such manuscripts. K.V. Sharma, who conducted a study of scientific texts in

Tamil Nadu and Kerala estimates that only 7 per cent of those have been translated and published. Amba's reference to millions of unread texts in Chapter 46, is based on this little known fact.

Dandaka: is mentioned in the Valmiki Ramayana, Book 2, Chapters 2 and 5. I have based the location of the Dandaka forest in this book on an excellent analysis of the geography of the Ramayana done by Arun Ramakrishnan, where he describes the ashram of the sage Suteekshina being located near Sarangpur village in Panna district. It is in the vicinity of this ashram that Lord Rama, Sita and Lakshman spent 10 years of their exile. All 14 years of their exile were spent in the Dandaka forest. And it is true that the Dandaka forest was created as the result of a curse by Shukra. The story of how this happened can be found in the Puranic Encyclopaedia, Pages 46 and 200.

The Seven Levels of the Netherworlds: and the details of their inhabitants are taken from the detailed description provided in the Srimad Bhagavatam, Canto 5, Chapter 24.

The story of Bali: can be found in the Srimad Bhagavatam, Canto 8, Chapters 15-23.

Attainment of the Siddhis : the Srimad Bhagavatam describes the Siddhis in detail and how they can be achieved, in Canto 11, Chapter 15.

The story of Tvasta: as narrated by Maya in Chapter 50, can be found in the Srimad Bhagavatam, Canto 6, Chapter 9.

The six categories of mantras: listed by Jignesh in Chapter 50 are purely fictional.

The missing verses of the Mahabharata: reference to this can be found (as reproduced in Chapter 56) in the Adi Parva, Chapter I, Verses 104-105.

The concept of the atma, the subtle body and the gross body: as described in Chapter 57, is based on the following references from the Bhagavad Gita and the Srimad Bhagavatam:

   Bhagavad Gita: Chapter 7, verses 4-5

   Srimad Bhagavatam: Canto 3, Chapter 5, verses 22-38; Chapter 26, verses 23-49

The shantaa-kaaram mantra: this is a real mantra and has been reproduced in the book in its real form, but the effect on Maya (enabling her *atma* to travel) is fictional.

The 'invented' mantras: the *laghu* mantras described in the book are purely fictional, except for the *laghu* mantra form of the Garuda mantra (see "Garudaya Trayambakaya" below). The following mantras are all invented by me, though the Sanskrit is real and each mantra has a meaning that is directly associated with its purpose, as you can see from the meanings below.

   Vikurute Vyapaniya: change the form to make it permeable

   Vidyutate: illuminate or shine forth

   Udnayate: raise or elevate

   Vegita Vriddhi: increase speed or velocity

   Gandharvo krpaya vishto: O Gandharvas, have compassion for me

Arjuna and the Vrishnis: the story of Arjuna's inability to recall his weapons when dacoits attacked the group of Vishnu women and children he was escorting is narrated in the Mausala Parva, Chapter 7, Verses 46-59. Verse 55 specifically describes how he fails to recall his celestial weapons. However, the 'storage space' or 'locker' for Kshatriyas weapons described by Virendra to Arjun in Chapter 63 is fictional, though inspired by this story from the Mahabharata — it is my way of interpreting the verses from the Mahabharata from a fantasy perspective.

The law of Karma: as mentioned in several places in the book is based on the following references from the Bhagavad Gita and Srimad Bhagavatam:

Bhagavad Gita: Chapter 14

Srimad Bhagavatam: Canto 1, Chapter 15, verse 18; Canto 3, Chapter 31, verse 1; Canto 11, Chapter 9, verse 26

It is very interesting to note that, in the story of Jara and Krishna, narrated earlier, the law of karma is seen in action, even for Krishna, who is divine. Krishna, in his earlier birth as Rama, had killed Vali (Sugreeva's brother) from behind. Vali was reborn as Jara, and he, in turn, 'killed' Krishna. The karma that Krishna had earned from his previous birth had an impact on him in his birth as the Krishna of the Mahabharata. It is a great example of how even the all powerful Krishna did not exempt himself from the working of karma.

Kadru: was one of the wives of Rishi Kasyapa, one of the Saptarishis, and the mother of the Nagas.

Takshaka and Parikshit: the story of Takshaka and Parikshit can be found in the Mahabharata, Adi Parva, Book 5 : Astika Parva, Chapters 42 to 43.

Dwarka: the verses quoted in Chapter 79 relating to the destruction of Dwarka can be found in the Mahabharata, Mausala Parva, Chapter 7, Verses 41 - 43. The 2003 discovery of the ancient, sunken ruins of a lost city in the Gulf of Cambay is fictitious, though inspired by the real life discovery of underwater ruins of two cities in the Gulf of Cambay, off the shore from Hazira in 2001. A detailed report on this discovery can be found in the BBC television series *Underworld*, by Graham Hancock, based on his book by the same name, including the discovery of the foundations of the cities. The description of the foundations in Chapter 78, of course, are based on my imagination of what they may look like, if actually discovered.

Sub bottom profiling: is a real technique for mapping what lies below the ocean bed.

Takshaka and Kasyapa: the story of Takshaka and Kasyapa, and the burning of the banyan tree by Takshaka, with the power of his poison, as described in Chapter 79, can be found in the Mahabharata, Adi Parva, Book 5: Astika Parva, Chapters 42 to 43.

The Nagas: the description of the Nagas that I have provided in Chapter 81 is completely fictional. The vermilion hue of the Nagas that I have mentioned in Chapter 74 is inspired by the description of Takshaka as he flees after killing Parikshit, in the Mahabharata, Adi Parva, Book 5 : Astika Parva, Chapter 44.

Garudaya Trayambakaya: this is a shortened form of the Garuda Mantra. The full form of the Garuda mantra is: om namo bhagawate garudaya trayambakaya sadhsttvastu swaha

Pronounciation Key

The following are the phonetic equivalents of the Sanskrit/Hindi words used in the book, listed as in order of their appearance in the book. I have provided both the Devanagari phonetic equivalent as well as the phonetic pronunciation in English, for ease of understanding, since English phonetics do not always lend themselves to an accurate pronunciation of Sanskrit or Hindi words.

	Word/phrase	Devanagari pronunciation	English phonetics
1.	Gana	गण	gʌnn
2.	Mahamati	महामति	mə:ha:mʌti:
3.	Sangha	सङ्घ	sʌŋ
4.	Kavach	कवच	kə:vʌtʃ
5.	Sadh	साध	sa:dh
6.	Preta	प्रेत	preɪt
7.	Udnayate	उद्रयते	ʊdnə:yə:teɪ
8.	Vegita Vriddhi	वेगिता वृद्धि	veɪgɪta: vrɪddhi:
9.	Vikurute Vyapaniya	वीकुरुते व्यापनीय	vɪkʊrʊteɪ vya:pə:ni:ɪə
10.	Vidyutate	वीद्योतते	vɪdyɔ:tə:teɪ
11.	Laghu	लघु	lə:ghu:
12.	Gandharva krpaya vishto	गान्धर्व कृपाय वष्टि	ga:ndharv krɪpa:y vɪshtu:
13.	Garudaya Trayambakaya	गरुडाय त्रमंबकाय	gə:rʊda:y trə:mbə:ka:y

Acknowledgements

The book you hold in your hands, dear reader, is the result of team-work. There are so many people who have contributed to give the book its final shape and I would like to acknowledge and appreciate their efforts and contribution.

As always, my biggest appreciation and gratitude goes out to my wife Sharmila and my daughter Shaynaya. They have supported and encouraged me throughout the time I spent writing this book, even though it took away from the time that I could have spent with them. Moreover, Sharmila, as always, was the first to read the first draft of the manuscript and give her feedback and Shaynaya, being a teenager herself, gave me some valuable tips on teenage behaviour in different situations.

It is extremely difficult to write a book using, as a base, ancient texts that are revered and followed even today. If I had been writing on Egyptian or Greek mythology, it would have been much easier. But the Vedas, Puranas, the Srimad Bhagavatam and the Bhagavad Gita, are all texts that are as relevant today as they were when they were composed thousands of years ago. As a result, while creating scenes, ideating or inventing fantasy elements, I wanted to stay true to the texts. This could not have been possible without the constant guidance of Shubha Vilas, who ensured that I stayed true to the texts and accurately reflected their teachings. Shubha Vilas has been studying and teaching the Vedic texts for the last two decades and is also the author of the *Ramayana: The Game of Life* series, *The Chronicles of Hanuman* and *Open Eyed*

Meditations. His expertise in Sanskrit was also invaluable in validating the mantras that I invented.

My thanks go out to Artika Bakshi, who also read the first draft, as always, and gave me her valuable feedback.

Anand Prakash, my friend and designer extraordinaire, continued his tradition of designing brilliant covers for my books by creating a cover that was in keeping with the very different theme of the book, while visualising some of the key plot elements. Ishan Trivedi, did the cover illustration and brought Anand's vision to life, for which I am grateful.

My thanks go out to Patricia MacEwen, Phyllis Irene Radford, John C Bunnell and Elizabeth Gilligan, fellow scribes in my writers' research group, who answered questions on key research topics that I struggled with at times.

With a book like this, illustrations can add to the reader's experience by helping them visualise things the way I saw them while writing. Priyankar Gupta, who has illustrated my previous books, once again delivered the goods with his illustrations of Egypt (the Sphinx and the Great Pyramid) and the Gurukul from Maya's viewpoint. Ishan Trivedi has vividly brought out the grandeur and beauty of The Pandava Falls and also brought to life my vision of Garuda fighting the Nagas.

A big thank you to all the people at Westland, especially Gautam Padmanabhan, Krishna Kumar Nair, Shweta Bhagat and the entire marketing team who have been tremendously supportive with this book.

As usual, Sanghamitra Biswas, my editor, did a wonderful and very thorough job of polishing my writing and making changes that ensured that the narrative was smoother and true to the plot.

Finally, I am deeply grateful to my parents for encouraging me to read and write from an early age and providing me with all the books I wanted to read as I grew up. It is only due to their encouragement and blessings that I have been able to fulfil my childhood dream of becoming an author.

While I acknowledge the contribution of everyone who has supported me, I take full responsibility for all errors and omissions of fact or detail in this book.

Have You Joined the Quest Club?

A word about the Quest Club, in case you haven't registered as a member yet. Membership is free and gives you access to Quest Club events—where readers interact with me both online and offline—that are held all over India. There will be free ebooks over the coming years, in addition to quizzes, puzzles, contests and exclusive previews of my future books for members of the club. Finally, you can join me, as I research my books, and gain free access to images, videos and my research notes. You could even learn more about characters, locations and events in my books. An exciting journey filled with adventure and mystery beckons all Quest Club members. You can register at: www. christophercdoyle.com/ the-quest-club right away for free.

Have you Joined the Quest Club?